SUGARCOATED

HOT CAKES BOOK ONE

ERIN NICHOLAS

ISBN: 978-1-952280-03-0

Editor: Lindsey Faber

Cover design: Angela Waters

Cover Photography: Lindee Robinson

Models: Chelsey Nicole, Adam Johns

SUGARCOATED

Hot Cakes Book One

A hot, funny brother's best friend rom com . . . with sugar on top!

She's his best friend's little sister. He's known her all his life. He's practically part of the family. There is nothing either of them could do to surprise the other at this point. Then she showed up in his bedroom in lingerie and asked him to take her V-card.

Okay, that was a surprise.

Aiden is pretty sure Zoe was equally surprised when he told her no.

To say that he didn't handle it well would be a massive understatement. Almost as massive as the amount of work he's going to have to do now to convince her that he wants her. Forever.

Right after he tells her that he's bought the company that's her bakery's biggest competitor.

Maybe if he tells her he's in love with her first, that will help sugarcoat the whole we're-rivals-in-business-now thing.

So, first "I'm in love with you", then "take off your clothes", then "I'm now your business adversary".

Sure. Piece of cake.

1

Zoe picked up the tray of little balls of cake and backed through the swinging door from the kitchen to the front of Buttered Up. She needed to dip them in their colorful coatings, add the sparkly sugar, and stick them on sticks, but she could do that on the prep table in the main part of the bakery while she watched for customers and waited on anyone who came in.

She and her best friend, Jocelyn—Josie to her friends—did most of the baking in the back, but they liked to frost and decorate the goodies up front where people could see what they were doing. It was where people really saw their talents and what all they could offer.

Honestly, Jocelyn was a better cake decorator than Zoe. If someone asked for something custom and elaborate, it was always Jocelyn who made it happen. Especially since the Great Hippo Cake Incident of last year. Zoe liked the more straightforward, simple icing jobs of their basic cakes, cupcakes, and decorated cookies. Tasks she'd been doing all her life. Well, since she'd been tall enough to reach the top of her grandma's worktable anyway. Even though that had required a stool at first. She could frost a cookie and add icing roses to cupcakes in her sleep.

But honestly? She was a girl who'd inherited a bakery and was tasked with keeping her family's legacy going, and she wasn't all that good at anything other than the essentials. So she stuck to the basics like peanut butter stuck to... well, everything.

Zoe noticed someone out of the corner of her eye as she set the tray down on the big prep table that sat in the middle of the area behind their L-shaped display cases.

When she turned, she was afforded a very nice posterior view of a man who was leaning over, studying their display of cake stands. She took him in from foot to head. Well, foot to midback. That was all she could really see with the way he was bending at the moment.

He was not the average Appleby-ite. The general male dress code around here was work boots, denim, and t-shirts. Henleys on occasion. Flannel when it got cold. Not this guy. He was in a freaking suit. Only Mr. Thompson, the bank president, wore a suit. Some of the guys wore slacks and button-up shirts—other bankers, the ones who worked at the insurance company, the school superintendent. But honestly, dressing up in Appleby mostly consisted of khakis instead of jeans. Ties were saved for funerals. Not even weddings a lot of the time. Things were very casual in Appleby.

This man wore a full-on suit. Pants, jacket, dress shoes. She could even see the end of a tie hanging. Red. The tie was red. Nice. As far as she could tell, this was a custom-tailored suit too because it fit *very* well.

She didn't know who he was, but she appreciated him stopping by. She liked a guy in jeans. Ones that were well-worn and fit nicely across the ass. Not the bagging, hanging-on-their-hips kind. But she saw a lot of jeans. She definitely appreciated finely woven Italian wool.

She sighed wistfully. But it wasn't just the suit that was making her study him. He was new. And there wasn't a lot of new in Appleby. Especially of the male, around-her-age variety. She cared about that more than she'd liked to admit. She hadn't before. But things had changed.

She'd become horny.

Not just oh-he's-kind-of-hot aware or even an oh-I'm-very-attracted-to-him realization. It was no-I-really-need-to-have-sex horny. She didn't know if it was hormones, or her friends who had active sex lives and loved to talk about it, or her friends who *didn't* have active sex lives and loved to talk about *that,* or her biological clock, or what. But she had sex on the brain now. All the time.

Which seemed odd for a virgin.

She didn't even know what she was missing, and was, honestly, a little uptight about finding out.

She sighed again. The truth was, she *did* know what had started it all.

Aiden Anderson.

And The Kiss. The stupid, what-the-hell-had-she-been-thinking-throwing-herself-at-him-Christmas-Eve kiss.

The best kiss ever. For sure in her life. She might be a virgin, but she'd kissed guys. A few anyway. And Aiden was the *best.* It had been romantic-movie good. R-rated romantic-movie good. *Definitely* not Hallmark.

Of course, she was never going to be able to face him again after that. Well, after the moment *after* the kiss anyway. But that was just something she was going to need to deal with. Somehow.

The guy she'd been studying from behind suddenly straightened and turned.

Zoe smiled and opened her mouth to ask how she could help him. But the words got stuck in her throat.

No. *No.* NO!

Seriously?

What was *he* doing here?

"Hey, Zoe."

Several emotions swept through her as she stared at Aiden. And his stupid, handsome face, and his sexy, things-are-totally-fine smile.

Shock. Happiness. Mortification. In that order.

She snapped her mouth shut, shook her head, turned, and headed back into the kitchen.

Jocelyn looked up from where she was cutting a 3D cat figure out of a tall cylinder of chocolate cake.

Zoe again opened her mouth, then snapped it shut, shook her head, and turned. She went straight for the freezer. She opened the big door, stepped inside, and shut it behind her.

Cold. She needed cold to combat that hot flush of humiliation that had just washed over her. And a huge metal door between her and Aiden.

She pulled in a deep breath of freezer air. The cold prickled her nose and was sharp in her lungs. She blew the breath out, studying the puff of white in front of her face. Then she did it again.

What was he doing here? Why hadn't he told Maggie he was coming? No way did her mother know Aiden was in town. If she knew, Zoe would have known.

Her mother always told her when he was coming to visit. The news of either of her boys—Aiden or Cam—coming home made Maggie giddy like a little girl. She cleaned and cooked at her house and then cleaned Zoe's house, since that was now where the guys always stayed when they were in town. Maggie brought over scented hand soap and new towels and filled the fridge with their favorite beer and juices, and the cupboards with chips and crackers. It was like a freaking bed and breakfast at Zoe's house when the guys were home. Which had never bothered her before.

But this time... this was the first time she'd seen Aiden since The Kiss. And there wasn't a single new towel or box of crackers in her house.

And even more importantly, now that he was here, how was she supposed to sit across her mother's dining room table from him and not shrivel up thinking about the fact she'd asked him to take her virginity and he'd said no?

She'd been dressed in lingerie. He'd kissed her as if he wanted to eat her up—in every single dirty way that could be intended. Then... He'd. Said. No. To. Taking. Her. Virginity.

Zoe put her hands over her face and groaned.

She'd known never seeing him again was impossible. He was practically one of her brothers. Which, yeah, sounded *ewww* when paired with the kissing and sex thing. But they'd grown up together. He'd more or less lived with them after his mom died. Zoe had known him her *entire life*.

And she'd never even thought about kissing him until about two years ago when he'd walked in on her ironing a dress. She'd been wearing only a bra and panties, and the look he'd given her had been holy-hell-melt-those-panties-right-off hot. She'd never seen him look like that. She'd never even imagined him looking like that. Certainly not at her. But that was the moment she'd stopped considering Aiden her older brother's best friend and started thinking of him as a very hot guy who she would like to get naked with. It had been like a light switch.

A very inconvenient light switch that had led to the most humiliating moment of her life. And that included the one time she'd tried to make a 3D custom-decorated cake.

Josie had been sick, and Angela Adams had needed the elephant cake. The elephant cake that had ended up looking like a hippo. A melted hippo. With an unfortunate snout deformity.

Zoe shuddered thinking about the fiasco. She'd been so

mortified. She'd had to deliver the cake. The horrible gray-blob-with-eyes cake. Angela had already paid for it, and there hadn't been time to make another.

There had been forty kids at that party. Forty kids who had moms who may or may not ever order a cake from Buttered Up again. Even now she blushed thinking about it.

But the moment after The R-rated Christmas Kiss with Aiden had been, amazingly, worse.

Suddenly Jocelyn whipped the freezer door open.

"What is going on? Why are you in the freezer?"

"I—"

"Hey, Josie."

Jocelyn swung around at the sound of Aiden's voice. "Oh! Hey, Aiden." She paused. Then said, "*Ohhhh*." She looked back at Zoe. "Never mind."

Zoe blew out a breath. "Yeah." Then she raised her voice. "Oh, here they are!" She picked up another tray of cake balls. After they were formed, they sat in the freezer until they got firm enough to work with. These needed sticks and the coating and decorations to officially be cake pops, and they weren't ready to be finished yet, but what, she was going to let Aiden think she'd run into the freezer to *hide* from him? Yeah, running and hiding wouldn't be embarrassing at all.

She'd just about used up her embarrassment quota with Aiden. For the decade. She needed to cover here.

Jocelyn stepped back as Zoe carried the tray out.

Zoe pasted on a bright, completely fake smile. "Hi, Aiden."

There. Just "Hi, Aiden" as if nothing at all was wrong. Or awkward. Or horrifying. Or even surprising. As if she'd known he'd be walking into her bakery, unannounced, looking amazing.

What the hell was he doing walking in here in a *suit*? He didn't want her to take her panties off for him? Then he needed to wear ripped-up blue jeans and an old hoodie.

She sighed internally. Even that wouldn't make her *not* want him.

But the suit was really unfair.

"Ladies." He gave them both a grin. "Just got into town and thought I'd stop in and say hi."

"Did my mom know you were coming?" Zoe asked. Maybe she did have a freshly clean house and lavender-scented sheets on her bed after all. She loved when Maggie spruced things up because she always washed the towels and sheets in every room and then spritzed all the beds with the Sleepy Time Lavender Sleep Spray she swore by.

"Last-minute decision."

"You just left Chicago and drove over on a whim?" Chicago was five hours from Appleby. "Is everything okay?"

Was he sick? He didn't look sick. He looked... really, really good. But maybe he wasn't feeling well. Maybe he needed some TLC. Maggie would make him soup and some of her menthol shower fizzies for any sinus issues. She'd gotten into Pinterest and Do-It-Yourself projects over the past couple of years bigtime.

He lifted a shoulder. A big shoulder clothed in expensive, charcoal-gray fabric. That probably smelled great. The fabric, not the shoulder. Though she wouldn't mind putting her nose against his shoulder either. Especially if it were bare...

"Everything's fine. Great. It wasn't really a whim, no. I've been planning the trip for a while."

"But you didn't tell my mom."

"No," he admitted. "I—" He shot a glance at Jocelyn. "I thought it might be best to surprise you."

Zoe blinked at him. Surprise her?

There were no surprises in her life. She lived in the same town she'd lived in since she'd been born.

She worked in her family's bakery, where she'd been

working since she was sixteen. But she'd been helping in this bakery since she'd been old enough to work a mixer.

She'd lived with her parents until two years ago when she'd moved into a house she knew almost as well as her own—the house Aiden had grown up in. The house his dad had given to her parents when he'd moved to Des Moines and that her parents had been renting out ever since. Which meant it was the house Zoe had helped clean and repaint several times over the years.

She used the same recipes in her baking her grandmother had used for over fifty years.

She saw the same people she'd been seeing for the past twenty-five years with very few exceptions.

Yeah, surprises weren't really a thing in her life. Especially from Aiden.

That's why she'd picked him to take her virginity. She knew him. Well. That had been a perk of the first-lover thing. She had no worries with Aiden.

Until he'd said no to the whole thing, of course.

Yeah, calling that a surprise was an understatement.

She didn't really like Aiden surprises, it turned out.

Zoe cleared her throat and moved forward, stepping around him to carry the cake balls to the front. The cake balls that would totally defrost before she had a chance to put a stick in them or dip them in the coating.

"Mom's going to be pissed you didn't warn her so she could scrub the bathroom and grocery shop for chicken alfredo ingredients." Maggie always made chicken alfredo for Aiden when he came home.

She stepped through the swinging doors with the big, useless tray of cake balls. Then froze.

Wait. The bathroom. The bed with the sheets Maggie was going to spritz for Aiden. The crackers. Those were all at...

No. No, no, no.

She turned quickly. The doors into the kitchen were still swinging, and she saw Aiden through them. Then she didn't. Then she did.

She was vaguely aware that a few of the balls had gone rolling off the tray with her quick turn.

She couldn't care about cake balls right now. Her whole world was rolling off the tray—so to speak. *Pull it together*, she told herself sternly. *Don't act like an idiot.*

"Where are you going to stay?" she asked. Dammit, her voice sounded funny.

"At the house," he said easily. "Of course."

But the way he was watching her told her that he realized there was nothing *easy* about that now. The house referred to *his* old house. The one she was now living in. Her and Camden's childhood home was only a three-bedroom house. Her younger brother, Henry, had slept in a bassinet in their parents' room until Cam went off to college. Then his old bedroom had become their little brother's. Her old bedroom was now Maggie's sewing room, and the guys were too old, and big, to sleep on couches and air mattresses.

Zoe's house, on the other hand, had four bedrooms. She used one as a library-slash-office, but the other two were, well, bedrooms. They still had all the bedroom furniture in them from when Aiden had lived there. It only made sense that her brother, and the guy who was practically a brother, would stay in those extra rooms. Hell, Aiden stayed in *his* old bedroom.

That had always been a perfect solution to the space issue around holidays and family get-togethers when the guys stayed for a few days.

Perfect until she'd made a complete and total ass of herself. In Aiden's bedroom. Hell, she still blushed when she walked past the room five months later.

"No," she said softly, shaking her head. She was aware she was not playing this cool as she'd wanted to. But her heart was suddenly pounding and she felt hot. She kind of wanted to head back to the freezer.

Aiden stepped through the doors into the front of the bakery. "Yes," he said. His voice was a little gruff and firm.

Her stomach flipped. Gruff and firm? That wasn't Aiden. But it was really working for her.

Uh-oh.

"We can't be there. Alone. Together. Now." She sounded like an idiot. But he knew very well what she was talking about. He'd *rejected* her. She'd made a fool of herself. She couldn't relive that with him every day for however long he was staying.

"Yes. We can."

Yeah, there was definitely a little huskiness in his voice. And her stupid stomach swooped again at the sound. This horniness was a huge problem, and when facing the man who had started the whole thing, it was simply the *worst* idea to have him staying with her.

Could she use her vibrator, knowing he was just down the hall?

Taking in the sight of him in that suit and tie, her first and only thought was, *Hell yeah, I can.*

"The idea of that is..." she started.

He gave her a slow, stupidly sexy smile.

"Horrifying," she finished.

2

Maybe not exactly the word he'd expected her to use, but Aiden understood where Zoe was coming from. He'd known this first time seeing her was going to be a little awkward. But they'd get past it. He just needed to tell her he'd worked everything out, and he was totally on board now. He would be *very* happy to help divest her of her virginity.

In fact, his entire body reacted to the mere *idea* of it with a hot, primal surge of *mine* that was actually shocking in its intensity.

But before he could tell her that—there was no point in beating around the bush after knowing her for twenty-five years and the brazen way she'd come into his bedroom on Christmas Eve—someone came through the front door of the bakery to pick up a cake.

Aiden moved to the cluster of little round white tables where people could enjoy their bakery items and coffee inside the cheery, iconic bakery.

He took a deep breath as he chose the table close to a window and sank into the bistro chair with the wrought-iron back that curved into a heart shape. He was here. He was home, and things were in motion. Seeing Zoe again had been step one. Well, after packing up most of his life in Chicago and driving back to Iowa. To stay.

The window was on the side of the bakery and looked out onto what was essentially an alley between the bakery and the antique store next door. The alley, however, was as wide as a street, paved in cobblestones, had little benches and planters full of flowers set along the length, and twinkle lights draped overhead between the two exterior brick walls. People used the alley to cut through from Main Street to Railroad Avenue, the street with the bar and café in this half of town. He had to admit, at night when the alleyway was lit up, it was pretty cool.

He smoothed his tie and sat back. Was he going to stick around and watch Zoe work? Yes, he was. He was going to talk to her the very first chance he had. If he had to wait for her to bake four cakes, frost six more, and wait on a hundred people, he would. She had to understand he was back for *her*. Before she found out about him buying Hot Cakes, the snack cake company that had been operating in Appleby since 1969.

The company had gone up for sale three days ago, and as soon as he'd seen the notice he'd known this was the way he was going to get back to Appleby and Zoe.

He was a millionaire. He and his best friends had developed the biggest online video game to hit the market in the past decade and had become wildly successful. And rich. He could have moved back to small town Iowa with nothing more than what he had in his bank account.

But he wanted more than that. He'd promised his mom before she died that he'd do something important with his life. That he'd make sure he did something that mattered. He'd been working on that since she'd died fifteen years ago. And for the past one year and eleven months—ever since he'd realized he was in love with Zoe McCaffery—he'd been trying to figure out how to do that in tiny Appleby, Iowa.

Now he knew. He had to buy the Hot Cakes factory, protect three-hundred-some jobs, and save his hometown.

And marry Zoe.

Which sounded easy enough.

If Hot Cakes wasn't her major competitor and if she wouldn't hate him for buying it and keeping it open, of course. And if she'd forgive him for turning her down for sex five months ago.

Yeah, he had some work to do.

"So who died?" Jocelyn asked as she approached with a cup of coffee.

She set it down on the tabletop for him along with a little silver pitcher of cream. Ah, Josie had remembered how he liked his coffee.

He ran his hand over his tie again. "No one. Came straight from the office."

He'd worn the suit on purpose. He knew Zoe liked him in a suit.

Aiden remembered the one time he'd been in a suit in Appleby. It had been for the funeral of a beloved teacher about year and a half ago. Zoe had been coming down the stairs and looked up from messing with her necklace on about the third stair. She'd seen him standing there and had nearly tumbled down the rest of the staircase. He'd caught her on the second step. Their gazes had met. Instant heat and awareness had sparkled between them. For just a second. Before her brother had said, "Jesus, Zoe, if you can't handle the heels, go put on some different shoes."

Had Aiden thought he needed an extra edge today, seeing her for the first time since she'd kissed him? When he was here to tell her he wanted her, forever? Oh, and that he was also buying her archenemy's company? And planning to keep it going?

Yes, definitely. He'd figured he should use any extra advantage he could come up with.

Judging by her reaction to seeing him in the bakery, that had been the right call. She was a little jumpy, and her skin was flushed and she was clearly worked up. This was good. So, so good.

"You came straight *here*, to the bakery, from your office in Chicago?" Jocelyn asked.

"Yep."

A metal tray clattered against the granite surface of the work island as if someone had just dropped it, and both Aiden and Jocelyn winced.

"You know that you embarrassed the hell out of her at Christmas, right?" Jocelyn asked.

Aiden grimaced. Dammit. Josie knew about Christmas. And Zoe's offer. And Aiden's response.

"She has nothing to be embarrassed about. I loved every minute."

Josie gave him a wow-you're-a-dumbass look. "I think it was the 'no' followed by you physically picking her up off of you and setting her on the floor that maybe made her think 'loving it' wasn't really where you were at."

Aiden coughed. Yeah, Zoe had definitely shared *all* the details.

He glanced at Zoe. She was working with her back to him and Josie. Maybe trying to ignore him.

Dammit.

He'd thought she'd be angry. *That* he could have handled. She was scrappy. She'd been raised, in part, by a grandmother who'd kept a personal grudge against her childhood best friend for over fifty years. But he hadn't expected Zoe to be *ashamed* of what had happened.

God, that night she'd been... everything he wanted wrapped in a hot-pink silk-and-lace package. But yeah, to be fair, who the hell turned that down? Who the hell turned down a gorgeous, smart, funny, sassy woman when she showed up in lingerie in his bedroom, *period*?

A guy who wanted a lot more than that from her. A guy who would want to marry her afterward. A guy who hadn't had any idea how to make it all work in that moment. Especially with the sight of her nearly naked scrambling his brain.

He hadn't handled it well. Clearly. But he was here now to make up for that.

"Okay, I get that I have some making up to do," he told Josie.

"It took you five months to figure that out?"

Aiden shook his head. "No. It took me about an hour to figure that out. It took me five months to come up with *how* to do it."

Josie frowned. "It took you five months to come up with apologizing?"

"Oh, I'm not apologizing," Aiden said.

Josie leaned in and lowered her voice. "You're *not* apologizing? We're talking about what happened Christmas Eve, right?"

"We are," he said. He looked past her at Zoe, who was boxing up cupcakes for a customer. But her body was stiff and her cheeks were flushed. She felt awkward having him here. But she was *aware* of him. He could work with that. "I'm not sorry about Christmas Eve." He met Jocelyn's gaze. "I'm sorry she was hurt by it, but I'm not sorry for saying no. That was the right call. I couldn't go there with her then. She'll understand why as soon as we talk."

Now Josie looked suspicious. "But you're planning to go there now?"

"And more."

One of Josie's eyebrows arched. "What's your plan?"

"Sweep her off her feet, of course," he said with a grin.

Josie's eyes widened. Then she straightened and gave a little laugh. "Oh. Of course. Well, good luck with that."

Aiden frowned. "What do you mean?" He didn't need luck. This was Zoe. And him. They were the perfect match, and now their timing was finally working out. But he felt a niggle of trepidation at the amused expression on Zoe's best friend's face.

"You were pretty good at scoring—lots of home runs and touchdowns, and you were the leading scorer in the conference in basketball for, what was it, two years?"

"Three," Aiden mumbled, suddenly feeling a little less optimistic.

"Right." She laughed. "I just think it might be entertaining to see the Golden Boy throw a few... pitches... that don't land just perfectly."

Aiden didn't like the way she said that. "Hey, I—"

"Try the cake pops," Jocelyn said. "They're great." Then she turned on her heel and headed back for the kitchen.

Cake pops? Aiden focused on what Zoe was doing rather than just on *her*.

They didn't have cake pops here. The menu at Buttered Up hadn't changed even once in all the time he'd been coming here. The way they iced and decorated the custom-made cakes varied, of course. If someone wanted Spider-Man, or the Eiffel Tower, or a fire truck, they got it. But the cake and icing always tasted the same. It was the best cake he'd ever tasted, and everyone he knew who had ever had a Buttered Up cake agreed.

What was up with the cake pops?

He'd been so tuned in to *her*—her light blond, almost white hair, that fell in waves to her shoulders, her bright blue eyes, her petite body with just enough curve to make his palms itchy to touch—he hadn't even really noticed what she'd been doing other than *bakery stuff*.

He quickly lost interest in the little balls of cake she was dipping into some kind of pink coating. Because studying Zoe would always be more interesting. She had a runner's body, trim and muscular. In bare feet, the top of her head came to his nose, so she wasn't exactly short. She was the perfect hugging height. He could easily kiss her on top of the head or on her forehead, but she'd have to be on tiptoe, or he'd have to lean in, to *really* kiss her.

If they were standing up.

Aiden shifted on his seat, suddenly thinking about the kiss she'd laid on him before he'd pushed her back. He hadn't had to bend over for that one. He'd been propped up on his elbows in bed, having just been awakened, and she'd climbed up on the mattress with him, straddling his thighs. She'd definitely been the one leaning in for that kiss.

Behind her bright yellow apron tied in a bow at her lower back, it was actually hard to make out much about her body. She was tiny through the breasts and hips and the apron covered both. But in pink lingerie, even in the dim light of his bedroom, he'd been able to see enough to haunt him for five months now. Every night.

He hadn't been with another woman since. Hell, he hadn't even been *with* Zoe that night. But he'd tasted her for the first time. He'd felt her silky, hot, bare skin. He'd seen her breasts and the hard nipples behind the filmy pink material of the teddy she'd been wearing.

And that had been more than enough.

That had done it. She was all he wanted after that kiss. Zoe McCaffery was the one.

"So you're just going to sit there?" she asked.

It took Aiden a second to realize she was talking to him. Her attention was still on the cake balls. But when he looked around, he realized the front of the bakery was empty except for the two of them.

"I'm going to sit here until you're done and able to talk."

"We can talk now. While I work."

"I don't know if it's a good idea to talk about this when you're within arm's reach of knives and forks," he quipped.

She looked up. "That's a good point."

Okay, so she really was mad. Too. Besides being embarrassed.

"Where exactly do you think this conversation is going to happen, then?" she asked. "I've got knives and forks at home too."

He gave her a smile. He understood he'd screwed up, and he was going to explain and make it up to her. But this was Zoe. She knew him too well, for too long, to stay mad at him. They had too many people in common. People who loved him and thought he was awesome. People who would be thrilled if they got together.

People like her mom and dad.

Them fucking around on Christmas Eve before he went back to Chicago? No. Not that. But long-term, forever? Definitely.

And there was always Henry, Zoe's little brother. Henry thought Aiden was a rock star. Aiden was one of the guys behind Henry's favorite video game after all. There was very little in the world Henry cared about as much as he did about *Warriors of Easton*. But Henry loved Aiden not only because he got tokens to unlock new levels of the game before they were even available to the public, but because Aiden had always been a part of his life. He was another big brother to the kid. Henry was one of Aiden's biggest fans. Henry would absolutely be a wingman if Aiden needed it.

But he really hoped he wouldn't need it.

"You wouldn't use a knife or fork on me," Aiden said.

Zoe dipped two more cake balls, rolling them in pink sugar, before answering, "Maybe I wouldn't use one on a major artery or anything. But I am mad at you."

Okay, she wasn't looking at him, but she wasn't yelling or throwing things either.

"I know."

"Actually, I'm... I wish I was mad. Or more mad. But I'm..." She let out a breath. "Christmas was humiliating. And I don't like having that between us. I can't avoid you, and it feels weird to... feel weird around you."

"You should *not* feel humiliated, Zoe. Christmas Eve was... amazing." That actually seemed like a weak word for the moment that had changed his life.

That sounded dramatic, he knew, but it was true. It might have taken him five months to figure out what *exactly* to do about it, but that night, kissing Zoe for the first time, had changed his course. Now he was here, on the verge of buying a business that would save his hometown, and able to dive in fully on a romance with Zoe.

Things were pretty fucking great.

Other than her deep hatred toward the business he was buying. But they'd get through that. Somehow. His plan for that at the moment? A lot of sex and sweet talk. Not necessarily in that order. Or maybe just at the same time.

She laughed lightly, swirling another ball on a stick through pink coating. "Pretty amazingly stupid and horrible."

"Stop."

She looked up at his firm comment. She shook her head. "You don't have to make me feel better about it."

"Fine. Maybe I don't. But I'm allowed to feel how *I* feel about it too."

She frowned slightly. "And how do you feel about it?"

"I feel like it changed everything," he told her honestly.

He rose from the table and approached the counter where they rang customers out at the register. There was a wide slab of granite and a few feet of the scarred wooden floor between them, but he still saw her draw her shoulders back as if preparing for a confrontation.

"I'm back," he said simply. "Things are different now than they were at Christmastime."

Her gaze went over him. "You had to wear a fricking suit, didn't you?" she muttered.

He grinned and smoothed his hand over his tie. "I just got in the car and drove straight here."

"Liar. You knew the suit would make me weak. Or you would have changed."

He definitely liked her admitting the suit was doing its job.

The clock over Zoe's head chimed and she glanced up. It was five o'clock. Closing time for the front of the bakery. His meeting with the guys had been at 9 a.m., as usual. He'd been on the road for Appleby by eleven. He'd rolled into town around four thirty, knowing Zoe would still be at Buttered Up but that she'd be closing at five.

"Hang on," Zoe told him with a little sigh. She wiped her hands on the towel lying next to the tray of pink-coated cake balls. She crossed to the swinging door that led into the kitchen and poked her head through. "Hey, Jose? You can head out. I'm going to finish the cake pops and then close up."

"You sure?" he heard Jocelyn ask.

"Yep."

"Is he still here?"

Aiden smiled. He wasn't going anywhere.

"He is," Zoe said, sounding resigned.

Well, resigned wasn't knife-throwing-angry.

"You sure you want to be alone with him?" Josie asked.

Zoe's shoulders lifted and fell as she took a deep breath. "Might as well get it over with."

"Okay. Well... call me later," Josie told her.

"I will," Zoe promised.

"Okay." Josie still didn't sound sure.

"She'll be fine," Aiden called.

"I'll hunt you down if she's not!" Josie called back.

He believed her. It should be funny. Jocelyn Asher was a tiny woman too. She was at least three inches shorter than Zoe, and though she had bigger boobs, she was very petite.

But he knew the protective streak in these women for one another was wide and intense. He didn't really want to test Josie's temper. Plus he liked her. And having Zoe's best friend on his side would be a very good thing.

Getting *Zoe* on his side might be a challenge, but he was up for it. He was a very successful guy. Things had always come a little easy to him—sports and grades and business achievements—but hey, he'd lost his mom as a fourteen-year-old kid. His dad had sunk into a workaholic daze afterward. It wasn't like everything had always been a piece of cake for him.

His gaze landed on the cake pops Zoe had been working on.

She might not be a piece of cake for him, either, but she'd be worth whatever work he had to put in.

Finally, Zoe turned back to him. She gave him a long look. Then she said, "Can you take those trays into the back?" she asked, pointing to the trays of cake balls and the already finished cake pops.

"Sure." He started around the edge of the counter.

She passed him on her way to the front door of the bakery. He lifted the first big tray as she turned the sign that hung on the big glass door from Top of the Muffin To You! to Bake Later! and locked the door. She flipped off the main overhead light, leaving just the lights in the display cases on. Anyone walking by would still be able to look in and appreciate the homemade pastries, cupcakes, and muffins Buttered Up had to offer.

Aiden took the tray into the back, setting it on the massive worktable in the middle of the kitchen. Over the fifty years of existing, they'd had to upgrade the appliances a couple of times, of course. The stainless steel, state-of-the art refrigerator and ovens were clearly high end. But the wood flooring was original, just like it was out in the front. The exposed brick walls were, of course, original, as was the worktable in the middle of the room. Zoe's grandmother had made cakes and pies and cookies on that worktable just like her daughter and now granddaughter. There were other little touches that spoke of the bakery's history. The light fixtures on the walls were the same. They'd added bright, overhead lighting at some point, but the sconces with their softer light made the kitchen feel cozy in spite of the overhead illumination, and even that came from a long, multi-bulb brass chandelier that matched the sconces pretty closely.

The oven mitts and hot pads and aprons hung on the wall were not fifty years old, but they were the same style and color Letty McCaffery had used, and bore Buttered Up's logo that had been the same from day one.

Aiden would also bet that several of the pots and pans hanging from the rack suspended over the center island were also Letty's.

It was an interesting space, a nice fusion of new and old, and he knew it took Zoe a lot to replace anything. Things had to wear out or break down before she'd get new. Her fierce protectiveness of the family business and Buttered Up's reputation was one of the things he admired most about her.

Zoe came into the kitchen with the other tray of cake pops that needed to be finished. "Okay, if we're going to talk, you're going to help me work so that we can get these done, and I can storm out of here when you piss me off," she told him.

He laughed. "Fair enough. I guess it doesn't matter that I'm staying at the house with you?"

"If I storm out of here mad, then you need to take your time coming to the house," she told him.

"I can always detour past your mom's house."

"You could also stay there."

Zoe set the bowl of cake pop coating—whatever it was—in the microwave to reheat.

"But you won't be there," he said.

"Exactly."

She still wasn't really making eye contact, but she was in here with him. The doors were locked. There was no countertop between them. They were alone, together. Something they hadn't been in five months. Something he'd wanted most out of this trip to Appleby.

Yes, the factory was important. A several-million-dollar investment was not a tiny, by-the-way kind of thing.

But Zoe was the reason he was here.

The microwave beeped, and she retrieved the bowl of pink liquid without saying anything.

She turned toward him, crossing the worktable. She set it down and braced her hands on the tabletop. Finally, she lifted her gaze to his. "Let's get this done."

"The cake pops?"

"The awkward conversation."

"You definitely want to talk here?"

"Definitely. As soon as my mom finds out you're here—which will be three minutes after you park your car in the driveway—she'll be over. She'll be flustered she didn't know you were coming. She'll want to clean everything and cook dinner and fuss over you."

Aiden grinned. He loved all that about Maggie. She was the best. And Zoe was right. His childhood home was on the block over from the McCafferys' house. Maggie could see the driveway from her kitchen window. She spent easily 80 percent of her time at home in the kitchen. He was certain she loved keeping track of Zoe that way, and it would take no time for her to notice his car.

"And, of course, Henry will want to come see you," Zoe said. "Then Dad will come too because he won't want to miss anything." She sighed. "If we want to have a honest conversation about why you don't want to have sex with me—and I'm not sure *we* want to have that conversation, but I know you're very used to getting your way so you won't let it drop—then we should do it here. On my turf."

Maggie had run the bakery with *her* best friend, his mom, for nearly fifteen years. They'd hired another woman, Alicia, after Julie had died, until Zoe was old enough to take over. Then Maggie had gone part time. Now Maggie only came in a couple of days a week. The bakery was definitely Zoe's turf. Even if most everything inside had barely changed and Zoe ran things much the way it always had been, she was still definitely the one in charge.

"The house you live in isn't your turf?" he asked. He maybe should have started with correcting her assumption that he didn't want to have sex with her, but they'd get to that. For sure. She would have *no* doubt about that soon enough.

"The house is..." She shrugged. "Still kind of feels like your house."

He liked that. The house had been where he'd spent all fourteen years he'd had with his mom. The memories in the last couple of years there weren't very happy, but they were mostly overshadowed by the ones that had been. That house was where he'd celebrated birthdays, Christmases, many of those home runs and touchdowns Josie had mentioned. The house was mostly full of great memories for him, and he loved that Zoe felt he and his family were still a part of the house.

"I love that you're living there," he told her, honestly. It was an aside to what he really wanted to talk about, but it was true, and he wasn't sure he'd ever said that. "It felt weird thinking about other people living there. I like knowing that it's still in the family."

She was watching him closely. "We are pretty much family," she said. "Is that why you don't want to have sex with me?"

"That is not..." He thought about that. "Okay, maybe a little of it."

She rolled her eyes and reached for a cake ball. She dipped the tip of a stick in the pink goo and then pushed it about an inch into the cake. She just let it sit like that.

"It's not what you think," Aiden said. "It's not because I think of you as a sister or something."

Zoe picked the cake pop up by the stick and dipped the whole ball into the coating. She twirled it, covering all sides, then she tapped the stick gently on the side of the bowl, getting rid of the excess coating.

"We know each other really well," he went on when she still didn't say anything. "But I'm definitely attracted to you."

She moved the ball to the plate of pale pink sugar next to her and rolled it, covering it with sparkling pink. Then she stuck it into a square of Styrofoam with the other completed cake pops so the coating could set up and harden.

"That's why I picked you," she finally said. She handed him a stick and gestured toward the bowl of pink goo. Clearly she thought he should know what to do now.

"You picked me for sex because I'm like a big brother to you?" He inserted the stick the way she had.

"Ew, of course not," she snapped. "But I picked you because I know you. Almost too well." She muttered the last three words.

"Almost too well?" he asked. He dipped the ball into the coating and swirled it to cover all sides.

She stood with her hip propped against the counter, watching him. "Make sure you tap it a little to get the extra off. You want the coating to be thin but to totally cover the cake."

He did as she asked, but tapped way too hard. The cake ball fell off into the goo. Zoe sighed.

"Yeah, see, I knew that was going to happen."

He frowned and started to reach for the ball.

She slapped his hand. "Don't stick your hand in there!" She grabbed a spoon to fish the cake ball out. "You always go hard. You just assume you'll be good at whatever you do. You believe everything will just work out. You don't think it through."

Aiden's frown deepened. "That is *not* true. I think things through. I manage our business by thinking through how everyone else is going to react to things and what they would be best at handling. I make sure everyone on our team is doing what they're best at."

Hell, thinking things through was most of what he did. He prided himself on reading the people and situations around him and making adjustments as things developed. He was the *most* thoughtful one, in fact.

He was the head of the company, the first contact, because Ollie would get in over his head saying yes to everything. Dax would get distracted in the midst of a project with something else. Grant would say no to everything right away. Camden would piss everyone off before they got anywhere just because he had to push buttons.

So no, Aiden didn't think things just worked out.

Much.

Zoe set the cake ball to the side and looked up at him. "Okay, then, maybe it's just with us. My family. This town. But you expect things here to always fall into line."

"Do I?"

"Don't you?" she shot back. "You think you can just walk back in here after five months, and I'll just forget what happened and forgive you and sit with you across the table at my mom's and sleep down the hall from you and share the coffeepot in the morning and everything just like it's always been? No awkwardness? No embarrassment?"

"No," he said honestly. "I don't think you'll forget what happened. And I want you sitting across your mom's table thinking about it. I want you sleeping down the hall thinking about it. I want you having coffee in the kitchen in the morning thinking about it. Because I sure as hell will be."

Something flickered in her eyes. But she shook her head. "What do you want?"

"You."

She blinked at him. Then frowned. Then blinked again. "What?"

Aiden braced his hands on the countertop and leaned in. "You. I want you. I'm here. To stay. I couldn't say that five months ago. But now I can."

"That's... I..." She took a deep breath. "That's not what I wanted you to say. I wanted sex, Aiden. Not a commitment. Oh my God." Her eyes widened that all seemed to sink in. "Is that what you thought? You thought I expected a *relationship*? No. Wow. No, that is *not* what I wanted."

Okay, she didn't have to be so adamant about it. "But that's how it would have to be with us, Zoe," he said. "I don't do casual and temporary."

That was for sure. Casual and temporary didn't really work in his life in general. When he dated, he did it for long periods and was always committed to the person for however long it lasted. Obviously, none of them had turned into forever yet, but he'd never had flings or one-night stands. He was a serial monogamist. And until Zoe had appeared in his bedroom like the Ghost of Christmas Fantasies last December, he hadn't realized the reason none of those had worked out was because *she* was the one he was supposed to be with. When the time was right.

Like it was now.

Losing his mom so young had taught him early that life went fast. You couldn't take things for granted. You couldn't waste days and opportunities.

Zoe took a deep breath. "Okay, I know you don't do casual. I get that. But... I picked you because..." She pulled her bottom lip between her teeth and looked up at him for a long moment. She had a smear of pink icing on her chin, and her cheek sparkled with pink sugar.

He wanted to kiss her. He wanted to lean across the work-table, cup the back of her head, and pull her in for a kiss. A kiss that would be surrounded by the scent of vanilla cake. He wanted to lick that icing and sugar off of her. And then keep licking.

"I needed to know what sex was like before I had it for real with someone," she finally said. "I picked you because I know you've done it—a lot—and I know you and trust you. I knew I'd be safe with you and you wouldn't make fun of me, and I could get the first time over with and not have to worry about running into you repeatedly afterward at the café or grocery store."

There was a lot there, and Aiden wanted to respond to all of it. He wasn't sure where to start. "What the hell do you mean you wanted to get it over with?"

That may not have been the *best* place, but it was one of the things that stuck out.

"And what do you mean before you had it for real with someone?" he asked before she could answer. It wouldn't have been real with him? What the fuck was that?

"I'm a twenty-five-year-old virgin," she exclaimed. "I have no idea what I'm doing. The whole concept of sex makes me a little anxious. I don't want to be awkward or do something wrong or stupid. So I wanted to get my first time out of the way, and I thought doing it with you was the best idea." She shook her head. "And then *that* was a humiliating disaster."

"I was going to be your guinea pig?" he asked. He was a little amused. And a lot ticked off. Because she'd clearly intended for it to be a one-time thing before she moved on to other guys.

And that was *not* okay with him.

"Kind of." She shrugged. "I figured you'd show me the basics, and I'd be able to get over the anxiety."

"The basics." He intended to show her a hell of a lot more than that.

"Yeah. I mean, I *know* the basics. In general. In my head. But I've never done them with another person." She shifted her weight from one foot to the other. "So yeah, I wanted to be prepared and figured you were a good person to help me with that."

He was momentarily distracted by the "with another person" thing filling his head with thoughts of the things she might have been doing alone. But he shook that off. He needed to focus. There was time for all that—and they *would* get to it—later. "Because you know me so well, you figured I'd be fine being your sex tutor."

The idea of that was a little hot, but he also ignored that. This was *not* a short-term, just-about-sex thing. Though tutoring her in sex seemed…

Focus, dammit.

"Look," she said, bracing her feet and squaring her shoulders. "Being a virgin at sixteen and learning about sex with other sixteen-year-olds who are virgins too, or at least not very experienced, is one thing. Being a virgin at twenty-five is different. The guys my age are probably not virgins and definitely have some experience. I don't want to be *bad* in bed, Aiden." She frowned at him. "This is a small town. That kind of stuff gets around."

He just stared at her for a long moment. "You're worried about getting a reputation for being bad in bed?"

"*Yes.*" She actually smiled at him as if relieved he was finally getting this.

He could tell her there was no way she was going to be bad in bed. She was passionate and sweet and smart and self-depre-cating and gorgeous. He could tell her that even when it was bad, sex was pretty damned good. He could tell her he was *certain* she was going to catch on right away.

"There's no recipe for it, Zoe. It's different with everyone."

She was already shaking her head. The idea of something *not* having a recipe she could follow was the easiest way to make Zoe McCaffery nervous. "There is a *basic* recipe," she said. "There's a starting place."

"Right. Tab A into slot B," he said dryly.

"And I want to know what it's like so I can be prepared."

She didn't even smile at his quip. She was totally serious. "Really romantic and sexy, Zoe," he told her.

"That's just it. I don't need it to be romantic and sexy the first time. I just need the *knowledge*," she told him. "That's why I picked you. And because you wouldn't talk about it around town after or make fun of me." That part seemed very important to her. What the hell was she doing even thinking about sleeping with guy who might make *fun* of her in bed?

But she'd picked *him* because she didn't want her first time having sex to be romantic or sexy. Oh, this woman had a lot to learn.

3

————

"Well, I'm here now and very happy to help with the virginity thing," Aiden said. "And I can fix all the rest too. I'll happily walk you through every fucking thing you want to try. Repeatedly. Until we're the best there's ever been." He gave her a wicked grin. He meant that to his soul. "There's also no way in hell I'm telling anyone a single detail, and Sugar, there is no damned way you're going to be bad at this. So no more worries about any of it."

She looked legitimately confused. "What are you talking about?"

"Everything is good now that I'm back," he said with a little smile. "You don't need to spend one more second thinking about or worrying about any other man ever again."

She slowly nodded as if catching on. "So we're just going to have sex every time you come home to visit. And I don't see anyone else? I just wait around for you? We'll have a long distance relationship from here to Chicago?"

He shrugged. It was not the time to tell her about Hot Cakes. It was definitely *not* the time. "Fuck, yes to the not seeing anyone else. Yes to the sex every time I come home. But no more visits, no more waiting around, no more long distance, no more Chicago."

"What?" She was clearly puzzled.

"I'm here now. To stay."

"Come on," she scoffed. "Sure."

"I haven't been able to stop thinking about Christmas," he said, letting his voice get a little husky and holding her gaze. "The kiss. Everything. I want it. All of it."

"Oh." She blinked at him. She frowned. Then her eyes got wide. Then she crossed her arms. "Well, you need to get over that." She swallowed hard at the end though.

That was the tell. The sign that she wasn't flippant about this. Or angry at his audacity. She was shocked, sure, but she wasn't nonchalant about this.

"Not gonna happen," he told her honestly.

"I can *not* have an *actual* relationship with you, Aiden."

"Of course you can. It's perfect."

"You really think you're just going to move here?"

She did actually seem confused by all this.

"Sure," he said simply. It was simple. This part anyway.

"How does *that* work?" she asked, clearly thinking he was nuts. "Your company is in Chicago."

"I've got a lot of money, Zoe," he said. It sounded arrogant, but it was also true. And with her, he could be a little cocky.

"Oh, great, I definitely want to date a guy who's just sitting around on his ass being rich," she said with an eye roll.

She knew he'd never do that. He wasn't wired that way. "You know, we just sold our company to a bigger gaming company," he told her. He and Cam had shared the news with the family at Christmas as a matter of fact. "They're taking over most of the operations. We're involved as much as we'd like to be, and we still get royalties, but we're not as busy with it now. We're in the midst of looking at new opportunities."

All true. No need to go into those specific opportunities—or the one that was in her backyard—at the moment. He really wanted to get a feel for the Hot Cakes situation and how the transition would work before he made a big deal out of it with the McCafferys. Yes, her whole family hated Hot Cakes, and more specifically, the Lancaster family who had started and owned and was now selling the company. He wanted to be able to assure them it was all nothing to worry about, and it wouldn't change their relationships at all, but he felt like he should at least set foot inside the factory before he said that.

"I can work from anywhere," he said.

That was true enough. He'd still have a hand—or at least a few fingers—in Fluke Inc., his company in Chicago. It was best when the five of the partners were together. It would be *best* if he was there with them, at least some of the time. God knew what Ollie would have them investing in next or who Cam would piss off if Aiden wasn't there some of the time. But Chicago wasn't that far away. Even if he was there once a week, he could keep them on track. Probably. Piper, their executive assistant, was there, at least. He could give her more authority and power to keep the guys in line. Especially Ollie. Grant, their CFO, had hired her as Ollie's direct assistant, though she definitely helped them all. If someone could just keep an eye on what Ollie was doing and knew when to alert Aiden, things wouldn't get too far out of hand.

"You're going to *move* here. We're going to have tons of sex. And then what?" Zoe asked. "How does that breakup work out? My family will be heartbroken. No other guy in this town will want to date me."

"Well, *excellent* on the second part," he said firmly. "As for the first—there's no breakup. Nothing to worry about."

"We're never going to break up?" she asked, her eyebrows nearly to her hairline.

"Right."

"You're crazy."

"Why? This makes total sense."

"It makes *no* sense. You can't just kiss someone, push them away, then come back five months later and essentially propose!"

He was getting a little irritated with her insistence against this. "Looks like I can."

She huffed out a breath while rolling her eyes. "Well, I'm not going to marry my brother's best friend. A guy I've known *forever*."

"Why not?"

Zoe propped her hands on her hips. "My entire life goes according to plan too, Aiden. But not just everything I touch turns to gold like you. I *make* it happen that way. But I live in the same town I've been in all my life. I took over my family's business. I moved into a house of a lifelong family friend. The people I work with and wait on are people I've known forever. The things I do at work go according to specific recipes that have been tried and true for *half a century*. There are very few surprises or bumps or glitches."

"And you love it that way," he pointed out.

She nodded. "Which is why I think having some surprises, excitement, adventures in my love life... and my sex life... would be great."

He lifted a brow. "Really?"

She tipped her head. "Yes. Really. Is that so hard to believe?"

"Yeah." He shrugged.

"Hey."

"You haven't even deviated from a recipe by a half a teaspoon in all your life," he told her with a little laugh.

"We're making cake pops now!" she said, gesturing toward the worktable.

"And I'll bet you one million dollars that it was all Josie's idea that the cake and icing and everything you're using is the same stuff you've always used, so that those things taste *exactly* like all the other Buttered Up cakes—which is a fantastic thing, by the way—and that even having those little balls of cake added to your menu makes you a little itchy."

She chewed on her bottom lip.

"Deny it," he challenged. "Any of it. You make those balls out of the same cake batter you do everything else, don't you?"

"No." She paused. Then she admitted, "We use the leftover cake Josie trims off the custom cakes she makes. And leftover icing."

"Ah-ha!" He knew this woman. She needed to realize that.

"It's a great way to reduce waste," she said.

"It is," he agreed. "And a great way to not really *change* anything."

She scratched her arm. "Even more reason to want an exciting sex life."

"The exciting, spontaneous sex life you wanted so badly but felt you needed to try out before doing it 'for real'?" He even made the air quotes with his fingers because he did *not* take seriously that sex between them wouldn't have been very real.

"Shut up," she muttered.

Aiden grinned. Zoe had never been good at admitting she was wrong or giving up a fight. Definitely something she'd inherited from her grandmother.

"Hey, no worries," he said. "That is *not* going to be a problem. I'm *all for* an exciting sex life. Whatever you want." His body stirred with the very idea of exploring anything and everything Zoe would want to try.

"Not. With. You."

She was so damned stubborn. "Zoe," he said, dropping his voice.

But she just narrowed her eyes. "Marrying a guy who's basically been a part of my family my entire life, who I know as well as I know my brother, who I already have years of memories with, isn't new or exciting."

"You've got to be kidding me," he finally said. "Knowing me, *liking* me, your family already loving me, having a history together—that's all counting *against* me here?"

She shrugged. "Yes."

"*That* is nuts," he told her.

"Actually, the idea of marrying the first guy I ever sleep with is so sane and normal and"—she wrinkled her nose—"*cliché*, it's ridiculous."

He straightened. "So the sex thing is still on the table though," he said, focusing on the part that would help him out most. Because the rest of it... well, she wasn't wrong. Falling for the first guy she slept with was absolutely a possibility, and Zoe was a forever kind of girl. Finding out she'd seriously dated and been intimate with only one guy would not have shocked him.

And now that the guy was going to be *him*, it made perfect sense.

Was he above taking her to bed and *then* pressing hard for more? Nope. Not at all. Zoe McCaffery was difficult. He wasn't sure why he'd thought she'd suddenly be easy for him. Oh yeah, the candy-pink teddy she'd worn into his bedroom on Christmas Eve. That whole thing had seemed *very* easy.

Forgetting about it had been the hard part. Impossible, in fact.

She flipped her hand as if waving it all away. "Oh, no. Don't worry. I'm good there."

He looked at her closely. "Good where?"

"The sex thing."

He sighed. None of this was turning out to be romantic or especially hot. He'd expected it to be sexy. He'd truly thought he'd show up, she'd be a little miffed, but he'd quickly wear her down. She wanted him. That was a well-established fact now. That kiss was not something either of them was going to be able to forget about. He'd really thought by this point of being alone with her, they'd be back at it.

"Look, I know you're ticked off and embarrassed that I turned you down," he said.

"Of course I'm ticked off and embarrassed!" she exclaimed. "I asked you for *one* little favor! We've been friends forever! You couldn't just do that one thing for me? Take twenty minutes out of your night? Instead, you had to make it this whole humiliating thing. Just no. That was all you freaking said, Aiden. Just no."

He opened his mouth then shut it and frowned. She really did make it sound like she was considering it a request she'd made of him like "Could you kill a huge spider in the bathroom for me?" or "Could I have a few of your frequent-flier miles?"

"Well, it wasn't exactly a *little* favor," he said, his jaw tight.

Her eyes dropped to his fly.

He was surprised. That wasn't what he'd been talking about. But it was good to know where her mind went.

Then she rolled her eyes. The way she'd done to him probably a million times in their lives. But this time his male ego got riled up. "And twenty minutes? You haven't even been reading good books about it or watching decent porn if you think it would only take twenty minutes."

Her eyes widened, then narrowed, then went normal sized, as if responding to a series of thoughts going through her mind.

All of which made him really nervous.

Her voice was completely calm when she said, "*Anyway,* you don't have to worry. That's all done. I'm good. I've got it taken care of."

"What the hell does *that* mean?" he demanded.

But he knew. It meant that some other guy had showed her what sex was all about so that she could "get it over with" before she had it *for real*. And now he was going to need names and addresses. Because Zoe McCaffery was *his*.

Not that he was going to say it quite like that to her. Zoe was very much her own woman. Hell, the sentiment would likely shock her. He wasn't that kind of guy. He'd certainly never been that kind of guy about Zoe.

Of course, if anyone had ever messed with her—teased her on the playground, been mean to her in high school—he would have been there to make that person sorry.

This was different. This was about someone touching her, her *wanting* that person to touch her, pleasure her, do things she'd never experienced before.

That was all supposed to be his territory.

She would *not* appreciate that sentiment from him at all.

The other men in Appleby would though. He'd be sure of that.

"It means I'm fine. Without you," she said. She cocked her head, giving him a little smile. "But really, thank you for your concern."

"You're fine without me?" His voice was low, and he was sure she could see his temper was rising too.

"What?" she asked, her eyes wide and blinking. "You thought I'd just be waiting around for you to come back?"

"Yes!" It was the wrong answer, he knew, even as he said it. But it was true.

"You are so full of yourself!" she said, immediately dropping the whole, obviously fake, you're-so-sweet-to-worry-about-me thing. She frowned. "You actually thought I'd be waiting around, pining for you, didn't you?"

Maybe not crying herself to sleep every night, but thinking about him? Yeah. Fuck. He hadn't been able to get her out of his mind for more than a few hours at a time. "It's only been five months," he said. "Is it really crazy for me to think that you didn't get it 'taken care of' yet?"

"Exactly! It's been *five months!*" she said.

"You went twenty-five years without sex, and you couldn't go five more *months?*"

"Well, it's not like you gave me an IOU!" she shot back. "I

had no idea when you were coming back, and I assumed your answer would have been the same. Not that you really gave me any explanation other than *no*. So yeah, I moved on, Aiden."

"Who was it?" he asked, noting his tone was suddenly a little ominous.

"I'm not telling you that." She looked at him like he was insane.

"Tell me, Zoe."

"*No.*"

"I'll find out. This is Appleby. I'll probably know by the end of tonight."

"You won't." She lifted her chin. "I can promise you that."

"Bet I do."

"Why do you really even care? Now you don't have to do it."

"Because you're mine."

Yeah, shit. See, he'd known that was the wrong answer to give. Guys didn't go around claiming women like they were property or possessions. He knew that. He'd never had that urge before. This woman was strong and independent and confident and certainly didn't *need* him for anything.

But the idea of another man touching her, seeing her naked, making her feel the ultimate pleasure, made his blood boil.

She stood, just staring at him. Then she picked up a cake ball. And threw it at him. It hit him square in the red tie and bounced back onto the table.

"You're a jerk."

Yeah, maybe he was. A nice guy would probably just take all her explanations and excuses about why they shouldn't be together and admit his idea was crazy.

He didn't say anything. He didn't wipe away the sticky crumbs the cake ball left on his tie. He picked up the ball and rounded the worktable.

Her eyes widened, and she backed up as he came closer. He kept going. Until her back was against the front of the fridge.

He didn't say a word as he stopped right in front of her, lifted his hand to cup her face, and leaned in.

Aiden ignored her hands on his chest. She wasn't pushing. She wasn't pulling him closer either, but she wasn't trying to get away. She wasn't lifting her knee to his balls. She wasn't saying no.

He stared into her eyes for a long moment. She could stop this. He knew she knew that.

She didn't.

So he kissed her.

He took her lips softly at first but then more fully. He stepped closer as he deepened the kiss, pressing her between the fridge and his body. He slid his fingers into her hair and tipped her head back slightly. Then he opened his mouth.

She gave a little sigh and followed suit. *Yes*.

He licked along her lower lip. She was so fucking sweet. She smelled and tasted like the cake and sugar and vanilla that surrounded her every day. It was like the scents had seeped into her skin and became a part of her. Appropriate. She and this bakery were connected in a deep way.

Aiden slid his other arm around her, pulling her up against him fully. He was careful not to crush the cake ball he still held. But his arm around her waist settled her against him. Her breasts pressed into his chest, their pelvises aligned, and he took the kiss deeper, stroking his tongue in along hers, tasting her fully.

She arched into him, her arms going up to encircle his neck as she went up on tiptoe.

Damn, he wanted her.

She slanted her head in the other direction and slid her hands up to the back of his head, pressing her body even closer.

She fit against him perfectly and he had a few options. He

could lift her against the fridge, put her up on the worktable and lay her back, or bend her over it to take her from behind.

He took the tiny step that brought her back against the fridge again and moved his hand from her hair to her ass. He lifted her easily. She was light enough and she definitely helped. She pulled herself up, wrapping her legs around his waist and giving a little moan that made fire lick through him.

Aiden leaned in, aligning his cock with the sweet spot between her legs, gripping her ass in one hand as she linked her ankles behind him.

He ground into her. He wanted bare skin, but he also didn't want to let go of her for a second. This spot—fitted against her like this in the middle of her kitchen—was ideal. In this moment, Christmas Eve, the past five months apart, the factory... none of it mattered. *This* was why he was here.

This woman, who he'd known his entire life and shared so much with, also made him hotter than he could remember ever being for another woman. He knew their history, their shared loves—her family, the town—and their shared desire for purpose and meaning in their lives and work were a part of that. How could he ever feel this way for someone he didn't know this well? That he hadn't known through triumphs and tragedies, victories and challenges? How could *she* want someone who she didn't know like that?

Exciting? Adventurous? Surprising?

Yeah, he'd give her all that.

He might be her brother's best friend, and this might sound a little cliché, but he didn't give a damn.

This was happening.

He pulled back and looked down at her, still holding her against the fridge.

She was flushed, her lips dark pink, her pupils dilated, and she was breathing hard.

She was also wrapped around him like a spider monkey on a banana tree.

Slowly she pulled in a deep breath and blinked.

"Surprised?" he asked, his voice gruff.

She licked her recently ravaged lips. And nodded. "Um, yeah."

Even the Christmas Eve kiss hadn't been this hot. In part because he hadn't been prepared for it. In the least. In part because he'd only let himself indulge for about ten seconds before he realized he had to stop.

This time he wasn't stopping anything.

He pressed her more firmly into the fridge to hold her up and brought the cake ball he was still holding to his mouth. He bit into it as she watched, her breathing still uneven.

He chewed, swallowed, and then gave her a cocky smirk. "I intend to have my cake and eat it too, Zoe."

4

I t took about three seconds for that to sink in.

Then she realized she was plastered against him like a sucker fish on the side of an aquarium.

Zoe unwrapped her legs and put her hands on his chest to push him back.

Aiden let her go and leaned back, allowing her to slide gracefully until her feet were on the floor.

She pushed her hair back and pulled in a deep breath. Well, *that* wasn't going to help her convince him she didn't want any of this.

Truth was, she wanted it so badly she was torn between pretending to be huffy and stomping out of here with her dignity slightly still intact, or stripping all her clothes off and begging him to resume the position.

Honestly, she'd only have to pull her panties down. This dress was very little barrier.

As she knew by the way the skirt had hiked up when he'd put her up against the fridge—damn, that was hot—and she'd felt every big, hard inch of him. Her panties and his suit pants were definitely not enough to hide that he was very okay with what had just happened.

Thankfully he said the thing about having his cake and eating it too. It was so classic Aiden. He'd really never *not* had his cake and eaten it too. It reminded her he'd pushed her away at Christmas when it wasn't convenient—or whatever—for him and *that* was *not* okay with *her*.

He thought he could just breeze back in here after five months? Of course he did. He was so... Aiden. The Golden Boy. The favorite son. The honor-student-class-president-star-athlete-debate-team-captain-perfect-commencement-speech giver. *Of course* he thought he could just waltz back in and say, "Okay I'm ready now. Take your panties off."

It really burned her up that she wanted to take her panties off so badly.

Because, of course, he was an amazing kisser.

Argh!

She was grateful for the cocky grin on his face at the moment because it was all that was giving her the ability to smooth down her dress, brush back her hair, and look him in the eye when she said, "Oh yeah, we should totally get married."

She *knew* he heard her sarcasm. But his grin grew. "I knew I'd bring you around." He reached for her face.

Zoe slapped his hand away. "You're insane."

"I don't think so." He stepped in and brought his hand up again. He ran his thumb over her cheek. "You're dusted with sugar." He put his thumb to his mouth and licked the sugar off.

Her nipples tingled.

"Hazard of the job."

"I like it."

She blew out a breath. "Knock it off." She pushed him back and slipped around him before he could touch her again. It was clear that *that* was going to be of the utmost importance—keeping a nice, big space between them.

Had he surprised her with the kiss? Yes. Yes, definitely. Had the heat of it surprised her? Yes, indeed.

Did that surprise make up for the fact that she knew everything from his favorite color to his favorite pizza toppings to his favorite church hymn? No, it did not. They had unexpected chemistry. Big deal. He was still the last person she should get involved with if she wanted surprises and excitement.

"I need to get going." She grabbed the trays of fully finished cake pops. Thank God she'd gotten a few of those done. She'd just store everything in the fridge overnight, and then she could finish the others tomorrow.

She turned. And stopped. Aiden was still standing in front of the fridge. The fridge they'd just made out against. The fridge she was very afraid she was now going to be unable to pass without thinking of him every damned time.

She passed by that fridge probably a hundred times a week.

Great.

"Excuse me."

He stepped to the side. "You're just going to leave? We're not going to talk?"

She looked at the handle on the fridge pointedly, and he reached for it, pulling the door open for her. She slid the tray in on the lower shelf.

"I think we both said plenty," she told him, turning back for the other tray. "You want to get married. I don't. I think that covers it, don't you?"

He laughed. "Yeah, not quite."

She grabbed the bowl of melted candy coating and stored it too. She should be able to remelt it in the morning. She couldn't deal with cleanup right now.

Slamming the door, she reached for the tie on her apron. "Really? What else do we need to cover?"

"The fact that I need to know who took your virginity," he said bluntly. Not smiling. "For one thing."

She rolled her eyes. Yeah, she wasn't telling him that, and there was no way he was going to be able to find out. Because the answer was *no one*. But she wasn't about to tell *him* she hadn't done a thing about her V-card in the past five months.

Mostly it was because of all the reasons she'd chosen him in the first place. She didn't know anyone else she could totally trust with her lack of knowledge and ineptness in that area. She *hated* being incompetent at anything.

That was actually something she and Aiden had very much in common. The difference between them was Aiden always thought he could *become* good at anything he wanted. Zoe was not at all sure of that herself. That was why she stuck with the things she knew she was good at.

The majority of which involved sugar, butter, and flour.

Definitely not sex. She wanted her first time to be with someone who could, and would, coach her through it, wouldn't think she was an idiot—or wouldn't let her know he thought that, anyway—and who would then leave town and wouldn't be running into her all the time and thinking about what a dork she'd been between the sheets.

Sure, she'd have to face Aiden again, eventually. She was going to have Aiden in her life forever. That was just a foregone conclusion. But it was *Aiden*. She'd truly thought they could have sex and then go back to things as they'd always been. He could do her a favor, help her out like he had when she'd been struggling with chemistry in high school, and after that one night, they'd just fall back into their regular relationship.

It had only taken one kiss to realize she'd really messed up that line of thinking.

Okay, yes, that had been a surprise.

And now that they'd kissed again... and this time *he'd* kissed *her*, which definitely made a difference... sitting across from him at her mother's dining room table was going to be difficult. Dammit.

"You have to know there is no way in hell I'm telling you who I've slept with," Zoe told him, putting her hand on her hip and summoning all her annoyance.

"I just want to have a little talk with him and let him know that you're now off limits."

She stared at him for a moment. Then she started laughing. "Yeah, sure, that's totally fine. You can absolutely go stomping around all over Appleby acting like a caveman who's marking his territory. Everyone will think that's adorable. Not to mention, totally in character for you. And I'll be paging through bridal magazines the whole time so turned on and ready to settle down with all *that*." She crossed the kitchen to the hooks by the back door. She hung up her apron and grabbed her purse. She looked back at him. "You coming?"

He had his arms crossed and was just watching her from beside the worktable. The worktable that was covered with drips of candy coating and a dusting of sugar. She was going to have to come in early to clean up tomorrow, but she couldn't be here, alone, with him any longer.

"Did you actually lose your virginity, Zoe?" he asked.

His voice was low and a little husky, and she felt a little shiver tickle down her spine. Bastard. He knew her. He could tell she was lying?

No way.

She gave him a bored look. A fake bored look—she couldn't deny her heart was pounding and she was having dirty thoughts about candy coating and sugar—but still. "You don't think so?"

He wouldn't know *for sure* either way. Maybe that would drive him even crazier. That seemed like it could be fun. Playing around with Aiden could be a good time. She hadn't had a good time in... a while. Maybe since planning her little Christmas seduction.

Which had turned into a huge humiliation.

She frowned.

He came toward her, almost like he was stalking her. Zoe felt herself straighten instinctively then told herself to relax. She didn't need to be defensive around Aiden. This was none of his business now. She just needed to remember that.

And remember to hate that he seemed to legitimately feel possessive of her. She did *not* like that. She didn't want some guy thinking he could control her.

But that's not how it felt. That's not how it would be with Aiden. He knew her too well for that. He knew she was *very* good with a paring knife.

Besides, she knew *him* too well. He was used to getting his way and having things just work out, sure, but he was a good guy. He'd always been a good boyfriend. She hadn't been close to any of the girls he'd dated in high school, being four years younger, but she knew he had a reputation for being charming and sweet and considerate, and yeah, good in bed. Or at least in back seats and on blankets down by the river. Rumors got around in a small town. Girls had known Aiden was Camden's best friend and that he was at her house a lot. They'd always wanted information about him. What kind of cookies did he like? Did he have a girlfriend currently? Would he be at her house after the basketball game? Would she take a note to him? Or a secret admirer gift?

It had been funny when she'd been twelve and he'd been sixteen.

She frowned a little. Now it wouldn't be so funny.

Now that she knew he was a good kisser. And that he wanted to sleep with her. And that he was feeling possessive of her.

Dammit.

He stopped right in front of her, totally in her personal space. Close enough for her to confirm, once again, that yes, he did smell as good as he looked in that freaking suit.

"I think if you wanted a guy, all you'd have to really do is snap your fingers, and you'd have a line out the door," he said. "But," he added. "I also think all the reasons you wanted me to be your first are still true. So I'm not so sure that you haven't just been waiting for me to come home."

All the reasons she'd wanted him to be her first were definitely still true. The bastard. He could have taken care of this five months ago, and she'd be over her hang-up about having sex for the first time at twenty-five and could maybe be dating someone now and having regular, fun sex and doing the relationship thing.

But no...

"It doesn't really matter if you believe me," she told him truthfully.

"You could still just tell me."

"It's really bothering you, huh?"

"It is."

"Then no, I don't think I will." She pulled the back door open, flipped off the kitchen light, and stepped out into the evening before he could say anything.

He stepped out right behind her and grabbed her upper arm before she could get too far. He pressed in close behind her and put his mouth against her ear. "I want to be your first," he said, his voice rough. "But more importantly, I intend to be your last."

Those damned shivers rippled through her, stronger and longer than before. She took a deep breath. "Your ego is out of control, Golden Boy."

But dammit, her voice was a little too breathless to really pull off the sass she'd wanted.

He chuckled, the sound low and delicious against her ear.

"Comes from years of getting my way. You should remember that."

She sucked in a breath then elbowed him in the ribs. "I think maybe you need someone who doesn't just fall to her knees in front of you."

Too late, she realized how that sounded. And with absolutely zero experience with blow jobs, she still had a pretty vivid picture of her and Aiden in her kitchen with her on her knees holding a jar of pink sugar.

Crap.

He chuckled again. "Believe me, getting you on your knees will be a pleasure, no matter what it takes."

She stepped away from him and he let her go.

"I've got to get going."

"You mentioned that."

She didn't look back. Or say anything more. What more was there really to say?

———

Zoe headed straight to her mom's house. She had dinner with Maggie and Steve a couple of nights a week. Not because she was lonely or hated cooking for one, but because she legitimately loved hanging out with her parents and because, well, why not? They lived a block away, and her mom loved to have her over. Jocelyn and Jane, her two best friends, joined them a lot of the time too.

They were careful not to talk about Jane's job with Hot Cakes too much. The snack cake company that was headquartered in Appleby was the McCaffery family's nemesis.

Zoe and Maggie didn't blame Jane for working there. The girl had to have a job. Zoe got that. But they just avoided the topic for the most part. It helped their friendship that Jane was a sugarholic and that she much preferred Buttered Up's sweets to the ones she made every day. They hadn't been close in high school because of their age difference, but once Jane had confessed her addiction, Zoe and Josie had become her dealers. She showed up at the back door of the bakery every morning at 6 a.m. sharp, just as they were opening, and they gave her a sugar hit for the day in the form of muffins, bars, cookies, cupcakes, and pie. Particularly strawberry pie. Zoe honestly believed Jane would kill someone for her if the payment was strawberry pie.

She was relieved to see Jocelyn and Jane's cars were both already in front of her mom's house. She needed some girl time. She needed to forget about Aiden for a little while. Then she needed to pull her friends onto her mom's back patio, tip some vodka into the lemonade Maggie no doubt had in the fridge, and ask them what she was supposed to do about Aiden.

She wanted to have sex with him.

She should *not* want that.

He'd had his chance. He'd turned her down. He'd left without any contact for *five freaking months*.

She should definitely not give him a second chance.

Especially when he was talking crazy about moving here and them having an actual relationship.

Unless she should.

She needed her friends to tell her what to do here. Both Jocelyn and Jane had dated more guys than Zoe had, and they would be objective about Aiden and all his nutso claims. At least, more so than Zoe was.

"Hey, everyone." Zoe let herself in through the back kitchen door.

Jocelyn had one of Maggie's favorite pink, polka-dotted aprons on and was stirring something on the stove. Jane was sitting at the table with a glass of the lemonade Zoe wanted to spike. Jane wasn't much of a cook. Jocelyn, on the other hand, was amazing. She'd practically grown up in Buttered Up too, working after school with Zoe at a young age.

They all gave her big smiles.

"Hi, honey!" Maggie leaned over for Zoe's kiss on her cheek. "Did you get my text?"

"Text? No." Hell, she wasn't even positive she had her phone now that she thought of it. She'd been way too distracted after closing time. "Why?"

"Oh, I was hoping you'd bring a pie home."

"I um... didn't check messages before I left the bakery," Zoe said. She shot Jocelyn a look that said, *Don't tell who I was with.*

"She knows," Jocelyn mouthed.

Zoe sighed. Of course she did. She should have known Aiden couldn't be within the Appleby city limits for more than fifteen minutes without Maggie knowing about it.

"Can you run back down?" Maggie asked. "You know the chocolate pie is one of Aiden's favorites."

Zoe rolled her eyes. Behind her mom's back, of course. Jane saw her though and smirked. "No, I'm not going to run back down to get a pie for Aiden," she said. Then she realized what Maggie's question truly meant. "He's coming over for dinner?"

"Of course he is." Maggie beamed at her. "I wish he'd told us he was coming home today, but as soon as he texted me I was able to hop over to your place and clean up."

Zoe tossed her purse onto the kitchen table—dinner would be at the dining room table with the nice dishes and even a tablecloth if Aiden was here—and slumped into the wooden chair across from Jane. "Great," she said. At least her sheets would be especially lavendery tonight. That could be helpful. She had a feeling she might have some trouble sleeping, what with the hot guy she wanted to get naked with right down the hall. And supposedly willing this time.

Jane gave her a wink. "Josie told us he stopped by the bakery. In a suit."

Jane and Jocelyn knew about Christmas Eve. Or The Great Seduction Debacle as they'd started calling it over hot chocolate and peppermint schnapps two nights later.

They didn't think it was quite as horrible as Zoe did. They were plenty protective of her and would absolutely give Aiden a hard time about it, but they thought his "no" made some sense. She and Aiden were longtime friends, and they'd have to see each other again—forever—afterward. She'd taken him by surprise. One night of sex to learn how to have sex with other guys was a strange request, and no way would Aiden Anderson ever be able to just casually have sex with her. They'd given her all those reasons.

Zoe hadn't wanted to hear any of it. Which had ended up with her being more hungover the next morning than she had been in a very long time. From schnapps. That was kind of hard to do.

But the part she *really* hated, was how their insistence that Aiden could never be casual about her had stuck with her. She'd assumed "he can't have casual sex with you" meant *he can't have sex with you at all, ever.* Not "he's going to want to have sex with you and only you. *Forever.*

That was nuts.

But it was also nuts that she couldn't stop thinking about it now.

"Yeah, he stopped by," Zoe said, trying to act nonchalant.

"In a suit," Jane repeated with a knowing grin.

Her back was to Maggie, so Zoe was the one who had to school her features. "Yeah, I guess he was wearing a suit, now that you mention it."

Jocelyn tossed something into the sink and turned on the garbage disposal. Because she was an awesome friend.

Jane leaned in. "She also mentioned he looked hot as hell in it."

Zoe glanced at her mom then at Jane. "So?"

Jane laughed. "You kissed him."

Zoe opened her mouth, then frowned, and said, "I kissed him *back*."

"And how was it?"

Zoe shrugged. "Fine."

Jane laughed. She sat back and lifted her glass. "You're a terrible liar."

She was. She said what she thought, and she had no poker face whatsoever. Which sometimes sucked. Like when she was trying to convince Aiden that she had no interest in picking up where they'd left off—where *he'd* left off—on Christmas Eve. "What do you mean?" she asked anyway.

"You haven't looked in a mirror?"

"So?"

"You've got frosting and sugar all over, and your hair is coming down."

Zoe's hands flew to her head. "So?" She'd just come from work.

"You were distracted when you left the bakery."

"And?"

"And I find it interesting that Aiden—a guy you've known your entire life—can suddenly distract you. He must have done something... unusual."

Well, that was a freaking understatement.

Jocelyn shut the disposal off and glanced over. She had a stupid knowing grin on her face too.

Zoe loved these women. Usually she loved that they knew her so well. Right now, though, she was trying to *not* give away the fact that she was having a hard time looking at her mother's refrigerator and not getting flushed.

"I'll be back in a minute." She quickly escaped the kitchen and headed to the upstairs bathroom, calling a "Hey, Dad!" to her father where he was coming down the hall from his office as she ran up the stairs.

She shut herself in the bathroom, leaning against the door, and squeezing her eyes shut. "Dammit, Aiden." Then she took a deep breath and opened one eye, moving to stand in front of the mirror.

Both eyes opened.

She was a mess.

She'd had an apron on, but she still had a smear of pink frosting on the top edge of her sundress. As Jane had pointed out, she had pink candy coating on one cheek, a dusting of sugar on her cheek and neck, and most of all, her hair, lips, and *eyes* looked like she'd been making out.

Of course, that was in part because she *knew* she'd been making out. But yeah, she looked like someone had had his fingers in her hair and his lips all over hers and... dammit, her eyes looked like she was maybe glowing a little or something.

Glowing? For Aiden Anderson? Seriously?

Zoe shook her head and turned on the faucet. She washed her face, pulled her ponytail out and brushed her hair. She slicked on some of her mom's pink lip gloss—that would at least be a better reason for her lips to be pinker than usual—and took a deep breath.

This was Aiden. She knew everything about him. His first dog's name had been Badger. His second dog had been Finley. She'd loved both of them. He loved asparagus and any movie Gerard Butler was in—which she couldn't disagree with, exactly, but was a little weird for a guy—and got motion sick on roller coasters.

That was *not* exciting. A guy who couldn't even go on roller coaster? Come on. She could do better than that.

Zoe stared at her reflection.

She really was a bad liar.

Even to herself.

Aiden Anderson was a good guy. Full of himself, yes. But a good guy, deep down. He'd been an amazing friend to her big brother, an awesome big brother to her little brother, a fabulous, practically adopted son to her parents, a wonderful real son to his own father. Things seemed to work out for Aiden, but he also worked hard and took things seriously. After losing his mom and kind of losing his dad—at least emotionally—Aiden had seemed to decide that he needed to make the most of everything in life. He'd been determined to leave Appleby and really do something big with his life.

He'd done that. He was a millionaire at age twenty-nine, for God's sake. And she knew he gave a lot of his money to charity. Not only because Camden gave him a hard time about it, but because the *Appleby Observer* was run by Aiden's great uncle, and he kept tabs on him and published all the great things he and Camden did, for the town and elsewhere.

Aiden was nearly a saint in Appleby. But she couldn't deny he deserved a lot of the accolades.

Still, if an exciting, surprising, adventurous love life was what she was going for, Aiden was not the guy. She knew he would add more pepper than should be allowed to his fettuccini. He'd eat only a few pieces of broccoli so as not to insult her mother even though he didn't really like it, and he'd drink at least three glasses of lemonade. Lemonade her mother made extra sweet for him. Yes, he also really liked chocolate pie. He liked most of the things they made at the bakery, but that was his favorite. He definitely had a sweet tooth.

She frowned. Yeah, there weren't a lot of surprises there. And his lemonade addiction was going to make having enough to spike later with the girls difficult.

Of course, him being here was going to make it difficult to sneak off with the girls and talk about him at all.

Finally, Zoe pushed away from the counter and headed back downstairs.

She heard his voice before she was even halfway down the

staircase. He was here. For dinner. The way he'd been hundreds of times before.

But she'd never felt her heart flip or tingles go through her body just hearing his voice.

She groaned. This was *not* good.

"*Purple* diamonds," Aiden was saying to her little brother Henry.

"No. Way."

They were in the living room, the room right off to the side of the staircase. Aiden was sitting on the couch, and Henry was on the ottoman facing him. She was sure Henry had come running the second he'd heard Aiden's voice. Not hers. He probably hadn't even said hello to Jane and Jocelyn yet. Of course, Jane and Jocelyn and Zoe never came bearing news, or even better, insider tips about *Warriors of Easton*.

Sometimes she couldn't believe these guys were actually famous. Cam never went to conventions or did interviews, but Aiden often accompanied two of their partners, Oliver and Dax, to fan events. She'd seen a few of them online. But it was always surreal to think about the two boys who'd built a tree house in her backyard and who got caught at fifteen with beer in her basement and who'd been hospitalized—in side-by-side beds—after a nasty dirt bike accident were guys people *thronged* to see and listen to.

Okay, so the "people" were mostly boys between the ages of eight and twenty. Still, Cam and Aiden were successful and famous, at least in their little corner of the world, and it was weird.

"Seriously. But not until September," Aiden said to Henry.

He must have seen her out of the corner of his eye or sensed her presence—or maybe he heard the fourth step from the bottom creak—but he looked over just as she stepped into the room.

For a second, she froze. Their eyes met. He stopped talking, and her stupid heart flipped again.

He'd stopped by her house. His old house. *The* house. She had a hard time referring to it as *hers*, considering it had been Aiden's house for most of her life.

He was now in a t-shirt and jeans, and his hair was slightly damp.

He still looked really damned good.

And there was something about knowing he'd been naked in the same shower she'd been naked in that morning that made heat curl through her stomach and dive lower.

She mentally rolled her eyes and made herself move into the room. He'd showered in that shower hundreds of times. Many before or after she did. Why was this an issue all of a sudden?

The. Freaking. Kiss.

And now there had been two.

She also wanted to smell his hair to see what his shampoo smelled like. She admitted she'd probably sniff his shampoo bottle the next time she was in there.

That was so damned stupid.

"Hey, Henry," she said.

"Hey." He barely glanced at her.

Yeah, well, she knew nothing about purple diamonds after all.

"Purple diamonds don't really sound very warrior-like," she said, passing the ottoman.

Aiden gave her a lifted eyebrow and half smile. "Hey."

"Hey."

Fuck breathlessness. Fuck. It.

"The diamonds are for the princesses," Henry said.

She turned back, mostly to break the eye contact with Aiden. "Oh, nice, that's pretty gender stereotypical, isn't it?" she asked, propping a hand on her hip. "Only princesses can have diamonds? I suppose the princesses just sit around and wait for the warriors to bring them diamonds and stuff?"

She doubted that was true. She didn't play the game, but she'd read enough about it—hey, it was her brother's company —to know the women in the game were every bit as kick-ass as the men, and the guys gave the women important roles throughout their virtual world.

Henry rolled his eyes. "The princesses get diamonds every time they bring a monster head to the queen. They get blue ones for troll heads and red ones for witch heads and black ones for dragon heads—only the bad dragons, of course," Henry said.

Of course. Zoe hid her smile. There was very little her baby brother was as passionate about as *Warriors of Easton*. Being Camden and Aiden's little brother basically made him famous with his friends and most of the boys his age from the neighboring towns. It was serious shit in his world.

"And the purple ones are going to be for the new monsters —the Rabid Arctic Rabbits." He said it like someone else might talk about the Ark of the Covenant. There was awe and excitement mixed with a solemnity that was unmatched.

Zoe turned wide eyes to Aiden. "Wow."

He nodded with a grin. "They're pretty horrible."

"The snow bunnies?"

He gave a little chuckle that tickled her stomach.

"Yep. They eat hot coals and breathe fire."

"Well, sure they do," she said. "I mean, they're *arctic*, right? They have to stay warm somehow."

"Right," Aiden agreed. "The burning rage against humans who've taken over their territories and driven them into the desolate, icy mountain ranges isn't *quite* enough."

"Huh," she said. "I don't think you should teach kids to underestimate burning rage."

He outright laughed at that. She really liked his laugh.

That thought seemed to come out of nowhere. She'd heard him laugh a million times. This post-Aiden-kiss period of her life was really getting annoying.

"I'll be sure to send Dax a note," Aiden said.

She'd never met Dax or Ollie or Grant, the other three partners in Cam and Aiden's business, but she'd read about them all, and Aiden and Cam talked about them when they were home.

"By the way, there's no dessert tonight," she said. "And you're going to think it was because I was distracted when I was leaving the bakery so didn't check my texts, but honestly, I don't have any chocolate pie so wasn't able to bring one. Because you didn't tell us you were coming home. So none of us were prepared."

Why did she feel the need to point all that out?

It wasn't as if Aiden would believe she hadn't been distracted. She'd *clearly* been distracted. And he obviously knew she was attracted to him. If not because of Christmas Eve, then by the way she'd wrapped herself around him in the kitchen like she was drowning in the ocean and he was her life preserver.

She could be upfront about that. She could face that. That was out there in the open and so what? That didn't mean he was going to get his way.

But it felt like he was going to get his way, and she kind of felt like she needed to keep reminding him—and herself—that she wouldn't be that easy for him.

"Oh, that's fine," he said, leaning back into the couch and draping an arm along the back of it, the picture of casual and content. "I had a taste of something a lot sweeter than chocolate pie earlier. Maybe I'll just have seconds of that. Later."

She blushed. Hot and immediately.

He was going to be at the house. With her. Just the two of them. With four beds and three showers and multiple other firm horizontal surfaces. Not to mention a big old fridge in the kitchen.

That was all she could think about.

He was watching her with a mix of heat and amusement and cockiness.

And she wanted to... climb into his lap and kiss the hell out of him.

Damn. Him.

5

She shot a glance at Henry—who, of course, had no idea what they were talking about—and then narrowed her eyes at Aiden. "Wouldn't want to overdo and get sick of it."

"Not one bit worried about that."

It was really good that eleven-year-olds were unable to pick up on innuendo and sexual undertones and things like husky, low voices that gave new meaning to every word they said.

She swallowed.

"Zoe! Henry! Aiden! Dinner!"

Zoe actually breathed out a huge, relieved sigh when her mom called from the kitchen.

Aiden gave her a knowing smile.

She was really getting tired of knowing smiles.

Then he stretched to his feet.

Zoe backed up, quickly. Clumsily. Stupidly. It wasn't like he was about to grab her or bite her.

Though that was kind of how he was looking at her.

Henry jumped up and ran past them.

Zoe started after him, not even willing to be alone with

Aiden in her mother's living room, with five other people in the very next room, for two minutes.

But he caught her by the wrist before she could escape.

She pulled in a deep breath but didn't look at him.

"You know we're not done."

Yeah, dammit, she did know that.

"You should let it go," she told him.

"I'm not going to do that."

She finally looked up at him. "Thought you were a nice guy."

"Well, *surprise*, Sugar, I'm not nice all the time." His voice was firm, and his expression said he was not teasing.

Well, she was sure surprised to find the way he said that pretty damned hot. And Sugar? Really? In her head she thought that should sound a little condescending. Especially coming from a guy who had never had a nickname for her before. But his tone and the look in his eyes did not allow that to sound like anything other than an affectionate-slash-sexy just-between-them name she wanted to hear him call her in bed. Low and husky. Maybe even a little needy. While he was licking her like he was licking sugar off of the cake pops they'd made.

Finally, she sighed. "Yeah, we're not done." She didn't know what she meant by that exactly. That they'd talk about it more? That she'd use him for sex tutoring after all?

But his expression went from surprise to victorious almost instantly. "That's—"

"What's going on? Come on, dinner." Maggie stuck her head around the corner from the dining room.

Zoe jumped. Aiden, of course, acted like he was totally in control and casual. He moved his hand from her arm to her lower back and nudged her in the direction of her mother.

"On our way, Maggie," he said. "Zoe was just apologizing for being too distracted to check your message about the pie."

Ugh. He was definitely *not* nice all the time. She elbowed him.

"He had cake pops at the bakery earlier. He's fine, Mom," she said, moving toward the table and taking a seat next to Jane, leaving two empty chairs across from them. She couldn't sit next to him. Because his shampoo did smell really good. And because she was afraid he'd find ways to "casually" touch her through the meal, and she'd be tearing her clothes off the second she hit the door at the house—that they were going to be sharing for the next who-knew-how-many nights.

"I definitely did *not* get enough at the bakery," Aiden said, pulling a chair out.

Jocelyn coughed slightly as she carried a big bowl of noodles to the table.

Jane outright laughed.

Zoe sighed. There wasn't enough vodka and lemonade in this house by far.

———

Teasing Zoe was nothing new in his life.

She'd had a crush on his and Cam's friend Dillon when she was ten. She'd written terrible, angsty poetry when she was thirteen. She'd gotten a horrible orange fake tan when she was fourteen. There had been a lot of wonderful reasons for two big brothers to tease her over the years.

Teasing her about sex though... yeah, that was new, and he was fucking in love with it. He intended to keep doing it. For a very, very long time. Like forever. Because even once they were sleeping together every single night, making her blush and stammer and drop her fork at her mother's dinner table was a hell of a lot of fun.

Aiden took the seat next to Henry, who paused talking about *Warriors of Easton* only to say grace and then finally stopped only after his father finally told him that every time he said the words troll, diamond, level, enchantment, or awesome, Henry owed him a quarter from his allowance. The kid would have blown through his entire allotment for the week before he was halfway through his meal.

Aiden chuckled and shared a look with Steve. Henry had been an "oops" baby, and he was beloved—and spoiled—but Steve and Maggie often commented about how there was a reason people had kids when they were younger. Henry was bright and energetic, and frankly, exhausted his parents a lot of the time. His mind went a thousand miles an hour all the time, and it was difficult to keep him from being bored.

Steve and Maggie loved when Cam or Aiden were home because then Henry focused all his intense, spirited, optimistic energy on them. Yes, Henry was an optimist. He insisted on happy endings. He was the ultimate *Warriors of Easton* fan, along with being their biggest critic. They'd made him an honorary member of the board and he used his Fluke Inc. coffee mug every morning for his orange juice.

Having Henry quiet and eating gave everyone else at the table a chance.

"How are things in Chicago?" Maggie asked him.

"Good. Great," Aiden said. "The big sale has been an adjustment though. We all have more time on our hands now. I think we're all feeling a little restless."

"That sale was a great decision," Steve assured him. "You guys should be proud of yourselves."

Aiden nodded. They were. Being bought out by a bigger gaming company had been a dream come true. The money that came with it was unreal, and the company's plan for expansion and development of the *Warriors of Easton* were amazing and far beyond anything he and the guys could have done. They'd pondered the offer for months. It had felt strange thinking of letting go of something they'd built together from the ground up. But it had been an offer they couldn't refuse. They'd finally decided it meant it was time for them to look at new opportunities.

Still, Aiden knew they were all feeling a little directionless at the moment. Hence, it was the perfect time to take over Hot Cakes. They needed a new project, and Hot Cakes and Appleby needed them.

"I think that's exciting," Maggie said. "We're very proud of you."

Aiden heard a soft snort from Zoe. He looked over at her. "I know you don't think my new... opportunity... is exciting, but I intend to prove you wrong." Did he mean his move home to be with her? He most certainly did. And she knew it.

She gave him a wide-eyed look as if she hadn't meant for him to hear that. She cleared her throat. "I, um... was laughing because Mom was practically scandalized by us adding cake pops to the bakery menu. But she thinks it's exciting that you sold a huge chunk of your very successful company and have no real plan for anything now."

"I do have a plan," Aiden said, looking at her directly, his tone low and firm. "I'm happy to go over it with you again if you've forgotten."

"No," she said quickly then glanced at her mom. "I mean, I know you think you do. It's just that your decision, which is a lot bigger and *crazier,* makes her proud but us adding little round versions of our cakes on a stick made her worry."

Maggie shook her head, seemingly too distracted by talk about Buttered Up to wonder what Aiden's big, crazy plan was. "The bakery is different. It's small and very dependent on this community. That means we have a much bigger obligation to give everyone exactly what they want and expect from us. We can't deviate or experiment much. We have a very focused brand."

"Yes, Mom, I know," Zoe said.

They all knew. This was the mantra that had led the McCaffery family and Buttered Up for over fifty years.

Maggie wasn't wrong. Their customer base was much smaller than Fluke's. That left less wiggle room when it came to giving their customers what they wanted. Aiden understood that. But it had always seemed extraordinarily rigid to him, especially when he'd started actually studying business.

"And you can't take a bunch of risks when you have Josie to worry about too," Maggie pointed out.

Zoe frowned. "I know that." She shot her friend a look. "I would never do anything to risk the business."

"I know," Josie said, looking uncomfortable. "Of course I know that."

"She can always come work with me," Jane said, taking a big bite of fettuccine.

"Hey, stop trying to poach my employees," Zoe said, elbowing her. "I've stopped pressuring you to quit Hot Cakes and come work for me, but don't flaunt your medical and dental in Josie's face or I'll start again."

Jane grinned at Josie. "Okay, I won't mention that I have no medical office co-pays and that I also have eye coverage. I definitely won't mention my paid vacation time, and I wouldn't dream of telling her about the big Christmas bonus we got."

Josie covered her ears with her hands. "Don't hear anything, Boss."

"I hate you," Zoe told Jane. "I worked her ass off at Christmas."

Jane put her head on Zoe's shoulder. "You know I love you, and working in the bakery would be a hell of a good time, but you get that I need the solid benefits and stuff."

Zoe put her head against Jane's. "Of course I do. And if I could, I'd offer all that and more. To you *and* to Josie."

Josie removed her hands from her ears and blew Zoe a kiss, proving she'd heard it all.

Aiden frowned, listening to the exchange. "You don't offer benefits?" he asked Zoe.

"There's no such thing as paid time off when you own your own business," she said. "Well, I mean, unless you're a millionaire. I guess you own your own business. And you're here. Out of the blue. For no reason. Taking time off."

He gave her a look. She knew very well why he was here. He'd been *very* clear. At least about her part in why he was here. He shifted, a little uncomfortable about the part she didn't know. But she would. Eventually. When it wouldn't ruin everything. "We have benefits though," he said. "Health insurance and stuff."

She glanced at Maggie and lifted her shoulder. "We're fine."

"But—"

"We have a plan," Zoe interrupted him with a look that clearly said, *drop it.*

"Zoe's still on my insurance," Steve said, taking a bite of garlic bread. "When she's too old for that, we'll look into a policy. It will be wildly expensive, especially for such a small operation, but she's saving and we're shopping around. Lance Gordon is our agent and he's helping us."

For not the first time, Aiden appreciated how open the McCafferys were with him. There weren't really any off-limit topics. He was part of the family. Even when it came to finances and business.

They needed more than a local insurance agent. Hell, Zoe probably needed a financial planner and business adviser. Things were vastly different now than they had been when Letty had started the business. They were different even from when Maggie had worked in the store. She'd had her husband's health insurance at least. His dad's insurance had covered his mom when she'd worked for Buttered Up. Zoe and Jocelyn didn't have that.

There was another good reason for Zoe to marry him. Even before her dad's insurance kicked her off.

Aiden frowned. He didn't like how unstable all this sounded. None of this was really news, but now he was looking at it from the perspective of a businessman, a guy who'd been running a company for nine years now.

"Anyway, I think it's safe to say we won't be taking any risks bigger than rolling our cake into little balls," Zoe said. "We all know what Buttered Up is known for and good at, and we're good if we stick with that."

"I trust you, Zoe," Josie said. "I really do."

"I know." Zoe gave her friend a smile, but Aiden could see there was a little worry at the edges.

He'd never really thought about Zoe as a business owner. That sounded stupid, even in his head. She'd been a business owner for five years now. But she'd just eased into it, taken over slowly, was doing something he'd watched her do for as long as he could remember. The bakery was such a fixture, in the town and in his life, that it never occurred to him it would be anything but solid, and yes, unchangeable. It had never dawned on him that she had business worries like he did. That probably made him kind of a jerk actually.

Zoe looked at Aiden. "I guess Aiden doing something big and risky like suddenly thinking he needs a new... opportunity... isn't that out of character."

Yes, she paused before *opportunity*, emphasizing it the way he had.

Aiden leaned in slightly, curious where she was going with this.

"Aiden and Cam really are the only ones who've ever done anything different or big and adventurous," she went on. "Leaving here. Starting a company. Traveling. Meeting new people. Trying new things."

She seemed thoughtful, as if she were just realizing all that, and Aiden lifted a brow. Yeah, maybe he wasn't as boring as she thought.

He could admit it bugged him that she thought that. He'd definitely done a lot over the past nine years. He'd been coast to coast, seen every major city, met celebrities and influencers. But surprising her was turning into a really good time.

"I guess it was inevitable that he'd get bored with things in Chicago and look for a way to shake things up," she said.

That was *not* what was going on here. Aiden gave her a look that said he realized they were having another conversation inside of the bigger conversation.

"Still, there's definitely something to be said for long history and stability and comfort," Aiden said. "Knowing exactly where you are and what you're doing and why, knowing the people you're with completely... that is all pretty damned great."

Zoe didn't frown at him the way he'd expected. He knew she knew what he was getting at. Them. Their history, how well they knew each other, how comfortable they were around each other. Other than the constant semi-erection he'd had since seeing her again today, of course.

Finally, Zoe nodded. "Yeah, you're right. I wouldn't change anything about what I've got."

He lifted a brow again, silently calling bullshit. She was the only one who needed to know he wasn't buying it.

She might not *want* to want to change things between them, but she wanted more of the heat and chemistry. She wanted more of what they'd started in the kitchen. More of what she'd started at Christmas. Building on everything they already had was going to make all that even better. He knew she could feel that.

"Um, so... speaking of shaking things up," Jane said. "Some of us might have to get used to change whether we want to or not."

Zoe frowned. "What do you mean?"

"Someone's buying the factory."

Suddenly a bite of fettuccini lodged in Aiden's throat. He reached for his lemonade, taking a quick drink. Then another. Fuck. The news was already out? Of course it was.

Aiden had called Eric Lancaster before he'd left Chicago, indicating he was interested and wanted to talk about a deal. But nothing was in writing, and Eric had been clear that until they signed on the line, he would still be entertaining other offers. Aiden understood, but it made him anxious. He needed to talk to his partners as soon as possible. Zoe had been his first priority upon getting to Appleby, but getting the deal done with the Lancasters was priority two. He'd also made it clear to Eric that he wanted to keep his interest in the company under wraps for a few days.

Dammit.

"Really? Wow," Zoe said.

Aiden focused on the conversation around the table. This was actually key. He needed to see their reactions.

Zoe was frowning. Maggie looked more curious than upset. Jane looked a little worried. Steve was definitely just interested. Jocelyn too. But Josie was a secondary nemesis to the Hot Cakes company. Like Aiden always had been, he supposed. She hated the Lancaster family because she loved the McCafferys, and the McCafferys hated the Lancasters.

"Who is it?" Zoe asked.

Aiden gulped more lemonade. This was it. Jane might be about to out him. To his family. Because they were. Not by blood, but by everything else that mattered in a family.

He did not want to hurt the McCafferys, and he did not want to lose them. He *needed* Maggie. She'd been his mom for longer than his own had, and had been there for him through his loss. The worst thing a kid could possibly go through.

Maggie had nursed him through illnesses, broken bones, a broken heart or two, definitely wounded pride. She'd encouraged him. She'd scolded him. She'd told him he could be whatever he wanted, but that he'd better want to be a good guy. Most of all, she'd talked with him about his mom. In a way no one else could or had been willing to. His dad hadn't been able to handle it. Maggie had known Julie longer than his dad had anyway. Maggie and Julie had grown up together. Maggie had memories to share with him that no one else could. And she had. She never shied away from helping him know his mom better, from remembering her, and he would be forever grateful to her for that.

Maggie McCaffery had helped him through the worst time of his life, and he knew for a fact that he would not be the person he was today if it wasn't for her.

He loved her to his very bones. He could not hurt her or lose her.

He focused on Zoe though.

Because Maggie would forgive him. Eventually. She might be angry. She might be hurt. It might take time. But she would forgive him, and they'd talk it out and they'd be okay.

Zoe was the one he wasn't so sure of. The woman was irrationally protective of that bakery. Nothing mattered to her more than her family's legacy. And she didn't have fifteen years of loving him like Maggie did. Zoe really might not forgive him.

Aiden held his breath, waiting for Jane's answer.

6

"We don't know," Jane answered.

Aiden struggled to hide his expression. He wanted to slump in his chair and suck in a relieved breath. Instead, he gulped more lemonade.

"All we know is someone made an offer. It hasn't been accepted or anything. We don't know who it is. But Melissa told Nancy who told Taylor who told Brianna who told me that Eric got a call from a guy who said he wanted to buy Hot Cakes, and Eric was in a really good mood when he got off the phone."

Eric Lancaster was Didi's oldest son and president of Hot Cakes. Melissa was his executive assistant. Melissa was the mother of one of Aiden and Cam's classmates. But that was as far as Aiden could follow the names. The rest didn't really matter though. Eric was happy about the conversation. That was the key takeaway here. That was good. That meant there wasn't another offer on the table. Yet. It meant Eric liked what he'd had had to say.

Aiden blew out a breath.

"Well, that sucks," Zoe said.

Aiden frowned. "It does? Why?"

"Someone is keeping Hot Cakes alive," she said. "Obviously, I was hoping that it would close and die."

Aiden cast a look at Jane. She was chewing on her bottom lip.

"That's not a very cool way to feel about your friend's job, is it?"

Jane had started working for Hot Cakes part time after school in high school and had stayed on. She had certainly been bright enough and had the grades for college, but she had a complicated home life, and college hadn't been a part of her plan. He remembered her telling him once that the more things could be simple and straightforward in her life—like a factory job that she knew inside and out and could depend on for decent money and benefits—the better.

"Jane knows how I feel," Zoe said, frowning at him and then looking at Jane. She grabbed her friend's hand. "I love Jane and want her to be happy, but she can do more than that factory. If they closed down, she'd be fine."

"Are you happy the factory is staying open?" he asked Jane directly.

She squeezed Zoe's hand and then said to him, "I am. Definitely. I don't want to make cupcakes at Buttered Up, and I don't want to work as an aide at the school, and I don't want to do farmwork, and I don't want to learn data entry for any of the offices in town... and that's pretty much all there is."

She was right. Small-town Iowa had limited job opportunities. It was just a fact. In fact, there were fewer jobs now than there had been ten years ago. Online shopping, faster shipping, and bigger stores in the next city over with more selection and cheaper prices made it almost impossible for small shops to stay open in little towns. The jobs in Appleby, like many towns in the Midwest, were teaching, healthcare, or working on the family farm. And even family farms were struggling. If Jane wanted to drive to the next city, there would be more jobs, but that would take job training, if not a degree, as well as time on the road and the expense of gas and more car maintenance along with the time away from her family.

Small Midwestern towns were dying. Young people went away to college and then never came back because there were no jobs. The cities in Iowa were growing, but the rural areas were losing population every year. It was one of the huge reasons keeping Hot Cakes open *in Appleby* was important to Aiden.

"You make cupcakes every damned day," Zoe said grumpily. She let go of her friend's hand as Jane reached for her lemonade.

Jane laughed. "Yeah, okay. But not *quite* the same way you do, Z."

The Hot Cakes brand snack cakes offered cream-filled cupcakes—Cupettes—in chocolate, vanilla, and red velvet. They were mini sized—about two bites each—and came in packs of four. They were nothing like what Buttered Up did.

"But you *could* do cupcakes with me and Josie. If you wanted to."

Zoe almost seemed a little hurt Jane didn't want to work for her.

"I don't even run the cupcake line," Jane said. "You know that. And even if I did, the machines do all the work. I can't stand in your cute little yellow bakery in your cute frilly little yellow aprons and make cupcakes into cats and baseballs and..."

"Poop emojis," Henry said helpfully.

Jane grinned at him. "And poop emojis."

"You're very talented and smart and awesome," Zoe insisted. "Josie and I could teach you. And you look great in yellow."

Jane shifted in her chair. "Z, I don't *want* to be creative like that. I like my job. It's... a job, and that's all I want it to be. I don't need to be creative or fulfilled by my work. I have plenty of problem solving and fulfillment *outside* of work. I just want to go do my job, not hate it, know what I'm doing every day, and collect a paycheck. I want that to be one area of my life that is steady and predictable and... boring." She frowned. "I just want it to still be steady with these new people."

Aiden didn't know Jane well enough to know *everything* about her personal life to know what all she was talking about, but he knew she had at least one younger sibling and that her father was sick with one of those horrible, progressive neurological diseases—he couldn't remember which one at the moment, and he made a note to ask Zoe about it.

Her job would still be stable though. It would be an even better job than it had been before. He'd be sure of it.

And that was the moment it really hit Aiden—he was going to be Jane's boss.

She was going to be working for him.

Well, that was... awkward.

Now when she bitched to her friends about work and her boss—because everyone bitched about work and their boss—it would be his company and him.

Hot Cakes had nearly three hundred employees. He'd briefly thought about the fact he would personally know many of those employees. That was one of the driving factors for him wanting to buy the damned company in the first place. To save those jobs.

But sitting across Maggie's dining room table and eating fettuccine with one of them while she worried about her job to her best friends was not something he'd thought through.

If she got pissed off at something at the factory, would she bring it up over dinner with Maggie and Zoe? Maybe. What about the other people at the factory? If they got ticked off, he'd probably hear about it at the post office and the diner and the corner of Depot and Main and probably in the bakery. Of course, that was assuming Zoe didn't ban him from Buttered Up for the rest of his life.

That was actually kind of how the town worked now. Among those who had deep roots in Appleby, the town was strictly divided, between those loyal to the Lancasters and those loyal to the McCafferys. The Lancasters had a larger number of employees and also a bigger network of people who wanted to be nice to them because of their wealth. Like the bank, the medical clinic they donated to, the various community groups they supported, the mayor whose campaign they'd contributed to.

But the McCafferys had what they called *true* friends because their allegiances weren't dependent on employment or donations. There were people who truly thought what Didi Lancaster had done to Letty had been a terrible betrayal and who distrusted the Lancasters' money and influence. It was also a fact that Didi's husband Dean and their son, Eric, didn't have a lot of actual friends. At least not the "regular people" of Appleby. Dean had always given off very elitist airs, and Eric had been an asshole as long as Aiden had known him. Aiden's dad had never liked Eric and had stories from high school of Eric thinking he was better than everyone else and getting away with a lot because of his daddy's penchant for getting out his checkbook whenever Eric got into trouble.

There was also a well-known policy at Hot Cakes that no employee there could do business with Buttered Up. It was ridiculous, of course, but no one had ever had the spine to challenge it. That meant all three hundred employees, plus their families, got their birthday and wedding cakes, muffins, cookies and so on from the bakery in the next town. Never from Letty, Maggie, and Zoe. It was why Jane's sneaking up to the back door of the bakery was a big deal. It was part of the Code of Conduct and was a fireable offense.

It would, of course, be the first thing Aiden changed at the company, but for now, it was one of the biggest things that kept the bitterness between the families alive and well. Just like the fact that none of the McCafferys' friends or family members bought or ate Hot Cakes products. The convenience store on this side of town didn't even carry the snack cakes.

It was all ridiculous. The companies were not actual competitors. A prepackaged snack cake someone stuck in their lunch box or grabbed during a road trip was hardly the same thing as a made-from-scratch and custom-decorated cake for a special occasion. There was room in people's lives for both.

Just not in Appleby.

"You do like your job there though?" Aiden asked.

He had to be careful pressing for information. He couldn't act too interested. But Jane was a friend. A friend of a friend, at least. And they were on the subject, so surely he could get away with a few questions without it seeming suspect.

"I do," she said. "Mostly."

"Except when they're making you do mandatory overtime," Josie said.

"Well, right," Jane said.

"And not when they're offering people early retirement and then not replacing them," Zoe said.

"Right." Jane sighed.

"And not when they're taking away the childcare center," Josie said.

Jane held up her hands and gave Aiden a weak smile. "I said *mostly*, right?"

He was frowning and worked on not acting completely pissed off about the things Josie and Zoe had revealed. "All that has happened?"

"It has." She shrugged. "Cutbacks."

"Why all the cutbacks?" he asked. "They netted five million last year. That's down a little over the past three years but it's still profitable."

They all stared at him.

Right. Why would he know that? Shit. "I was curious when they went up for sale," he explained. Which was true. He'd wondered if they'd been losing money or if someone had been embezzling or just what the hell was going on.

Jane leaned in. "Eric was hanging on, doing the bare minimum, until his dad died. Then he just let it go. Didn't invest, did as much cutting as he could. It's clear he's completely over it. Everyone was sure he was just going to close it up."

Aiden knew all about Eric's attitude. But he hadn't known about the cuts and early retirements. Because he hadn't asked.

He realized he'd come in here thinking he'd be the big hero, but just keeping the factory open was not the whole story. There was a lot more that needed to be done to make Hot Cakes a great place to work.

He was going to do it. He had to. Not just because this was his hometown and people he knew, but because how could he not? How did someone pocket five million dollars while their employees, the people actually doing the work, worked mandatory overtime and lost their childcare?

"I know you're worried," Zoe said to Jane. "But just know my offer stands."

"And I love you for it, and if these new people are horrible, I might be begging on your doorstep," Jane said with a smile. "But I'm hopeful it will be okay."

"You can't employ them all," Aiden said. Without really thinking. But even as Zoe frowned at him, he didn't regret it. He lifted his eyebrows. "You can't absorb the entire Hot Cakes workforce, so that's not really a solution to this problem, is it?"

"So?" She sat back in her chair and crossed her arms.

"That's a lot of people out of work if this new buyer hadn't come along."

"Not really my problem," she said. "They all chose to work there. People think a big company is going to take care of them, but sometimes they learn the hard way." She glanced at Jane. "Sorry, babe. But you know I'm right. Big companies are less intimate. They care less about individual people. There's less loyalty. It's about the bottom line."

"It doesn't have to be that way," Aiden protested.

"I suppose it doesn't," she allowed. "If rich people weren't assholes who only think of themselves."

He narrowed his eyes. "Referring to anyone in particular?"

"You and Cam are pretty generous," she said. "But tell me, Aiden, do you *like* being rich?"

She was such a brat. "I do. Because then I can give it away."

"Sure. But you still make more than fifty grand a year, right? And you don't worry about things like your farmland flooding or your kid getting a basketball scholarship because that's the only way you can afford college, or you being off work because of a horrible case of pneumonia and using up your sick days." She leaned in, pinning him with a serious look. "Your money doesn't just give you *money*, Aiden. It gives you privilege. Privilege to not worry. To not be scared. To not lie awake at night and wonder what you're going to do. To not be at someone else's mercy. You work your ass off and you're rewarded for it. You don't have to sit around and wait for someone else to notice you're working your ass off and feel generous toward you."

Her eyes were glittering and her cheeks were pink. She looked a lot like she had after he'd kissed the hell out of her against the fridge. Or when she'd been pissed at him for telling her they should get married.

But this was even hotter in a way. Because now she was riled up on someone else's behalf.

"You're right."

Her eyes flickered with surprise at his response.

But she was right. "You're absolutely right." He looked at Jane. "The first thing you need to do when new people take over is make an appointment to talk to the CEO. You've been there a long time. You know all the people who work there. You know the place inside and out. Tell him you have some ideas and demands. Tell him you can be a resource. And tell him there needs to be some changes."

Jane's eyes had gotten progressively wider as he spoke. Then she laughed. "Sure. Okay, Aiden, I'll do that."

"Trust me. Someone needs to speak up for the employees." He frowned.

"I told her she should be the union leader," Josie said.

Jane gave Josie an eye roll. "Yeah. I don't want that at all."

"Why not?" Aiden asked.

"I take care of and worry about a lot of people outside of work," she said. "I don't want to be in charge of worrying or taking care of people *at* work too."

"You already do," Josie pointed out with an affectionate smile.

Jane sighed. "I just want to go to work, get paid, and go home."

"But you can't, because you're strong and smart and loving," Zoe said. "You care about the work conditions and how people are treated and if they're happy. You can't help it. You might as well be in a position to *do* something about it."

Aiden nodded. "You really need to at least get your current union leader to meet with the new management."

With him. Aiden realized it was strange he was giving her this advice. Eventually, she would find out it was *him* he was encouraging her to meet with. But he really did want to hear this. He wouldn't be waltzing into a company that was perfect and running smoothly, obviously. But if he knew the problems, he could fix them. Hopefully.

"We don't have a union leader right now," Jane said.

"Then you need to do it," Aiden told her. Jane was perfect for it. She was smart and dedicated and no-nonsense. She knew the factory inside and out. If Aiden wanted to know what was really going on, Jane was exactly who he should be talking to. "As a guy in management, I can tell you people like you are invaluable to us."

"I'm not some geeky computer programmer who knows all about dragons and trolls." She gave Henry a wink. "I'm just a girl who knows how to push buttons and pull levers."

Aiden dropped it. For now. His pushing was going to seem suspicious. But he needed to get into the factory, see how it worked, figure some things out, dive into the employee benefits. And more. There was a lot. He was going to need his partners.

They could look at benefits, even talk to employees. Cam would review the contracts, of course. Grant could help look at new benefit plans and do some cost analysis. The Fluke team could definitely make this happen.

"Well, Letty is probably frowning down from heaven, convinced Didi waited to sell until Letty was dead," Steve said with a little chuckle. Clearly, he was trying to lighten things up and divert the conversation from all of Jane's worries.

Maggie shook her head. "Didi probably did."

"Oh, come on," Steve said.

"You come on," Maggie told him. "You always said there were two sides to the story, but she named it Hot Cakes. You know that made Letty almost crazier than anything."

Aiden looked from Steve to Maggie and then back. "What do you mean? What about the name made Letty crazy?"

He'd heard some of the stories about Charlotte "Letty" McCaffery and Dorothy "Didi" Lancaster, best friends growing up, who started the bakery together—and then Didi's betrayal —but it was very possible there were family stories he didn't know. Now, more than ever, he was curious about the feud.

"Once it was doing well and she was getting ready to incorporate and make it an official business, Didi went to Mom and asked if she'd be her partner," Steve said. Letty was his mother, but he'd had no interest in the bakery as a full-time job. Fortunately, his young wife had jumped at the chance to work with Letty and had eventually taken it over.

"Wait, Didi asked Letty to be her partner in Hot Cakes?" Aiden asked. He'd definitely never heard that part of the story.

Steve nodded. "Yep. They hadn't spoken in months, but Didi credited her success to Mom's recipe and told her, 'They're selling like hotcakes, Letty. Come on, let's do this together.'" He shook his head. "Mom told her she could shove her hot cakes straight up her ass. So Didi went on and filed her official paperwork, including trademarking the original recipe, and the name Hot Cakes. When they first painted that on the side of their factory, I thought Mom was going to have a stroke."

Aiden's eyes were wide, he knew. Everyone around the table was listening raptly. "I have never heard this part of the story," Aiden said.

He glanced at Zoe. She shook her head. Josie and Jane looked just as surprised.

"What I've heard is that the most popular cake among the men who would stop in before their work shifts was the butter cake," Aiden said. "One day, one of the men asked Didi and Letty if they could wrap up several pieces and bring them out to the factory—when the farm implement factory was still here."

Steve nodded. "He said if they could bring them out there, right to the men, they could sell a lot more. Mom, of course, said no. That would mean one of them needing to leave the bakery, and she had no way of knowing how much more to make and a dozen other excuses."

"So Didi did it on her own. Just to see what would happen," Aiden said. "She made extra cakes the night before at home, wrapped up individual pieces, and took them out there."

"And sold out," Steve said.

"But she couldn't tell Letty because Letty would have been upset with her," Aiden went on with the story he knew. "And she wanted to be sure it wasn't just a one-time stroke of luck.

She did it again. But word had spread and she ran out. Men promised to buy them if she'd bring extra the next day. She did. She made a couple of other kinds of cake too. Everything sold out. Then people would stop her and ask if she could come by their place of work to sell them some. It was the convenience of it that they liked. Pretty soon, she was doing it every morning before work. It went on for over a month before she told Letty about it. She was sure Letty would be excited because it was new business—people who didn't have time to stop by or a way to get to the bakery before work but who wanted the cakes for lunch or snacks."

"And Letty was absolutely *not* excited. She was furious. They had a huge fight about Didi going behind her back and using her recipes," Steve said. "But Didi knew it was a great business plan."

"So she kept doing it. With Letty's butter cake recipe," Maggie said.

Steve nodded. "She used other recipes for the other cakes, but that was the most popular one and the one people asked for when she tried to leave it off her menu. She adapted it a bit, but everyone—including Letty—knew it was essentially Letty's recipe and the whole reason things took off for Didi."

Aiden sat back in his chair. "But she offered Letty a chance to go into business with her and Letty turned her down."

"She couldn't have said yes to that," Zoe said from across the table. "Didi took her recipe and then kept selling the cakes even after she knew Letty was upset. Didi chose making money over their friendship."

"Or was she just embarrassed Didi's idea was better than her own?" Aiden asked.

"Better?" Zoe asked with a frown. "We make cakes that *mean* something. We make birthdays special. We're a part of celebrations like weddings and graduations and retirements. People come to us for special occasions. Not just a wrapped-up snack cake people don't think twice about when they wolf it down at lunch."

Aiden took a deep breath. She was right. He wasn't wrong. Didi hadn't been wrong. But Letty hadn't been wrong either.

"But Letty was too proud to expand her business and save her friendship," Aiden said, his eyes on Zoe.

Zoe met his gaze. "Or was she brave enough to realize maybe that friendship wasn't what she thought it was and to let it go in order to keep doing what she believed in?"

Okay, that was another way of looking at it.

He turned to Steve. "Was that why Letty never changed anything at the bakery? Because she was proving what she'd been doing from day one was right just as it was?"

"You've got it," Steve said with a nod. "She wouldn't even want to add a new pie after that because people might not like it. And that would be like admitting Didi had been right in thinking the bakery wasn't already everything it could be."

"Wow." Aiden shook his head. Then looked at Zoe again. Surely, she could see that *that* level of stubbornness was too much.

Zoe just looked back at him, leaning on her forearms on the tabletop.

"Grandma told me if someone makes fun of you, you have to act like you love whatever they're making fun of."

Everyone looked at Henry as he scooped the last of his noodles into his mouth.

He had been, for the most part, ignoring everything they were talking about. Or at least, he'd seemed to be. Henry's future plans had nothing to do with the bakery. He fully intended to come work for Cam and Aiden and one day take over their company. Probably by the time he was twenty-five, if they were all being honest.

"When did she tell you that?" Aiden asked.

"A kid at school was making fun of this part of my hair that always sticks up." Henry flicked at the cowlick on the back of his head. "I told her it was making me mad and asked her to cut it off. She said no way. The best way to get back at that kid was to get some gel and make that part of my hair *really* stick up and then tell everyone how much I loved it. She said people won't make fun of things if they think it won't bug you."

Steve and Maggie both smiled at Henry. "That hair *shouldn't* bug you," Maggie said. "It's just hair."

Henry nodded. "Yeah, and when I made it stick up on purpose, that's kind of what everyone figured out."

Aiden thought about that. It was all very interesting. Didi had proposed change, and that change had worked out. She'd made a point of that with Letty, even naming her company Hot Cakes because her cakes were selling like crazy, and in response, Letty had dug in, deep, on exactly what she'd been doing, absolutely *not* changing a single thing.

They started clearing the dishes from the table and conversation diverted to lighter topics, probably by Josie and Maggie, until eventually, Aiden found himself in the dining room with Zoe alone, picking up an empty breadbasket and a handful of forks.

"I assume you still want to get in my pants?" she asked.

Maybe being in the dining room alone with her wasn't an accident.

"With everything in me," he said sincerely, looking at her across the table.

"Then I would suggest you quit thinking my grandmother was crazy and stop defending Didi Lancaster and Hot Cakes to me," she said.

Aiden sighed. "Zoe, come on. You know the factory needs to stay open. You have to be able to sympathize with all those people. This town. The *town* would be affected if that factory closed."

"They're our competition, Aiden."

"They're not really. And you know that."

"The Butter Sticks should have been ours."

He sighed. "That may be true," he admitted. "But those don't actually compete with anything you sell now."

"You don't think people sometimes grab Peanut Butter Pinwheels or Fudgie Fritters rather than coming in for peanut butter cupcakes or fudge brownies from me because they're easier and already packaged and cheaper?"

He thought carefully about how to answer. Finally, he just went with honest. "Okay, yeah, they probably do."

"Of course they do," she said with an eye roll.

"But if Hot Cakes was in another town or even state, it would be the same thing. You could say the same thing of Hostess or Little Debbie. You don't consider them competition, do you?"

"I do," she told him stubbornly. "But, of course, Hot Cakes is different because all that could have been ours."

He didn't believe that, actually. Even if they'd kept the original butter cake recipe, they never would have packaged them individually and sold them in gas stations. He studied her for a moment. "So why don't you do that?"

"Do what?"

"Prepackage some stuff and make it cheaper."

"I don't have the machines or capacity to do something like that."

"You could figure it out. Just wrap or box things individually."

"Extra packaging costs more money. I have to cover my costs."

"Then make the stuff smaller. The Fudgie Fritters are way smaller than your brownies. For a reason," he said.

"The other reason is they're mass produced and they can negotiate for bulk ingredients," she said. "There's a limit to what I can do."

"But you could do *something*. If your quality is better—which it is," he said quickly, holding up a hand, "then people will pay more. Prepackage some stuff, and mark it down a little, and talk to the convenience store about some shelf space."

"How does marking it down help me make more money?"

"At a lower price you could sell greater quantities." She knew this, but he was willing to talk it out with her. "Or if you don't want to do that, add some new products."

"I did. We're doing cake pops now."

"With the leftover cake and frosting you already make. And only because Josie pushed. And you kind of hate them," he said.

She didn't deny it.

"Maybe you could offer something like cake-decorating classes instead."

"And teach people to make everything for themselves instead of paying us to do it?"

"You have an excuse to avoid every single idea." She was incredibly obstinate. But she made his heart pound. She didn't think he was always right or perfect or some kind of savior. And that was probably good for him.

"They're all risks," Zoe said.

"You mean they're all changes."

She frowned.

Aiden smiled. God, she was stubborn. And gorgeous. And a pain in the ass. And he'd never wanted a woman more.

"So about me getting into your pants..."

"Not tonight," she told him with a look that said *that* should have been obvious.

"And why's that?"

"You've been arguing with me all night. And judging me. I'm not taking my clothes off for you after that."

But that sure as hell sounded like there was a chance that was going to happen in the future. If he toed her line. He grinned internally. He'd do whatever he had to. He could work on softening her feelings toward Hot Cakes more slowly.

"For future notice, if I want to get you naked, I need to always go along with whatever you say, do whatever you want, and generally agree that you're always right."

She nodded. "Yes. Definitely. Absolutely." She tilted her head and looked him up and down. "And wearing a suit doesn't hurt."

Then she turned on her heel and headed into the kitchen.

He looked down at his t-shirt and jeans. And chuckled.

But if she thought she'd just stumped him there, she was *very* wrong.

He had plenty of suits. And as she'd pointed out, plenty of money to get more.

Was that also privileged of him? Yes, yes it was. Because getting Zoe McCaffery naked was absolutely going to be a privilege.

7

She'd totally lied to him.

Aiden did not need to agree with her and think her ideas were all brilliant for her to want to sleep with him.

In fact, arguing with him about things of substance—business and employee benefits and the effects of Hot Cakes on the town and people of Appleby—had been... interesting.

And surprising.

It wasn't that they'd never argued. Lord Almighty. They'd argued about Hawkeye football play-calling and if pineapple belonged on pizza—it definitely did—and if she'd cheated at poker—another definitely. But this was different. This felt grown-up. Important. Challenging.

She'd liked it.

She *hadn't* been lying about the suits though. Him wearing a tie definitely made her more inclined to take her clothes off. Whether or not she wanted him to take the tie off in bed remained to be seen.

The dining room and kitchen were finally cleaned up, and the huge perk of her family loving Aiden became apparent when her mom and dad and Henry all settled in the living room with him and started chatting. It gave Zoe the perfect opportunity to pull Jane and Josie out onto the back patio after all.

"Tell me what to do," she demanded of her friends as soon as she slid the glass door shut behind them.

"About?" Jane asked. But she was already smiling.

"Aiden. Living with me."

"Be grateful for all the water you're going to be saving?" Jane suggested.

Zoe frowned at her. "What?"

"By showering together."

Jocelyn giggled.

"That's not helpful," Zoe muttered.

"True. The showers will be probably even longer if Aiden is in there with her," Josie said to Jane.

"Good point," Jane said. "Well, less laundry because you'll only be washing the sheets on one bed?" She shook her head. "No, because you'll probably be getting those sheets even dirtier than usual, so you'll have to wash them more often." She shrugged. "Sorry, I've got nothing. There is *nothing* good about Aiden living with you."

Zoe huffed out a frustrated breath. "I know."

Josie and Jane both laughed.

"Come on," Jane said. "Aiden's awesome. And clearly he's regretting his Christmas decision. That's got to feel good, right?"

Zoe sighed. "That's the thing. He doesn't regret it. He's not sorry for turning me down at Christmas. Thinks that was the right thing to do."

"What's he want now, then?" Jane asked.

"Her."

Zoe shot Jocelyn a look. "What?"

"That's what he told me. I asked why he was here, and he said he's going to sweep you off your feet."

Zoe felt her heart do a little flip. She frowned. That was so annoying.

"Wow." Jane looked from Josie to Zoe. "Well, awesome, now you can get rid of that pesky V-card, once and for all, just like you planned."

"Shh!" Zoe glanced at the house. There was no way anyone inside could hear them. "You can't let him know that's still a thing."

"But..." Jane frowned, confused. "Wait... what?"

"He thinks maybe I already got rid of it." Zoe winced after she said it.

Jane's eyes widened. "Why would he think that?"

"I might have insinuated that."

"*Why?*" Josie asked.

"I can't have him think I've been pining away for him for five months!" Zoe said.

"But..." Jane looked at Jocelyn and then back to Zoe. "You haven't been *pining* for him. But you haven't been with anyone else either. There's a lot of space in between those two things. Why can't he know that?"

Zoe sighed. "I don't know. I sort of... panicked, I guess. He just struts in here after all this time and says 'Okay, let's do this,' and I'm supposed to just melt. That's so typical. And insulting." She crossed her arms. "Especially when he turned me down so easily before."

Jane grinned at her. "That's your ego talking."

Zoe rolled her eyes. "Well, yeah."

"How is that really different from what he's doing?" Josie asked. "You expected to walk into his bedroom at Christmas and say, 'Hey, could you give me a quick orgasm, please?' and he was supposed to just be all in without a single thought."

Zoe stared at her. "Well, first, I didn't expect an orgasm." She knew enough about sex to know those didn't happen every time, and very often they didn't happen the first time.

"And second... yeah. I did expect him to just be all in. It's sex."

"It's sex *with you*," Josie said. "We told you even back then that makes it all different."

"Argh!" Zoe let her head fall back, covering her face. "I thought going to someone I knew so well would make it easier. Instead, it's complicating everything. Now he thinks we need to get married!" She looked at her friends. "I need a one-night stand. With a stranger. Who's not an ax murderer but who I will never see again. Can you help me out with that?"

Josie's eyes got wide. Jane started laughing.

Zoe propped her hands on her hips. "What?"

"That is the *last* thing you need," Jane informed her.

"You would be *terrible* with a one-night stand," Josie said.

"Excuse me?"

"Seriously," Jane agreed. "You're not one-night stand material, Z."

"I. Just. Need. Sex." Zoe was gritting her teeth. Good Lord. Everything in society made it seem that a young, healthy, relatively decent-looking, willing woman could have sex—especially no-strings-attached-sex—*very* easily. That was very much not turning out to be the case.

"I know you think so," Jane said, a little sympathetically now. "I understand everything you've said about being a twenty-five-year-old virgin and everything. I do. But honey, you don't do casual. You don't do short term. You don't do superficial. I mean, the guy you thought of to take your virginity is literally the one nonrelative male you've known the longest."

"Because I can trust him."

"Exactly," Josie said. "There is no way in hell you could go to a hotel room with some guy you just met at a bar and get naked. No. Way."

Zoe frowned at her. "And you could?"

"Maybe." Josie lifted a shoulder. "He'd have to be a *very*

good flirt. Very charming. He'd have to be funny and make me laugh. He'd have to do something sweet—like rescue a kitten or help an old lady carry her groceries or something. But I wouldn't have to know his whole history." She nodded as if thinking it all over. "Yeah, a funny, cute, sweet guy could definitely get me naked on the first date. If he was wearing a t-shirt that said something like 'I'm very good with my rod. I make fish come,' I'd be all over him. Even if it was one night."

Zoe actually snorted at that. Josie was sweet. Like *sweet*. But clearly she'd given this some thought.

"I saw Sam Carson wearing that shirt the other day," Jane said. "Naughty girl." She gave Josie a grin that looked almost proud.

"Sam is definitely someone who would be fun. For one night." Josie winked.

Sam was a nice guy. Funny. Goofy even. But he wasn't all that bright. Josie would be bored with him after one night for sure.

Zoe immediately thought of Aiden. She wouldn't get bored with him.

Wait. What? She *would* get bored with him. Right? She knew everything about him. How was that *not* boring?

But bantering with him was fun. Sassing him was fun. Kissing him was definitely fun. Seeing him with her family made her happy. And listening to him talk business tonight had been interesting. Arguing with him was fun. He took her seriously and listened to her, even when he didn't agree with her.

Sure, he thought her beloved, recently deceased grandmother was crazy. But... he'd still loved her. He would have still sat at the dining room table with her tonight and been respectful and sweet and teased her and made her laugh. He might have even gotten away with teasing her *about* being so stubborn and a little crazy. He *might* have even gotten away with teasing Letty about Hot Cakes. If anyone could pull that off, it would have been Aiden.

He had a way about him. A way that even Letty McCaffery wouldn't have been able to resist.

Zoe sighed. He definitely had a way with *her*.

Could she come home at night and talk about her day with him? Not just about how they were making poop emoji cupcakes for some kid's birthday party, but about things like how amazing all the reviews for her last wedding job had been or how she was worried about her favorite vendor increasing prices on her?

Yes.

She didn't even have to think about it.

Talking about muffin pans and spatulas might not seem *exciting* exactly, but being able to share her business, her day-to-day thoughts and issues would be nice, and yeah, Aiden would get it.

He'd care. He knew what Buttered Up meant to her and her family and respected that. He knew the bakery inside and out and understood their business, the town they did it in, the people they dealt with. He also understood business on a big-picture scale. Profit margins, dealing with vendors, taxes, and everything else that went into it all.

"Did you sleep with Sam Carson?" Jane demanded of Josie.

"No." Josie laughed. "I'm just saying I wouldn't rule it out." She focused on Zoe again. "But Zoe would definitely rule Sam out."

"I'm not attracted to Sam," Zoe said.

"Sam is *hot*," Jane said.

Zoe thought about that. Yeah, he was. She frowned.

"But you could never be comfortable enough with Sam to get naked," Josie said.

Jane was studying Zoe. "But she knows Sam really well."

Sam was just a year older than Zoe and Josie. He'd grown up in Appleby and farmed with his dad.

"She does," Josie agreed.

"And Sam is a nice guy," Jane went on, almost contemplatively. "He wouldn't talk about their one night together."

"Nope," Josie agreed again.

"I'm not attracted to him," Zoe repeated.

"I know," Josie said. "Makes you wonder, doesn't it?"

"Wonder what?" Zoe asked.

"Why you're not attracted to him."

"Yeah," Jane agreed. "He's got everything Aiden does. Except the money."

No, he didn't. He didn't have a history with her like Aiden did. No one did. Dammit.

"Because..." Zoe just shrugged. "Attraction is hard to explain, isn't it? It's a chemistry thing."

Josie grinned as if Zoe had just given the perfect answer. "It really is. And more goes into chemistry than good looks or someone being nice or how well you know them."

Zoe sighed. Two people she knew *very* well were these two women. "You're trying to make a point."

"Yes I am."

"Can you just get to it?"

Josie nodded. "Fine. I think you need to think about *why* you're a twenty-five-year-old virgin and why Aiden was the one you thought of to change that."

"Yeah," Jane said, joining in. "I mean, you've dated a few guys. Some who really liked you a lot. Some who I'm *sure* would have helped you out there."

"I'm a virgin because I've never been with anyone I thought I could be with long..." Oh. Damn.

Josie nodded. "Exactly. You didn't think any of them would be long term. You've always been thinking along those lines. But you want to sleep with Aiden."

Zoe felt her stomach flip, but she shook her head. "I just went to him for a one-time tutorial."

"I think that was a *really* good excuse you came up with to make yourself get into that lingerie and walk down the hall," Josie told her with an affectionate and gentle smile.

Yeah, it had been. She'd been repeating it over and over as she'd listened for him to shut the shower off and open the bathroom door and walk down the hall over the creaking floorboard and then shut his bedroom door. She'd repeated it over and over again as she waited the thirty minutes for him to relax and maybe even start to drift to sleep. And as she'd gotten dressed. And as she'd approached his door.

Dammit.

"Josie's right, you know," Jane said. "You weren't just mad when he turned you down. It wasn't just an ego thing. You were *hurt*. You'd been waiting for him, and you finally got your nerve up and then he shot you down."

Zoe grimaced. "Okay, we all know. No need to rehash."

Jane put an arm around her and gave her a side hug. "I'm just saying that it meant more than you're admitting. It wouldn't have hurt you if it hadn't."

Josie reached out and squeezed her arm with a smile. "Zoe, you're not a casual kind of girl. Like Jane said. There is nothing in your life that is short term. Your business, where you live, your friendships, your *recipes*... everything has history and is a true part of your *life*. Sex is going to be like that for you too. And that is not a bad thing. But you have to accept that before you jump into it. Because Aiden's already realized it," Josie said. "And I think that's pretty amazing. Even with you half naked and in his bed, he still *knew* that it was not going to be casual for you."

Zoe felt a jolt of... something... shoot through her. Aiden had known that about her?

But yeah. She realized a second later that, of course he would have known that. If Josie and Jane knew that about her, then Aiden would. It wasn't just *her* that knew everything about *him*. She was certain she could ask him right now what her least favorite food at Thanksgiving dinner was and he would know. He'd also know her favorite card game, and she was sure he knew she'd chosen a pink teddy because she loved the color. And it was his favorite. No, pink wasn't commonly a guy's favorite color, but it was Aiden's. Not that he admitted it readily to his buddies. But she knew.

She also knew it was because of the bakery. His love of pink had started young when he'd come to Buttered Up with his mother. He associated the color with frosting and candy and cupcakes and happiness and sweetness and the fun and laughter that had always been part of the bakery. And especially the strawberry cupcakes that had been his mother's specialty. He'd been requesting those for his birthdays even after he was a teen. Right up until his mother passed away. Zoe doubted he'd eaten a strawberry cupcake since.

"And once you sleep together, you're going to have to be ready to at least give it a chance to really work," Josie added after letting Zoe think for a moment.

Zoe felt like her whole body was swirling with emotions. And realization. Which wasn't an emotion exactly, but she felt like someone had turned on a bright light in a previously dim room. Why had things felt so hot with Aiden? And so painful when he'd turned her down? And why hadn't she gone out and found someone else in the past five months since she'd made this huge decision to end her virginhood? And why had it taken twenty-five years to get to the point where she wanted to end it?

Now she knew.

Josie was right. She didn't do casual. And without even fully understanding it, when she'd decided it was time, she'd gone to the one guy who was the most long term in her life that she could actually get naked with. Who also didn't do casual.

She blew out a breath.

"But," Jane said, her grin sly, "that doesn't mean you can't torture him a little for turning you down the way he did."

The way he'd done it had been born of sleepiness and shock, Zoe knew. When she wasn't being irrationally angry at him about it. But he'd been pretty blunt about the no. And he *had* waited five months to come back and fix it.

"Yeah?" she asked, interested.

"For sure," Jane said. "You'll be living together. And Aiden will never do anything you don't want him to do. So if, for a few days, you eat breakfast in your shortest nightgown, or take your bra off first thing when you get home from work, or blow dry your hair wrapped only in a towel with the bathroom door open..."

"I already do all those things," Zoe said.

"Exactly." Jane gave her a wink. "And why would you stop just because the guy, who's practically like a brother to you and who was very clear about *not* wanting to sleep with you, is staying there."

Ah. "He did say no," she mused.

"Yes, he did." Jane's smile was devious. "And I can tell you from personal experience that really pent-up, waiting-forever-for-it sex is *soooo* good."

"Almost as good as make-up sex, which this also will be," Josie piped up.

Zoe was going to have to take their words for it, but she liked this idea. A lot.

Okay, so she wanted Aiden. And Aiden knew it. And she hadn't actually gotten rid of her V-card yet. And Aiden at least suspected that.

That didn't mean she had to just let him pick up where they'd left off without a little pain of his own.

But she was going to let him pick up where they'd left off.

Where they'd left off in her bakery kitchen earlier tonight, as a matter of fact.

She couldn't get that pink candy coating and the pink sugar out of her head.

———

*Z*oe took her bra off the second they stepped through the back door of the house.

The house.

The house where he'd grown up and where she was now living. The house where she'd tried to seduce him five months ago.

The house where he fully intended to make her his and then raise their children and live well into their old age together.

Yes, his drama about this whole situation had gotten more intense since actually getting to Appleby, seeing her again... and having her tell him he was insane.

He watched as she reached down the back of her dress, unhooked her bra, and then pulled the straps down one arm and then the other, pulling the pale pink bra fully off and tossing it toward one of the kitchen chairs. The tiny piece of silk caught on the back of the chair, swinging there, taunting him. Probably still warm from her body. Probably smelling like cake. And Zoe. Which was kind of the same thing.

He propped a hip against the counter just inside the back door and watched her cross to the fridge. She pulled the door open and took out a bottle of water. She bumped it shut again with her butt as she twisted the cap on the bottle. She took a long drink, meeting his eyes over the bottle.

After she'd swallowed she asked, "What?"

"Just waiting for you to keep going."

"Keep going with what?"

He let his gaze drop to the front of her dress where her nipples were prominent now without the bra. Then he glanced at the bra on the chair.

"Oh. I didn't even think," she said, waving her hand like it was no big deal. "That's always the first thing I take off." Then she kicked her shoes off. "Then the shoes."

"Don't let me being here stop you."

She gave him a smile. "I won't."

"And don't worry about picking your shoes up from in front of the fridge so I don't trip on them and break my neck." He looked at the shoes.

She took another drink from the water bottle and lifted a shoulder. "It is my house. And you think you want to just insert yourself in my life... well, this is what it's like."

Uh-huh. That's what he'd thought. In all the times he'd stayed over here, and previously at Maggie and Steve's, Zoe had never taken her bra off in front of him. She didn't exactly treat him like a *guest*—they were hardly formal—but she did act like he was a guy who... well, who she didn't take her bra off for.

"Good to know," he said. He crossed to where she stood. She straightened as he got closer, awareness flaring in her eyes. But he simply bent and picked up her shoes. He tossed them over by the door, out of the way of foot traffic. "I mean, if *this* is what I can look forward to around here"—he let his gaze drop to her breasts again—"I'm never leaving."

He was never leaving anyway.

She started to lift an arm, almost instinctively, as if to cover herself, but then she thought better of it. Her arm dropped and she took a breath.

"I'm glad you're fine with us just both being... ourselves. Comfortable. Just doing whatever we usually do," she said.

"Of course. Wouldn't have it any other way."

She nodded. "Okay. I'm going to take a shower and go to

bed, then." She turned and headed for the hallway and presumably the stairs up to her bedroom.

"Zoe."

His low voice stopped her in the kitchen doorway. She looked back at him over her shoulder.

"Sweet dreams."

"Yeah. You too, Aiden."

She headed down the hallway and then turned up the staircase.

He leaned around the door, expecting to see at least one more tease.

He wasn't disappointed. Her dress hit the hallway floor when she was far enough up the stairs that he couldn't see anything more than her ankles.

And then a scrap of pale pink silk floated down on top of the dress.

She was a brat. And she was going to torture him over turning her down at Christmas. Make him horribly sorry. Maybe even get him begging before she gave in. Make him come to her this time.

"Can do, Miss McCaffery. Can do," Aiden said softly as he snagged the panties and dress on his way up to his bedroom.

He tossed the dress in front of the bathroom door, which was already closed with the sound of the shower running behind it. His body responded to the thought of her naked and wet just behind a slab of wood. Not that he'd ever do anything he wasn't absolutely sure she wanted him to do. And he wasn't *absolutely* sure she wanted him to join her in the shower tonight. Besides, shower sex wasn't first-time, take-her-virginity kind of sex. It was on the list for eventually, of course, but that wouldn't be their first time.

Yeah, he was 90 percent sure she was still a virgin.

But he intended to find out for sure. Before he took her to bed. He was taking her to bed either way. He'd meant it, absolutely, when he'd told her he now intended to be her last. But if he was her first—and good God, he wanted to be her first—then their first time needed to be even *extra* special.

Okay, really, he needed to know so he could be a little more careful. He wouldn't want to hurt her, and with how he was feeling about her, he wasn't so sure words like "ravage" and "pounding" wouldn't be applicable. He needed to know how easy he needed to take her the first time.

They could work up to ravaging and pounding.

His body liked that idea too.

He looked down at the panties in his hand, then at the bathroom door. The tease. Well, two could play this way. He tucked the panties into his pocket and headed for his bedroom.

This was going to be a hell of a lot of fun.

As long as his balls didn't explode before he teased her out of her panties when she was within reach.

8

S he was pretty sure he'd kept her panties.

After her shower, she'd found her dress outside the bathroom, obviously tossed there by Aiden. His bedroom door was shut, and she hadn't heard him stirring around in the bathroom until after she'd paraded down the hallway in only a towel, changed into her pajamas, and gotten into bed.

Her bra was still on the chair in the kitchen when she went down for coffee in the morning.

But she couldn't find her panties anywhere. Which sent her thoughts spinning. If he'd taken them... why? What was he doing with them? Why was that hot?

She was thinking about all that, staring at the Keurig while stirring hazelnut creamer into her coffee, when she heard, "'Mornin,' Zoe," in a deep, rumbling voice behind her.

She jumped and turned.

Okay, he'd taken the "do whatever we usually do" thing to heart. It looked like he usually grabbed his first cup of coffee dressed in only the boxers he'd slept in. She knew he slept in only boxers because of last Christmas.

Or he was just torturing her right back.

That was equally possible.

Though she wasn't sure she minded. At all. Because he looked very, very good in those boxers. At Christmas the room had been dark, and she hadn't fully appreciated just how hard and long he was. She'd felt some of it. But she'd been so worked up about the whole situation and nervous and then distracted by the kiss and then by him saying no and physically setting her back *off* of him that she hadn't really taken time to *feel* him the way she would have liked to.

She could make up for that right now. If she reached out right now and put her hand on his chest—his wide, hard, probably hot-to-the-touch chest—he'd welcome it. He might grasp her wrist with his big hand and pull her close. Or maybe he'd move in and press her against the counter like he had against the fridge last night.

It was a thrilling feeling knowing she could reach out and run her hand over his abs, and lower, and this time he'd absolutely take her up on it.

That was a *really* thrilling feeling. Whatever crazy thoughts were going through his head, one was clear—he wasn't going to push her away this time.

It was also a heady feeling knowing she could pretend this was all no big deal.

She could keep him guessing. She was in control.

But she could also parade around her kitchen in a t-shirt and panties and ogle him in his boxers and think dirty thoughts and flirt and not worry.

This was Aiden. She could be different with him than with any other guy. She could... practice. Flirting, teasing, being sexy, having fun. It wasn't *meaningless* the way she'd made her thoughts about Christmas sound. In fact, it was more meaningful. Because she could be herself. She might be awkward or clumsy about it, but that would be okay. Then again, maybe she'd be good at it. That would be okay too. She didn't have to worry about leading him on, hurting his feelings, giving off mixed signals.

Because she would mean everything he thought she meant.

She took a deep breath and gave him a bright smile, leaning back against the counter nonchalantly. She was wearing only a big t-shirt, which hit just below the curve of her butt, and a pair of red panties this time. They matched the sparkly words "Inside" and "Hot" on the front of her t-shirt. Zoe braced her hands on the counter behind her so Aiden could better see the shirt she'd worn just for him. There was an oven and a cake pan. The oven said to the cake pan, "I want you inside me." The cake pan responded, "That's hot."

Aiden definitely read it. Or at least, he looked at it. She wasn't wearing a bra now either, and he took his time dragging his gaze over her breasts. She was hardly well endowed but he didn't seem to mind. His attention lingered there nice and long. Her nipples responded. Which made his gaze stay. But eventually the corner of his mouth quirked up, and she assumed he'd taken in the whole shirt.

"Good morning," she greeted. "I didn't know you'd be up this early."

She went to the bakery at six every morning except Sundays.

"Well, I knew if I wanted to catch you in your skimpy pajamas, I'd have to be up."

He moved closer and she caught her breath. But he only reached past her left ear to the cupboard that held the coffee cups. She didn't move though. There was no reason to move. She wanted to be this close. To smell him. Feel his heat. Tease him.

And herself.

But after he'd retrieved a mug, he didn't move back. He stayed way closer to her than was necessary to put the pod into the coffeepot and pushed the buttons.

As the fresh brew poured into his cup, he put a hand on the counter next to her hip and leaned in. She looked up, tipping her head back.

"And I definitely wanted to catch you in your skimpy pajamas," he said, low and husky.

He smelled good. She felt his body heat soaking into her skin.

She took a big, deep breath. "Well, it's not a pink lace teddy. But I'm glad you like it."

He definitely liked how she was dressed. His erection was obvious. The boxers wouldn't have hidden it anyway, and he was doing nothing to shift the hard length away from her hip where it was pressed.

His hand skimmed down her side to the edge of her t-shirt, and he inched it up, then looked down. "There's some lace." He dragged his finger over the lacy top edge of her panties.

Zoe felt tingles trip through her, her nipples beading even tighter as she sucked in a deep breath.

"And you in a sassy t-shirt is a lot more appropriate than a teddy."

She narrowed her eyes. "So if I'd worn this into your bedroom at Christmas, you would have taken my virginity?"

When she said *taken my virginity* heat flared in his eyes. Interesting. He liked that idea. He'd been acting all jealous and possessive yesterday, but she'd been so flustered about seeing him and her own reactions to him and just general surprise over him assuming they'd now get married, that he hadn't *really* thought about that.

"I still would have said no," he said, his voice gruff. "But..." He looked like he was fighting the instinct to keep talking.

Zoe pressed against the erection that was hot and hard against her. "But what?"

"I would have kissed you longer and touched you a lot more first," he admitted. "I might have even slipped a finger into these silky panties." He ran his finger down the front of her panties now, pressing against her clit, before sliding under the elastic edge and brushing over the hot, now wet, folds between her legs.

She gasped, then moaned, reaching up to grasp his opposite arm.

He leaned in, putting his mouth against hers. "I might have even—I *should have*—made you come before I sent you back to bed."

Her body shuddered. With need. And irritation.

Only Aiden could make her feel both of those things at the same time.

"I could have had an orgasm except I wore the wrong outfit?" she demanded. Or tried to demand. Being breathless with her heart pounding made it difficult.

"That teddy just brought home how unusual it all was and kept reminding me," he told her, brushing his lips over hers and his finger against her clit without any silk between them.

Zoe realized she could get a before-work orgasm. She was apparently dressed correctly this time. That wasn't exactly her "usual morning routine" but damn, it could be. It really freaking could be.

"You're an idiot," she told him. Then she wrapped an arm around his neck, arched closer, and kissed him.

Aiden must have decided not to be an idiot *again*, because he kissed her back. Deeply. Hotly. While sliding his finger into her in one smooth, firm, but gentle thrust.

Just one finger. One long, thick, knowing middle finger. But wow. She had a great dildo. She had her own fingers. *This* wasn't exactly virgin territory—so to speak—but no guy had ever had his fingers there, and now she realized *she* was the idiot. She should have been asking guys to put their fingers there over and over.

Okay, no, that wasn't true. She would never let another guy

do this to her. That thought hit her even as a spiral of pleasure shot from Aiden's finger to her toes, literally curling them.

She was probably uptight or a prude or weird or something. But it was true. She couldn't imagine letting anyone else put his hand where Aiden's was right now.

He slid his finger in and out, then brushed his thumb over her clit at the same time and Zoe felt even her scalp tingling.

She would never admit it, but she really hadn't known that this could feel like this and be this good. It was just his finger. Just one finger. And she was going to insist—probably pathetically, with lots of compliments heaped on—that he do this to her all the time now. Maybe hourly.

Zoe pulled her mouth away and gasped. "Aiden. Oh my God."

"Damn, you feel so fucking good," he rasped against her neck. "You're so damned tight."

She gave a half laugh, half moan. "Is that good?"

Now it was his turn to give a choked laugh. "Fuck, you have no idea."

No, she didn't. That was kind of the point. Which reminded her, that if he wasn't an *idiot* who got hung up on things like her wearing a teddy instead of a t-shirt, she could have felt this *five months* ago and been feeling it repeatedly since then.

But that was when the *real* realization hit. If she couldn't imagine anyone but Aiden Anderson putting his hands in her pants, then it wouldn't have been repeatedly even if he had done it five months ago. He'd left. He'd gone back to his life in Chicago. Just as he'd *planned*. That had been part of why he'd seemed so perfect. But truthfully? That would have been... horrible. She would have felt all this amazingness then realized it could probably only happen with him, and she would have been cut off. Or driving to Chicago every other day and begging him for orgasms. Which would have been humiliating.

Not to mention hard on her business.

And her car.

Dammit. Aiden had been right to say no.

Oh, she really hated that.

She started to squirm, intending to push him away, too confused and annoyed to really focus on here, on what was happening now.

But then it didn't matter.

Aiden curled his finger in just a certain way and shifted his hand just so and pressed against her clit just right, and suddenly Zoe was pulling him closer and grinding against his hand and gasping his name along with, "Oh, yes, please," and then her body pulled tight, like someone was stretching a rubber band inside her and then let go, like they'd shot it across the classroom—and she was flying.

Pleasure flooded through her scalp to her toes and back again. Heat and relief and want and an insane desire to thank him and beg him to start all over again washing over her, and all she could do was grip his arm and try to stay upright.

Aiden pulled his hand from her panties and wrapped a big arm around her waist, pulling her against him, his other hand going to the back of her head. He hugged her as she struggled to catch her breath, running his hand over her hair.

"You're so amazing, Zoe. Damn, that was hot. Holy hell, girl, that's so much better than coffee."

He said it all against the top of her head, kissing her and stroking her, and making her feel amazing and hot and like maybe *she'd* just rocked *his* world. Which was crazy. But damned if her ego wasn't ballooning up like he was pumping helium into her.

Along with his fingers.

Suddenly she giggled. It was adrenaline and a little feminine empowerment and endorphins like crazy, she knew. But she pressed her face against his chest and giggled.

She felt the rumble of a chuckle from him.

"Okay, well, laughter might not have been what I was going for."

She tipped her head back, looking up at him. "I think you know this is the wrong place, and I'm the wrong girl to be expecting to hear 'Oh, Aiden, you're a god.'"

He grinned down at her, his gaze hot, but affectionate at the same time. "I've got time, and the patience and inclination, to work on that."

Heat fizzed through her bloodstream, but she managed to not melt into him. Somehow.

"I need to get ready for work."

"I need coffee."

"Okay then."

But before he let her go, he leaned in and gave her a hot but sweet kiss. Unlike the others. All their kisses, even the surprising one, had been hot. This one was... different. There was a lot of lip, a little tongue, breaths mingling, tasting, arching closer. But it felt... slower. And intentional. And like he wanted to keep doing that for a very, very long time.

Maybe forever.

He lifted his head, looked into her eyes for a long moment, then stepped back.

She brushed her hair back, took a deep breath, and said, "Right."

Right? Right about what? What did that mean?

"I know," he said.

Then he gave her a cocky grin.

Dammit. He thought she meant *he* was right. About all of it. Everything. That saying no at Christmas had been the right move. That things between them should get serious now. That she wasn't going to be able to resist him.

And... she thought that was maybe what she meant too.

———

He jacked off in the shower to images and thoughts of Zoe.

Not that it was the first time. He'd been *very* good about pushing thoughts of her out of his head if they tried to wander there before last Christmas. And they had, on occasion. But after Christmas? It had been impossible.

Now, though, there was no holding back or even a flicker of guilt about it.

He'd just made her come, in the kitchen where he'd grown up, before he'd even had coffee.

And it had been the hottest thing he'd ever experienced.

He hadn't intended to touch her like that this morning. He hadn't really intended to touch her at all. He'd *wanted* to, but he knew she had some plan to tease and tempt him for a while first, and he was very willing to play along.

That had all gone up in smoke in about ten minutes.

She'd looked so fucking hot... and adorable. That was the problem. It was that combination. Because Zoe McCaffery was a lot of things—sassy, smart, fierce, stubborn, funny, loving. But she wasn't very often adorable. That came with a hint of vulnerability and sweetness which was at odds with the woman he knew.

It was the idea that there were sides and layers he didn't totally know, which made his heart really race. He wanted everything he already knew about her. He wanted her exactly as she was. But the idea that she would show him some new things, let him get closer, be even more real with him in a way she hadn't been with her brother's best friend before, made everything in him shout *yes!*

That was what the virginity thing had been about. It had hit him as he'd slid his hand into her cherry-red panties and felt her sweet, hot wetness for the first time. It had nearly brought him to his knees. *That* was a place they'd never gone before, a place they'd never really imagined in all likelihood. Had they recognized the other was attractive? Sure. That was just one of those things that registered and then sort of went out of mind. Zoe being beautiful was like saying Zoe was wearing a green dress or that she made the best lemon bars in the state.

But being intimate with her like that was something new. Something that had thrown him for a huge loop five months ago.

Something that he was all fucking in on now.

And now that he'd touched her, felt her sweet pussy clench around his finger, heard his name from her mouth as she came, seen the dazed look of pleasure, and yes, surprise, dammit, in those big blue eyes when she'd looked up at him after... yeah, he was done. Addicted. Whipped. A goner. Going to fight to have that for the rest of his life. She was his.

Aiden stepped out of the shower and grabbed a towel, drying off quickly. He wasn't walking around with a raging hard-on now, but he was far from satisfied. He wanted her. And it was more than physical now. There was this nagging need that went beyond needing to sink deep and thrust hard and feel all that amazing tight, wet heat around his cock. Though he definitely wanted all that. It was this need to be sure she was on this same page with him. That Zoe knew what had happened in the kitchen this morning was the start. To... everything.

That no one else would ever touch her like that. That he would never touch anyone else like that again. That he might not finger-bang her *every* morning before work, but they would be in their kitchen together every morning before work from now on. Their kitchen. Yeah, that was now *their* kitchen. And that they would be going down to that kitchen from *their* bedroom upstairs.

That was a lot to lay on the woman today. He knew that.

But the quick finger fuck had to help his case.

He grinned as he brushed his teeth, shaved, and finished

getting ready for the day before heading down the hall for his clothes. He didn't hear anything in the house, and he looked out his bedroom window to find Zoe's car was already gone from the driveway.

That was fine. They needed to drive to the bakery separately today anyway. He needed to try to find a way to get over to the Hot Cakes factory later without being noticed if possible.

But he was definitely going to the bakery. He was going to use Zoe's Wi-Fi and hang out while she worked today. Because she was the reason he was in Appleby right now, and the more he was with her, the faster he could convince her this was all meant to be.

And then he could tell her about Hot Cakes and wouldn't have to find ways to sneak around over there.

He had some business to do before he could stake out a spot at the bakery though.

He'd sent his partners a message before he'd gotten in the shower, so they should all be logging into their video conferencing service by now.

The Fluke Inc. guys weren't early-bird-gets-the-worm types. They were much more night-owls-get-the-juicy-mice types. Plus owls were fucking majestic as hell. But if one of them needed the others, they'd be there.

Aiden settled into a chair at Zoe's kitchen table and connected to the call.

"Where the hell are you?" Camden McCaffery asked, squinting at his computer screen from where he was lounging on his couch in Chicago.

Aiden was five feet from where he'd made Cam's little sister come before he'd had his first cup of coffee.

He was not going to tell Cam that.

He was already pushing his luck asking them to all be on a video call this early. His four partners were not morning people. This would have been better around the table in their conference room in Chicago rather than with him in Zoe's kitchen and them all in their apartments almost two hundred miles away, but he wasn't leaving Iowa any time soon, and he needed to fill them all in ASAP.

"Appleby."

"What the hell? Is everything okay?" his best friend since childhood asked. Cam was frowning. Aiden understood. The only people in Appleby that Aiden came home to see were Camden's family members.

"Everything is great," Aiden assured him. "I'm just... moving back."

Cam blinked at him. "When?"

"Yesterday."

"To *Iowa*?" Oliver Caprinelli asked. Then he yawned. "*Why*?"

To marry Cam's sister, actually, but he was going to hold off on that information for a bit as well.

Oliver was propped up in his bed, his laptop propped on his thighs. He looked truly confused about why anyone would ever utter words that were even close to, "I'm moving to Iowa."

Grant Lorre, Fluke Inc.'s CFO, was at the breakfast bar in his ultra-modern kitchen. He was dressed to head to the gym after the call. He simply lifted his coffee cup, listening.

"Well... Hot Cakes." Aiden hit a button, sending the article about the sale of the factory to his partners' phones.

He gave them a second to scan the article. Ollie was actually the one who was going to be most in favor of this. Ollie was always in favor of the crazy ideas.

Ollie looked up. "Okay, and...?"

"It's for sale. You want in?"

"It's in Iowa?"

"It is."

"Well... I'm a little tied up right now... and possibly allergic to pigs..." Ollie trailed off without finishing the thought.

Aiden looked at Cam. He would know why Hot Cakes being for sale was important. And complicated.

Grant lifted a brow. "You eat a lot of bacon for a guy who's allergic to pigs," he said to Ollie.

"Wide-open spaces, then," Ollie said. "They have a lot of those there, right?"

"A lot of those," Aiden agreed dryly.

"Why are you into this?" Grant asked simply, his attention on Aiden.

Cutting through the B.S. was one of Grant's roles in the group.

Okay, well, the short answer to that was *Zoe McCaffery*. But that wasn't a *simple* answer. Grant and Ollie didn't know anything about Zoe other than her name and that she was Cam's younger sister.

"The Hot Cakes factory went up for sale this week. I think this would be a great investment for Fluke." Aiden put on his CEO voice. He wasn't CEO of Fluke because he was smarter or more driven than any of these men. But Aiden was a natural leader and manager. He'd brought these men together and knew how to handle them. He knew them each very well and knew and appreciated each of their strengths. And weaknesses.

"Why?" Ollie asked.

"Hot Cakes makes Butter Sticks, Peanut Butter Pinwheels and..." Aiden paused for emphasis. "Fudgie Fritters."

Ollie sat up straighter. "Shut the fuck up."

"Seriously."

"Hey, sorry I'm late." Dax Marshall, their fifth partner, logged on. He was in a shirt and tie and had a to-go coffee cup in hand. Of course, it was the same shirt and tie he'd been in yesterday before Aiden had left for Iowa.

"She didn't even make you coffee before kicking your ass out?" Cam asked Dax, watching him toss back two ibuprofen tablets and wash them down with coffee.

"Never get coffee from 'em," Dax said, after he'd swallowed.

"Because?" Cam asked.

"Coffee is to sober up, to focus, to get *work* done. I take my work with coffee. I like my girls with tequila."

"Coffee is too serious for you and your girls?" Grant asked with an eye roll.

Dax grinned. "Yep. I save all my good, really strong coffee time for you." He batted his eyes at Grant.

Grant flipped him off. "I'm so blessed."

The term "herding cats" could have easily applied to day-to-day operations of Fluke. And Aiden was the master herder of these tomcats.

He oversaw the nerdy dreamer, Ollie, the everything's-a-party playboy, Dax, the arrogant, spoiling-for-a-fight lawyer, Camden, and the serious, not-everything-is-a-fucking-game-you-guys CFO, Grant. Which was one of their favorite things for Grant to yell because Fluke was, first and foremost, a game company. They'd created *Warriors of Easton*, the fastest-growing online video game in the world. Much to all of their surprise on a daily basis.

Dax pulled something out of a plastic grocery bag and started unwrapping it, making a lot of noise. It was a Cinnamon Curl. A mini coffee cake. Made by Hot Cakes.

Aiden chuckled as Dax bit into it. He looked up. "What?"

"You've got impeccable timing," Aiden told him.

"Check your phone," Ollie said to Dax.

Dax picked up his phone, moving his thumb over the screen while still eating with the other hand.

"Okay. Why do I care about Lancaster Foods and their factory being for sale?" Dax asked.

"They make Hot Cakes," Ollie said.

"No way," Dax replied.

"So we're buying it," Ollie told him.

Yep, that was exactly the type of spontaneous, sudden-pivot,

I'll-brave-pigs-to-save-my-fritters kind of reaction that was classic Ollie.

"Cool." Dax bit into the Cinnamon Curl.

And *that* was probably as much a reaction as they would get from him. Dax was a roll-with-it, up-for-anything guy.

"We're buying a failing company?" Grant asked. "A company that does something we know nothing about?"

"I'll have you know, I've eaten my weight in Hot Cakes in my lifetime," Ollie said.

"Same," Dax agreed around a mouthful of cinnamon crumbles.

"That doesn't actually make you qualified to run the company that makes them," Grant said, his tone long suffering.

"You sure?" Dax asked with a grin. "I mean, we made a pretty great video game company, and all we knew how to do was play video games."

"And draw cartoons on the computer," Ollie added. "Don't sell yourself short."

Dax nodded. "Thank you. You're right. I can draw cartoons on the computer really, really good." He even made the cringeable grammar error just for Grant.

Grant sighed. But he didn't argue. Because Dax was right. The game Ollie had come up with and Dax had designed—and that Cam, Aiden, and Grant had marketed and sold—had accidentally become an overnight sensation. It had been a total fluke the five of them had become rich and successful. Hence, the company name, Fluke Inc.

"The company isn't failing," Aiden inputted. "The grandfather, who was the head of the company, died about a year ago, and the son wants out. His big project now is in Texas. He wants to get rid of this part of the company quick and focus his time and energy in Dallas. They're still in the black. Profits were down this past year a little, but they're still doing well."

"Then someone will come in and buy it up. The Peanut

Butter whatevers will be safe. If it's a solid product they shouldn't have any worries," Grant said.

"*If* it's a solid product?" Ollie protested. "Peanut Butter Pinwheels are the best thing anyone ever did with a nut butter."

Okay, *that* was not true. Hot Cakes were great, but they were individually packaged snack cakes sold in grocery and convenience stores. They were bought in boxes of twelve or twenty-four and stuck in lunch sacks that spent the day in school lockers. They were tossed up on counters with beef jerky and energy drinks when paying for gas. They were great. But they were hardly changing the world.

Nor were they anywhere near as amazing as the peanut butter chocolate bars Zoe made at Buttered Up.

The crinkling of the plastic wrapper around Dax's second cinnamon curl seemed extremely loud in the microphone suddenly.

"Someone *will* buy it," Aiden agreed. In fact, he was afraid someone might just come in and do that today. Right out from underneath him.

That's what had prompted him to get in his car yesterday and head straight to Appleby after he'd read about the news. "But it will likely be a competing food company. They'll absorb the products into their existing lines and probably move production out of Appleby. That would mean over three hundred people out of work and a huge hit to the town."

"But the Fudgie Fritters will be safe?" Ollie asked.

"We can't let someone else buy it," Aiden insisted. "They... uh... might change the recipe." He had to get the guys on board. He could do this alone, but he'd feel so much better if he had his partners with him.

"*What?*" Ollie said, looking horrified. "No. I won't let that happen."

Yeah, Aiden needed Ollie's drive and fuck-it-let's-make-this-amazing attitude. He needed Dax's laid-back, fun attitude. He needed Cam's who-do-I-need-to-call-and-yell-at attitude. And he needed Grant's let's-look-at-all-the-possible-scenarios attitude. They were all pieces to one big whole.

The kind of overnight success they'd experienced as a bunch of young twentysomething guys had, predictably, come with a few hiccups. Aiden had kept them together through it all and made sure their friendship was always the top priority. He made them work together as a team that, frankly, when they were all at their best, kicked major ass.

"Why do you really want to do this?" Grant asked, watching Aiden carefully.

Grant always paid attention and never missed details. Like the fact that Aiden cared about more than Fudgie Fritters.

"Appleby is our hometown," Camden said before Aiden could respond. "And that factory has been there since 1969."

He was lounging on his sofa, his feet propped on his coffee table. In a t-shirt instead of his usual dress shirt, his tattoos were on full display. He looked completely nonchalant. But Aiden knew better.

Besides being Letty McCaffery's grandson and Zoe's big brother, Camden had a long, not-great personal history with the Lancaster family. Primarily the family's one and only granddaughter and heiress apparent, Whitney.

"No shit?" Ollie asked.

Camden shook his head. "No shit. It's been for sale for about two days now. I'm sure everyone in town is panicking."

Technically, it had been for sale for three days, and it was starting to make Aiden itchy. He wanted the company. He would have had this meeting three days ago if he'd known Eric wanted to sell. But he wasn't plugged into anyone who would have told him the news. Because they wouldn't have known he wanted to know the news. He hadn't seen the announcement in the *Appleby Observer* until yesterday because his hometown newspaper was a weekly publication, and he had to wait to get it in the mail. Two days after, everything in it was old news. But he still liked to flip through it. After all, it didn't really matter that he missed the notice of the chili feed for the football cheerleaders or that the dentist was changing his office hours.

Getting the news from Appleby two days late had never mattered. Until yesterday.

Now, the company he hadn't even known he needed until twenty-five hours ago, had been on the market for three days, and he was certain another food company had their eyes on it. Maybe more than one. Hot Cakes was no Hostess, but they did fine. Like millions of dollars' worth of fine every year. They were not going to be unclaimed for long.

They were not going to be unclaimed by *him* for long. He was giving his friends about thirty more minutes to get on board here.

"I need you to do your numbers thing right away, Lorre," Aiden told Grant.

"My numbers thing?" his much more serious partner asked.

"The thing where you add and subtract shit until you say, 'Yeah, we can do that,'" Aiden told him.

"It's only been up three days," Grant said. "Why don't I call over there, feel them out? Maybe they're willing to negotiate—"

"No," Aiden said simply. "I want you to make this happen. Today."

"Why are you in such a hurry?" Grant asked.

Zoe was never leaving Appleby. So Aiden was now never leaving Appleby. So he needed a job. And now, especially after talking to everyone last night, including one of his soon-to-be employees, it needed to be *this* job.

It was pretty simple, really.

It had gotten that simple over the past few months after realizing he was in love with Zoe. Or maybe it had always been that simple and he'd just been very slow realizing it.

Zoe had been ten when Aiden's mom had died, and he'd

more or less moved in with her family. She'd been his little sister as much as she'd been Cam's.

Until she hadn't.

Until that Fourth of July almost two years ago when he'd walked in on her ironing a dress in the kitchen wearing only a bra and panties.

Until he'd finally admitted she was the funniest, most interesting, most amazing woman he'd ever known, and that he could no longer shut down his inappropriate thoughts about what she looked like without her clothes on once he'd actually *seen* the sight. There was no forgetting that.

Or the way she'd confidently faced him in only her underwear, not acting embarrassed or like he should *not* be seeing her that way. But also not at all like someone she thought of as a brother who had just walked in.

But she was also the reason this was all so fucking complicated.

Instead of all that, he said, "Someone has to save the factory and all those jobs. If that factory closes because some other company buys them out and relocates the production, it will devastate my hometown. I can't let that happen."

"Yeah, I definitely want in on this," Cam said. He was sitting forward now. He looked serious.

Aiden sighed. He'd been expecting this.

Cam cared about the impact to the town, no doubt. But Cam would want to buy the business for the same reason he'd donated money to build a new baseball field—that had turned into an entire youth sports complex. And the same reason he'd donated money to the school for a scholarship. A full-ride scholarship. In his name.

Appleby was a small town. The kind of small town you never truly, fully escaped.

Cam would want to do it to be a big hero and to show the Lancasters up.

Which was very complicated.

"You *sure*?" Aiden asked. "*Really* sure? This won't be easy."

"Totally sure," Cam said resolutely.

"You both want to be the big hero," Ollie said, grinning. "You small-town boys are so cute."

Aiden felt a mix of relief and trepidation. He wanted his friends and partners with him, but it wouldn't be a cakewalk for him and Cam... pun intended.

"Oh, I'm totally in too," Ollie said. He pointed into the screen. "Lorre, you won't want to be around me if I can't have Fudgie Fritters."

"What makes you think I want to be around you anyway?" Grant asked, sounding bored.

He was almost always bored with Ollie's big ideas. Except when those big ideas were costing him money. Which was often. Or when those ideas ended up with Ollie and Dax stranded in a foreign country and needing money for plane tickets. And new shoes. That was a great story though.

"You do," Ollie said confidently. "Without us you'd be sitting on Wall Street, hating your life, drinking every night, and wondering why you don't have any cool friends."

Grant didn't say anything to that. Aiden thought he was maybe thinking he should give the Wall Street thing a try.

"Snack cakes and video games... seems like a great combo for our brand," Dax said.

Aiden frowned. *Is that really making the world better?* a voice asked in the back of his head. Getting kids who were sitting around playing with virtual people instead of real friends to eat more sugar?

But it was bigger than just the snack cakes. People depended on that factory for their livelihood, to keep their families supported. If those people couldn't work in Appleby— something he knew all about—then they'd move. They'd take their tax dollars with them. They'd take their money from the grocery store, from the hardware store, from the cafés, from the gas stations. The whole town would be affected.

"Can we find a potato chip factory to buy too?" Ollie asked with a grin. "Or soda. We should absolutely own a soda factory. Fluke Soda. That has a ring to it. Hell, we should *start* a soda company."

Grant sighed and finally set his cup down and leaned in. The sign things were serious now. Because in spite of the grin, Ollie definitely now wanted to start a soda company.

"Okay, gentlemen, let's dial it back," Grant said.

Everyone knew that "gentlemen" meant Ollie *and* Dax.

Dax was, no doubt, quietly thinking of the different flavors of soda he'd want them to offer. At least one would be something bizarre like *Unicorn Piss*. Dax was very proud of the fact that he made Grant reach for his antacids more often than anyone else. He kept a tally of Grant's Tums ingestion on the whiteboard in his office.

Grant wasn't wrong—Aiden had no idea how to run a company like Hot Cakes. Fluke had literally started in a dorm room and had grown with them. They had employees, but they had been relatively small, and things had always been very casual. They'd recently sold to a bigger company which had reduced all their roles, and now they were all trying to figure out what to do next with their time and energy. This was the perfect thing.

Probably.

Maybe.

Aiden wanted to shrug out of his jacket. He was suddenly hot. This idea was complicated. He didn't even really know where to start, but he had to hope a company that had been running for this long would be easier to step into than starting something from scratch.

Of course, the McCaffery family feud with Hot Cakes made

it more complicated. And for Aiden and Camden to come in and save Hot Cakes would be... yeah, complicated.

But he wanted to do this. He wanted to be in Appleby, and this was his shot at having an actual purpose here. He wasn't a farmer. He couldn't open a business fixing anything or selling anything—they had everything they needed there already anyway—and he wasn't a doctor or teacher. That was why he'd headed out when he'd turned eighteen. He'd wanted to own his own company but one that served more than the seven thousand people who lived in and around Appleby. He wanted to do something bigger.

"Don't call anyone," Aiden said to Grant. "I'm going to go meet with them in person and make an offer. Just figure out how to make the money work."

"You're really moving there?" Dax asked. "For good?"

Aiden nodded. "I'm not leaving Fluke. Just Chicago. I'll come back for meetings and things as needed. But"—he took a breath—"yeah, I'm moving back to Iowa."

"Okay, I changed my mind," Ollie said. "Let go see some pigs and wide-open spaces and save the Fudgie Fritters." He picked up his phone and started tapping it. "Piper," he said a moment later. "I need to reschedule Thursday."

Their executive assistant also didn't start work this early. Though Ollie called her at all hours.

"Ollie, *no,*" Aiden said firmly. Of course, Ollie was ready to just pack up and go to Iowa.

Ollie looked up, his phone at his ear. "What?"

"Let me start on this. Just me. Quietly," Aiden said, trying not to look like he was panicking at the idea of Ollie charging into Appleby and announcing they were there to save the day. He had to hope no one gave Ollie the idea to ride into town and down Main Street on a white horse.

"You want to make the announcement?" Ollie asked. He

nodded. "I guess that makes sense. Hometown boy comes home to save the day."

"Actually, no. I just need a little time to..."

"Figure out how to keep my mom and sister from hating him when he tells them that we're their major competitor now," Camden said.

"Wait, Hot Cakes is your family's major competition?" Grant asked, frowning.

Aiden sighed. Camden was a McCaffery through and through. He might not live in Appleby anymore, but he'd been ingrained to hate the Lancasters. Even when he'd been kissing Whitney Lancaster and trying to talk her into running away with him after graduation.

Aiden wondered if Cam knew the story about Didi offering Letty a partnership. Or her naming it Hot Cakes to rub it all in when Letty turned her down. Or that everything in the bakery was exactly the way it had always been because everyone was now completely scared of trying anything new because of the risk of looking like fools.

"It's... a long story," Aiden told Grant. "But yes, this could be a little complicated with Cam's family. Just let me... ease them into the idea."

"You can do that?" Grant asked. He looked at Camden. "You sure you want to do this?"

Cam shrugged. "I'm not gonna lie to you—the idea of coming in and buying Hot Cakes away from the Lancasters and then making it even bigger and better is like fucking karma filled with cream and wrapped in chocolate."

"But your family." Grant looked legitimately concerned.

Camden looked at Aiden. "The Golden Boy can deal with them. They like him better than they like me anyway. Let him hang out with my family for a couple of weeks. I'm sure he'll find a way to sugarcoat the news."

All he really wanted to coat in sugar was Cam's little sister. Again, probably no need for him to share that.

But if anyone could convince the McCafferys that this would be okay, it was Aiden. He really was their favorite son— Camden could be a rebellious pain in the ass, and Henry had only had eleven years of charming them. Aiden could make them understand that this was a good thing. He and Cam were saving the town. Maggie and Steve could even end up *proud* of what Aiden and Cam were doing.

Of course, Zoe also needed a lot more sweet-talking before he dropped the, "Oh, by the way, I own your major competitor."

The kitchen orgasms were a great place to start.

He could easily follow that up with, "I'm in love with you."

Then maybe a, "Take your clothes off."

Then, "I'm now your business rival."

Sure. That would be a piece of cake.

9

Aiden grabbed another cup of coffee on his way out the door, feeling good about the meeting with the guys. With them on board with him, everything was going to work out. He'd written an email to Eric Lancaster as soon as he'd hung up with the guys, making the official offer. He expected the deal would be finalized by the end of the day.

On impulse, he pulled his phone out. It was still early. But he could leave a voice message.

Much to his surprise, Whitney Lancaster answered on the second ring.

"This is Whitney."

She didn't sound like he'd awakened her either. He'd grabbed her number from the company information before he'd left Chicago. He knew it was a cell number but wasn't sure if she used it for business only and what hours she kept. Still, he'd figured he was the best one to make the first contact. They knew each other. They'd gone to school together. He'd known her in kindergarten, and they'd walked across the stage to graduate together. He'd been a friend of the family that hated her family, but he'd also been the best friend of the man who'd been head over heels in love with her. Aiden had been the only one who'd known about Whitney and Camden for a very long time. He'd like to think, even with how things had turned out between her and Cam, that she would consider *him* a friend. Or at least a used-to-be friend.

Aiden had been plenty pissed on Cam's behalf when things had gone to hell between him and the woman he'd thought he was going to run away with, but they were all grown-up now.

He hoped.

"Hi, Whitney. It's Aiden Anderson."

He heard her take a deep breath. "Hi, Aiden."

"We should probably chat."

"Yeah." She didn't go on.

"Is this a good time? I know it's early."

"I'm not in the office yet, but yes, this is probably the best time actually." She paused. "I thought someone from Fluke would probably be calling. I'm glad it's you."

Aiden lifted a brow. "You thought it might be Cam?"

"He's your attorney. It wouldn't be crazy."

But it would be crazy to think he'd want to have personal contact with her. Camden would deal with her attorneys, but Aiden couldn't imagine Cam would want to talk to Whitney herself.

Then again, this was his never-back-down best friend. He loved to push buttons. He loved a good fight. He probably wouldn't get a better fight or bigger buttons to push than he would with Whitney Lancaster when he was helping Aiden buy out the business that had kept them apart once upon a time. The business she'd chosen over being with him.

Aiden hadn't *really* thought that through. Camden had been plenty agreeable to the idea of buying Hot Cakes, but Aiden had assumed Cam would continue to avoid Whitney at all costs. As he had for the past eleven years.

Aiden might have miscalculated.

"I heard that word's gotten out that you've got an offer and thought maybe we should talk before more information got out," Aiden told her. "Assuming your dad agrees to the deal I just sent over."

"He will," Whitney said. "He's very pleased with the idea in general. I can't imagine what would stop him from agreeing."

Aiden felt a rush of relief go through him. "That's wonderful. I'm very pleased as well."

"So yes, I suppose we should discuss how you want to roll this out."

Aiden nodded even though she couldn't see him. "I don't want to roll it out. Yet."

"What do you mean?"

"I need to keep the buyers, including me and Cam, under wraps for a little longer."

"So it *is* you *and* Cam?" She didn't sound surprised. Nor did she sound thrilled.

"And our other partners."

There was a pause on her end. "The McCafferys don't know yet?"

He blew out a breath. "How did you guess that?"

"Why else would Cam not already be here trumpeting in the town square about how he's saving hundreds of jobs and pointing out to me that he's saving my family from being even more hated and going deeply into debt?"

Well, at least she realized what they were doing for the town and for her. "Cam's not..." But Aiden stopped mid-defense.

Cam would love to do all that. Camden had never had any trouble pointing out all the things he'd done for Appleby over the years and the chance to have something to hold over Whitney Lancaster's head. Yeah, Cam might be older, a little wiser, and a tiny bit more mature than he'd been at eighteen, but maybe not *that* much. No one had ever gotten to him like Whitney had, and he'd never gotten over that. Or over her.

"We're not ready to tell them everything yet," Aiden amended. "But we knew we needed to step in with Hot Cakes now rather than waiting. We're ready to move forward with the sale. We just need to keep the details private for a little longer."

"Fine by me," Whitney said. "I'm in no rush to admit that the town's favorite sons are once again saving the day. This time by bailing the Lancasters out."

"Your dad won't say anything?"

She laughed but didn't sound amused. "He honestly couldn't care less," she said. "He moved on a long time ago. I'm handling all this. He just wants it done. He doesn't need or want the details other than how much we're getting and when."

"Great," Aiden said. "We'll keep working on the details and keeping things moving. Just without any publicity. For right now." Cam would never go for keeping things on the down low for good. He'd want to make a splash, let Appleby know they were here, and that it was all going to be amazing from here on out. In their humble opinions, of course.

"Fine." She paused. "Will I be dealing with you, then?"

Unspoken was the question about when and if Cam would get involved. "For now." He hesitated. "Could I stop by later on and get a copy of employee manuals and all the compensation and benefits information?"

"Of course," she said. "Or I can just email it all to you. We wouldn't want someone to see you walking in over here."

Aiden almost heard the smile in her voice. This was complicated and just plain weird, but at least they could all acknowledge that. "That would be great to start with. Thanks."

"I'm happy to go over any of it with you. And we can do that off-site too. Of course, we'd probably have to go out of town."

He actually chuckled at that. "I promise this isn't going to be a secret for long."

It couldn't be. He had a lot to do. The business had been neglected by Whitney's father for some time now. He needed to get the lay of the land and figure out how to bring it all back. And then some. Aiden knew Camden and Ollie well enough to know that by the end of the day, they would already have schemes to make Hot Cakes even bigger and better under their ownership. In fact, with Cam in Chicago with Ollie and Dax—the big idea guys—and without Aiden keeping track of them, God only knew what they might be cooking up. A bored Oliver Caprinelli was a dangerous thing. Egged on by a troublemaking Camden McCaffery... Aiden shuddered. The only good thing was that Grant was there and would put the kibosh on anything too crazy. Dax, of course, wouldn't stop a thing.

Aiden rubbed the middle of his forehead. He needed to get this thing with Zoe locked down, so he could dive into Hot Cakes before his friends bought a Hot Cakes blimp or something.

But he probably needed to call Piper first. She needed to keep even closer tabs on Ollie for a few days.

Did that mean he was going to instruct her to get into Ollie's emails and listen in on his phone calls and absolutely keep track of *anything* he and Cam did together? Hell yes, it did.

"Well, I know I'm listed as the VP of Sales and Marketing," Whitney said to Aiden, returning him to their conversation. "But I really know the business inside and out. That's just... a title. I mean... I do marketing. Of course. I deal with all our accounts. But I do... more than that." She sighed. "I feel like I'm applying for a job with you and failing this interview."

Aiden knew that technically Whitney was put in charge of marketing mostly because she was beautiful and charming and smart and knew everything about the business. She could easily sell it to anyone. She hadn't actually gone on to get a degree, having been given her position as soon as she turned eighteen and having learned what she needed to know by working in the company alongside her father.

"You don't have to interview, Whit," Aiden said, reverting to the nickname she'd gone by with friends in high school. "You can be as involved with the company as you want to be for as long as you want to be. We want to preserve *all* the jobs there, and we know that you're a valuable asset to us. We've all eaten plenty of Hot Cakes, but that's kind of the limit to our knowledge about the company."

"I doubt very much that Camden's eaten plenty of Hot Cakes," Whitney said. She sounded like she might be rolling her eyes. But she also sounded a little sad.

She was right. Cam avoided all snack cakes from the Hot Cakes company.

"Camden is only part of the ownership," Aiden felt compelled to point out. "We're equal partners. You don't have to worry about him interfering with this going through or him firing you or anything like that."

"I'm actually more worried about working for him than being fired," Whitney said. "But I can't not work for him. I don't know how to do anything else."

Aiden realized that Camden being her boss might be... interesting. Especially with their history and Camden's propensity to provoke people. Aiden might need to especially review any sections in the employee manual about harassment. If nothing else, they would need to have a talk about how Camden was going to act with and treat Whitney.

"I've got your back, Whit," Aiden told her. "You don't have anything to worry about."

"I don't know about that."

"I'll admit there are a few... complicating factors."

Camden, for one. Definitely. But also Zoe.

Whitney laughed lightly. "That's a nice way to say it." Then she said, "But really, Aiden, thank you. I'm glad you called. I've been worried, and it's good to know we've got a place to start."

"You bet. And you can reach out to me anytime too. I'll text you my email address."

"Great. I'll send all those materials over as soon as I get into the office."

Yeah, Whitney and Eric might be the only people in Appleby who knew the names of the new owners at this very moment, but they couldn't keep it under wraps for long. He needed to get to work on Zoe.

He grinned at that thought. That was hardly going to be *work*.

"I'll talk to you soon," he said to Whitney.

"Sounds good."

They disconnected, and Aiden headed for Buttered Up.

He parked in the back and started for the door. And ran into Jane.

"Uh, hey."

She smiled up at him. She had on a hoodie, the hood up, and was dressed in running clothes. She was leaning against the bricks beside the back door. "'Morning."

"What are you doing?"

"Waiting for Zoe to bring me my breakfast."

"By the back door?" Aiden grinned.

"I can't be seen out front." Jane shrugged. "Against company policy to shop here. It's a gray area, since I don't actually *pay*, so I'm not sure it's really shopping, but you can't be too careful when it comes to crazy family feuds."

She was right. She was also about to be one of his employees and was breaking company policy right in front of him.

Yeah, that was the first policy he was going to look at when Whitney sent the materials over. They were axing that clause, first thing.

"Want me to go in and get her?"

Jane looked at her watch. "Nah, there's another minute before our meet."

"Does she pass it to you in an unmarked brown paper bag?"

Jane laughed. "She does."

Aiden shook his head, smiling. "You're both crazy."

Jane shrugged again. "Don't want to get fired but can't live without my Buttered Up sugar fix. It's a tough position to be in." She gave him a mock frown. "You can't tell."

"Of course not." He started to move past her to the back door but then slid her a glance. "So you haven't seen Zoe yet this morning?" Did he want to know how Zoe was acting after their kitchen tryst? Yes, yes he did.

"Nope."

"Huh."

"Have *you* seen Zoe yet this morning?" Jane asked, clearly fighting a smile.

"I... have."

"And was she in a good mood?" Jane asked.

"She was... after her... coffee."

"Her... coffee." Jane nodded. "Yeah, she hasn't had any morning... coffee... from a guy in... a long time."

He immediately turned to face her. "How long?"

Jane blinked at his sudden intensity. "Um." It was clear she was trying to figure out how much to say. "Not sure."

"Jane," Aiden said, in his low, firm, I'm-not-fucking-around voice he had to use with Dax at least twice a week. "Get sure."

"Well, if we're talking about *coffee*..."

"We are *not* talking about coffee."

Jane's eyes got wide. "Are we talking about..."

He let her trail off and then lifted a brow. "Not quite. Somewhere between that and... actual coffee."

Jane grinned. Aiden couldn't help but grin back. He liked Jane.

"You got up early," Jane commented.

"Zoe gets up early."

Jane nodded. "And if you wanted... coffee... with her, you'd have to be up early."

For some reason Aiden laughed. "You missed the emphasis on *up*. I mean, as long as we're doing this insinuation and innuendo thing."

She gave him a huge smile. "I'll bet *you* didn't miss the emphasis on *up*. Am I right?"

He laughed then shook his head. "You're not going to help me out at all here?"

"If you want to know something about Zoe and her coffee, you're going to need to ask her." Jane pushed away from the wall and turned to face him. "But you do already know she takes her coffee very seriously."

He did, actually. "Then why was she so pissed at me about not wanting Christmas coffee and wanting more serious coffee?"

Jane shook her head. "Because she had a recipe and now you're throwing new ingredients in, and she has no idea how this is going to end up... tasting." She sighed. "I'm not going to give you the info you want, but I'll tell you this— because it's something you already know—Zoe is really good at what she does. But what she does is what she's always done. On purpose. Because she knows how that will turn out. She knows exactly how much butter and sugar and flour to put in and what temperature to bake it at and how long to leave it in the oven. She will have to really trust someone to change anything up and risk it turning out badly."

Aiden thought about that. He glanced at the back door of the bakery. "She would also have to really trust someone to change up her... coffee routine."

"You've got it," Jane said with a little nod.

"But I really need to—" He was cut off by the back screen door to the bakery whacking him in the back.

"Oh, geez!" Zoe gasped. "Aiden! You can't stand right in front of the door."

Soft light and the scent of vanilla and buttercream and cinnamon drifted out, like Zoe was an angel arriving on a glowing cloud of sugar and spice.

"Um—" He tried.

But all he could think about was how he'd had his hand in her panties and her moaning against his mouth just a couple of hours ago.

"Here you go." Zoe handed a plain paper bag to Jane through the door. "Double chocolate muffin."

Jane took a deep breath, her eyes sliding shut in bliss for a moment. "I love you so fucking much."

Zoe chuckled. "Get out of here before someone sees you." She shot Aiden a look. "Someone else."

"See you later, babe," Jane said. She gave Aiden a wink. "You too. Enjoy your next... cup of coffee."

"Oh, I will," he promised. He watched her jog down the alley and turn the corner. Then he looked over at Zoe. "She parks a couple of blocks away?"

"She jogs down here from home," Zoe said, pushing the door open wider so he could step inside. "That way people think she's just out for a run. She tucks the bag inside her jacket on the way home."

"It's so dumb she has to sneak around like that," he commented.

"Of course it is," Zoe said. "But I guess if Josie came in here munching on a Cinnamon Curl from Hot Cakes, I'd be a little annoyed."

"You wouldn't fire her though," Aiden said, shutting the door behind him as Zoe moved across the kitchen.

Zoe shrugged. "I'd tell her I didn't want it to happen again."

"If you found a bunch of Hot Cakes wrappers in Jocelyn's car, you'd be upset and have a talk with her with the expectation she stop eating them?"

Zoe looked at him across the worktable, and for just a second he flashed back to last night then to that morning in the kitchen. He could smell her, feel her, hear her all over again, and he lost his train of thought.

Damn. This woman. How had this all happened so fast? Suddenly, almost overnight, he couldn't even keep track of a conversation while standing in a room where he'd kissed her.

Then she said, "By eating those, she'd be supporting my enemy. Yeah, I would ask her to stop."

And he was right back on what they'd been discussing. He sighed. "Your enemy? That's a little strong."

She shook her head. "This again? Already? Everything was going so well between us too."

He moved farther into the room. "You mean when I was making you come?"

She sucked in a quick breath. "Uh... yeah. I really liked you right then."

He grinned. "I can make you like me a lot. Often. And even more."

Her eyes were wide as he came around the corner of the worktable and into her space. She swallowed hard. "I would be okay with that."

"I would be very okay with that too." He lifted a hand and dragged his thumb along her jaw. She was so soft. He wanted to touch her all over.

"Aiden?"

"Yeah, Zoe?"

"You better never show up eating a Hot Cake in front of me."

Dammit. This really was stupidly complicated. It shouldn't

be. It didn't need to be. He really wanted to fix it. But right now, it was.

"You're saying that if I had one hand in your panties and the other holding a Mint Munchie, you would tell me to stop fingering you?"

She wet her lips. Her pupils were dilated. But she nodded. "Yeah."

He braced his hand on the worktable next to them and leaned in. "You're saying that if I broke open a Hot Cakes cupcake, took that cream filling, painted it over your nipples and then licked it all off, you'd still push me away, because it was Hot Cakes cream?"

Her chest rose and fell with her deep breath. But she nodded again. "Yep."

"And if I dipped my finger into a Strawberry Swirl and then *swirled* that strawberry filling over your sweet little clit and then wanted to suck it clean, you'd say no because it was Hot Cakes strawberry filling?"

It took her a little longer to reply that time. She cleared her throat. But then slowly nodded. "Yeah."

Her *yeah* was very breathless.

He didn't believe her. He shook his head, making sure he looked regretful. "That's too bad."

"But I make cream and strawberry filling," she said quickly.

He grinned. There was no question Zoe's was superior to the Hot Cakes fillings. Those fillings were mass produced and needed preservatives, so they had a longer shelf life. Zoe's were fresh and made by hand in small batches. Which was the entire point. They weren't the same thing. They weren't competitors.

Though both would work for nipple and clit sucking.

"But I probably won't have your filling in my glove compartment, convenient for when we're randomly out parking by the river and the need to lick your nipples and suck on your clit comes up."

God, he loved talking dirty to her. This was Zoe McCaffery. He'd known her forever. Five years ago, he would have *never* thought about talking to her like this. He would have never imagined anyone talking to her like this. Actually, if he had, he would have wanted to punch them in the face. Hard. Repeatedly.

But that was because he'd never seen her cheeks flush pink or her lips fall open or her nipples bead behind her light blue t-shirt.

She loved it too. Clearly.

"You can't just lick my nipples and suck my clit without cream or strawberry filling?" she asked.

Aiden felt heat jolt through him. Zoe had just said *clit* to him. And talked about him sucking on hers.

"Oh fuck yeah, I can." He started to lean in.

She gave him a smile. "Exactly. So you better not show up with any Hot Cakes, and you better not have any in your glove compartment."

Then she slipped around him and headed for the front of the bakery.

Aiden dropped his head. She was such a brat.

And he wanted her so damned much.

Grinning, he turned, intending to follow her out to the front.

The back door opened just then, and he glanced over to see Josie coming in. She stopped, clearly surprised to see him.

"Good morning," she greeted.

"Hey, Josie."

She looked toward the door that led to the front of the bakery. "Zoe made you come in and work this morning?"

He chuckled. "No. Thought I'd steal your free Wi-Fi and maybe some coffee and muffins."

She nodded, hanging her purse on the little hooks by the door and then grabbing an apron. She slipped it over her head and tied it behind her. Then she crossed to the sink to wash her hands. "Well, you better get out there, or there won't be much of any of that left. Zoe's fan club is about to arrive."

"Her fan club?" Aiden felt his frown.

"Oh yeah. Mornings are our busiest time in the front."

"But everyone is coming in for muffins and pastries, right?" he clarified.

Josie tossed him a smile as she dried her hands. "That definitely seems to make sense."

He planted a hand on his hip. "But that's not it?"

She lifted a shoulder. "I'm just saying that—as you know—the recipes for the stuff we sell here haven't changed at all over the years, but since Zoe took over, business has picked up in the mornings. Especially with the males in the twenty-to-forty-years-of-age demographic."

"Forty-year-old men are coming in here because Zoe is waiting on them?" Aiden asked, scowling now. "What the hell? They're a little old for her, aren't they?"

"Too old to start their day with a cute girl serving them sweets?" Josie asked. "Is any man too old to want that?"

Aiden narrowed his eyes. "You're a cute girl who serves sweets in here too. What makes you think they're not in here for you?"

She laughed and started toward the front. "I didn't say they *all* come in here for her." Then she pushed through the door, letting it swing shut behind her.

Aiden shook his head. These two girls. They weren't above flirting and smiling and curling their hair to sell a few additional muffins, huh? That was good. That was business. It was for good reason you never saw ugly, grumpy people doing commercials.

But he didn't like it.

Aiden followed Josie through the swinging door out of the kitchen. He came up short immediately. It was only ten past six.

They'd just opened the front door for business. And there was a line. Literally out the door to the sidewalk.

And they were almost all men.

Josie shot him a glance that said, "Told you."

Aiden crossed to the coffee station, where the line was only slightly shorter. It wasn't until he was in line for coffee and scoping out the tables where he could set up his computer for the day to make Buttered Up his makeshift office, when someone noticed him.

"Aiden Anderson!"

He turned to find Jerod Carpenter and Carter Jackson behind him, smiling huge smiles. Jerod worked at the bank and was one of the two men—including Aiden—in suits in the bakery. Carter was a good friend of Jerod's and farmed his family's farm just north of town.

"Jerod." Aiden took the other man's hand. "Carter." He shook the farmer's hand next. "How are you?"

"We're just fine. Haven't seen you in a while," Jerod said. "How are things?"

Aiden glanced over his shoulder to where Zoe was bagging muffins and laughing and chatting with her long line of customers.

"Good. Really good." He was. He'd just had his hand in Zoe McCaffery's panties. It didn't get much better than that.

"How long are you in town?" Jerod asked as they all moved up closer to the coffee station.

Aiden assumed the other guys had already paid for their coffees, but the counter that held the tall carafes and all the accompanying sweeteners and creamers just sat there opening inviting anyone to help themselves. He'd have to mention to her that she should at least store the cups behind the counter and hand them over only after they'd been paid for. Anyone could come in here, help themselves, and walk out with free coffee.

Like he was going to do.

But he was staying. He'd slip a twenty in the register or tip jar later. He'd been mooching off the bakery all his life. He hadn't paid for a cookie or cupcake in... ever. But now it felt strange.

The bakery had always been successful. As far as he knew. But he'd never really asked or paid attention, or hell, even thought about it, honestly. Now, overnight, this all looked different. Who repainted the trim when it chipped? Probably Zoe and Maggie and Steve. Had they always offered both a light and a medium roast? Had they always offered three kinds of cream? Who thought through the details of how many kinds of cream to offer so that people felt like they had a selection, but they didn't overdo on inventory? Maggie probably. They probably hadn't made hazelnut creamer when Letty had run the bakery. And Zoe didn't change things. Probably not even the creamer. He sighed even as he thought about how much he liked the stubborn little blond baker he'd known all his life.

She was stubborn, but it was born of a fierce determination to take care of her family and her family legacy. But it wasn't all pink sugar and frosting and sprinkles. Suddenly he was looking at all the ways it could be complicated and stressful.

"Aiden?"

He focused on Jerod and his questioning look. Then remembered the man had asked how long he'd been was in town.

"I'm here for good, as a matter of fact. Just moved back."

Might as well lay that out there. Especially among the twenty-to-forty-year-old male demographic that seemed to be Zoe's most enthusiastic customers.

Not that anyone here would have any reason to think his moving back had anything specifically to do with Zoe. But once they all saw him with her constantly, knowing he was here to stay, people could start putting two and two together. He was fine with that.

"No kidding," Jerod said, clearly a little surprised. "No more Chicago?"

They moved up another spot, and Carter reached for a coffee cup.

"Been there, did what I needed to," Aiden said. "I wanted to get out there and try some new things, and I've had a lot of amazing opportunities."

That was all certainly true. He and Camden had both wanted to leave Appleby and do something big. They both felt like they could honestly say they'd done something big and impressive.

But when they'd gotten the offer to sell, Aiden hadn't balked for even a second. He'd been ready to move on. Even before Zoe had shown up half naked and turned everything in his mind in a new direction, filled with a new possibility, he'd been ready for something else. Something more.

His mom had told him to make something of his life, to make it matter. He'd been struggling with the idea of *Warriors of Easton* really *mattering* for a while. It had given him money to donate to worthy causes. It had made lots of kids happy. Those weren't nothing. But were they big enough?

They weren't as big as Hot Cakes.

He didn't mean monetarily or fame-wise. Saving the town, saving those jobs, *mattered*. Being someone who didn't turn his back on his hometown, who used his good fortune—and his actual fortune—to make things better for people here *mattered*.

"Now there's stuff here you need to do?" Jerod asked as he and Aiden took their turn at the coffee station.

Yes. There was. Save Hot Cakes—and the town. Convince Zoe to marry him. Just to name two.

He glanced over at the bakery counter where Zoe and

Jocelyn were boxing and bagging treats for their long line of customers.

"Yeah. I guess I felt like it was time to come home," he said.

Jerod followed his gaze and his eyebrows went up. "Jocelyn?" he asked. "I didn't know the two of you were a thing."

Okay, so now he had a choice. He could shake that off and insist he was just friends with both women—which was true enough—and downplay what was going on with him and Zoe. Especially considering she hadn't admitted anything was really going on with them.

Then again, she had been more than fine with what had happened in her kitchen at home this morning.

Or he could use this opportunity to tell Jerod—one of the men within the exact demographic of guys who possibly came in for more than muffins—that Zoe was off limits now. That she was *his*. Jerod would probably spread that news around like it was butter on these muffins everyone loved so much.

"Not Jocelyn," he said, reaching for the coffee carafe and pouring sixteen ounces of nice, strong brew into his cup.

"Ah. Zoe." Jerod nodded. "That makes sense."

"Does it?" He sure as hell thought so. Maybe he'd have Jerod go tell Zoe. Aiden added a top to the cup and turned to watch Jerod add cream to his and then a lid as well.

"You've known each other forever. You're with her family and at her house whenever you are home," Jerod said with a nod. "And she's never been serious with anyone here. Guess I just never put that all together."

She's never been serious with anyone here.

Aiden knew the caveman part of him who liked that *very* much was over the top. But he couldn't help it. He wasn't 100 percent certain she was still a virgin. If he were a betting man, he'd say she was. But this was Zoe. She was goal oriented. Annoyingly so. If she really wanted to get rid of that V-card, she would do it. That thought tightened his gut.

But the idea of her being emotionally close to, spending quality time with, talking and laughing with someone else as she would in an actual relationship, made his *chest* feel tight.

"That's great," Jerod said, clapping Aiden on the shoulder. "Welcome back, man."

Jerod was now assuming Aiden and Zoe had an ongoing relationship that had been spanning a long period of time and was closer than the friendship that had been a part of him being so close to her family.

He was good with that.

They had a more serious relationship than she'd had with any other guy around here. He knew her. He knew her dreams and plans and likes and dislikes. He'd been there when her grandfather died. She'd been there when his mother had died. She'd been a kid, but they had that history. They were close. And dammit, they were now sleeping together.

Or would be.

Soon.

Very, very soon.

"See you around," Aiden told Jerod.

"You bet." He and Carter headed out of the shop.

Aiden went to stake out his table by the far window that looked out over the alley. He plugged his computer in, opened his email, and glanced over at Zoe, who was smiling and laughing and bouncing around behind the glass cases full of her homemade treats—though becoming less so by the minute —and sighed. He might have to become a morning person if he was going to be with her.

That was going to suck a little bit.

But then she stretched to reach up into a high cupboard behind the front counter, and his gaze dropped to her ass.

Yeah, sucking. He could get into *sucking* when it came to Zoe.

He quickly became aware, however, that he wasn't the only

one enjoying the view. A couple of the guys in line at the register elbowed each other, and one actually leaned in to see around the two men in front of him.

Aiden's eyebrows shot up.

Then evidently not finding what she was looking for in that cupboard, she stepped back and bent over to search a lower cupboard.

A couple more men leaned to get a look.

Yeah, no.

Aiden got up, shrugged out of his jacket and draped it over the back of his chair. He pulled his tie off and tossed it over his computer. Then he headed behind the counter to join Zoe and Josie.

Looked like they needed some help.

He rounded the end of the counter to join the ladies.

He moved in behind Zoe and when she rose, put a hand on her lower back—yes, it was a possessive gesture especially for the guys watching from behind her—and said near her ear, "Let me get it."

They were far enough away from the register and the line of customers-slash-admirers that no one could hear their conversation. But they could see.

She looked up at him, clearly surprised. Then her eyes narrowed. "You don't know what I'm looking for."

"I know if it involves you stretching and bending in front of a bunch of other men, I'm going to get it."

She rolled her eyes. "You want to just pee on me to mark your territory and get it over with?"

"I don't think that's necessary." Then he leaned in and kissed her.

10

It wasn't deep or long, but it did the trick.

It also caused her to relax into him, her lips softening. For just a couple of seconds.

He pulled back before she could push him away, because he sensed she was about to. That wouldn't help with his narrative here at all.

She pressed her lips together briefly then shook her head. "My mom's going to hear about that."

"I don't care."

"What if I do?"

"Shove me. Slap me. Throw a cake in my face. Yell. Tell me to leave you the hell alone in front of all these people."

He could tell she was thinking about it for a moment, probably playing each of those out in her head and maybe enjoying them a bit, but she didn't do any of them. The surge of satisfaction and *hell yeah* was strong as he realized this was a big win.

"My mom would hear about that too," she finally said.

"Yeah."

"She'd be mad if I slapped you. Or wasted cake. Or swore in front of customers."

"Uh-huh." Those were all true. And not at all why she wasn't doing them.

"I need more plastic containers for a half-dozen muffins and cupcakes," she said. "They're not up here, so we'll have to get them from the back."

"You go," he said. He glanced behind them. The line was still there. Most of them were staring with their mouths hanging open. "I've got this."

"Oh, I don't—"

"I can get cupcakes and muffins and scones out of the case."

"Bet you don't know how to run a cash register," Zoe said.

"I... don't." Aiden frowned. He'd never run a register.

"Bet you also can't smile and flirt them into buying double what they came in for," Zoe said, giving him one of the smiles that probably got guys buying by the dozen.

Considering 90 percent of the line was male, that was a pretty good bet.

"Fine, where are these containers?"

She grinned, clearly pleased with herself. "Storeroom, second shelf, right-hand side."

He went after them, returning with a huge stack only two minutes later. It was still enough time for Zoe to dive right into waiting on people again. With a big, bright I'm-so-happy-you're-here, you're-so-funny-and-charming-and-handsome smile.

"He's back to stay, then?" Garrett Green was asking her.

Aiden set the containers next to her.

"I guess," Zoe said, looking up at him.

"I am," Aiden confirmed. "To stay."

"I see," Garrett said. He didn't look happy.

Aiden didn't really fucking care if Garrett was happy. About this or anything else.

"What can I get you?" he asked the next guy in line. The man looked familiar, but Aiden wasn't sure who he was. It wasn't like Aiden knew *every* person in Appleby. Even in a small town, if someone had been behind him in school four or five—or more—years, he wouldn't have been on any sports teams or in class with them, and he wouldn't have really known them. It was also possible, of course, people would have moved to Appleby since Aiden left.

"Need a blueberry and an apple cinnamon," the guy said, making direct eye contact but without a smile. He looked almost annoyed.

"That it?" Aiden asked.

"Yeah."

Aiden started to turn toward the case to grab the guy's order.

"Oh, Caleb, that will only get you through your first cup of coffee," Jocelyn said, coming up next to Aiden. "Especially because Brian will take the blueberry if you don't eat it first."

Caleb's expression softened and he smiled at Josie. "Yeah, you've got a point. I should eat that one first for sure."

"Or get two and then tell Brian he owes you one when he comes in on Thursday," Josie said with a wink.

A wink. Aiden rolled his eyes. He would put very good money down on the fact these men intended to buy more when they walked through the door but wanted Josie and Zoe to flirt with them before they increased their orders.

Dicks.

Caleb chuckled. "Yeah, okay. Two blueberry, an apple cinnamon, and you better give me a lemon poppyseed or Dan will be mad."

Aiden shook his head. Transparent dicks.

Josie nodded, punching that into the register. "That's more like it." She looked up at Aiden. "You know which ones are which?"

"Guessing the blueberry have blueberries in them and the

lemon poppyseed have poppy seeds?" His tone was dry as he moved toward the case.

Josie grinned and handed him a pair of thin plastic gloves to wear. "Wow, quick learner."

He pulled the gloves on and grabbed all the muffins and a bag, wrapping them in the paper on top of the case before stuffing them in the sunshine-yellow bag that said Buttered Up on the side and handing it over to Caleb, who had moved down after paying Josie.

"Thanks," Caleb muttered.

"My pleasure," Aiden muttered back.

Had Caleb wanted to take Zoe out? Had he been flirting every morning, working up to asking her out? *Had* he taken her out? Had Caleb been the guy to make Zoe "good" with the virginity thing as she'd put it last night?

"Hey," Aiden said to Caleb.

The other man turned back.

Aiden glanced over to where Josie and Zoe were waiting on new customers.

"You have a problem with me?" Aiden asked.

Caleb looked surprised. "Should I?"

"I'm here. Back in Appleby. And I'm with Zoe now."

Caleb looked over at Zoe. "Okay."

"You sure?" Aiden said. "You're okay with that? No issues?"

"Issues like what?" Caleb asked.

"Issues like maybe you thought something was going to happen with her, and now I'm here fucking that up for you."

Caleb shook his head. "You're not fucking anything up for me."

That wasn't exactly a denial of him wanting something to happen. It also wasn't a confirmation that he thought Aiden was a threat. Just that he wasn't worried about Aiden being here. He could take that a few ways. "Good to hear."

"Yeah, I've got what I want from Zoe."

Caleb waited a beat—just long enough for a wave of rage to wash through Aiden and his blood pressure to spike—then he lifted his bag of muffins. But then he smirked. So obviously Aiden still wanted to punch him in the mouth.

"Fucker," Aiden breathed.

"Um, calling our customers fuckers is really not the image we'd like to project here. Nor is the general body language that makes it seem like you want to fight them," Josie said. Her voice was low as she reached past him for two scones, a muffin, and a cinnamon roll.

"Did they date?" Aiden asked, still glaring at Caleb's back as the man exited the shop.

"Caleb and Zoe?" Josie said. She frowned. "No."

"Is he the one she finally slept with or something?"

Josie frowned harder. "No."

Well, that was something. "But he wants to."

"Maybe," she said with a shrug.

"That's not okay."

"It doesn't matter, Aiden. If *she* doesn't want to, then it doesn't matter if he wants to."

Yeah, okay, that was true. "Who was it?"

"Who was it what?"

"Who did she sleep with?"

Jocelyn shook her head. "You need to have *that* conversation with Zoe. And you know it."

"She won't tell me."

"Then maybe you don't get to know."

"I should get to know."

"Just because you want to?" Josie put a hand on her hip.

"Yeah. Because I care. Because she matters to me."

Aiden looked over at Zoe. She was now talking to Lucy Scranton. Lucy was old enough to be her mother.

Or her mother-in-law. Her son, Luke, was about Zoe's age. Good-looking guy. He was the basketball coach and taught history. That was pretty great. Noble and stuff. The kind of guy that could marry the beautiful small-town, family-oriented, never-leaving-home baker.

Aiden shook his head and scrubbed a hand over his face.

He was losing it. A little. Luke wasn't going to marry Zoe. Neither was Caleb. Or anyone else in here. Or not in here. Except him, of course. He needed to cool it.

But again, when he looked at Zoe, the word *mine* went through his mind.

"Aiden," Josie said. "I think you need to do two things."

"Okay." Aiden squared up to her, ready for the advice.

"One, realize that Zoe is sugar *and* spice. Being in a relationship with her—of any kind—is dealing with her humor and intelligence and drive and willing to work her ass off for what she wants, but also her sass and her stubbornness and a lot of I'll-just-do-it-myself and I'm-always-right."

"A relationship like a friendship and working together too?" he asked with a slight smile.

"You've got it." Josie sighed but also smiled. "She's a lot. Of everything. You could try to give up the spice, but without her, life becomes a lot less flavorful."

That was all very accurate in his experience as well. Josie had known Zoe since kindergarten and now worked with her every day in this bakery. Just the two of them. It was probably safe to say Josie knew Zoe almost better than anyone did.

"And what's the second thing I need to do?"

"Stop threatening and insulting our customers."

Right. "You feel sorry for Caleb?"

"Nope. But you being annoying to the customers will be annoying to Zoe, and that will prolong the time it's going to take you to get her naked. And that girl needs a release. More than beating eggs and whipping cream and kneading dough can give her."

"Are those euphemisms?"

"I almost wish they were," Josie said, then she took him by the arm and turned him toward the register.

"Are you saying..."

"Go wait on someone," Josie said. "And if they don't walk out with at least a dozen of something... you're fired."

Aiden did. But he couldn't get it out of his head that if *kneading dough* was not a euphemism for sex—and Zoe needed a release—that meant Zoe definitely going to bed alone every night.

———

He was so distracting.

She'd known him all her life. She'd been ignoring him for a large portion of it. She'd been blocking out the sound of Aiden and Cam chasing each other with Nerf guns, playing video games, watching football on TV, and generally rough-housing and being boys in her house for years.

But at the moment, he was sitting at a table near the window of the bakery, quietly working on his computer while she frosted sugar cookies, and she could barely focus on what she was doing.

What the hell was that?

It was the kiss. Out of the blue. In front of everyone.

Okay, it was the kiss and having his fingers in her panties first thing that morning.

And how he'd looked in only his boxers, walking into that kitchen as if he was completely comfortable with them being half naked together.

At least it *should* have been all that. That was all part of it, for sure. But it was also the way he'd come behind the counter and started helping out that morning.

Staking his claim.

It had been clear as day that's what he'd been doing.

To everyone.

She knew because she'd already ignored two calls and three texts from her mother.

What happened this morning with Aiden?! Lucy said he KISSED you in front of everyone!

Zoe Marie! What is going on! Are you dating Aiden?!

WE WILL TALK.

Oh, she was sure they would. She just knew she needed to have some answers before they did.

Not answers from Aiden. He'd actually been very clear about what he was thinking and wanting.

She needed answers for *her*. If they were just going to sleep together, that would be one thing. Something they could keep between just the two of them. Something that wouldn't involve her entire family, all their friends, and the whole town.

More than that would... involve everyone.

Was that what she wanted? That wasn't a fair question. Until yesterday, when he'd waltzed back into town and announced he was back, to stay, and wanted to be with her —*with her* with her—she hadn't known that was an option. So she'd never thought about it.

The bakery was mostly empty during the day. Between the breakfast rush and people picking orders up later in the day, it was quiet with very few exceptions. There was a book club that meant once a month and a group of young moms that got together every Tuesday and Thursday while their toddlers were at playtime at the preschool. There were occasionally people in and out, but for the most part during the day it was Zoe and Josie and George and Phil.

George was a retired banker who'd lost his wife about a year ago. He came every day at 10 a.m. in the suits he'd worn to work for forty-five years. He sat at the table closest to the coffeepots with his two newspapers. He barely said a word other than giving his muffin order. His snowy-white hair was a sharp contrast to his ebony skin and his kind, if slightly sad, brown eyes.

Phil was a retired over-the-road trucker. He, too, had lost his wife a little over a year ago. He came in wearing jeans and a t-shirt, also with two newspapers. He had leathery tan skin from years outside loading and unloading his trucks, and his long gray hair was always gathered in a ponytail.

The two men looked very different and had very different backgrounds. But they both liked coffee and muffins and reading the paper in the morning. They would sit at neighboring tables, not speaking, but after they each finished their first newspaper, they would pass it to the other.

Their little ritual always made Zoe smile. They clearly didn't want to chat in the mornings, but they also didn't want to have coffee and read the paper completely alone.

They hung out until about eleven thirty, then they both cleaned up their tables, tucked their newspapers under their arms, and headed out.

Zoe liked both men a lot, but she'd been antsy waiting for them to leave today so she could talk to Aiden.

The door had just bumped shut behind George. "You know —" she started.

Just as Aiden's phone rang.

He looked up at her. The phone rang again. "You okay?" he asked.

He was giving her the choice of talking instead of taking the call? That was nice. She waved her hand. "Go ahead."

He picked his phone up. "Hey." He was still looking at her. "Nice of you guys to finally get to work. I see what happens when I leave the office."

Zoe went back to applying blue frosting to the cookie flowers that Janice Murphy was coming to pick up later that afternoon, but she couldn't help but hear what Aiden was saying. Clearly, he was talking to his partners. Which probably included her brother.

"I'm going to tell her you're going to call. She can go over all that with you," Aiden said.

Zoe kept working, but with it being only the two of them in the front of the bakery, it was impossible for her to not hear him. There was soft music playing overhead, but that hardly obscured his voice. She could turn it up, she supposed, but at the same time, Aiden wasn't acting like he minded that she could hear him.

"Because I need someone else to take the lead on that," he said. "I can't do it, and I think you'd be the best for that anyway, Dax."

He was definitely talking to his partners.

"Fine, but Cam needs to stay out of it," Aiden said. "He knows why."

Zoe glanced over at her brother's name. Aiden was now standing and looking out the window, away from her.

She took a second to check him out. His jacket was still hanging on the back of his chair and his sleeves were still rolled up on his forearms, but he'd put his tie back on after helping behind the counter. Why? He was in here alone and obviously his work activities were all being conducted via computer and phone today.

Probably because he knew that tie got to her.

Then again, watching him moving behind the bakery counter, bagging muffins and scones, catching whiffs of his cologne whenever he passed her, had also gotten to her. She wasn't used to having that extra pair of hands. Or such a big body in that space. It had seemed he was always in her way. He'd been helpful though. Kind of. After Josie had had a little talk with him about the glowering he'd been doing.

Zoe wasn't sure what Josie had said exactly and Zoe hadn't asked. Aiden hadn't been *friendly* to the rest of their morning customers, and he was nowhere near the salesperson Josie and Zoe were when it came to talking customers into adding to their orders, but he hadn't messed anything up and hadn't scowled anyone out of the store. He had also seemed intent on keeping the line moving and none of the guys lingering too long at the counter with Zoe and Josie. They'd had the morning crowd taken care of thirty minutes earlier than usual.

Of course, they couldn't let him keep helping if that was going to be the case. When the guys lingered, they bought more. The bakery did better business when the customers had a chance to talk with Zoe and Josie, laugh a little, flirt a little, have a sample of the day's special, be reminded it was a coworker's birthday—cause for a surprise muffin—or that their assistant had brought them a cinnamon roll last Wednesday and they should repay the favor.

Yes, Josie and Zoe knew who their customers worked with, who got along with who, who didn't, who was allergic to walnuts, who hated anything flavored with pumpkin, who was likely to choose a cinnamon roll with more frosting, or one with less. It was good business. And inevitable after living here and waiting on these people for *years*.

Aiden didn't know those things. That meant this morning, Bud Wilmer had walked out with only one cream cheese Danish rather than the dozen he should have, considering it was his best carpenter's first day back on the job after his wife had given birth to their first daughter. Zoe could have easily convinced Bud to take Danish for the whole crew as a mini celebration. Travis Buckley had also walked out with a banana muffin for his partner, Dana. Dana hated banana muffins. That was going to be awkward.

Aiden definitely couldn't help anymore.

But he could sit his nice ass at one of her tables in his suit and tie and work with her Wi-Fi any time he wanted.

"Oliver, we need to know all about the benefits they have

now so that Grant can look into improving their plans." Aiden paused. "Yes, I want you to start comparing plans now." He listened for a few seconds. "You can start with that, but we need to go bigger. I'm not sure we know enough." Another pause. "Because we want to do better. We want to *improve* things." He let out a sigh. "Sure. If everything is fine, great. But Dax will be able to tell us that. I don't want bottom line and numbers and lists of services to be our only consideration, Grant. I mean it. I want Dax to talk to the employees. See what they want and need. Let's show them they matter."

He paused again and turned to pace to the front door of the bakery then back to the table.

Zoe kept icing cookies, but her mind was only half on her task. Not even half. Because her mind was 80 percent on Aiden. Which left only 20 percent for the... what was she decorating again? Oh yeah, flowers.

This was interesting. She'd never seen Aiden working. Not like this. Not real work.

She'd seen him mowing grass around town as a kid. That had been before he'd developed any muscles to speak of and long before she'd developed any appreciation for guys with muscles, so seeing him with his shirt off in the summer had done nothing for her.

She'd seen him serving ice cream and making milkshakes at the drive-in by the highway a couple of summers, mostly because her friends had thought he and Camden were *so cute* and always wanted to go there. What *she'd* seen was a couple of guys who laughed at fart jokes and who never left any mashed potatoes for her and who flirted with the same girls they said were bitches behind their backs. She had not been impressed by Aiden's sundaes either. He skimped on the caramel and thought chocolate ice cream with marshmallow topping was the best combo, which was *not* true. Clearly he was not an ice cream sundae connoisseur, and she had no idea why all the girls thought he was so great behind that counter.

But what he was doing this morning in the bakery was real work. He was a grown man now. He made a lot of money. His company was very successful. Additionally, it was clear, even from just this side of the conversation, that he was kind of the one in charge. At least, he was the one making assignments for the rest of the guys.

Plus, dammit, he looked hot in that tie. And when he was talking business and bossing people around, his voice seemed deeper and firmer.

Zoe shifted a little as her nipples tingled. That was stupid.

"Great. Having you on-site would make it all even better," he said into the phone. He slid back into his chair and tapped on his computer keyboard. "I need a few more days." He paused and typed something in. "I know that." More typing. "Fine, that will work. But not Cam."

Zoe grinned as she finished off the petal on the last cookie. Cam was a stubborn ass and didn't listen very well to many people. Aiden Anderson might be the one person who could get Cam to do what he wanted. Or to *not* do what Aiden *didn't* want him to do.

"Call me when you know." Aiden paused. "Okay, sounds good. Let's get this done right."

He disconnected, and Zoe glanced over to see him run a hand through his hair. She pressed her lips together, moving the freshly decorated cookies to the tray with the rest of the finished ones. She looked over at him again. He was typing on the computer, intent on the screen. Then he sat back, breathing out.

"You listened to Jane," she commented.

He looked up, almost like he'd forgotten her for a moment. "What?"

"Sorry, I couldn't help but overhear," she said, gesturing toward his makeshift workstation in general.

"Oh." He glanced at the phone then back up at her. "Right. Sorry."

"Didn't bother me," she said. She propped her hip against the worktable. "But it sounds like the things Jane said last night made an impression."

"What things?" he asked.

"About benefits and how nice it would be if management would just talk to their employees and listen."

Aiden swallowed. "Oh. That. Yeah, I heard her."

"I think it's cool you would take something a friend tells you and apply it to your company. You're using her to help you look at your own company through an employee's eyes and experiences rather than as management." Zoe lifted a shoulder.

She hadn't really thought about the fact that her brother and Aiden had employees. She knew that, of course, but she hadn't thought about them having people who actually depended on them and that they had to make decisions like benefits that could help or hurt the people who worked for them. That was very grown-up. Responsible. Probably stressful.

She only had one employee, and she was thinking about Jocelyn and how Buttered Up, and its successes and failures, affected her all the time. She worried about it and felt guilty she couldn't provide her amazing employee—and best friend— with a robust, secure, awesome benefits package. The best she could really do was pay her a decent wage—for Appleby, Iowa —give her time off when she needed it, and keep her in cupcakes and pie for life.

She made great cupcakes and pie. But that didn't exactly equal a 401(k) and dental. In fact, cake and pie kind of worked against a dental plan in some ways. Or maybe they made a dental plan even more important.

Aiden was watching her closely. "I want the people who work for me to be glad they're working for me."

"Well, the best way to know how to make them glad is to ask them," she said. "That's a great first step. Do you think the plan you have now isn't good enough?"

"I have reason to think it can be improved," he said. "And after listening to Jane last night, I'd like to know more about things like childcare needs and other benefits that could make a real difference in their lives." He was looking at her with a strange expression. But he kept talking. "There are long-term things that matter. Things like retirement and life insurance and covering time off for jury duty, things off in the future or that don't come up very often. But I'm aware there are day-to-day needs that impact people's lives that can really make them feel taken care of on a more direct level."

She thought about that. Childcare definitely seemed to fit that description. "Like what?" she asked.

"Transportation," he said. "Some people are limited to where they can work, or what hours they can work, because of sharing cars or needing public transportation."

Zoe nodded. She'd never thought about that. "What else?"

"The chance to go to school and advance in the company for additional training or certifications or degrees," he said. "Pay advances or reasonable loans or even grants for emergencies like the furnace going out in January or a kid wanting to go to summer camp."

Zoe's eyes widened. "Really? You do that? You give an employee money to send their kid to summer camp?"

"Why not? Summer camp is awesome. Every kid who wants to go should get to."

Wow. It turned out Aiden and Cam were not only grown-ups with employees who needed things like reasonable pay and medical coverage and a way to take Christmas off at least every couple of years, but they—at least Aiden—were realizing there was more to those people working for them than just product makers.

"So you're the one who's in charge? With your company? With the other guys?" she asked.

He'd definitely sounded bossy on the phone. And hot. She hadn't seen that side of Aiden before either. He was generally easygoing. He would get a little worked up on the basketball court or football field. He and Cam had definitely had a few fights—that got physical at times—over the years. Her brother was a stubborn, opinionated, cocky, not-really-easygoing guy, so he and Aiden had clashed at times. Usually when Aiden was trying to tell Cam to stop being a jerk or to pull his head out of his ass about something. But for the most part, Aiden wasn't *bossy* exactly. He didn't need to be. Things worked out for him without all that much effort.

"I'm... the organizer," he said, finally settling on a word.

"What does that mean exactly?" she asked, intrigued suddenly by how his company ran.

He and Cam had owned their company—she couldn't even think of the name of it at the moment—for nine years. She'd never been all that curious about how it all ran, what they each did day to day, or even how they really felt about it.

"The guys are each really good at specific things. They're very talented and they're very passionate," Aiden said. "When you get four strong-willed, talented, and passionate people together, it's a good idea to have someone who else who can... steer the ship."

"You're not talented or passionate?" she asked. She gave him a teasing smile. He was definitely both of those things. There was no question about that.

He grinned. "Brat. I like to think I'm both. But I'm a good... offensive coordinator." His smile grew. "Like on a football team. You need a great quarterback. You need talented running backs. You need a solid offensive line, and you need gifted receivers. But you also need a coordinator who can put them all together. Who can come up with a game plan and put everyone where they're going to be the biggest asset and then make changes as needed as the game goes on. Someone needs to call the plays."

"You call the plays," Zoe said. "You're the one putting the plan in place."

He nodded. "Dax is definitely a receiver. He goes out, runs the route we need him to, always makes the catch. The flashy stuff. The big yard gains."

Zoe grinned, enjoying Aiden's analogy. It worked for her. She'd grown up watching Cam and Aiden play as well as following the Iowa Hawkeyes. She knew football.

"Is Cam the quarterback?" she asked.

He laughed. "No. Cam is the offensive lineman. He's the one knocking people down who get in our way, breaking open holes to help us get ahead."

She nodded. "I can see that. Who else?" God, she couldn't even come up with the other guys' names. That was terrible. These were her brother's best friends.

"Grant. He's our money guy. He's like the running back. He makes smaller gains, safer plays, not the flashy, go-for-it stuff like Dax. But he's tough, and he'll fight for every yard for us. And he'll protect that football. Nobody will get it away from him."

"Who's the quarterback?" Zoe asked. "There has to be a quarterback, right?"

Aiden nodded. "That's Ollie. Oliver. He's the visionary. The one who sees the whole field, who is up for whatever it takes to make the biggest play. He looks at every play as a chance to make a touchdown. He's also the one who will generally follow the game plan—my plan—but you never know when he's suddenly going to tuck it and run himself or throw a Hail Mary pass. He's smart and cocky, and you wish like hell you could bench him for his stunts, but without him, the whole thing falls apart."

She smiled. Aiden wasn't looking at her now. He was studying the cookies in front of her. Though she didn't think he really saw them. He was thinking of his friends. Affectionately, clearly. But also with some exasperation.

"Sounds like a great team."

"When we're on the same page, we're amazing," Aiden said without any conceit. It seemed he was just stating a fact. "But we have our disagreements, of course. And..." He was thinking hard about something.

"And what?"

"I don't know that we've ever *really* been challenged." He looked up at her. "We're talented, and we balance each other out, but the truth is, we're all also pretty charmed."

She nodded. "You always have been."

He didn't disagree. "We still have a lot to learn about running a business and being bosses. At least, being good bosses. Our company started out with just the five of us. We didn't need childcare, and healthcare for young, single guys is different than for other employees. When I had to get my appendix out, our plan didn't cover much of it, but I could afford the huge deductible and co-pay."

"Wait a second," Zoe interrupted with a frown. "You had your appendix out?"

"Yeah. Three years ago. Almost burst. The guys actually rushed me to the hospital from a basketball game."

"You were playing *basketball* while you had appendicitis?" Zoe asked. She hadn't known any of that and that bothered her. A lot. "That was stupid."

"I didn't *know* it was my appendix," he protested.

"Did your stomach hurt? Did you feel like crap?"

"Yes. But..."

She lifted her brows. "But what?"

"We were in the finals in the tournament."

She rolled her eyes. "Do you have a life insurance policy that would have covered you if you would have *died*?"

"Yes."

She stopped and met his eyes. She let out a breath. Of course he had a life insurance policy. He knew better than most that sometimes you needed that long before you planned on it. "Sorry."

"Don't be," he said. "It's fine. Yes, I have a life insurance policy. Also a will and lots of paperwork covering what happens with the business if one of us dies or quits."

It was a big-time business. A true corporation. They needed that kind of paperwork. Zoe... didn't. The bakery would probably go back to her mom, who might run it for a while and keep Josie employed. Maybe they'd sell to Josie eventually. Though she had no idea if her friend had that kind of money, and it would be very weird for the Buttered Up to *not* belong to a McCaffery.

But if Zoe keeled over from a ruptured appendix, that whole thing would be up in the air.

Damn. She'd never really thought of that.

"If you're just going to stand there, distracting me, you could at least come back here and help me frost cookies," she finally said.

He straightened, and his hands went to his tie.

She watched, almost mesmerized, as he unknotted it, pulled it loose from his collar, then tossed it to the table he'd been using.

That was hardly real *undressing*. He'd been a hell of a lot more naked in the kitchen at home that morning. But there was something about how he took that stupid tie off that made her stomach feel warm and twisty.

Wow, she really did need to get laid. It was *stupid* to get worked up about Aiden taking his tie off.

He came around the counter and stopped next to her at the worktable.

"You really want me to help with this?" he asked, looking over the cookies she'd already done.

He smelled so good. She took a deep breath then said, "Sure, why not?"

"Because I haven't frosted cookies in years."

She smiled. "It's like riding a bike. And I'll let you do the easy stuff."

This was all pretty easy. Josie did the *hard* stuff. Zoe was amazed by her friend's talents and knew she and Buttered Up were totally screwed if Josie ever left her. Zoe could do round cakes and square cakes. Period. She'd once tried an octagon for a stop sign cake. She'd ended up cutting the corners off to make it a round cake and had drawn a stop sign in the middle of it.

The largest area of the cookies were covered in blue icing, and then she added embellishments with other colors over the blue. Aiden could swipe blue icing on, surely. She showed him what she wanted him to do with one then picked up a tube of pink frosting.

She started adding pink piping around a few of the petals as she cleared her throat. "I have to admit I was surprised to hear you talking about childcare and having Dax go meet with people. I've always pictured you guys sitting around in beanbag chairs, playing games, and talking about your new t-shirt design as your biggest item of business."

"Well, we talk about the new diamond colors and monsters too. The princesses have to cut the heads off of *something*," Aiden said as he spread blue frosting over the cookies. He did so carefully, swiping the edges to make them even and smooth. Just the way Maggie had taught them all when they'd been helping in the kitchen as kids.

"Right," Zoe said. She watched him, a little distracted. "And childcare."

"That's actually a new thing," he said. "I hadn't thought of that until Jane said it last night."

He was clearly concentrating on the cookies, but he kept talking. This felt very natural. They'd helped with cookies and cupcakes and other things over the years, but Zoe didn't remember a time it had ever been just her and Aiden. This was nice.

It also occurred to her he'd always taken this seriously. He didn't take seriously her dislike of the Lancasters or the idea of Hot Cakes being a true competitor for Buttered Up, but he did take the bakery and their business and what they did seriously —even down to making sure the blue icing on the cookies was smooth and even. She appreciated that.

He didn't have to. A lot of men in his position probably wouldn't. He was a millionaire, running an internationally known, highly successful business. That was all still very hard for her to remember. Which she supposed was a good thing. He didn't act like a guy with a lot of money. He didn't try to buy his way into or out of things. He didn't flaunt it, or take things for granted, or act like he was better than anyone else. He was the same guy she'd always known. More confident. More commanding. More experienced and smarter. But still the same guy deep down.

That was... important. It hit her squarely. The idea that Aiden was truly the same person, after all this time and after everything that had happened to him, really mattered. She was, after all, the woman who really liked things that stayed the same.

She took a deep breath and tried to focus on pink piping. It was difficult. Because suddenly she was distracted by how small the cookies were in his big hands, how delicate they were but how careful he was being, and how cute he was when he was earnest about a task. His brow was furrowed with concentration as he turned the cookie this way and that, making sure the

icing was perfect. He wanted to get it right, and that made her...
want to cover his naked body in blue icing.

She swallowed. "Really?" she finally said in response to his
comment about daycare for his employees. "I think that's great
you took that all so seriously," she said sincerely. "I mean, I've
never given that stuff a lot of thought either. Jane talks about
work at Hot Cakes some, but she doesn't need childcare, and
the most we've talked about benefits is when she tells me I can
no way match what she gets there so, no, she won't work for
me." Zoe bent over a cookie, swiping a thin pink swirl on the tip
of each petal of the flower. "I've only got the one employee, and
I just..." She shouldn't say the rest of that sentence.

She knew a lot of people—okay, her brother and Aiden and
Jane and Josie—thought she was a little stuck. They understood and supported her in wanting to keep her family's legacy
alive and to keep Buttered Up the Appleby staple it had always
been. But they also thought her *strict* adherence to keeping
everything the same always was a little crazy. But it wasn't *their*
shoulders where the family legacy rested. If she did something
new and it didn't work, it wasn't just an embarrassment to her.
It was the whole Buttered Up reputation at stake.

Why would she not stick to the recipes and routines that
had been *proven* to work? She really had it pretty easy here. She
literally had the recipe to success. More than one recipe, even.

Aiden stopped his knife and looked at her. "You just?" he
prompted.

"I just keep doing what's always been done," she said,
staring at the cookie. "I just keep doing what works."

"But needs change over time no matter what stays the same
inside this bakery—the paint colors and the recipes and the
menu—the *people* change. Your customers change. And your
employee will change." He paused then apparently decided to
go on. "I know Buttered Up has been run by a McCaffery
woman and her best friend from the very start. But... if you

think about it... Didi changed. Or something changed. That's what started the whole feud between Letty and Didi."

"Didi got greedy," Zoe said with a frown. That was always the way Letty had told it. Didi saw a way to make more money, and instead of adhering to quality and tradition, she'd sold out.

"Or she was willing to take a chance Letty wasn't," Aiden said.

"She gambled her lifelong friendship on that," Zoe said. "And lost it. She has snack cakes—had," she corrected. "She *had* snack cakes. But now look at her. That business is being sold off to someone else. The Lancasters will no longer have it, while Letty's bakery is still going strong. Just as it *always has*."

Aiden turned toward her and leaned a hip into the worktable. He waited until she looked up at him. Why? So he could see her eyes? Read her expression?

"Didi has made more money in one year with Hot Cakes than Buttered Up has *ever* made," he said.

He didn't say it cruelly. He said it matter-of-factly. Then seemed to watch her closely.

Zoe straightened too and faced him. "Yes, I know. But Letty had something Didi doesn't. Something worth even more."

"What's that?"

"Her integrity."

Aiden nodded slowly.

"And loyalty," Zoe went on. "Sure, Didi has people on her side, but Letty has *true* customers. People who come back over and over, for every occasion that matters to them, to *this* bakery. People send people they love our cakes and cookies and pies. People want our products to be a part of special days like weddings and birthdays. When people come in here they know exactly what they're going to get. With Hot Cakes... people stuff those in their lunch boxes and glove compartments—" She gave him a little frown. "No one sends those to their moms for Mother's Day or with engagement rings baked inside or with

It's a Girl frosted on top. *We* have people's hearts. They just have their wallets."

Zoe felt her heart racing. Dammit. Why did he set her off? He knew all those things and how she felt about them. Why was he pushing these buttons?

"Remember what I said about defending Hot Cakes and getting into my pants?" she asked him crossly.

"I do," he said. He leaned in slightly. "So panties don't count as pants? Because I remember, distinctly, getting into your panties this morning."

11

---

*Z*oe felt as if she'd just opened the industrial oven and had been hit by a wave of hot air. She swallowed. "I'm glad you remember it *distinctly*," she said somehow. "Because if you keep talking about how great Hot Cakes is, you're not going to have anything *but* a memory."

The corner of his mouth curled. "Well, you're right," he finally said. "No one would compare Hot Cakes to Buttered Up."

She narrowed her eyes. That wasn't exactly admitting Buttered Up was *better*.

"And I might only have one employee," Zoe went on. "But she knows I want to take care of her. She knows I'll cut into our profits to make sure she has what she needs. She knows I'll work extra if she needs time off. I really doubt the Lancasters have taken a cut in their own pay to increase the amounts in their employees' checks or ever rolled up their sleeves and done any of the work themselves. I'd be shocked if Whitney can even turn one of their machines on."

That actually got a frown from Aiden, but he looked more thoughtful than anything. "You're probably right." He straightened again. "But it's easier to take care of one person than three hundred-some."

Zoe shrugged. "Not if you have three hundred times the money and resources."

Aiden didn't say anything to that.

Zoe turned back to the cookies, feeling less defensive as he continued to seemingly think about what she'd said. "Your dad's job was pretty stable, right?" she asked. "Healthcare and vacation time and all that?"

Aiden also faced the worktable again and picked up another cookie. "Yeah. Very. And his seniority with the company mattered to them too. Even when he started drinking hard, they gave him a lot of chances. He had an assistant and coworkers who covered for him and a boss who was sympathetic."

Zoe swallowed hard. She remembered when Aiden's mom had died. She'd been devastated. She had only been ten and hadn't really realized moms *could* die. Not that young anyway. She remembered seeing Aiden torn up, sad, angry. She also remembered her own mother being almost manic—cooking, baking, cleaning, *doing* things because if she sat still she'd have to think about losing Julie. It had been an awful time all around.

Zoe also remembered the change in Aiden's dad. Dan had always been a wonderful guy. Happy, friendly, outgoing. He'd coached the boys in baseball from peewees until they started playing on the official school team. He'd been the one to allow a trampoline in the backyard and had assured Zoe and Josie that, no matter what the boys said, they were welcome to jump on it anytime they wanted. He'd been the one to pick Zoe up and carry her home after she'd fallen out of his tree and fractured a rib.

Then Julie died, and Dan had changed overnight. He'd been sad. All the time. Quiet. He didn't go out, didn't want to socialize. And he'd started drinking. Zoe hadn't really known what that meant, but he'd started snapping at the kids when they were around, so obviously, they'd stopped going over there.

She remembered one day Maggie had asked her to take some leftovers to him. Zoe hadn't wanted to go. Dan might bark at her. Or he might not even answer the door. She didn't know how to act around him. He was a different person than the man she'd known. But Maggie had seemed so tired when she'd said, "Just do it, please," so Zoe had trudged across the yards.

She'd found Dan crying at the kitchen table. She'd seen her mom cry. There had been tears on her dad's cheeks at Julie's funeral. But she'd never seen an adult man sob. Dan had been sobbing as if... well, as if his heart was broken.

"There's a lot more to people's lives than work," she said, running her finger through a smudge of frosting on the worktable.

Aiden gave a soft chuckle. "How would *you* know?"

She looked up. "I don't work *all* the time." But she did. She worked all the time. Her work was her life. "Yeah, okay. But when you're the boss, it's different."

He nodded. "It really is."

She studied him. "You work a lot?"

"All the time."

"Really?"

He nodded again. "I make myself go to the gym and take time off. I make the other guys take time off too." He paused and smiled. "Okay, Dax makes us take time off. But I back him up. He's the one who reminds us when we've been at it for too long, and I always agree."

She smiled. "Dax needs a break more often?"

"He believes in a healthy balance between work and play," Aiden said. "He's got articles and everything. He's gone to conferences."

"In warm, sunny places?" she guessed with a grin.

"Of course," Aiden said with an answering grin. "Then again, a lot of our work feels like play. Kind of like making cupcakes and cookies for a living. But it's important—according to Dax—to not forget that just because you enjoy what you do, it's still work, and you need more in your life."

"You believe him?"

"I do. I haven't been very good about it," Aiden admitted. "I kept telling myself, in one more year I'll take more time off. Or after one more project I'll relax a little. Or that I would just know when it was time." He met her gaze for a long moment. "I think that last one was the one that finally came true."

Zoe felt her heart flutter. Actually flutter. This guy was the same guy she'd always known. The one who she'd thought could never surprise her, never be exciting, never be the kind of thrilling she wanted from her love life, and yet he was making her heart flutter. On a regular basis.

He was definitely surprising her.

"What?" he asked after she'd stared at him for a few long seconds.

"I'm just looking at you and seeing an adult businessman with responsibilities and people who depend on you and that you're actually taking that seriously and... it's just weird."

It was hot was what it was. And kind of awesome. Okay, really awesome. She liked this side of him. It was a little discombobulating, maybe, but no more so than having him kiss her in front of the entire morning rush. Or finger her to orgasm before her second cup of coffee.

No, seeing him in businessman mode was *more* discombobulating than that. Because she'd imagined the other stuff before. Vividly. She hadn't really thought of him as an employer and an in-charge corporate guy. At least not a kick-ass, in-charge corporate guy with a heart.

At times, she'd pictured him and her brother with their

money from their online game buying stupid things like too-expensive cars and high-tech refrigerators that told them the day's weather and stock market news, kept track of their grocery list, made perfectly round ice, and practically brushed their teeth for them. In other words, stupid shit no one actually needed.

But it turned out Aiden was taking his position as a boss seriously and was looking at ways to make things better for his employees.

That was, strangely, sexy.

He took that in and then gave her a low smile. His eyes dropped to the front of her apron. Her breasts, kind of, but then he said, "Well, don't get too freaked out. I still like to play with food."

She frowned and looked down. Her apron was streaked with frosting. Her body got a little warm and she looked up. "Whew, that was a close one."

He reached out and ran his finger over the frosting that was smeared over the top of her left breast. It was about two inches from her nipple, but the tip hardened, begging for him to give it some attention too. Then he lifted the frosting to his mouth, sucking it from his fingertip.

Oh yeah, her nipple definitely wanted some of that action.

She had to get these cookies done. And she and Aiden were in the front of the bakery. The area with the *big* windows. And Josie was in back. And... those were the only excuses she could come up with for not stripping her clothes off right then and there. They were big ones, sure, but she was already thinking about how the front door was locked and how if they were on the floor behind the counter no one would be able to see them and how Josie could definitely have the rest of the day off.

"We need to frost the rest of the cookies," she said. Maybe Aiden could help her out with some willpower here. "Mrs. Murphy will be here in about two hours."

"We do," Aiden said. With a smirk. He knew what she'd been thinking.

What else would they have been doing other than frosting cookies? No one had suggested anyone take any clothes off. At least not out loud. But he knew what she'd been thinking.

So she gave him a wink, took in his surprised reaction, and then bent over the cookies again. They frosted, side by side, in companionable silence for a few minutes. But her mind was spinning.

Finally, Zoe said, "You know, we're actually a lot alike with our businesses."

"Yeah?" he asked, nearly done with his cookies. He smoothed the edge of a final blue flower and set it with the others for her to decorate.

"Yeah, we both came into our jobs really easily. I took over my family's bakery—where I've been working all my life—and you and Cam and the guys kind of accidentally made something that became popular."

He gave a little chuckle, but he didn't dispute that. He reached for one of the blue flowers he'd finished icing and picked up a tube of yellow buttercream with a star tip.

"And we were both young when we started in our businesses," she continued. "And it seems we're having to grow up and get more responsible and serious at the same time."

"You're right," he said. He looked over at her. "I guess we've got something in common there. That's pretty cool."

"It is." She smiled. "Maybe we could... talk more about it. I'd like to hear more about what you figure out with your employees. And maybe you could look at our books, and we could talk about some ways to make something work for benefits for Josie."

He looked genuinely surprised and straightened slightly. "Really? You'd want my input?"

She shrugged. "I don't know if I can afford anything at all, honestly. And I'm nowhere near the scale you guys are. But I wouldn't mind having someone else looking at it with me. Mom never dealt with this stuff. Dad doesn't look at this stuff from an employer standpoint. It would feel weird to let any other business person I know look at all my books. I definitely want to ask Josie what kind of stuff she would need, but I don't know about really diving into all the numbers with her." Zoe frowned. "I'm really the only one who deals with *all* of it now."

But she could trust Aiden with it. The bakery didn't bring in millions of dollars, and there were good and bad months, but it didn't bother her to think about letting Aiden see that. Hell, he might have some advice. He'd said Grant was their money guy, but she was certain Aiden knew plenty about the financials of their company.

Aiden seemed to think that over, then he nodded. "I'd be very happy to help you with that. Of course. Whatever you need."

There was a huskiness in his voice almost as if her asking meant a lot to him. She felt another little flutter like before, but this one she felt in her stomach. It felt like a combination of anticipation and happiness because she'd have some help but also like pleasure because she'd made *him* happy by asking.

She smiled. "Thanks."

This felt really good and natural, actually. Talking to Aiden about the bakery would be completely comfortable. He was a businessman, but more, he knew this bakery and he loved it. He had a personal interest in it. He always had. When his mother had worked here and because he considered Letty a second grandmother and Maggie a second mother. But now, looking into his eyes, standing here frosting cookies, talking business, teasing about frosting, Zoe definitely got the feeling there was even more personal here. That he cared because of *her*. Not because he considered her a friend or a little sister.

It felt like more than that.

His gaze dropped to her mouth, and the warm flutter of pleasure quickly turned to a hot jolt of lust. She felt her lips part and her heart trip. She really wanted him to kiss her. *Really* wanted that.

"We need to frost the rest of the cookies," he said. "Mrs. Murphy will be here in about two hours."

His attention was still on her lips.

"We do," she agreed. It was true, of course. But clearly, he was thinking about other things. And knew she was too. Again.

He leaned in and she held her breath. He brushed his lips over hers then said gruffly, "But we need to be a little stingy with the pink frosting, okay?"

"Why's that?" she asked, breathlessly against his lips.

"Because I want nothing more than to put you up on that worktable in back and suck pink frosting off your nipples."

She couldn't help the little moan that escaped. "That back worktable? Not this one?"

"Gotta admit the idea of all the men in Appleby seeing that, and knowing you are now *mine*, is pretty fucking tempting."

Zoe sucked in a quick breath. She'd *never* considered herself an exhibitionist, but she definitely liked having her baked goods on display and having people exclaiming over them. Maybe this would be the same. She giggled.

He pulled back a little to look down at her, smiling. "That's funny?"

"I was just thinking about how much work I put into all the things I put pink frosting on and how much I like having people look at them."

He laughed. "Forget it. You and your nipples and all the parts of you I can cover in frosting are all for me."

Again, his possessiveness, even when it was playful, surprised her. As did how hot it made her.

Yes, Aiden Anderson was surprising her in many ways. Much to her surprise.

ERIN NICHOLAS

"Frost those cookies," she said. "I suddenly want to close early." She looked up at him from under her eyelashes. "And I *never* close early."

"Well, your workaholic heart can relax a little," he said, lifting a hand and running his thumb over her bottom lip. "It's not like you're going to be *leaving* the bakery early."

She blew out a little breath. "I guess that's true."

He leaned back, giving her a little room. "But definitely ease up on the pink."

"It has to be the pink we save?" she asked, amused by that.

"For some reason, yeah," he said.

"You don't know why?" She did.

"It's my favorite color, and I've always associated it with this bakery and all the sweet stuff inside."

So he did know.

He leaned in again. "And nothing's sweeter inside this place than you."

This time it was Zoe that stretched up on tiptoe and met his lips with hers in a quick, sweet kiss.

"You *are* kissing?"

They jerked apart at the sound of Maggie's voice. They both swung to face the kitchen door where Zoe's mother stood, staring at them.

"You're just standing around in the front of the bakery, during business hours, when anyone could walk in, *kissing*?"

They hadn't heard her come in because she'd come in the back. Of course she had. She'd been coming in the bakery through the back door all her life.

Zoe felt her cheeks heat. "Mom!"

"Zoe," Maggie said. She looked at Aiden. "Aiden."

"You already heard about that, huh?" Aiden asked.

Zoe looked up at him. He looked... amused.

"Of course I already heard about it!" Maggie exclaimed. "My daughter and the boy who's practically my *son*, *kissing*, in my *bakery*, in front of the entire town?" There might have been a question mark at the end of that sentence, but she wasn't asking a question. She was making an accusation.

"Mom," Zoe started. But she really didn't know what to say.

"It seemed like the fastest and easiest way to spread the news," Aiden told her. Calmly.

He wasn't embarrassed. Or worried. Or apologetic. At all.

Zoe looked at her mom again.

"Well, it was that," Maggie said, her tone a little calmer. She crossed her arms. "So you *are* together?"

Suddenly Zoe realized she needed to be the one to answer that. She met her mother's eyes directly. "Yes. We are."

She felt Aiden's hand slide across her lower back to her hip. He drew her closer to him and squeezed her hip. He was pleased. That was good. She liked that. He'd been staking his claim on her, and she could have been annoyed and angry and offended. Instead, she was glad because she wouldn't have gotten there on her own probably. But now, she could give him some of that back.

"How long has this been going on?" Maggie asked. "How long since things changed?"

"Christmas," Zoe answered honestly. Things hadn't gone according to her plan on Christmas Eve, but that was definitely when things had changed. Or started to. Actually, things had *really* changed when Aiden had come back to Appleby and started surprising her. But Christmas Eve had started things in motion.

Maggie looked from one of them to the other. "And now what?"

"Now we're together," Aiden said. "I'm back in Appleby to make this work."

Maggie looked at Zoe. All Zoe could do was nod. That's what he'd told her too. Honestly, at this point, if he said he was leaving, she'd be... brokenhearted. Not angry and hurt and embarrassed like at Christmas, but actually heartbroken. Which meant in the span of a few hours, Aiden had made her at least start falling for him.

Of course, having a lifetime together already made that easier. Knowing him, him being a part of her life already, made it so they could skip ahead several spaces on this particular game board. But now that she'd opened up to this whole idea, her feelings had started to change quickly.

Maggie just watched them both for a long moment. Then she nodded. "Wonderful. I love you both very much."

Stunned, Zoe nodded. "I love you too."

"Love you too, Maggie," Aiden said.

"Now, can you keep your hands off each other long enough to get your work done, or do you need some help?" Maggie asked, eyeing the cookies behind them.

"Well, since you offered, I can think of a few other things I'd rather be doing, as a matter of fact," Aiden said.

Maggie actually laughed at that.

Zoe elbowed him. "We're fine, Mom. Of course we'll get these done. And Aiden has actually been doing his own work." She nodded in the direction of his computer.

"All right," Maggie said. "Then I'll leave you alone. But," she said as she paused in the open door to the kitchen, "no more big news delivered via grapevine. I fed you chicken fettuccini, and you didn't tell me you were in love with my daughter," she said, pointing a finger at Aiden. "That means when you propose, I'd better be the second person to know after Zoe, or you're going to be cut off from pasta at my house."

Zoe felt a jolt go through her at hearing her mother say Aiden was in love with her then another at the mention of him proposing. Whoa. That was... not as crazy as it should be.

"But you can't cut me off indefinitely," Aiden said. "Wedding planning goes especially well with spaghetti and meatballs, and I'm sure your grandkids will *love* your lasagna."

Zoe saw her mother's face first register shock and then soften into a mix of emotions. Her eyes actually filled with tears. "Grandkids," she said softly. Then she shook her head. "I never could stay mad at you anyway," she told Aiden. "But that's a pretty potent argument."

He grinned. "I was always your favorite. Imagine once I'm the father of your grandchildren."

Zoe's breath caught in her chest. She honestly couldn't have responded to that if she wanted to. She had no air. But damn, *grandkids*? *Her* kids. With Aiden. Wow.

Maggie swiped at her eyes. "You're so much trouble," she told him, but her loving smile told them how she really felt. She looked at Zoe. "I'm so happy for you both."

Yeah, Zoe was feeling pretty... happy. Or something. Dang. This was going so damned fast. But it felt so good. Right.

Maggie headed back out through the kitchen, and Zoe watched the door swing back and forth behind her three times before it stopped.

Then she looked up at Aiden.

He was watching her. Probably waiting for her reaction. Him walking back into the bakery yesterday had gotten a reaction. Him declaring they were going to be together had gotten a reaction. Him kissing her in the bakery in front of everyone had gotten a reaction. This...

"We definitely need to save lots of pink frosting," she said.

"Yeah?" He lifted a brow.

"I think *you* might look good with some pink in some sweet spots too."

His eyes heated. "Let's get to work."

He let her go just like that and turned to the worktable.

She watched as he started decorating the cookie. Her heart was pounding from, just, everything. He was suddenly here, back in her life, and when she thought *in* her life, she realized *really, really in.* Her head kept telling her it should feel crazy, but it didn't.

That was the crazy part.

Her eyes widened as she watched him place perfect frosting embellishments on the petals, then switch tubes to apply green piping down the stem and leaves the way she'd been doing.

He stepped back, and she glanced up to find him looking at it with satisfaction.

"Wow," she said simply.

Aiden grinned, his eyes meeting hers. "That's exactly what I was thinking."

She knew he wasn't talking about the cookies. She knew he knew *she* wasn't talking about the cookies.

And her heart fluttered again. Much harder and for much longer this time.

12

Dax Marshall drove a 1960 MGA roadster in Old English White with black leather interior and classic silver wire wheels. He also wore a dark gray felt fedora when he did it. But not just any dark gray felt fedora. This was the dark gray felt fedora that Frank Sinatra had worn in his last starring movie role as Edward Delaney in *The First Deadly Sin*. As he would explain. Ad nauseam.

He'd bought the hat at an auction with a winning bid of over five thousand dollars. Dax considered that a bargain. Wearing a hat that had once graced the head of one of his personal idols—fifth on the list behind Fred Rogers, Robin Williams, Tom Hanks, and Derek Jeter, in that order—was a true privilege worth any price. That he looked "fucking dashing as hell"—his words, *not* Aiden's—was simply a bonus.

Aiden was less enamored with the hat, but he had to admit the car was awesome. Classy, distinctive, extremely cool, the car turned heads.

Especially in a small town in Iowa that mostly saw pickups and SUVs. Practical vehicles. Vehicles that were used for work and hauling things and getting people from one place to another. Did the guys in Appleby pick out their favorite colors for their F-150s? Sure, sometimes. If their favorite color was black, white, silver, red, or blue. Did they take a little time over things like adding satellite radio and lining the truck bed and matching floor mats? Maybe. But that was as flashy as things got.

No one drove around in classic convertibles that seated two and had only enough trunk space to hold a spare tire and nothing else.

It wasn't practical. Iowans, especially those in Appleby, were nothing if not practical.

So when a white 1960 MGA roadster rolled past the Buttered Up bakery driven by a young guy in a dark gray felt fedora like Frank Sinatra would have worn, Aiden groaned.

Dax honestly didn't know the meaning of inconspicuous.

Dax believed in fun, living in the moment, and making the best of everything. In fact, he believed in making everything better. It was one of his best traits and the main thing that had drawn Aiden and Dax together initially. Aiden believed in doing big things, leaving the world better than he'd found it, making his life count. They'd seen that all very similarly, and Aiden still appreciated that about his friend.

Except, of course, when Aiden wanted to keep a low profile in his hometown regarding Hot Cakes.

A young guy cruising into town in a shiny, classic convertible with a fedora was going to stand out among the pickups and seed company caps, and people were going to want to know who he was and what he was doing here.

Which was fine. As long as Dax didn't mention Aiden. Yet, anyway.

Aiden kept from lunging out of his chair, barely, but he stood and frowned at his phone as if he'd just gotten an important text. Which he should have. One from Dax saying he was on his way and he'd meet Aiden at the hotel. In the next town.

Where Aiden had specifically asked Piper to make reservations for both Dax and Ollie.

"Hey, I need to head over to Dubuque for a meeting," he said to Zoe.

She was the behind the main counter now, decorating cupcakes. They'd finished the cookies, and Mrs. Murphy had been thrilled with how they'd turned out. Josie was in back manning the ovens and sculpting a cake into a kangaroo. He hadn't asked why. And Zoe was doing the basic cupcakes frosting and watching the front.

"Oh? Really? Why?" she asked, looking up.

He'd been settled at the table by the window on his computer working since finishing the cookies. Away from the smell of Zoe. And out of touching distance. Because neither of them had been getting much done—at least not very efficiently —when they were within touching distance.

But she'd told her mom they were together. *That* was productive.

Every time he thought of that, he felt like someone had sucked the oxygen out of his lungs. And he wanted to put Zoe up on that worktable and do all the naughty frosting things they'd teased about. He also wanted to add in sprinkles. He'd always loved sprinkles.

He also wanted to beat his chest like a caveman and take out a billboard down by the highway and maybe just stand in the town square with a bullhorn.

He wanted to buy a diamond ring.

Hearing her claim him, to her mother, and seeing Maggie's face when she registered that, had caused an avalanche of emotions to crash through him he'd been unprepared for. He'd had five months to think about Zoe and how he felt about her and what he wanted from her. He'd had five months to mentally restructure his life around everything and to imagine what it would be like to be back in Appleby with Maggie and

Steve and everyone. But he hadn't given any thought to how it would feel to be on the receiving end of their words and emotions.

Or maybe he'd thought he knew what it would be like.

Zoe had come to him for sex. That had felt pretty damned good. After the shock, of course. But she'd wanted him. He'd thought *a lot* about how that had felt.

Maggie loved him. Steve loved him. Henry loved him. He'd figured there would just be, well, more of that.

He hadn't been prepared, at all, for how it would feel to see Maggie's absolute *delight* at the idea of him and Zoe together. To see her eyes well up with tears. To see her nearly overcome with the idea of grandkids.

Hell, *he* hadn't even thought of kids.

But now he wanted that. Them. Lots of them.

He also hadn't been able to truly imagine how it would be starting his morning in the kitchen with Zoe. Because he *couldn't* have imagined that. His attraction to her was real enough, but he couldn't have been prepared for how touching her, kissing her, hearing her, and tasting her would seep into him and become an addiction the very first time.

Even more, he would have never been able to prepare for the way it would feel to have her looking at him with admiration. Or how it would feel to have something like their businesses in common. Or how natural it would feel to hear her sharing things about her business, and asking about his, and talking about real things like employees and how they both wanted to be good to the people who depended on them. Sharing something like that with her, something that was new to him and that already meant a lot to him, something that was already giving him a little anxiety, truth be told, had felt... good. Different. New for them. He and Zoe hadn't talked about things like that before, but it had been effortless to slip into that conversation.

Now he wanted to talk to her about Hot Cakes. He wanted to tell her he was nervous about introducing new owners to a company that had belonged to the same family for over fifty years. He wanted to tell her how he wanted to find out what the employees needed and how he wanted to actually blow their minds with all the amazing things working for Hot Cakes would mean for them. He wanted her to look at him with admiration for his plans and goals and know they were about Hot Cakes.

But he was scared.

Of losing her.

More now than he had been before. Before he knew how much he really wanted her. Before he'd realized that, as much as he'd wanted to be with her, he hadn't fully realized all their relationship could truly be. Laughing and teasing in the morning, flirting fun even when she was annoyed with him, him helping in the bakery, sharing their thoughts and feelings and plans about their work.

"Yeah. I've got a meeting with a guy about a new business venture in the area," he told her. That was completely true.

She smiled. "You do?"

"Yeah." He crossed to the counter.

"You really are planning to stay," she said. "I mean, I know you said that. A few times. And I know you have plenty of money. You don't have to work. But that just..." She sighed. But it sounded happy. Not like the exasperated ones she so often gave him. "That just makes it feel really real."

He braced his hands on the counter between them and pinned her with a look. "It *is* really real, Zoe."

"I'm starting to get that."

Thank God.

He'd only been in town for two days. Really just short of twenty-four hours if they were being very technical. But there was no reason for them to tiptoe around here or take their time or be subtle. He was back in town. To stay. Because of her.

"Good. Because I'm way past *starting to*, and I'm pretty sure your mom is all in." He gave her a grin.

She rolled her eyes. "She snuck up on me. I wasn't prepared."

"So the truth came out because you didn't have time to cover."

Zoe just looked at him for a long moment. Then she nodded. "Yeah."

Everything in him went hot and hard. But she was still working, and he needed to make sure Dax went to the hotel and they had a full plan for how to approach the Hot Cakes employees. And that he got a rental car. "I'll be back around closing time." His voice was a little gruff.

Her smile grew. "You'll notice I'm not using any pink frosting on these."

He had noticed. "Good girl."

She bit her bottom lip. Right where he wanted to bite. And suck. He gave a little groan. "Lose the good girl thing by the time I get back," he told her.

Her eyes widened.

He chuckled. "What?"

"I might regret admitting this, but... you've definitely been surprising me. The dirty talk in particular."

He fucking liked that a lot.

"I'll keep that in mind."

"Please do."

Again, he had to resist rounding the counter and saying to hell with his meeting with Dax. And the big windows at the front of the bakery.

Yeah, Zoe McCaffery had a few surprises as well.

She liked dirty talk? They were a better match every time they spent time together.

At least, until they got to talking about Hot Cakes.

With that not-so-pleasant thought in mind, he gathered up his stuff and headed for the Hilton in Dubuque. He put a video call in to Piper on the way.

"You need to get him a different car," he told their assistant.

"He's picking it up in about thirty minutes," Piper said.

She was wearing her glasses, clearly still at work. She was only twenty-three, but she ran the office, and the guys' lives—especially Ollie's—like she was much older and wiser than any of them. Because she was. Wiser, anyway. More mature. More practical. More capable. The woman was like Mary Poppins, Martha Stewart, and Super Nanny all rolled into one. She knew everything, was always two steps ahead of the guys, took care of things efficiently and effectively. Interestingly, she ran the office and their schedules like a drill sergeant, but she did it while dressed in what she called "pinup-girl dresses" that were always in bright colors and patterns and emphasized her curves.

She looked twenty-three though. She had long, dark hair, streaked with blond and red highlights that hung nearly to her ass when she didn't have it up in a curly, tight ponytail or bun—which was 90 percent of the time. She had huge brown eyes, made even larger behind the large-framed colored glasses—coordinated with her outfits, of course—she wore in the office. She was short so she wore heels. Or maybe she just wore them because she liked them. She dressed smart and professionally but also gave off a fun, confident vibe. Everyone loved her, and Fluke, and Oliver Caprinelli specifically, would fall apart without her.

"Really?"

"Of course, he can't be driving that roadster around," she said. "I told him he could drive it to Iowa, to the hotel and around Dubuque, but *not* in Appleby."

Aiden really liked Piper. "Well, he just drove it down Main Street."

She sighed. "Was he wearing the fedora?"

Aiden chuckled. "Of course."

"He better not have stopped," she muttered. "We had a long talk about how it might not go over so well if five rich, hot, young guys come strolling into town, taking over the factory that's been there for so long and employs so many people, thinking they're all that and doing everyone a favor."

Aiden nodded even though he had to admit that he'd been feeling a little bit like he might have been doing Appleby a favor. He didn't like admitting that. Especially now after hearing Jane say that things at the factory weren't quite hunky dory. Now he wanted to fix it all. And he had no idea how to do that.

"Great, thank you," Aiden told Piper. "Text me the hotel address?"

"Sure." She paused, then Aiden heard his text notification ding. "Done."

He grinned. "When will Ollie be here?"

"Tomorrow. He had to finish some things up for Grant before he could leave," she said.

"I've got an in-office suspension until I get it done."

Aiden heard Ollie's voice but he was outside of the frame. Piper looked over to her right.

"Yes, you are. You're staying right there until you're finished. And no more meatballs until then."

"He's sitting by you so you can make sure he's working?" Aiden asked. This wouldn't be the first time.

"Yes. He's on the couch with his laptop."

They had a couch in the reception area outside of their main offices. Piper manned that desk. She was so much more than a receptionist, but all the other women they'd hired for the job had been too easily charmed by both Dax and Ollie.

The guys' schedules and to-do lists had gone out the window with just a grin and a wink. There were also a number of girls who delivered from nearby restaurants, the printing place they worked with, and a couple of PR firms they outsourced to that would come by to talk to Dax, Ollie, and even Cam at times. When the other, equally charm-susceptible receptionists were at the desk, they let those girls past or called the guys to the front, and suddenly the guys were missing phone calls and meetings and not getting shit done.

None of that was a problem when Piper sat there. She'd taken that desk back about a year ago, and things had been smooth sailing ever since. Though Cam grumbled about not getting free extra egg rolls, and Dax made excuses to stroll down to the print shop himself on a regular basis, now.

"She made sweet-and-sour meatballs, Aiden," Ollie called. "She gave me one and then told me the rest had to wait until I'm done. They're sitting on the edge of her desk mocking me."

Piper was a hell of a cook, and her meatballs were Ollie's favorite.

"It's Aiden's fault." She looked back at Aiden. "You got him all riled up about getting to Appleby to save the day. He's got two conference calls and a packed inbox he needs to deal with before he can leave and get all wrapped up in this new project. You know he'll totally lose track of everything else once he's there."

"Well, I do need him," Aiden said. "We need a plan for this new company. We have a lot of files to go over, and we need to research benefits and—"

"I already went through the files you sent to Ollie and Dax," Piper said. "I highlighted the things you should review first. I also sent you a few articles I think you'll find interesting. And I set up a call for the three of you tomorrow afternoon with a Duncan Prestor. He's going to talk you through some employee benefit plans and help you with an intake survey to help you get a better idea about what you'll need."

Aiden blinked. Piper was a force of nature.

"I don't think we can do an intake survey yet. We need to talk to the employees."

Piper was already clicking on her keyboard. "I'll let him know that. Do you still want to do the initial call with him to go over some plan options?"

"That... might be a good idea?" Aiden was aware that sounded like a question.

"I agree," Piper told him.

Okay, then it was a good idea.

"I'll let him know you're going to wait on the employee survey." She stopped and focused on Aiden. "Do you want me to write up a more general survey? Maybe ask them about general satisfaction? Changes they might like to see?"

"That would be..."

"I think it could be a good place to start. Especially paired with the information I sent you about current benefits."

"Then yes," Aiden said.

"Great. I'll tap into my network and see who's done something similar and can give me some direction." She was typing this up as she spoke to him.

"Hey, Piper?"

"Yeah?"

"Do we pay you enough?"

She paused in her typing and smiled at him. Then she glanced at Ollie. Then back to Aiden. She had a strange expression on her face when she said, "Working with you guys is a dream job."

Aiden studied her for a moment. He'd always thought maybe, just maybe, Piper had a little thing for Ollie. But Ollie treated her like a sister at best. A nagging assistant at worst. Hell, she made dinner reservations for him and the women he took out. Aiden was pretty sure she'd sent flower arrangements and possibly even a birthday gift or two on Ollie's behalf as well. Knowing Piper, *she* was the one who remembered there were birthday gifts that needed to be sent.

Oliver Caprinelli would be a very hard man to be in love with. His head was in the clouds 99 percent of the time. Getting his attention would be a feat. He would forget about you the second even the spark of a new idea came to him. He'd close himself in his office to brainstorm and not emerge for hours. He'd forget to eat. He didn't always go home to sleep. He missed phone calls, dinners, and yes, birthdays.

It was even hard to be his *friend* sometimes. Aiden couldn't imagine being a girlfriend. Or a wife.

And no one would know that better than Piper.

"That wasn't really an answer to my question," Aiden pointed out.

She grinned. "I'll let you know when I'm ready for a raise."

"No raises for wenches who dangle meatballs in front of their bosses," Ollie groused from off camera.

Maybe she should try dangling other things in front of him, Aiden thought. Then frowned. Piper didn't need to go out of her way to get Ollie's attention. She was amazing and beautiful, and every other man who walked into their office noticed everything she had going on. If Ollie wasn't smart enough to notice Piper, that was his own damned fault.

Besides, if they did hook up and Ollie pissed her off or broke her heart, then Fluke would lose Piper, and they *all* needed her. Aiden should be working to keep Ollie completely distracted from Piper as a woman. She was his nagging assistant. That was perfect.

"Just type the email, Oliver," Piper said in a very old school-marm tone. In spite of her cherry-red glasses that matched the red cherries that dotted her white dress, she pulled off the I'll-rap-your-knuckles-with-my-ruler attitude very well.

"Don't give him the meatballs even when he's finished," Aiden said. "His attitude is crap."

"It is," she agreed.

"Don't you have a cute cupcake baker you need to be covering in frosting?" Ollie called.

Aiden froze. "What?"

Piper frowned at Ollie. "Keep typing."

"What's he talking about?" Aiden pressed.

"Cam got a call from his mom a little bit ago," Piper said. "She asked if he knew about you and Zoe."

"Oh." Shit. Aiden thought fast. Cam did *not* know about him and Zoe. Cam was protective of Zoe. To an extent. If someone hurt her, Cam would absolutely hurt that person. But Cam wasn't the type to punch Aiden for kissing Zoe.

He didn't think.

"What did he say?" Aiden finally asked. Cam hadn't called him or Zoe about it. What did that mean?

Piper chewed on her bottom lip for a moment.

"Piper?"

"He didn't call you?"

"No."

"Text? Email?"

"No. No."

"Oh." She sighed. "All he said to me was to book him a room at the hotel too."

Aiden frowned. "He's coming to Iowa?"

"Yeah. He left right after Dax did."

"But he's staying at the hotel? Not in Appleby?"

Piper shrugged. "He asked me to book him a room, so I did."

What the hell? "Okay. Well, I guess I'll see him soon enough, and I can ask him what's up." Aiden wasn't looking forward to that reunion. "Did he seem... angry?" Aiden asked. He really liked this tie. If Cam was going to punch him, he didn't want to bleed on it.

"He seemed... resigned?" Piper said. She ended that with a question mark though. She looked at Ollie. "Didn't you think?"

"Determined," Ollie said. "Or... annoyed. Yeah, maybe a little annoyed too."

Great. A determined and annoyed Camden McCaffery. That wasn't as bad as a pissed-off, unreasonable one, but it wasn't great either.

Aiden reached up and pulled his tie loose.

Dammit.

———

Twenty minutes later, he strode into the lobby of the Hilton Hotel in Dubuque, Iowa.

He'd texted Dax that he was here, and Dax had replied with a simple, "1247."

Of course Dax was on the top floor. He did love a great view. And Dubuque might be in what some people considered a flyover state, but it was right on the Mississippi and definitely had a pretty view. If you were into rivers and bluffs and trees and rolling hills and stuff.

Aiden was. He'd missed his home state. Chicago was a great city, and he'd loved city life at first. Chicago and its many resources had been an important place for them to be as they got Fluke off the ground, and trusting Grant to take them back to his hometown had been a good move.

But Aiden was ready to be back in Iowa.

And yeah, he did have a cute cupcake baker to be covering in frosting as a matter of fact.

He thought about Zoe as the elevator climbed to the twelfth floor. Cam would get over it. Or used to it. Or whatever. Aiden and Zoe were together now, and Cam would just have to deal. That wasn't really Cam's strong suit—dealing with things he didn't like—but this was his best friend and sister. He wouldn't want to lose either of them, and if Aiden could prove he was the best thing for Zoe and that he really wanted to take care of her and love her, then Cam would be good with it.

He would definitely need to leave out the frosting stuff though.

The doors swished open, and Aiden blew out a breath. Cam was very likely in there with Dax. They'd probably already raided the minibar and had room service on its way up.

The thing about hanging out with Dax... he didn't let you let things like practicality and huge price tags and it being 2 p.m. keep you from enjoying yourself. Two p.m. on a weekday? Why *not* have a T-bone steak with the works? And dessert. Especially dessert. Dax was a dessert-first kind of guy. Not because of a sweet tooth exactly. More because of a life philosophy. Live life to the fullest. Get what you wanted when you wanted it. Always.

Aiden rapped his knuckles against the door to Suite 1247. The corner suite. Of course.

Dax opened it with a flourish a moment later. He was wearing one of the hotel robes. And probably nothing else. Aiden didn't need to know.

"Hey." Dax stepped back to let Aiden in.

Clearly room service was not on its way up. They'd already been there. Dax picked a french fry off the plate as he passed, tossing it into the air and catching it before settling back on the couch, propping his feet on the coffee table, and pointed to the remote and the gigantic television. He shut it off.

"I see you've settled in easily," Aiden said, taking the armchair perpendicular to where Dax sat. Dax's robe was loose around the waist, and he didn't want to accidentally catch a glimpse of anything underneath.

"I think best when I'm comfortable," Dax told him with a grin.

Dax was very rarely *uncomfortable*. Physically or emotionally. Zoe's assumption about the guys sitting around their office in beanbag chairs was true if she was referring only to Dax's office. He had two oversized beanbags in there, and he claimed he did his best thinking in them. As a group they never met in Dax's office. Grant refused to do serious work while sitting in a beanbag chair in an office with a cappuccino machine in the corner. Grant Lorre was very much a black-coffee kind of guy. Strong black coffee.

And yes, Dax claimed cinnamon sprinkles on top of his cappuccino helped his creative process. Just like the gummy bears in the glass candy jar on his desk did. Just like the music from the Rat Pack—played on vinyl on an old turntable—did. Just like the daily ping-pong game against Elliot, one of their best graphics guys, did.

But the truth was, bugging the shit out of and getting smiles out of Grant, helped Dax's creative process and all that—from the Rat Pack to the gummy bears—did *that*.

Yes, hanging out with Dax Marshall was a little like hanging out with a thirteen-year-old with a credit card and no limit. Or being stuck in one of *The Hangover* movies.

Still, the guy made a kick-ass video game and was the star at every con he'd ever been to. Aiden knew Grant would never admit it, at least not where Dax could hear him, but Dax and his YouTube videos and his appearances at conventions and his insistence on high quality, unique merchandise, had made them more money than anything Aiden and Grant actually did for the company.

Bottom line, *Warriors of Easton* wouldn't even exist without Dax. Ollie was the storyteller, the world builder, the visionary, but Dax made it all real. He took Ollie's ideas and made them come to life. On screen anyway. He put movement and color and sound to everything, and without him, *Warriors* would have never come to be. He worked his ass off, honestly, to make *Warriors of Easton* everything it could possibly be.

Aiden, Grant, and Cam were completely worthless when it came to all that.

They were the paper and money and regulations and business guys. Sure, the company needed them too, but Ollie and Dax could have found three other marketing and business majors just by throwing a rock. It was a good thing Aiden, Grant, and Cam had found *them* and had recognized brilliance when they saw it.

"Have you seen Cam?" Aiden asked, propping one of his feet up on the coffee table next to Dax's bare foot.

Dax also rarely wore shoes around the office. That also bugged the shit out of Grant.

"Yeah, he's on his way. Went to upgrade his room." Dax grinned.

"Upgrade?"

"Piper put him in the executive suite down the hall. Figured we'd want to be on the same floor to work. There's only one of these deluxe suites on each floor. He's down there working to get a deluxe on another floor. Can't handle me having a better place than his."

Aiden rolled his eyes. That sounded exactly like Cam. "He's not planning to stay in Appleby?"

"Said he didn't want to walk in on you banging his sister on the kitchen table."

Aiden started choking. On nothing. He coughed hard and sent Dax a glare.

Dax waited for him to quiet then gave him a grin.

"Did he actually *say* that?" Aiden asked.

"I sure fucking did."

Aiden looked over his shoulder at Cam. Who evidently had a key to Dax's room.

13

———

"Uh, hey," Aiden greeted Cam.

"Yeah, hey." Cam dropped into the chair opposite Aiden. He glanced at Dax. "Jesus, cover your junk, Marshall."

"You're in *my* room," Dax informed him, leaning to grab a package of M&M's—that probably cost thirteen dollars—from the spread on the coffee table. "You don't want to see all my glory, go to your room."

Cam grabbed the throw pillow from behind him on the chair and tossed it at Dax. "This must be what it's like to hang out with rock stars who think they're hot shit and that everyone should just let them do whatever they want."

The truth was, Dax was kind of their rock star. He was the face of the company—and it was, by all accounts, a good-looking face—and he was the freaking Wizard of Oz. The guy who made the magic happen. That was why Grant went along with all the stupid shit Dax claimed he needed to *be creative.* The same reason Grant often, and always, begrudgingly, accompanied Ollie and Dax when they traveled. Grant was protecting his investment.

Dax just nodded. "Probably." He looked from Cam to Aiden. "I prefer to travel with Ollie. He gets me."

"Translation, 'Ollie is as *special* as I am,'" Cam said in his usual imitation of Dax. Which sounded nothing like Dax and completely like a California surfer dude from a bad beach movie. Dax was from San Francisco, actually, but was apparently a terrible surfer.

"You *say* I'm special, but I don't think you mean it," Dax replied, pretending to be hurt.

Cam rolled his eyes and slumped back in his chair. "Oh, I mean it. I just don't mean that I think you slide to work on a sparkly rainbow or that your farts smell like cookies."

Dax grinned at him. "Good thing millions of boys between the ages of ten and twenty-five, not to mention a fairly significant number of guys twenty-five to forty, think both of those things about me."

"Metaphorically, anyway," Cam said.

"Bet I could convince a chunk of them those things are actually true," Dax said, almost thoughtfully.

It was never a good idea for Dax to get thoughtful when the topic of conversation was ridiculous. Thank God Ollie wasn't here, or they'd end up with a fucking plastic rainbow running from the parking garage into Dax's office window that he would literally slide in on every day.

"We need to talk about Hot Cakes," Aiden said, trying to steer the conversation.

"Or we could talk about you banging Cam's sister on her kitchen table."

Aiden stared at him. They could find another computer genius, right? Surely there was another one in the world that could pick up right where Dax left off when Aiden killed him.

"The only thing I have to say about that—" Cam said, his voice deep and firm from across the coffee table and a pile of Dax snacks.

Aiden looked up at his best friend reluctantly. They'd done a lot of awesome things together. Not the least of which was harnessing Dax and Ollie's brilliance. A huge, amazing, multi-million dollar business. They'd always been honest with one another and they trusted each other completely. He couldn't lose Cam.

Unless it came down to Cam or Zoe.

The revelation hit him hard. He'd never thought about it. Had never let himself think about it. Cam was not an easygoing guy, but he also wasn't the type to get all riled up about his sister's sex or love life. If the guy treated her badly, then definitely Cam would make him regret it. But if Zoe chose to be with someone, Cam trusted her to make that decision.

Probably.

It had never really been an issue before. Aiden had never heard Cam talk about Zoe's dating life or any guys she'd ever been involved with. Then again, she hadn't dated much.

But yeah, if Cam was going to be a dick—and that was something Cam McCaffery did very well—then Aiden was going to lose one of his best friends and business partners.

Fuck.

"I'm never eating at that table again."

"I love her, man."

They spoke at the same time. Then stared at each other.

"What?"

"What?"

Again they spoke simultaneously.

Then Aiden took a breath. "I love her."

Cam just nodded. "Good."

"Yeah? That's it? Just good?"

"Yeah. I love you both, and I know you'll be good to her. And as long as I don't have to hear about your sex life... or *hear* your sex life." He frowned. "Fuck. Where am I going to stay when I come home now? I can't stay at the house."

"You can stay at the house," Aiden said.

"I can't listen to the headboards banging or come down the hall knowing you're in the shower together." He shook his head. "Dammit. I'll have to stay at Mom's."

Aiden laughed. "When you stay over, I'll sleep in my own room."

"So what?" Cam asked. "That didn't stop her from sneaking in there on Christmas Eve."

Aiden froze. "What?"

Cam gave him a "come on" look. "Yeah, I saw her coming back out of your room."

"You didn't say anything," Aiden said carefully.

"I thought maybe you were just screwing around that one night or something," Cam said.

"And you didn't care?"

"You're both grown-ups," Cam said with a shrug. "Who the hell am I to be judging other people about relationships?"

"That is a really good point," Dax said.

"This from a guy who likes to bang chicks who dress up like fairies and princesses?" Cam asked. "That *he* created? That's kind of creepy, don't you think?"

"It's fucking awesome," Dax said. "I draw stuff in a notebook, and six months later that drawing is showing up in the flesh at cons and thinking my farts smell like cookies." Dax crossed his ankles on the coffee table and grinned. "It's like magic."

He wasn't wrong. Aiden had seen Dax's creations walking and talking—and fawning all over him—at cons all across the country and at one in London.

"And by the way, my fairies and princesses and warriors really like it when I refer to my cock as my staff. What do you think of that?"

Cam looked like he was also wondering about finding a new brilliant computer genius to take Dax's place.

"Anyway," Cam finally said. "I figure if you do anything to mess up with Zoe, you've got my mom and dad and Josie and Jane to deal with, and they're going to give you a lot more trouble than I ever could."

Ugh. Aiden nodded. "Yeah."

"Who are Josie and Jane?" Dax asked.

"No one you need to worry about," Aiden told him quickly.

Cam laughed. "Oh, I don't know. Josie and Zoe keep saying Josie needs a sugar daddy to take care of her."

"I've got tons of money," Dax said. "Who's Josie?"

"Zoe's best friend and assistant at the bakery," Cam said.

"She bakes?" Dax asked. "I'm in. Set me up."

"Hell no," Aiden told him.

"Why not?"

"Because I like Josie," Aiden said. "And you're... a lot. Josie is too... sweet for you."

"I'm a lot of fucking fun," Dax said. He dropped his feet to the floor. "I'm a goddamned delight. Women love me. *I* am sweet." He pointed at his phone. "I can get twelve women on the phone right now who would tell you I'm sweet as hell."

"Yes. Until they need you to be serious about something," Aiden said. "You're allergic to serious."

"I'm not *allergic.*" But Dax wasn't nearly as emphatic now.

"You pretended to get into a car accident so you couldn't make it to a girlfriend's uncle's funeral," Cam said.

"Great uncle," Dax said. "And it wasn't pretend."

"You braked for a squirrel, and a bicyclist ran into the back of your car," Cam said.

"I had to be sure he was okay."

"He was fine."

"But I had to be *sure.*"

"And you broke up with a girl in college because she was homesick," Aiden pointed out.

"She was going to drop out after the semester. The relationship was doomed."

"It was September," Aiden said.

"She wasn't embracing all that college life had to offer. She never wanted to go and try to meet new people. She cried every day."

"She was sad. And you broke up with her." Aiden and Cam had been juniors when Ollie and Dax had been freshmen. Ollie and Dax had hit campus ready to live it up and have the time of their lives.

"We were clearly mismatched," Dax said dryly.

"What did you see in her in the first place?" Cam asked.

"She was splashing around in the fountain in the middle of campus. I thought that seemed like fun. Like she was kind of a risk taker or something." Dax sat back and put his feet up. "After I found out she was just in there to get her hat back after it had blown off her head, I thought I should at least give her a chance."

Aiden and Cam both snorted. Dax grinned. "I like fun girls. That's not a crime. Is Josie fun?"

"Josie is *sweet*," Aiden emphasized. "And Zoe's best friend and someone I care about, so you are not going to do anything with her."

"Jane could handle you though," Cam said.

Dax perked up. "Jane? Okay, who's Jane?"

"Zoe's other best friend," Aiden said.

"But she's not really *fun*," Cam said.

"Jane's awesome," Aiden protested.

"She is," Cam agreed. "But she's... practical. Definitely serious. She doesn't have time for video games and dressing up like fairies, and she'd think you and your beanbag chairs and gummy bears are all ridiculous. She's not your type at all."

The thing was, Dax probably needed a girl like Jane. Someone to keep his feet on the ground. Grant did that for him, in a fatherly or annoyed-big-brother way. Dax probably needed a long-term relationship with a girl like Grant. Someone who appreciated his brilliance but didn't let him get too full of himself. Which actually made Aiden instantly turn back to the entire reason for his visit to the hotel.

"Okay, about Hot Cakes," he said, sitting forward in his chair. "You can meet Jane, actually. She works at the factory, and we need to talk to her more about employee satisfaction and benefits and the things we can do to improve things there."

Dax dropped his feet to the floor again and sat up straight. "Go into the factory and make it more fun to work there."

"That's not what I said," Aiden told him.

"Are you sure?"

"The factory doesn't need to be *fun*," Aiden said. "It needs to be safe and efficient and..." He shrugged. "It would be great if it was pleasant. Or at least didn't suck."

"Pleasant, fun, unsucky. All kind of the same thing," Dax said.

Yeah, well, Aiden had seen Dax in fun-mode. It was his default mode, actually. "We don't need plastic rainbow slides inside or a candy bar. We need..." Aiden trailed off. "Fuck. I don't know what we need. That's the point. I haven't even been inside the factory we now own. I know we need to do some work on the benefits and making the workers more stable and happy, but I can't do it. And Cam can't do it."

"I'd love to do it," Cam said. His voice was low and didn't sound joking. At all.

"No."

"Let me go in and find out from the horse's mouth all the ways they've failed," he said. "Now *that* sounds like fun."

"What's going on?" Dax asked.

"Whitney is the VP of sales and marketing at Hot Cakes," Aiden said, watching Cam.

Cam's jaw ticked at the mention of her name.

"Whitney the ex?" Dax asked. "That's right."

"So Cam can't go in there," Aiden said again.

"I can't go inside the building that houses the company I now own twenty percent of?" Cam asked. "That sounds like bullshit."

Aiden rubbed the middle of his forehead. "One thing at a time. You can't go because everyone knows you." Aiden blew out an exasperated breath. "Look, I know I can't keep you and Whitney apart forever. Hell, she knows that too."

Cam's eyes snapped to his. "She said that?"

"Pretty much. She's resigned to this. Not happy, of course, but she is grateful the company isn't going out of business entirely and that we're saving the jobs. She was honest about the fact her dad has let things go because he doesn't care about Hot Cakes anymore, and things aren't how she'd like them to be. She's also grateful we're keeping her employed. She acknowledges we don't have to do that."

"Good," Cam said simply.

"But let's not rub it in," Aiden said.

"Oh, I'm rubbing this in," Cam said. "Sorry, buddy, but there is no way I'm not going to gloat over the fact that the fucking company she chose over being with me is now only staying afloat because of me. That is definitely going to come up in conversation."

Aiden sighed. As much as he wished Cam could get past all that, he couldn't completely blame his friend for his bitterness. Whitney *had* chosen the business and her family over Cam. And now he was a huge success and that company and family needed bailing out. By Cam. It was kind of beautiful in a way.

"You can't go in there *yet*, then," Aiden said. "We need more information and a plan before we announce anything and let everyone know who we are."

"You haven't told Zoe and my mom and dad yet, have you?" Cam asked.

"No."

"You waiting for the engagement party or what?"

"I'm waiting to have a *plan*. I want everyone—including them—to fully understand our intentions."

"Our intentions are to keep Hot Cakes open. And success-ful. Even more so than they've been up to this point," Cam said. "That's *my* intention anyway. I want to make that company bigger and better than it ever was under the Lancasters."

"I want something new to do," Dax said, shrugging. "I need a new challenge."

And Grant and Ollie fell into those two categories as well. Grant would want to build this investment into something even bigger. Ollie needed a new place to put his creative energy.

"Great," Aiden said. "But we need to be able to show the employees that things are totally stable *and* going to improve. And we need the town"—he looked at Cam—"including your family, to understand that what we're doing is *good*. That it's important to the town, and we're doing it for noble reasons."

"Fine. Then how do you want to do this?" Cam asked, giving in.

"We need to talk to the employees, get a feel for the physical plant, meet everyone from the factory workers to the office staff. You and Grant and I need to go over the financials, the benefits, look at the suppliers. Anything we can do that doesn't involve someone local. If it has to do with the banks or anything, we'll get Grant to do it. Just for a few more days. I just need to have a clearer direction before I let Zoe and Maggie and Steve in on everything. I want them to all know that I'm serious about this and to know our goals and plans so I can prove this isn't a threat to Buttered Up."

That all sounded great. Practical. Reasonable.

But those were things Zoe was *not* when it came to the bakery and her family legacy.

"Okay, I'm going to meet with Whitney. Alone." He slid a

look at Cam as he got to his feet. "For now, you guys read up on everything. Start thinking about how you think we should roll this out." He pointed at Cam. "Maybe take the chip off your shoulder for a second and think about how we should best approach this with Appleby."

Cam frowned, but he didn't dispute the chip on his shoulder. "Okay. I'll talk to Dad about it. He'll have some ideas."

"Cam," Aiden said with a sigh. "He doesn't know."

Cam rolled his eyes. "*Fuuuuuck.* Can you get that taken care of?"

"Yeah. I'm... working on it." His thoughts went directly to Zoe.

Zoe who had told their mom she and Aiden were together. Zoe who had let him touch her in the kitchen that morning. Zoe who had let him kiss her in front of everyone at the bakery. Zoe who had liked hearing that he had business nearby that meant he really was staying.

Yeah, he was working on it. He was making progress.

But dammit, the closer he got to her, the more he realized that messing this up and losing her was not an option. He wanted her even more than he'd known, and he had to make her see that they could have it all.

"You guys work on this stuff, and I'll talk to you tomorrow," he said. He started for the door but turned back. "And stay out of Appleby."

"They don't know me there," Dax said.

"You don't need anything in Appleby," Aiden said. "Dubuque has everything Appleby does and much, much more."

"We'll go to the brewing company downtown," Cam said. "Awesome beer and pizza."

"Fine. I just thought I could look around the town," Dax said.

"You can't drive the roadster if you do. Or wear the fedora."

Dax looked at Cam. "Can we take the roadster downtown?"

"Fuck yeah," Cam said.

Dax looked at Aiden. "Fine, I'll stay away from Appleby for now."

"Thanks," Aiden said dryly.

He pulled his phone from his pocket as he crossed the lobby a few minutes later, preparing to call Whitney and see if she could meet briefly, but the phone dinged with a text before he could dial.

It was Zoe.

Got an emergency order for butterfly cupcakes. Pink. I'm out of pink frosting. She included a sad-faced emoji.

But her second text made him feel a hell of a lot better.

But they're cream-filled cupcakes, so I'm making extra filling. Maybe we can make do with that. For tonight.

He stopped walking, nearly getting plowed over by a woman rolling two oversized suitcases toward the front desk.

"I'm so sorry," he apologized, stepping out of her way.

But Zoe had just propositioned him. With cream filling. How had the rest of the world not stopped and just observed a moment of awe like he had? When they'd talked about cream fillings, it had included the word clit.

That meant Zoe McCaffery had just invited him over to suck on her clit.

That's what he'd read in that text anyway. He would be very happy to explain that to her too, when he saw her.

But before he could text something back, his phone rang. It was Whitney. She was available to meet right now.

He blew out a breath. Fuck. He really needed to talk to Whitney. Hot Cakes was depending on him.

The cream filling was going to have to wait for a few hours.

He'd survive.

Probably.

14

Could a woman get blue balls?

Obviously not, but what was the equivalent? Blue clit? And what was the appropriate reaction to—or punishment for—a guy causing it for the same woman *twice*? A woman he claimed to want a relationship with? After he'd already proven that the orgasms he could give were so much better than the DIY ones she was used to?

These were the things Zoe contemplated as she kneaded dough, chopped fruit, and whipped frosting over the next three days.

Three. *Days.*

None of it had worked off her frustration.

Aiden had texted her from Dubuque the day Maggie caught them kissing to say he was so sorry, but his meeting was going to go late. She'd thought he meant maybe seven or eight. She'd stalled at the bakery—with the cupcake cream—until seven thirty. She'd fallen asleep at home at ten. An hour later than she usually went to bed so she could be up at 5 a.m. She hadn't heard him come home and only knew he was there the next morning because his car was in the driveway.

The same had happened the next two nights.

He'd come to the bakery around six thirty, looking like he'd barely gotten any sleep, and parked his tight, suited-up ass in one of the chairs and supervised the morning rush. He didn't help, but he kept his eye on the guys in line.

When they'd cleared out, he'd come to her, kiss her until her toes curled, and apologize with a "this new project has just gotten crazy." Or something similar.

She said she understood. She did. This was the job that was going to allow him to be in Appleby with her. She understood how much owning a business could take out of a person. At Christmastime she was sometimes at the bakery until midnight and then back by 5 a.m. to fulfill all the orders. She actually liked seeing him working hard and taking it all so seriously. She liked that they had a devoted work ethic in common.

She just didn't like going without orgasms. Now that she'd *really* had a taste, she felt itchy and hot and jittery all the time thinking about it. One definite disadvantage to being able to do all her work on autopilot by now was that it left a lot of time for thinking about other things.

Like the fact they hadn't had time to sneak in anymore hands-in-panties time. The morning rush kept her and Josie on their toes and then George and Phil were at their tables. Aiden was busy on his computer and phone almost nonstop anyway. Then around four o'clock, he'd pack up and head to Dubuque. Apparently, the guy he was meeting with also worked during the day and could only meet after hours.

Aiden had, however, given her a folder with some small business resources for employee benefits and had asked her to send him her books for the past two years. She appreciated he was still thinking of her and Buttered Up in the midst of the project that had caused him to miss dinner at her mom's house last night and her invitation for pizza and beer with her, Jane, and Josie the night before. The project that was also making him look constantly worried and down four cups of coffee every morning.

She glanced up as he sat back in his chair with a sigh and scrubbed a hand over his face, putting his phone down for the first time in almost an hour. He'd mostly been listening to whatever was being discussed, but he'd been frowning a lot. She'd never seen him so... bothered. Things usually worked out for Aiden. He really had always seemed to have a golden touch.

Maybe this was good for him. Humbling, perhaps. Though the only two things he'd seemed totally confident about since coming back to Appleby was that she would open her arms— and legs—for him. And that she had no reason to hate Hot Cakes. Well, he'd been right about one of those.

"You know," she said, piping vanilla frosting onto the strawberry cupcakes and tiny strawberry pies on the table in front of her. "You don't have to come in here so early every morning." She looked up to find him watching her. "You could sleep in."

George and Phil had left a while ago, and they were alone in the front of the bakery.

He gave her a smile that looked tired but sincere. "I like being here," he said simply.

"You mean you like staking your claim," she said. She liked him doing that too.

"That too," he agreed.

She ignored the curl of heat in her stomach. "I think you've done that. Mom and Dad both said people have asked them about us. Jane and Josie too."

"I like being here with you," he said. He rose and approached the counter. "I like watching you work. I love the smells and sounds here. They're... comforting. I like you filling me in on everyone as they come in and out." He braced his hands on the counter. His dress shirt was rolled up on his forearms, and his tie was present but loose.

It was probably the tie that was making it hard for her to not be constantly horny.

"But mostly I like watching you work," he said again.

She felt warm—even though she was frustrated. "You're not watching me. You're on your phone and computer." She hoped he wasn't watching *too* closely. She was trying something new, and she didn't want him to notice and ask her about it. It was probably a dumb idea and wasn't going to go anywhere anyway.

His gaze went over her. "I'm watching, Zoe. I'm aware of every move you make."

She smiled. "Okay."

"Did you know you make this little growling sound when something doesn't turn out?"

She frowned. "No, I don't."

"You do." He growled softly, clearly mimicking her.

"And 'son of a damned fudge stick' is your favorite curse while you're working and you don't think anyone is listening."

Okay, that she did say. A lot. Under her breath. Or so she'd thought.

"And when something turns out well, you give this happy little sigh that sounds like the sigh you make when I kiss you."

She frowned at him. "You can't talk about kissing me."

"Why not? All this—the little frown you wear when you're decorating, your smile when one of your customers compliments you, the way you and Josie talk and joke, the way you look in that damned apron—" Again his gaze went over her. "It all makes me hard. All day long. I love just being here with you in your element. Working side by side."

She liked that too. But she gave a little half sigh, half groan. "*Aiden.*"

"What, Sugar?"

"You can't talk about being hard and kissing and stuff." She glanced toward the kitchen where Josie was working on a wedding cake with five tiers for that weekend. "If you're not going to do anything about it, you have to stop turning me on."

His smile was slow and sexy. "I'm sorry you're all worked up, babe." He didn't really look sorry.

"After all the frosting and cream-filling talk the other night?" she asked. "And the kitchen the other morning?"

He nodded slowly. "I'm *very* sorry. This has all kinds of blown up. Our timelines got sped up, and there are more issues than we expected."

"I get it. I do understand," she said. Then she dropped her eyes to study the flecks of icing on the tabletop. "But the other morning didn't take very long."

Suddenly Aiden was around the counter and crowding her against the worktable. Her breath caught as she looked up at him. He looked hungry and as wound up as she felt. "You need some relief, Sugar?"

She nodded mutely.

"Tell me what you need, Zoe," he said, his voice dropping to a husky drawl.

She wet her lips. "Well, you're kind of the expert."

He gave her a half smile but shook his head. "I think you know what you want." He dragged his hand from her shoulder to her wrist, brushing his finger over her pulse point. "And I'll do whatever you need. Can't have my girl unsatisfied."

"I'm definitely that," she told him, liking the *my girl* thing more than she would have expected. "I've been so..."

He lifted a brow when she trailed off.

She lowered her voice. "Horny."

Aiden's eyes flared with heat even as his grin grew. It was surprised and cocky at the same time. He leaned in. "I'm sorry." He seemed sincere now. "You're so busy when we're here together, and our schedules have been so off. But hopefully not for much longer."

"You could wake me up when you get home," she said, hopefully.

He gave a soft laugh. "The first two nights were way too late. And I tried last night."

Her eyes widened. "What?"

He nodded. "I came in, gave you a kiss, hoped you'd wake up."

"You did not." But it was possible. She slept like the dead, and she definitely had a hard time even seeing nine thirty most nights.

"Totally did," he said. "And I tried to meet you for... coffee... the last two mornings, but girl, you get up early."

She smiled. Aiden and Cam had never been morning people. She'd been surprised and pleased to see him at the bakery as early as he'd been coming in the last few days.

Zoe lifted a hand to his face. "It's okay. It really is." She'd gone this long without sex. She could wait until he had this project under control. Probably. "I'll wait for you."

He took her hand and turned his head to press a kiss to the palm. "It's not okay," he disagreed. "We're both busy, and you're on deadline when we're here, so I haven't wanted to interrupt. And I've been busy every evening. But if you need me to help you take the edge off, I'm more than happy to take you into the storeroom and give you some relief."

She wanted that. So much. "Sex in the storeroom?" she asked, her mind spinning with images. "There's not really a flat surface or empty wall. It's all shelves."

He chuckled. "Not sex. Not like that. Yet," he added. "But I can get my hand in your panties in the storeroom and have you coming hard and fast." He ended the offer with a hot, deep kiss.

She wasn't too proud to not grind against the hard length behind his zipper before pulling back. "Why not sex?"

Aiden dragged his thumb over her bottom lip, his pupils dilated. "Not your first time."

"Oh." That made sense. That was sweet.

"The first time calls for lots of space—and lots of *time*," he said huskily. "I've got a very long to-do list for that."

"Okay." She was breathless.

And when a glint of satisfaction flashed in his eyes, she realized what she'd kind of admitted. Or what she hadn't denied. This would be her first time. "The first time for *us* together, you mean," she said.

"Uh-huh."

She grinned. She wasn't confirming a thing. Because she loved seeing possessive Aiden rear his head once in a while.

He shifted back, a "got ya" look on his face that made her feel very warm.

Then her gaze dropped to the worktable, and another surge of warmth went through her. She'd been trying something new. Because of him. And she wanted him to know it.

"Would you... try something for me?" she asked.

"Of course."

She leaned to pick up one of the little mason jars and held it up.

"What's this?" He took it from her.

"Cupcakes in jars. And pies," she said.

She watched him lift it up, studying it.

"Is this... strawberry?" he asked. His eyes went to hers. Questioning.

She nodded. "Yeah." Because those were his favorites. She hadn't intended to show him this. Certainly not to have him try the cupcakes. But she'd still made it with him in mind. "It's a thing. People do cupcakes and pies and cobblers in jars. Makes them into instant individual servings. Very easy to ship and transport."

He picked up a strawberry pie in a jar as well. "You haven't done these before."

"No."

"Why now?"

Her eyes dropped to the deep-green silk of his tie instead of his gaze. "I guess I was thinking that if people *were* to buy things that had real frosting or cream topping—not the plastic, preservative-filled crap *some* people put on their cupcakes—to put in their lunches or maybe even their compartments—not that they would last too long, but people would *want* to eat these right away and wouldn't forget they were there or whatever—then jars might be better than boxes or plastic containers. Because you can bake them right in the jars. Then they're not loose inside the container and sliding around and getting smooshed. Plus that saves us work and time, because we don't have to cut them and transfer them to new containers. And jars are different from what anyone else is doing around here. And they're reusable and recyclable. We could even have people bring them back in for 'refills' for a little discount or something. Or just to be used again. I mean, once you wash and sanitize them, there's no reason to not use them again, so that could allow us to keep costs down and..."

She trailed off realizing that he was just standing there. She lifted her eyes to his. He was staring at her. But grinning.

She crossed her arms, suddenly feeling very vulnerable. She'd been rambling but it was because she had a lot to say about the jar pies. Evidently. "What?"

"That's amazing, Zoe." He was practically beaming. "This is a fantastic idea. For all those reasons. You're thinking about ways to expand. That's so great. Are you going to go talk to Tom down at the store about shelf space? I'd go with you. I bet you could even talk to the convenience store. And you could do something at the farmers market. You could maybe even set up some kind of profit-sharing fundraising thing with the school. These would be amazing things to sell for something like that. Unique but something that everyone would want."

Now she was the one to stare at him. But she *wasn't* grinning.

"No." She shook her head. "No. No. Definitely not. I just tried it. This one time. This is the first batch of anything I've made."

"Did it work?" he asked.

"Well... yes. I mean. They turned out."

He set the jar down with the pie and then looked around. He grabbed a fork from the counter and then dug into the cupcake. He took a huge bite, watching her while he chewed. But suddenly he stopped and swallowed with some difficulty.

Her eyes grew round. "Oh my God! Is it horrible? Did I mess it up?"

He swallowed again and set the jar down, wiping a hand over his mouth. "No." He cleared his throat. "No, definitely not. It's... perfect."

"Then why do you look like that?" Not believing him, she picked up the fork and took a bite for herself.

But he was right. It was perfect. Delicious even. Moist, fluffy, wonderful strawberry flavor, perfect creamy icing.

"It just... tastes exactly like the ones my mom made here," he said, his voice gruff.

Her eyes flew to his face.

"It just hit me. Hard. All of a sudden," he explained. "The smell and the taste and everything at once."

She swallowed, also with difficulty, and nodded. "I know they're your favorite. I always associated them with you."

"They are. Were."

Zoe suddenly felt tears stinging her eyes. Maybe she shouldn't have picked strawberry. "Have you had one since she died?" she asked softly.

Aiden shook his head and cleared his throat again. "No."

"I'm... sorry. I guess, for some reason, that was just the one I started with when I was trying this out. And strawberry pie for Jane."

He smiled and reached out, pulling her in. "It's delicious. And perfect. And I fucking love that the first thing you do when you're trying something new is something that makes you think of me."

She wrapped her arms around him. "Well, you *are* the one who gives me the hardest time about not trying new things."

He hugged her tight for a moment. Then his hands slipped to her hips, and he pressed her against him. She could feel he was partially aroused.

By strawberry cake in a jar.

God, he was easy. She grinned, rubbing her cheek against his tie. Then she wiggled her hips against his.

He gave a soft growl. "Yeah, I'll give you a *hard time* trying new things later on, Sugar," he teased huskily.

"Thank God," she said sincerely.

He chuckled. Then he kissed the top of her head and let her go. "I'm proud of you for trying this." He nodded at the jars of cake and pie.

She sighed. "I'm not really trying anything, Aiden. They're the same recipes I've always used."

"You put them in new containers. That's actually pretty huge. Around here anyway."

She laughed. "Well, maybe. A little huge."

"And did you have to adjust the baking time at all?"

"A little."

"There you go. You're doin' it."

Lord, he really did seem proud. "But I'm not ready to go to the stores with them or do fundraising drives or any other crazy thing you have spinning in your head," she warned him. "I'm going to put these out here in the bakery for now and just... see."

"What's the difference?" he asked. "Except if they're in the store, people can get them more conveniently, grabbing them off the shelf while they're also picking up chicken and potatoes for dinner. Or they can grab them on impulse while they're paying for gas and lottery tickets at the convenience store. Or they can be talked into buying them by their grandchildren who need new soccer uniforms. Expanding your audience, getting more people to taste your products, taking it to them so they don't have to come to you, making it available at eight o'clock at night when you're already closed. I mean... other than all those things... what's the difference?" But he was grinning.

She shook her head. "Okay, I can kind of see why your gaming company is so successful."

He laughed. "And Dax is even more charming than I am."

"Lord help us all."

"I could take him some cupcakes in a jar..."

"No." She slapped his hand away from the jars. "Just... I'm not ready."

"Why not?" He seemed sincerely curious.

Zoe blew out a breath. "Because if the jars are sitting on shelves in other stores, in public, then everyone can see them *not* selling. Just sitting there. People can see other people reaching past them for Strawberry Swirls from Hot Cakes instead."

He sighed. Then he nodded. "If it doesn't go well or take off then everyone knows. If you keep it in here you can control that."

"Of course. I can display just two or three items and make it seem like we're almost sold out. I can dump the stuff that doesn't sell. And no one is reaching for anything else in here. If they come through the door, at least I know they're here because they want my stuff."

"Got it."

That surprised her. "Really?"

"Sure. I understand. That doesn't mean I don't think you should take a chance."

"Yeah, well... taking chances and making cakes of any shape other than round or square are *really* not my strong suits."

He gave her a very affectionate look. "You take your time with this. But," he added, grabbing the cupcake-in-a-jar he'd already sampled, "this is fucking delicious. The second-best thing I've had on my tongue. Ever."

"What the first best thing you've had on your tongue?" she asked. He really liked her chocolate pie.

"*Your* tongue."

Before she could respond, the door to the bakery opened with a little jingle. They stepped apart, and Zoe took a deep breath before turning to greet her new customer.

It was Jane. She was dressed in her work clothes—jeans and black polo shirt with the bright pink and white Hot Cakes logo on the left side—and she was coming through the front door. Jane never came through the front door. Hell, she never came through any door to the bakery.

Zoe was immediately concerned. "What are you doing here? And coming in the front?"

Jane waved that away. "The new owners got rid of that rule."

"Wait, what?" Zoe asked. "You mean, you can shop here now?"

"Yep. No problem."

Zoe felt a jolt of surprise, then excitement. "Really?" Wow. That was a lot of potential new customers.

"Really." Jane braced her hands on the counter. She was frowning.

Which distracted Zoe from the thought of needing to up the muffin inventory. "What's wrong?"

"Can I talk to you?" Jane asked. But she was looking at Aiden.

Aiden straightened. "Um... of course."

Jane nodded and headed for the table where Aiden's computer was set up. Aiden shot Zoe a puzzled look. She shrugged. But she moved to the bakery case as Aiden started for the table. She grabbed a jar with a strawberry pie in it and a fork. Jane looked curious when she set it down.

"Trust me. You'll love it," Zoe told her. At least she knew that was true.

Zoe grabbed a cup at the coffee station and filled it with a dark roast and a splash of cream. She set that down for her friend too. Jane gave her a grateful smile.

"You okay?" she asked, her hand on Jane's shoulder.

Jane nodded. "Yeah. I'm... pissed off and worried."

"About what?" Zoe asked.

"The new owners," Jane said with a frown. "They sent out a big welcome email to everyone, but all it really said was there were going to be some big changes. Everyone's freaking out." She played with her fork but had yet to take a bite.

That was a sure sign things were not okay.

"They want me to go talk to the new owners on everyone's behalf. I don't want to, but everyone is so worried, and no one else is really willing to confront them." She sighed. "I feel like I have to." She focused on Aiden. "I was hoping you could coach me."

"Coach you?" he repeated. "What do you mean?"

"On how to talk to management. How to get them to listen? Do I act meek and submissive and beg for mercy? Do I go in guns blazing, demanding they listen? What?"

Aiden grimaced. "Somewhere in between those. Even if I thought you could actually pull off meek and submissive."

That got him a tiny smile and Zoe felt relieved. Jane didn't need any more stress or people to worry about. But Aiden would help her through this. That was also very sexy.

15

"**N**ight, Zoe! See you tomorrow!"

Zoe looked to where Josie was leaning through the swinging door to the kitchen. "What?"

"I said, good night. I'll see you tomorrow. You almost done?"

Josie glanced toward the table where Aiden and Jane were still sitting. Typically he left for his meetings by now, but he'd either canceled them or at least pushed them back to stay with Jane.

"Not quite," Zoe told her.

"What's going on?" Josie asked, stepping out from the kitchen.

They'd been talking for over an hour. Zoe had tried to give them space. She'd waited on a couple of customers. She'd even decorated some more cake pops. But she'd been very interested in Jane and Aiden's conversation. Evidently several employees had come to Jane with concerns, practically begging her to talk to the new owners. They thought, and Aiden agreed, that they should bring up the things they loved and the things they didn't about working for Hot Cakes before the owners started making changes. She'd apparently sent an email requesting a meeting to someone higher up and they'd agreed. Now, Aiden was coaching her in how to approach the whole thing.

"Aiden's giving Jane advice about the new Hot Cakes management."

Josie nodded. "That's good."

"Is it?" She was truly interested. "You think he'll have good advice?"

"Sure. But mostly she just needs someone to tell her she's right to ask for everything she wants. You know Jane. She's kind of a cynic. She'll assume they don't care and won't tell them everything."

"Aiden will help her with that?" Zoe asked, looking over at them again.

Jane was smiling now. That was good. Josie was right. Jane was a natural pessimist. Her dad's illness and her stepmom's attitude toward it had changed Jane. Her stepmom, Cassie, had decided Jane's dad would be better off in a nursing home as his condition progressed and he needed more help. The truth was, being a caregiver got in her way. She couldn't take her girl trips or go to four-hour-long coffee dates or on all-day shopping sprees if she had to be at home taking care of him.

Jane had never liked Cassie, but that had made it all so much worse and had made Jane a little depressed and a lot pissed off. She'd looked into moving her dad in with her, but her work schedule kept her from being able to be the caregiver he needed. So she also felt guilty.

But Jane was strong and smart and had a huge heart and if her fellow employees—many of them friends after working together for so long—thought she'd be the best one to represent them all, she'd take that seriously and would want to do a good job. If Aiden could make her feel more confident and even hopeful about the meeting, then he'd be a hero. Something he was really good at. Something he really liked to be.

Seeing him reassuring Jane and building her up, giving

advice as a person in a powerful position, trying to truly help, did something to Zoe. Something that felt stronger than turned on. That was there too, but this was more.

I love him.

It hit her squarely as Jane pushed her chair back, smiling.

Jane gave Aiden a quick hug and he said, "You're going to be great."

Yep, Zoe loved him. She'd loved him in a brotherish way for a long time, but now... this was different. It was deeper. More. *He* was more. She wanted him badly.

"Bye, girls!" Jane called to Zoe and Josie.

"Bye!" Josie returned.

Zoe waved, but her attention was on Aiden. He'd followed Jane to the door.

Aiden held the door for Jane, then shut it behind her, twisted the lock and turned the sign to closed.

"Yeah. Okay," Josie said, backing toward the kitchen door. "So I'm going to... just go."

Zoe didn't look toward her friend. She knew Josie was already gone. The look on Aiden's face said it was time for them to be alone.

Her whole body flushed with heat, and her heart started pounding even harder and louder.

She'd talked big in her text three days ago. She'd flat out told him she was horny a couple of hours ago. Now he was here, looking at her like he definitely wanted to eat her up. She was suddenly feeling jittery, and she had no idea what to do.

He rounded the counter and came straight for her. Zoe turned, the edge of the worktable against her lower back and held her breath just waiting for whatever was about to happen.

He crowded close. He didn't touch her. He just looked down at her for a moment. Then he said, "You ready?"

Oh, God. She was ready. She was so *not* ready. She wanted

this so much. She wanted him. She wanted this. That was the only thing she knew for sure.

"I think so," she said softly.

He leaned in, bracing his hands on the table on either side of her. His lips were nearly against her. "Need you sure."

He was giving her a chance to say yes. Or no. To really decide. He wanted to make sure everything about this was intentional on both their parts.

That was really sexy.

"I'm sure that I've been thinking about this for days. And I'm very hot and wound up about it. But I'm also jittery and a little nervous about it." She could be honest with him and it felt amazing. This was Aiden. He'd never tease her. Not about this. Not in a mean way anyway. Maybe in a really hot way. But he'd never make her feel bad or silly about being nervous.

He shifted, running a single finger over the back of her hand where she was gripping the edge of the worktable and then up over her wrist and up her arm. Goose bumps broke out, tripping up her arm and down her body.

"I like that you've been thinking about it. I like that you're hot. I even like that you're a little jittery and nervous," he said, watching the goose bumps.

"You do?"

He met her gaze. "It means this matters to you. And I love that. Because this matters so damned much to me, I don't even have the words."

She read his sincerity in his eyes. He really meant that. "This definitely matters to me," she said, putting as much earnestness into her tone as she could.

He ran his finger up and down her arm, the corner of his mouth curling. "Because you're a virgin? Or because you're a cream-filling-on-your-clit virgin?"

She sucked in a sharp breath as heat arrowed through her.

"Well—" She swallowed hard. "Both. But because it feels like this, with you, with us, is more than just sex."

His grin was sexy, and cocky, and triumphant all at the same time.

Triumphant? She tilted her head.

And then it hit her.

She'd just confirmed she was, in fact, still a virgin.

"You're such a jerk," she said.

But he pressed in closer, his big body giving her not an inch of air that wasn't filled with the smell of him. The *heat* of him.

"You have no idea how fucking hot it is that I get to be your first, Zoe," he told her, his voice gruff.

She felt like he was touching her, running rough palms over her skin, but he wasn't even touching her arm anymore.

"You have no idea how much I want you. No matter what. But to know that I get to take you through this for the first time..." He pulled in a deep breath. "I have never wanted anything more in my entire life."

Suddenly she didn't care he was so smug about her not getting rid of her V-card between Christmas and now. She didn't care if he thought it was all about him—it was mostly all about him anyway. She didn't care if he thought she'd been sitting around, just waiting for him to come home again. Maybe deep down she had been.

None of that mattered now. He was here. She was a virgin. And she really, really wanted him to change that. Right now. Right here.

Well, maybe in the kitchen away from the front windows.

"I don't know what to do," she said, almost in a whisper.

He swallowed hard. He clenched his jaw.

She lifted her hand to his face, frowning slightly. "What? Are you okay? I'm sorry. I mean, I know the basics but..."

He grabbed her wrist and pulled her hand to his mouth. He pressed a hot kiss to her palm again and then put her hand over his heart, his hand covering it. "I was going to say, 'You just do whatever I tell you to do' in some attempt to be really hot and sexy and dominant," he said.

She widened her eyes as tingles went from her nipples down her belly to her clit. "That would have worked."

He gave her a little smile. "But the truth is, you can't do this wrong, Zoe. Not with me. Whatever you do, however you do it, as long as we're doing it together it's going to be amazing. You have to know that. I want you to do whatever feels good, whatever you want to try, whatever you've fantasized about. I'm all yours."

Her eyes widened even farther. Yeah, that was even hotter. Her nipples, belly, and clit were suddenly on fire. Throbbing. Wow. Suddenly her mind was spinning through a whole reel of fantasies and things she'd read about like a movie reel going double time.

"Aiden?" she said, her voice breathless.

"Yeah?"

"I'm *totally* ready."

This grin was big. Immediate. Wolfish. A shiver of hot anticipation went through her.

He grabbed her wrist and pulled her after him, into the kitchen. He stopped by the worktable and tossed two things onto the top.

One was a package of chocolate cupcakes. The other was a strawberry pastry. From Hot Cakes.

She narrowed her eyes. "Those were in your glove compartment?"

"Oh, no, I stopped for those special three days ago on my way home."

She looked up, ready to tell him that this was *really* not the way to get on her good side. But he'd just pulled the knot loose from his tie and was sliding the tie from around his neck. He tossed it next to the snack cakes and then flicked open the top button on his shirt. He was watching her, and she could tell he expected her to say something sassy.

Instead she turned on her heel and marched to the fridge. She pulled it open, reached for the bowl of extra cream filling she'd made—also three days ago—and then bumped the door shut with her butt. She brought the bowl to the center island and set it next to the snack cakes.

He'd untucked his shirt by the time she got there.

Unfair.

She looked up at him.

"Battle of the cream filling," he said.

She lifted a brow. "Oh yeah?"

"Bet I can make you *love* this stuff." He pointed to the chocolate cupcake.

A Cupette. That's what Hot Cakes called their bite-sized cupcakes. It was such a stupid name.

"Not more than this." She pointed to her bowl.

"Let's find out."

And just like that, all the butterflies and jittery feelings were gone. She was in her kitchen, teasing and flirting with Aiden. This was familiar. Fun. Hot. This was the stuff that had been surprising her since he'd returned to Appleby but that she was getting used to very quickly.

"Yeah, let's find out," she agreed.

His eyes were hot, and he started unbuttoning his shirt. She felt her pulse start racing, but she nonchalantly dipped her finger into her bowl of cream filling and then lifted it to her lips, sucking the sweet concoction off while watching him.

He shrugged out of the shirt, letting it fall to the floor.

Then he unbuckled his belt and pulled it through the loops. Zoe caught her breath as the buckle hit the tile with a clank. This was getting real. He popped the top button on his pants. Then stopped.

He reached for the cupcake. Zoe felt her nipples tighten as

the package crinkled. Oh, boy. He could *not* train her body to respond to Hot Cakes. That would be so unfair. She couldn't get hot and bothered when faced with their bright pink and black logo or their fake, plasticlike frosting. That would be so bad. He couldn't buy them in bulk and bring them home to sexually torment her. She couldn't contribute to their bottom line because Aiden Anderson...

He broke the cupcake open, revealing the white cream inside. Then he lifted it to his mouth and licked the cream out with a swirl of his tongue, his eyes pinned on hers. He licked the dab of cream from the pocket of chocolate cake with a confidence and skill that she didn't have to be experienced to understand.

Her clit ached. She wanted his tongue doing that to *it*. She'd never had anyone's tongue do that to *her* before, yet she knew Aiden's tongue doing *that* right *there* would be freaking magical.

Dammit. She was going to give Hot Cakes money. Because they were now a part of this.

She swallowed.

"You want some of this?" he asked. Taunting. Teasing. But with a smile that was full of affection and heat.

"The cupcake?" she asked. "Looks like you got that pretty well taken care of."

There was no cream left in that half of the cupcake. None. He'd licked it clean. She felt a little shiver of desire go through her.

"Well, the beauty of eating cupcakes—" he said.

And yes, *eating cupcakes* sounded totally dirty and made her hotter. Zoe shifted her weight as she felt the urge to grab him and beg him to put his tongue on her.

"Is that there are ways to get more cream as you go." He reached for the bowl in front of her, took a huge dollop of cream on his finger and then spread it into the middle of the cupcake he'd just licked. With his big, long finger. Slowly and with a little extra circle at the top.

Holy crap. Zoe felt her face flood with heat. He hadn't used any specifically dirty words. He hadn't even touched her. But that was the dirtiest thing anyone had ever said to her.

She was never going to be able to look at half a cupcake with cream filling without thinking about female body parts and sex. Great. That was going to make her job as a baker of cupcakes with cream filling a little difficult. Or at least uncomfortable.

"I'm going to be blushing every time someone wants cream-filled cupcakes forever now, aren't I?" she asked. "I'll be making chocolate cupcakes with green cream middles for Halloween and *still* thinking dirty thoughts."

He gave her a wicked grin. "Oh yeah." Then he licked the cream he'd just added out of the cupcake.

Zoe felt her inner muscles clench. Damn, he was good at that. Or seemed good at that. *Looked* good doing that. She'd love to know if he was as good as he appeared to be.

"And you're right," he said. "You do have the best cream in town."

She swallowed hard. "Wow."

"What?"

"I would have been even more pissed at Christmas if I'd known this about you."

"What about me?" He licked a chocolate crumb from his finger.

"How dirty you are. How good you seem to be with your tongue."

He put the cupcake down and came around the edge of the table to her side. Zoe had to force her feet to stay put. She wanted to bolt. Which was stupid. She *wanted* this. Him. His hands and mouth and tongue on her. She wanted him talking more. A lot more. Dirtier. But for a second there, she felt like she should run.

Everything was about to change.

She didn't like change. Change meant she might make a mistake.

Until now. She wasn't going to mess anything up here. She could *feel* it.

"*Not* showing you how good I am with my tongue and how dirty I can be was the hardest thing I've ever done in my life," he said. His voice and expression were dead serious. He lifted a hand and ran his thumb over her cheek. "I'm still not entirely sure how I managed it. I've been thinking about you nonstop since Christmas. I've been waiting to get back here every fucking day. I've never needed someone like this."

Zoe felt her breaths coming in fast little pants. She was staring at him but she couldn't make herself stop. The look in his eyes was too good, too delicious, to interrupt with even a quick blink. He looked, yes, hungry. Needy. A little pained. Like the past five months really had been difficult.

"I haven't been with anyone since that night," he said, his voice gruff, his thumb now dragging along her jaw, his fingers sliding into her hair. He tipped her head back. "There's no one else for me anymore, Zoe."

She pulled in a breath. He meant it. She could see it. Hear it in his voice. He had his shirt off and was touching her now, but they weren't really *doing* anything, and yet she felt like he was already making love to her.

Holy crap, this guy was good. She was so out of her league. In over her head. In way too deep.

And she loved it.

"Please let me cover you in cream and lick you like a cupcake," he said.

There it was. Dirty and sweet, teasing and serious, just like she wanted it, just like she knew Aiden would give it to her.

"If you don't, I can't be responsible for what I'll do to you with my rolling pin."

He gave her half a grin, but his fingers tightened in her hair and he tugged slightly. Her nipples tingled sent sparks to her clit and she gave a little gasp.

"I'm going to need you up on this worktable."

"We're going to have to really sanitize this thing after," she said, already bracing her hands on the edge, preparing to lift herself up.

"I'll buy you a whole new one if necessary." His big hands settled on her waist and he lifted her, practically tossing her onto the tabletop. "Maybe we need two. One for baking and one for sex."

She smiled. "We could go back to the house." There were, after all, four beds, two huge couches, a couple of tables, and several countertops there.

"I need to taste you here for the first time," he said without even considering her offer.

She and Aiden had history in a number of places. If they were going for some kind of nostalgic, meaningful moment, there were several choices, probably. Most importantly, they could have a redo of Christmas Eve in his bedroom at the house. Get it right this time.

But maybe—just maybe—they'd gotten it right last time. Not that she'd ever admit that to him, but he'd turned her down because it couldn't be just a quickie, just a practice run for her with other guys, just a one-night thing. And he'd known that. Even half asleep and totally ambushed.

That made her love him even more.

Aiden had done it right at Christmas.

Now, here in the bakery, this felt right too, and if he wanted to associate her and sex with cream filling and pink sugar and candy sprinkles and the smell of vanilla and cinnamon and buttercream, she wasn't going to argue. Because this was a part of her life. Would be a part of *their* life. They might move to another house. She'd get new lingerie. There would be many holidays. But this bakery would always be a part of their life.

He moved to stand in front of her and she parted her knees. He immediately moved between them. She took his face in her hands and looked into his eyes. She nodded. "Yeah."

His eyes heated, and he reached for the back of her neck where her dress tied. It was a halter style, so when he pulled the string, the bodice fell away, baring her breasts. Her breasts were small. Something she'd always hated. But her friends had assured her that not having to wear a bra unless she wanted to was the luckiest thing in the world.

At the moment, with Aiden's hot gaze on her, she felt pretty perfect.

"Damn, you're gorgeous." He lifted a hand and ran a thumb over her nipple.

She shuddered, her whole body reacting to the touch.

He leaned in and took her mouth in a deep kiss as he played with her nipple, making her wiggle on the table, the heat between her legs building. Her eyes were closed, and she was so lost in the feelings, she didn't notice him reaching for the other half cupcake that was just behind her. But she felt it.

She pulled back as she felt him pressing the cupcake to her other breast, the cream center over her nipple. She looked from it up to his face, but he was watching as he smeared white cream and chocolate cake over her breast.

Hot Cakes cream and cake, to be exact. She opened her mouth to protest. Probably. Though protesting anything about being half naked and having Aiden touching her seemed like a stupid idea.

Then he lowered his mouth to that breast, licking and sucking, and she didn't care about anything but his hot mouth and tongue doing *exactly* what they were doing. He was absolutely going to win this argument. She didn't care about that either.

"*Aiden.*" Her hand went to the back of his head. Just in case he thought about stopping. Ever.

But he did stop. Kind of. He switched sides anyway. That cupcake half was pretty smooshed, but that didn't slow him down. He swiped his finger through the bowl of cream she'd made. He painted it over her other nipple and then licked and sucked it clean.

She was officially needy and hot and wet and wriggling by the time he finally lifted his head. He took her mouth in a greedy kiss, and she put both of her hands on his head, fingers deep in his hair, holding him still. She arched closer, wanting to be against him, to rub and grind.

"God," he said, his voice almost pained as he spoke against her mouth. "I want you so damned much. You're so sweet. And we're just getting started."

"Started?" she asked, trying very hard not to pout. "I'm so ready, Aiden."

"Oh, but there's so much more."

"I can't take any more." She arched, rubbing her naked breasts against his chest.

"You can," he told her. Firmly.

"I'm *so* ready," she insisted, kissing him. She stroked her tongue along his, wrapping her legs around him, pressing against his hard fly.

He kissed her back. He gripped her hips, grinding into her. Then he pulled his mouth away. "So. Much. More."

"I'm almost there now," she said, definitely pouting now. "I swear I could come just like this."

He gave a little growl, that yes, pushed her even closer to that edge, and kissed her again. Deep, hot, hungry. But he pulled back *again*. "Then come. I'll get you there again."

"Oh God, Aiden," she half gasped, half groaned.

"Yeah, I'm going to be needing to hear a lot more of that."

Suddenly Zoe found herself tipped back onto the worktable and her skirt up around her waist.

"Pink panties. Thank you," he said. He ran his big hand, brazenly over her hip and around to her ass, then down to the back of her thigh. He lifted her knee toward her chest. The whole time he was studying her panties and everything they covered, and the stuff they didn't.

"Thank you?" she teased.

"Pink is your color, Zoe," he said sincerely.

She tried to respond, but he ran his finger under the edge of her panties and over her bare skin. The hottest, wettest bare skin on her body. Her breath rushed out of her lungs in a long breath.

"Grab the cream," he told her gruffly.

Blindly, she grabbed the bowl with one hand and the edge of the table with the other. Her eyes were squeezed shut as he stroked the pad of his finger back and forth over her slick center. She didn't even really know what she was doing. She just knew that as long as his finger stayed right there, she was happy to comply.

"Need some right here." He circled her clit.

She picked the bowl up and held it for him.

"Nope. You."

Her eyes flew open. One knee was nearly to her chest, the other leg hung off the edge of the table. Her dress was bunched at her waist. She was still wearing panties, but it did not matter considering where his finger was.

This was already the most shameless she'd ever been. Especially under fluorescent lighting. And she had a feeling this was truly just the start.

"Me?"

"Yep." His finger brushed over her clit again. "Right here. Let's get you nice and creamy."

She gave a little laugh that was partially amused, partially scandalized. Still she heard herself say, "I'm not good enough yet?"

Wow, where had that come from.

He gave a groan. "Jesus, Zoe." Then he bent his head, pulled her panties to one side, and took a long lick, right up the middle and over her clit.

She cried out, arching up off the table. That was the most incredible thing she'd ever felt.

"More."

Yeah, that was her voice too. She felt her cheeks heat. But she definitely didn't take it back.

He licked again and then gave her clit a little suck.

She felt the tightening of an orgasm, already. Wow.

Then he lifted his head.

Her eyes flew open again, and she lifted her head off the table. "Wha—"

"I almost forgot."

"Forgot? You didn't forget anything! You're doing great! It's *so* good."

He chuckled and reached past her head. "I almost forgot I'm supposed to be proving to you that you can love Hot Cakes."

Her head thunked back onto the table. "You did *not* just say those two words to me while I'm like *this* and you're doing *that* to me."

He grabbed the Strawberry Swirl, letting her panties slide back into place. That was *not* okay. Of course, she couldn't quite bring herself to move. Because spread out, half naked, on her worktable with Aiden Anderson half naked and really, really good with his fingers and tongue, she could stick around for a little longer and see what he had in mind she supposed.

His eyes were still hot and on her as he lifted the package to his teeth and tore it open. Okay, that was a little hot. And he couldn't have done that with one of her cupcakes.

Then he bit into the Strawberry Swirl. Whatever it was. It

wasn't really a cake. It wasn't a pie. It was a weird pastry thing with strawberry filling and a white icing swirl over the top.

His bite exposed the bright red filling—probably containing artificial coloring—and he dipped the tip of his finger into it. She remembered exactly what he'd said he was going to do with it. She probably shouldn't want that artificially colored and flavored stuff on her body, especially her most sensitive, private parts. But then he pulled her panties to the side again and ran his finger over her clit.

Yeah, she didn't mind. It was fine. Totally fine. Better than fine.

He lowered his head to suck the strawberry filling off, adding a lot of licking to it, and Zoe felt everything in her suddenly tighten, and then Aiden slipped a finger into her.

Just one. One finger. One slide. One little hook with the tip. Another suck.

And she was flying. Her orgasm crashed over her and she cried out.

"Fuck, yes," was all she heard from Aiden, before he was pulling her up and crushing his mouth to hers.

Dammit. He'd made her come with Hot Cakes strawberry filling.

But she kissed him back as if he was her favorite person on the entire planet.

Because he was. He *so* was.

She reached between them and pulled his zipper down, slipping her hand into his pants and wrapping her fingers around his cock.

His breath hissed out, and he pressed his forehead against hers. "Zoe."

"Now I need to prove how good my cream filling is."

He pulled back and ran a thumb over his bottom lip giving her a very sexy grin. "Oh, I know very well."

She'd been expecting that. She reached for the bowl of

cream and scooped out a dollop with two fingers. "You're telling me you *don't* want me to cover your cock in this and then lick it off?"

His grip on her hip tightened. "You have no idea how much I want that."

"Then back up."

He looked at her for a long moment as if weighing his options. Finally, he sucked in a breath. Then stepped back.

Zoe's heart skipped. She hadn't done this before. But wow, did she want to. She started to pull her dress back up but he shook his head.

"No way." He reached for her and slid her off the table. When she was on her feet, he pushed the dress to the floor to pool around her shoes.

She lifted a brow, and stepped out of it. Then she slipped her panties off too.

"You are... everything," he said.

Her heart turned over again. His words gave her the little push she needed to go to her knees and reach for his fly.

He helped her push his pants and boxers out of the way, and she took a moment to just drink in the sight of him. The first time she'd seen him naked. Fully aroused. All hard, hot man. Right. In. Front. Of. Her. Face.

She did the only thing she really could.

She reached out and touched him.

He groaned and Zoe looked up at him. He looked like he was in pain, but he was watching her intently, not making a single move to stop her. She stroked her hand up and down his length, watching his face.

His jaw tightened, and he didn't seem to be breathing.

She squeezed.

"Fuck, Zoe," he said softly. Gruffly.

The sound made all the happy sensations that had just been coursing through her with the orgasm come to life again.

Her nipples tightened, her belly got hot, and her inner muscles clenched.

She squeezed and stroked again and then leaned in to taste him. First without the cream. She wanted to know what *he* tasted like. Purely Aiden.

She licked up the length of his cock and then over the head.

"Christ." It was almost as if he were talking to himself.

He only moved a hand and that was to bring it to her head, tangling his fingers in her hair. Maybe he was going to help? Show her what to do? But he did nothing but rest it there, a hot weight against her scalp that sent tingles clear to her toes.

"Are you okay?" she asked, looking up at him.

He gave a bark of laughter. "I can honestly say that there is only one way I could be better than I am at this moment."

"What's that?" She wanted that. Whatever it was.

His gaze heated, and his fingers tightened in her hair. "If I was buried balls deep in your sweet pussy."

Zoe felt her mouth drop open. She was really going to have to get used to this side of the Aiden she knew. The Aiden she thought she knew. The Aiden she was discovering now. Then again, she loved the ripple of surprise followed immediately by the wave of heat.

"Oh," she said. Or almost said. It was so quiet she wasn't sure it counted as actually *saying*.

"How about you get back up on that table?" he asked, his gaze pinned on hers.

"Just a minute." She wiped the cream, that was starting to melt in her fingers, along his shaft, then leaned in, licking and sucking the way he'd done to her.

"Zoe." His voice was gravelly, his body tight, his fingers curling into her scalp.

He definitely wasn't pulling her away.

She looked up at him and then took the head of his cock between her lips. She really had no idea what she was doing.

She'd only read about this. But it seemed kind of common sense. When he'd been using his tongue and mouth all over *her* it had felt amazing. It stood to reason that the same would be true for him.

She licked him and then sucked him into her mouth.

"Fuck," he said tightly. Then he pushed forward. Just slightly. Slipping farther into her mouth.

That ignited a flame in her belly. She could just follow his lead. Do whatever made him sound like that again and again.

She sucked and drew him farther into her mouth, the hard, hot length of him sliding over her tongue. He was big, and she had to open farther to take him in. There was no way to take all of him, but he didn't seem to mind. He pulled back a little then eased in again. Slowly and easily.

She loved the sounds he was making, the feel of him taking pleasure from her like this.

"Fuck, Zoe. That's... so good. Too good." He pulled back, slipping out of her mouth.

She ran her tongue over her bottom lip. She tasted the cream but also Aiden. She wanted more.

He was staring at her, breathing fast. "You don't even know, do you?" He shook his head.

"Know what?" Had she done something wrong? Was she supposed to be doing something now?

"How fucking hot you are right now. What you're doing to me."

"Oh." She couldn't help the slow smile that lifted her lips. "What am I doing to you right now?"

He leaned over and grabbed her by the waist, lifting her and turning to set her on the edge of the table. "Making me lose my fucking mind," he growled, before kissing her. It wasn't a slow, romantic, sweet kiss. At. All. He *took* her mouth. It was all tongue and lips and even a little teeth. It was like everything he'd done between her legs.

She wrapped herself around him, arms around his neck, legs around his waist, pressing close, opening for him, returning his strokes, needing to be closer. They were both totally naked now. His cock was rubbing against her clit every time she pressed forward and she wanted *more*.

"Please, Aiden," she said against his mouth, running her hands up and down his back.

"I can get you off again. Tongue, fingers, whatever. We don't have to do... this," he said, his voice gruff.

"This?" She pulled back. "You mean sex?"

He gave her a lopsided grin. "Well, some people would consider all of this sex."

"What you're saying is that we don't have to have *actual* sex. Where you put your cock inside me?" she asked. That didn't sound sexy. Or romantic. But they really needed to be on the same page here.

His eyes were hot anyway. "That's what I'm saying. I don't have to be inside you tonight." He gave a little laugh that didn't sound at all amused. "I don't know what the fuck I'm saying. I've never wanted anything more. But this is a big deal. Your first time." For a second he paused, their eyes locked.

Finally, she realized he was reveling in that. She rolled her eyes. "Yes, Aiden. My first time. You will be my first." She leaned in, putting her lips against his ear and squeezing his ass. "Please be my first. Right here. Right now. In my bakery. With us both covered in cream—of all kinds."

He took a deep, shuddering breath and then reached up to cup her face in both hands. "I had to give you one more chance to back out. Because this *is* a big deal."

She nodded. Kind of. With him holding her she couldn't do much more than just stare back at him. "It is."

"Because I'm also going to be your last," he said, his voice thick with promise. And lust. And maybe something else. Like love.

A shiver went through her. Heat, need, and a sense of *oh, yes* that she realized in that moment was exactly what every woman should feel the first time—every time—she had sex. *Oh, yes, this is right. Oh, yes, this is the one. Oh, yes, this is what I want. Oh, yes, I have power here and I'm choosing this for me.*

"Oh, yes," she finally said. "I want this."

There was a beat of silence. Then he nodded, stepped back, reached for his pants, and pulled out a condom. His gaze was back on hers immediately as he ripped it open and rolled it on.

Wow. Even that was sexy. She hadn't thought much about condom donning and doffing. She knew it was important, and it would be something that needed to happen, but she hadn't really thought about who would do it, how it would look. She'd definitely never thought watching him do it could make her whole body get even hotter and tighter.

Aiden stepped back between her thighs, putting a hand on each knee and spreading her legs. He swept his gaze over her, then ran a finger over her clit and then down into her wetness. He slid a finger deep. "You ready?"

"I've *been* ready," she told him. "Since Christmas," she added.

He gave her a you're-such-a-brat look. "Okay, time for me to make up for that."

"Damn right it is."

16

Aiden cupped her ass and pulled her to the edge of the table. He kissed her. "Wrap your legs around me," he told her huskily.

She did. Her heart was pounding. She was very glad she was on a steady surface and that Aiden had a good hold of her. She *was* ready, but she wasn't positive what to expect, how this would feel. She had an inkling it might hurt.

He reached between them and took hold of his cock. He slid the head through her slickness, teasing her opening and rubbing over her clit. "We'll take it slow," he told her.

"Okay."

"Zoe."

"Yeah?"

"Open your eyes."

She hadn't realized she'd squeezed them shut. She opened them and looked at him.

"Watch," he told her, looking down.

Oh, God. Could she watch?

"It's hot," he told her. "I'm definitely going to watch as I ease into your sweet body for the first time. I can't wait to stretch you, nice and slow. Feel your pussy tight around me. Feel your muscles gripping me. Feel you come all over me."

His words made her melt, heating her up, and relaxing her. With her hands on his shoulders, she leaned back a little so she could see. He pressed forward, the head of his cock pushing into her. She felt a little stretch, a little pressure, and she felt her body responding, wanting to pull him deeper. She wanted this connection, wanted the fullness that seemed *right there*.

She put a hand behind her, bracing herself on the table and leaning even farther. He grinned. "Nice."

She looked up. "Yeah?"

His gaze swept over her face, her breasts, her belly, down to where they were joined. "Fuck yeah."

She leaned a little more. But not so far that she couldn't see. "More," she told him.

"Gladly." He pressed forward, sliding a few more inches inside.

She felt her body stretching, the fullness amazing, her nerve endings singing. "Oooh," she said softly. "Yes."

"Tell me if you're not okay," he said.

She looked up. His jaw was tight. "Are *you* okay?"

He laughed lightly. "Sugar, it's taking everything I've got not to thrust hard and pound into you. I want you so fucking much and you feel like heaven. You're every damned fantasy I've had."

"You've had *this* fantasy?" she asked. "Me and this work-table? Right here?"

"About a hundred times."

She liked that. A lot. A burst of confidence went through her and with it came the uncontrollable urge to tease. "Did it include going slow and gritting your teeth and holding back?" She wiggled her hips against him and felt him sink in another inch. Oh, that was nice.

He gritted his teeth harder. Then managed, "It most definitely did not."

"Then this isn't really a fantasy come true, is it?" she asked. She wiggled again. Another inch.

"Zoe," he said firmly. "You gotta let me take the lead here."

"Why? Because you've done this a million times? Because you're the expert? Because you're the big, strong man who's taken so many virgins?"

His teeth were grinding now. "Because I might hurt you."

"Oh, wouldn't you love that? For me to tell my friends how big and rough you were and how you did me so hard I could barely move after." She wiggled again, arching her back slightly.

He slid deeper, and she felt pleasure ripple through her.

"Dammit. Don't mess with me. I'm trying to be a good guy here," he said, frowning. "Considerate and sweet and gentle and shit."

She laughed, feeling a euphoria she hadn't expected to come from something other than an orgasm. She and Aiden were doing the most intimate thing imaginable—under very bright, hide-nothing lights, in a place where they would both be frequently, unable to forget—and they were still laughing and teasing and taunting each other.

It would never be like this with anyone else.

She tightened her muscles around him and he groaned.

"I'm not delicate, Aiden," she said. "I want you as much as you want me. If I'm a little sore tomorrow, then I'll just be thinking about you even more." She squeezed him again. "Every time I move just right or sit down or—"

Aiden suddenly gripped her hips and thrust, burying himself the rest of the way inside her.

Zoe gasped and for just a second thought she'd made a huge mistake. Emphasis on *huge*. That did hurt. That was a *really* tight fit. This was obviously very new.

But then he pulled back and thrust again. Then again.

Maybe the idea of making her think about him with every

step around the bakery tomorrow was what did it, but whatever it was, Zoe was pretty quickly thinking she was brilliant for teasing him. Because This. Was. Amazing.

He filled her up in a way her fingers, her favorite vibrator, nothing ever had or could. He was hot and hard and huge. The friction was unmatched, the angle was perfect, the... everything was unlike anything before. Especially the way he was watching her, still with jaw clenched, his eyes on hers.

"God. Aiden. I—" She tipped her head back and opened her legs even farther.

"Zoe," he bit out. "Dammit."

It was a good, dammit. Somehow she knew. She arched her back. Hot sparks shot through her body from where Aiden was buried, to deep down to her toes and up to her scalp.

"This is so good," she panted.

"Fuck yeah, it is."

She liked that. She knew *he* was no virgin, and she wanted this to be good for him too. She had no idea how to really make that happen, but she wanted it. She looked up at him. "Tell me what to do."

"Just fucking lie there, and look like a damned goddess, and let me worship you." His voice sounded different as if he was feeling a whole bunch of stuff that was all trying to come out at once.

She knew the feeling.

"Just lie here?" she teased. "Easiest gig ever."

He ran a hand from her belly up between her breasts to cup one. He plucked at the nipple as he thrust then circled his hips.

"Oh, God," she moaned.

"Yeah, just lie there," he said, his grin cocky.

Well, she'd let him be cocky with this. He was earning it.

He ran his hand back down and rubbed his thumb over her clit. She shuddered. "Oh, more of that."

"I love that you're vocal," he said. "But I could tell that was good."

He did it again, and she felt her muscles tighten around him.

"Yeah, milk me with that gorgeous pussy," he muttered as he worked her clit again.

As if she could help it. Her head fell back again. She was all his. She didn't have a ton of leverage here anyway, and she was quickly losing the ability to function beyond remembering to breathe. Even that was becoming secondary to chasing the orgasm that was tightening low and deep.

"I'm never going to get enough of you," he said.

"I hope not. I'm going to need a lot of this," she said, breathlessly.

He groaned. "I might have created a monster."

"Yeah, you did," she told him as he did some magical swirling thing over her clit while pumping deep.

"But you're *my* monster," he told her. He thrust again. "Only mine. All mine."

"Oh my God, yes." She couldn't imagine being like this with anyone else. Letting someone else see her, touch her, *taste* her the way Aiden had. "Only you."

That made him give a growl that shot straight through her and her muscles tightened. He picked up his pace, still circling her clit. She lifted her head as she felt everything begin to coil.

Their eyes locked.

"Let go for me, Zoe," he said roughly. "Let me feel it."

She couldn't have held it back if she tried. "Aiden!" she cried as the orgasm seemed to start in her toes and work its way up to where he was buried deep. She clenched around him, gripping his shoulder with one hand, trying to grip the tabletop with the other, but finding no purchase.

Which was no problem at all. Aiden was holding her so tightly she wasn't getting even an inch away from him. He clutched her hips, pulling her against him as he pumped deep and then came, shouting her name, pulsing inside her.

Add that to the list of never-befores. Feeling Aiden's climax, feeling him coming apart inside her was almost as good as feeling her own.

Almost.

Because her own orgasm with Aiden deep inside her was absolutely the best thing. Ever. Full stop.

"I can *not* believe I waited so long for that," she said, sitting up and throwing her arms around his neck giving him a big hug.

The change in positions, shifted him inside her and she felt ripples of pleasure even from that. She wiggled.

"Wow, could we go *again*?" she asked.

He laughed, the sound rumbling against her ear, and squeezed her ass. "Give me a little bit. But yeah. We're *going to* go again."

Her inner muscles responded to that with their own little, "yay!" He must have felt it because he groaned.

"Monster. Definitely created a monster."

She pulled back. "That was *so* good." She frowned. "You denied me *that* at Christmas? You are such a jerk!"

He shook his head. "That was unbelievably good. I can't believe I denied us both *that*."

"But—" She thought about that. "Are you saying it was only that good because it was us?"

"That's what I'm saying." The look in his eyes was softer now. Affectionate. Sweet.

She smiled. "Oh." Then she frowned. "You still have kept that from me for *five months!*" She slapped him lightly on the chest.

"Can you imagine having this and then having to wait five months to have it again?" he asked. He shook his head. "I wouldn't have survived. I had to wait until I was here and could give it to you over and over again."

He kissed her. It was deep and slow but sexy as hell.

"You knew it would be this good?" she asked when he lifted his head.

"I had a pretty strong inkling," he said, seeming totally sincere.

"How?"

He shrugged. "It's you. Even kissing you. Seeing you in that lingerie. It was stronger than anything else I'd ever felt."

That was a pretty good answer. "Maybe you would have been inspired to come back sooner. Maybe it wouldn't have taken five months."

He seemed to think about that for a second. He frowned slightly. "Maybe. This business opportunity just really... made sense now."

She lifted a brow. "I wouldn't have been enough to bring you back?" She was teasing. Mostly. But it did occur to her that it was a fair question. Sure, the guy needed to have a job. Well, he didn't *need* one like most people did. But he probably needed something to do. Still, he claimed he'd come back because he was ready to be *with* her. He'd made it sound like Christmas had started him thinking about them as a couple, and he'd decided he was ready for that to happen so had come back to Appleby for her.

"Come back and be your sex slave?" he asked as he pulled back. "That does sound like my kind of gig."

She watched him take care of the condom, even taking the bag out of the trash can by the back door and tie it up, presumably to take it out with them when they went to their cars.

She supposed she wouldn't want Josie to find that. Not that she didn't have *every* intention of telling Josie what had transpired here. After she reassured her she'd fully cleaned and sanitized everything. Which reminded her she needed to do that.

Zoe slid to the floor and grabbed her panties and dress, pulling them back on. Aiden started dressing as well. She took the bowl of cream filling to the sink, giving the Hot Cakes wrappers and leftover cakes a little frown.

Dammit. He *had* made her think more fondly of them. She'd see them in a gas station now and probably get a little hot and bothered.

"So what is this business thing you're working on?" she asked as she washed the bowl out and loaded it into their industrial dishwasher. That was definitely something they'd added over the years. Letty was still jealous of the thing. She had come down occasionally to do dishes, just so she could use it and be in awe.

"We're... acquiring a local company," he said.

Zoe looked over her shoulder. "Really? Local like Dubuque?"

He blew out a breath. "Actually, I've been meaning to talk to you about it."

She shut the water off and grabbed a towel, drying her hands and turning to face him. "Okay. I'd love to hear about it."

"The guys and I—" Just then his phone rang. He hesitated, clearly debating about answering it.

Zoe waved her hand. "Go ahead."

He was still watching her, a strange expression on his face, as he reached for where he'd evidently set his phone earlier on the counter near the ovens. He glanced at the number then frowned, lifting it to his ear. "Hey." He paused, listening. Then he looked surprised. "Now?" He glanced at Zoe again. "This is *not* a good time."

She smiled. "I'm okay."

She was. She was *so* okay.

"Hang on," he said into the phone. He lowered it. "What do you mean you're okay?"

"I mean, I'm spectacular. I've never been better. I feel so damned good I think I'm going to be able to float home."

He gave her a bemused grin. "Yeah?"

"Dude, I just had *sex* for the *first time*."

His grin grew. "I'm aware."

"And it blew my mind."

"Yeah?" he asked again.

"Definitely. I probably need a little recovery time. You know from all the big, hard thrusting and pounding and stuff."

His gaze heated but he did say, "Are you sore?"

"In such a very, very good way," she assured him.

He blew out a breath. "We need to talk about a few things."

"You know where to find me. If you need to go do something with this fabulous new company takeover or whatever you're doing, then go." She crossed the tile to where he stood, lowering her voice a little so the caller wouldn't happen to hear her. "If I go to bed before you get home, I'll go to bed naked. You know which door is mine."

His gaze heated. "Open invitation?"

"Oh yeah."

He lifted his hand to her face. "I'm crazy about you. I really need you to know that."

Her heart flipped in her chest, and she felt another of those surges of, *oh, yes*. She turned her head and kissed his palm. "I do. And same."

"Really?"

"Really. I'm all in. I know I gave you a hard time at first and I know I said this was too boring and cliché and all that but... you're the one, Aiden. I think you've probably been the one for a long time."

Emotions swirled through his eyes. Surprise, heat, affection, lust, and something else. Something that looked like concern. But that didn't make sense.

He lowered his head to kiss her before she could really study his face. The kiss was hot and sweet, longer than she'd expected. He lifted his head reluctantly.

"Okay, I'm going to go take care of this," he said. "But I'll see you later."

"For sure," she said. "We have a lot of laters, Aiden."

He gave her a smile that looked like he couldn't quite believe she was saying this stuff.

Well, he'd convinced her. What could she say? She could admit when she was wrong. And when she'd thought a relationship with Aiden would be predictable and boring, she'd been *very* wrong.

He kissed her again. "God, I don't want to go."

"Then hurry up so you can get back. Text me when you're on your way. I'll probably be at Jane's. Or Josie's."

"I didn't know you had plans with the girls. What if I was going to take you home and ravish you all night?"

"I didn't have plans. Until now."

"Now that I'm leaving you alone?"

"Now that you're leaving me alone and I have a huge story to tell them!" She laughed. "But even if I did have plans with them, I would have canceled. No problem. I would have sent them a message that said, 'Can't make it' and an eggplant emoji." She grinned. "They would have been fine with it."

He laughed. "That's all it would have taken?"

"Totally. I would have gotten high-five emojis back. Or maybe the one that looks like a noisemaker with confetti. Or maybe the honeypot emojis. You know what those mean, right?"

He nodded with a half grin. "I definitely do."

"Of course, after I tell them our story, we're going to start using the cupcake emoji."

He lifted a brow. "You're going to tell them our story?"

"That's why I'm going over there," she said. "I'm *definitely* telling them this story."

"*All* of it?"

"Well, the highlights. And that the cupcake emoji definitely needs to be added to the sex emojis." She grinned and couldn't help but hug him again. "It was so good, Aiden. Oh my God, I'm getting hot again just thinking about it."

He squeezed her ass. "Same."

"Good." She gave him another quick peck. She wanted to do so much more than that, but she stepped back. "Now I have some deep scrubbing to do on this table," she said with a grin. "Go."

He blew out a breath. "Okay." He lifted the phone back to his ear. "I'll meet you in twenty minutes."

Then he was gone.

Zoe had never grinned so much, or gotten so horny, cleaning up her kitchen.

She really hoped he'd hurry home.

———

He shouldn't have slept with her before he told her about Hot Cakes.

Aiden realized this insight was one, too late, and two, probably shouldn't have been a huge revelation actually. It seemed obvious now. After the fact. He should have definitely told her before taking her on her worktable. With Hot Cakes cupcakes. Definitely.

Dammit.

But he hadn't had a real *plan* for when to tell her. He hadn't had a specific plan for sleeping with her either. Not one that went beyond *I'm definitely going to do that*. Well, and okay, the cupcakes. Those had been part of the plan from the day he'd promised to make her love that cream filling.

But he should have told her he was now in charge—sort of —of the production of that cream filling. Before he'd smeared it on her breasts.

That did seem obvious. Now.

The last few days had been so damned nuts that both of those things—confessing his new business deal and finally making love to the woman he was falling more in love with every day—had simply been "Get to that ASAP" in his mind. They hadn't been really related.

Except now he could see that one should have definitely come before the other.

If just one damned thing with taking over Hot Cakes would have gone smoothly, then he might have gotten it right. If things had fallen into place the way he'd expected, he could have gone to her and said, "So there's this thing I've been working on" and told her everything, *before* getting the best blow job of his life.

"We should have a town hall."

Aiden looked up at Dax, refocusing on the conversation.

"I was nearly driven out of the building with pitchforks," Ollie reminded him. "So naturally, you want to call even *more* of our new employees together in one place and ask them how they feel about things?"

Ollie had gotten to town about an hour ago. He'd flown. Using the private jet they owned but rarely used. He'd then gone straight to the Hot Cakes factory. Because he could never just fucking chill.

Apparently, his arrival had not been met with a red carpet and champagne toast.

Now he, Dax, and Cam were all checked into the hotel in Dubuque, and the four of them were sitting around Dax's suite with Grant on Skype trying to figure out what to do next.

"Pitchforks?" Dax asked. "Come on. People found out the

new owner was in the building and they had some questions."
He shrugged. "Makes total sense to me. Besides, it was only the
business office people and one of the foremen, right?"

"Fore*woman*," Ollie corrected. "Though she's also the new
union leader, I guess. Gorgeous redhead. Riled up, gorgeous
redhead."

"That's the best kind of redhead," Dax said.

Ollie shook his head. "She had a ton of questions, and I
think she kind of hates me now."

"Why?" Aiden asked. It was Jane. It had to be Jane. She'd
gone in to talk to Ollie. Good for her. "What did you say?"

"That I didn't have any answers," Ollie said. "Which is true."

Aiden could understand why that would have frustrated
Jane. The employees were already worried about this change,
and to hear the new guys in charge didn't have a clue, wouldn't
make anyone feel better. "You should maybe let Whitney
handle this stuff for a little while," he said. "She's at least good
at PR."

"I'm good at PR," Ollie protested.

"Standing on a stage at Comic-Con and throwing t-shirts
out to the crowd isn't really *PR*," Aiden said.

"Public relations," Ollie said. "Our relationship with our
public is great."

"But we're talking about relationships with our *employees*,"
Aiden said. "That's different. They want us to be serious. And
knowledgeable. And reasonable."

"Maybe we should make t-shirts and take them to our next
employee meeting," Dax said. Aiden shot him a look. He put
his hands up. "Just kidding."

He had maybe been *half* kidding.

"They want benefits and time off and fair overtime pay,"
Aiden said. "Not t-shirts and cappuccino machines in the break
room." Yes, Dax had suggested that as well. "These aren't kids
blowing off steam by chopping troll heads off and earning

purple diamonds. These are real people with real issues that they're counting on us to solve."

What had he gotten into? Aiden wondered for the forty-seventh time over the past two days. What the hell was he doing buying and trying to run Hot Cakes?

"By the way, we're promoting Whitney," he said firmly. "To VP."

"She's already a VP. What's she going to be VP of, now?" Cam asked.

"Everything," Aiden told him with a scowl. "VP of Every.-Fucking.Thing. We need her. She's the only one with a clue about how that place runs."

"Yeah, sounds like her family did a hell of a job," Cam said dryly.

"She wants to do things different. She's on board with what Ollie and I have discussed with her."

"You've met Whitney?" Cam asked Ollie. Then looked like he regretted letting that slip.

Ollie nodded, giving Cam a grin. "Now I see why you date the girls you do."

Dax looked from Ollie to Cam and back. "What's that mean? From what I can tell, Whitney is nothing like the girls Cam dates."

"Exactly," Ollie said. "You like them a little more... submissive now, don't you, Cam?"

"Fuck off, Ollie."

Which was *you've got me all figured out* in Cam language.

This was getting so complicated. Aiden scrubbed a hand over his face. He'd just given Jane a pep talk and advice about confronting her new bosses. Including *him*. She'd told him about Heather, who had the perfect work hours to allow her to pursue her paralegal degree. She'd told him about Albert, who was seventy and had a bad knee but still had to work to afford to support his wife and their developmentally disabled adult son who lived with them. She'd told him about Mathias, whose wife was a nurse who picked up all holiday shifts so she could get extra holiday pay. That meant Mathias needed to be off on those holidays to take care of their two kids.

None of them *loved* Hot Cakes, but they had worked out their schedules and the jobs they could each do so they could be there for their families and work on improving their lives.

Apparently, Whitney had been the go-between for the workers and management so her father was never aware there were jobs Albert couldn't do because of his knee or that Mathias and three other men often traded shifts without formally being approved.

They were all worried about the idea of changes. They were all in precarious positions, balancing their work and their lives, and fearful their new bosses wouldn't be as understanding and flexible.

Aiden rubbed the center of his forehead where a headache was definitely brewing. He'd left the guys alone for a few hours, and already things were more complicated than they had been that afternoon.

"Full steam ahead," Cam said. "There's no reason to mess around. Let's just do this. Let's get in there and do things and not talk it to death."

Full steam ahead should be fine. There was no reason to be taking this easy or rolling this out slowly. Hot Cakes needed overhauling. They all needed something to do, and hell, Aiden was all in. He was madly in love with Zoe and was moving his life back to Appleby. Might as well jump into his new business venture with both feet.

Too bad he hadn't told her about it *before* he'd fucked her on her worktable, had the most amazing sex of his life, and basically convinced her she was in love with him and ready to say *I do*. He hadn't proposed, but she'd said she was all in. She'd said he was the one.

Fuck, she thought he was the one.

He knew *she* was the one, and he wanted to be the one for her.

But the one didn't go behind her back to rejuvenate the company she thought was standing in her way of being more successful.

Even if it wasn't true.

"Fuck." He pushed himself up from the chair in Dax's suite and paced to the sliding door that led to the balcony.

"We *have to* talk about it," Dax said.

"We do," Ollie agreed. "I wasn't ready for that today. That's on me. But these people are worried."

"Of course they're worried," Aiden said. "They've never worked for anyone else. Whether they love or hate the Lancasters, that's who they know and who they're used to. I doubt anything in that factory has changed in ten years. The employees may not like it, but at least they know what to expect. People, by nature, don't like change. If they've had a hard time getting management to listen to them, then they're not going to trust us when we say not to worry and that it's all going to be all right."

"Then you think a town hall is the right thing to do?" Ollie asked.

Damn. A town hall. Inviting everyone who wanted to come to see them. Meet them. Talk to them. Pummel them with questions.

"We have to be open with them." This came from Grant. "They're not going to trust us if we keep things hidden or make it all a big secret."

Aiden winced. Exactly. Hiding things and keeping secrets was a really bad idea.

"Then we just go in and prove it will be different. We make the changes and *show* them it's better," Cam said. "They'll balk at the start, but once it's all in place, they'll see it's fine."

"What if they quit? Or picket or something?" Dax asked.

"They're not going to quit," Cam said. "Where would they go? There aren't that many jobs around here. They'll stay. They'll bitch, but they'll stay."

"You really think bulldozing them is the way to go?" Ollie asked. "Wouldn't it be better to talk and listen and negotiate? Long term, that will build trust. We ask what they want. We tell them what we can do—and we're honest about what we can't— and then we deliver. That will build trust. And loyalty."

"It will also take forever," Cam said. "People can adjust. The faster we get it done, the sooner they'll see it's better, and the sooner the complaining will stop."

"That will be cheaper too," Grant said. "Drawing it out, doing focus groups and town halls and whatever will take time and money. If you just go in, implement things, and hang on for a few months, it will be more efficient."

Aiden took a second to appreciate how even this meeting highlighted how each of his partners was different and how their varying perspectives worked to make the bigger picture more complete.

Ollie shook his head. "This is a small town. This is Iowa. Honesty and integrity are really important if we want to get anywhere. If we want to be here long term—and I assume that's our goal here—then we need to do this well."

Yeah, yeah. Okay, Aiden thought. He got it. Honesty and integrity mattered for long-term relationship building. Aiden looked skyward. If the universe or God or whatever was trying to drive home that point, *it*-slash-*He* was doing a great job.

"Fine." Cam shrugged again. "I think it's going to be a bigger pain in the ass that way, but whatever."

"And you're going to come back to Chicago with me and Grant and observe all this from afar, right?" Dax asked, eyebrows up. "You sure? Because you sure seemed interested in the reports and articles you were reading earlier."

"Only to the extent that I want to see the Lancaster empire taken completely apart and everyone saying what we're doing is four million percent better than anything they ever did," Cam said. Without a single ounce of humor.

"Four million percent?" Grant echoed, though his tone was dry. "In year one or by year five, or what are we talking here?"

"The sooner the better," Cam said, again without even a curl to his lip.

Ollie gave Aiden a wide-eyed look. Yeah, it was really better that Cam stay in Chicago as they took over Hot Cakes from the Lancasters. And worked with their new VP of Everything, Whitney Lancaster.

Grant sighed from the computer screen. "Which means, as usual, I'm the only one considering cost? Because it sounds like, as long as whatever you do is four million times better, Cam isn't going to blink at spending money."

"Oh, we're spending money," Cam said. "Benefits, gutting the plant, new technology, fucking new name tags, if needed. Whatever it takes to make Hot Cakes bigger and better and *the* best place anyone has ever worked and the product the best fucking thing anyone has ever eaten."

Everyone seemed taken aback by how adamant he suddenly was.

He looked around. "Reading everything over the last few days shows me there are a *ton* of improvements that can be made. There are a lot of holes. Things they've half-assed. Because they were the only game in town. In the area really. But they haven't expanded their products in years. They haven't gone after any new markets. They haven't done any upgrades in almost a decade. There's a lot of potential."

"And you want to make these improvements because..." Ollie prompted.

"Because I want everyone to know that the second a McCaffery got involved, things got better. That a McCaffery will do things the Lancasters never did. That a McCaffery is the one who gives a shit."

Ollie nodded. "Got it. But *we're* the ones who are going to be here dealing with it all in person while you're in Chicago?"

Cam shrugged. "I might hang out in Appleby more than I thought."

Oh. Shit.

Aiden stared at his friend. "Really?"

"If we're having a town hall and having the entire town show up to see what we've got planned and who's involved, I'm going to be there," Cam said.

Aiden blew out a breath. He needed to talk to Zoe. She had to hear this from him. Before there was a fucking town hall.

"I need twenty-four hours." God, he was going to need more than that, he had a feeling. "No announcements of any kind for at least that long," he told his partners.

"Whitney thought Thursday next week would be good," Ollie said. "And she thought having it at the plant would be perfect. Plenty of room. She said we can bring in chairs and refreshments. We open it up to everyone, even people who don't work there. They meet us. We present our plan. We take questions. Then everyone is talking about it over the weekend."

"You want them talking about it?" Grant asked.

"Of course. Because we're going to wow them," Ollie said, clearly fully on board.

Aiden's stomach was in a knot. He cast a glance at Camden. This was it. Soon everyone would know. They'd see them as heroes. Or villains. Depending on who was looking at the situation.

"You worried about your family's reaction?" he asked.

"Sure," Cam said. "They're totally stubborn and unreasonable. But we're in too deep now."

"You don't believe Hot Cakes is a competitor of Buttered Up, do you?" Aiden asked.

"No."

"You think you can convince your mom and sister of that?"

Cam snorted. "No."

Aiden sighed.

"But hey, now that you're sleeping with Zoe, they can't stay pissed at us forever, right?"

Fuck. He hoped that was true.

But that sounded horrible. That wasn't why he'd slept with her.

Was it? The knot tightened further. It wasn't. Of course. He'd wanted her long before he'd thought about taking on Hot Cakes. He'd decided to buy Hot Cakes because it was a way for him to come home and be with her. *She* was the reason he was home. Hot Cakes was secondary to that.

But he'd definitely slept with her *before* confessing about the business. That could have easily been his subconscious trying to hedge his bets.

Dammit.

He had to tell her. Tonight. Right now.

"You better sit down," Grant told Aiden. "We need to hash out this town hall."

Well... shit.

This was going to be bad.

17

"I can't believe you never told me sex was *that* good," Zoe said. For the fifth time.

Jane laughed and leaned over to fill Zoe's wineglass again.

They met at Maggie's for dinner at least once a week, but it was nice to hang out at Jane's and Josie's sometimes instead because they could drink without Mom's looks. And they could talk about sex.

"I really feel like we were quite honest about sex being good," Jane said, setting the bottle on the coffee table.

Josie was in the armchair and had her feet tucked up under her butt. She nodded. "We really were. Though in my defense, I haven't had *that* much, and I don't think I've ever had sex I couldn't shut up about." She grinned at Zoe. "But I'm very happy for you."

Jane nodded. "I haven't had like a million experiences, and none were *this* gushworthy, but yeah, it's pretty great. I can't believe you waited this long."

Zoe gave what was surely a swoony sigh. She wasn't sure she'd ever been swoony before. She was pretty sure she'd never swoony-sighed. But that's how it felt when she thought of Aiden. "Well, it was *so* good."

"Yeah, yeah, cupcakes and cream filling and all that," Jane said taking a swig of wine. "I'm totally jealous."

"And now you're getting married or what?" Josie asked. "I mean... it's Aiden, so you are, right?"

Zoe felt her stomach flip. "Yeah. I guess we probably are." That didn't feel as weird to say out loud as it maybe should have.

Josie laughed. "That's great. He's an amazing guy."

"He's got some business thing going, and he's definitely moving back. He's been pretty clear about that. And I told him I'm all in. That he's the one." Zoe sat back in her chair feeling warm and happy. "My mom knows and is thrilled. My dad surely knows by now too and I'm sure he's happy. Everything is perfect." She thought about that then gave a little laugh. "Wow. I mean this has all happened so fast, but it feels so good."

"It hasn't been all that fast," Josie said. "You've known him forever. You're a friends-to-lovers story. Those are the best." She gave a swoony sigh too. "I love romances like this."

Jane snorted. Josie was definitely the romantic of the three of them.

"What? You don't think friends becoming lovers and then falling in love is romantic?" Josie asked.

"It is," Jane said. "It makes total sense, actually. I'm just thinking of the guys I've known my whole life and... well, I've kissed a few of them but can't imagine spending the *rest* of my life with any of them."

"Well, a handsome stranger coming to town and sweeping you off your feet is a possibility too," Josie said with a grin.

Jane frowned.

"What?" Zoe asked.

"There are strangers coming to town all right. And two of our new bosses were in today."

Zoe leaned in. "Really? They've already come to town?"

"Yep. I was on my way home after talking to Aiden, but I got a call from Danny. He said I needed to get my ass back down there. The new guy was in the office. Just waltzed in like he was big shit." She was frowning. "He was, of course, meeting with Whitney. God knows what she's going to tell him. If they keep running things as they have been, it's really going to suck."

"But what if they change a bunch of stuff and that sucks worse?" Josie asked.

Jane nodded. "I have a ton of really worried people."

"Is this the guy who agreed to meet with you?" Zoe asked.

"I don't think so. He didn't seem to recognize my name." Jane grimaced. "I'm not sure I made a very good first impression though. Instead of waiting for that meeting, I stomped in there today. I was riled up after meeting with Aiden."

"Oh... no," Zoe said.

"No." Jane shook her head. "Aiden gave me the confidence to go in there. That was good. I just might have gotten a little loud."

"How did the new guy respond? Are you in trouble now?"

"No." Jane chewed on her bottom lip for a second then said, "He seemed surprised. Which makes me nervous. He didn't seem to know there were any problems."

"Well, the Lancasters probably wouldn't admit that, right?" Josie asked. "They're not going to tell the new buyers they're inheriting a bunch of trouble."

"It's more that the Lancasters didn't care there were problems," Jane said.

Zoe frowned. She hated seeing her friend worried like this.

On one level she'd definitely hoped that Hot Cakes would bite the dust. But she knew that was selfish. Aiden had made her face that. He'd seemed almost frustrated with her when she'd refused to admit they weren't her competition.

But they were. She'd been taught that from birth.

So why did Aiden have her doubting things?

They made different products. Their products were for different purposes.

Hot Cakes might have started with Letty's recipe but even the Butter Sticks, their original cake, was different now than when Didi had started out. Nothing else they made even came close to resembling Zoe's cakes and pies and cookies.

If the new owners made Hot Cakes a miserable place to work—or an amazing place to work, for that matter—how did that affect Zoe and Buttered Up?

Not at all.

Except for her friend being unhappy.

That bothered her far more than thinking about the money the Lancasters had made over the years or Didi stealing Letty's recipe. Yes, that had been a betrayal of their friendship. But it was *her* friendship with Jane that was Zoe's concern now.

She wanted her friend happy and fulfilled. She didn't want Jane stressed and worried. She didn't want Jane driving to another city for work. She didn't want Jane losing sleep. She also loved seeing Jane getting a little feisty and more involved. Jane tried hard to keep work just work. She really did just want to go, do her job, and go home. There was nothing wrong with that. Zoe supported it fully, if that was how Jane would really be happy. But Zoe suspected having a bigger mission at work, something more to do when she was there than—as Jane put it —push buttons and pull levers, would make her even happier.

Zoe's phone dinged with a text just then.

Very distracted by all her thoughts, she glanced down. It was Aiden.

I'm going to be late again. I'm so sorry.

As much as she wanted to see him, she didn't mind. She knew she couldn't leave Jane right now.

It's okay, she sent back. *Jane needs more jar pie and wine anyway.*

I'm glad you're able to provide for her. See you later.

She sent him a heart emoji in return. Then she sat back, feeling strangely satisfied. She was happy to think it was *her* strawberry pie that made Jane feel better. Jane claimed it was even better in the jar. Zoe wasn't so sure about that, but Jane wasn't eating Strawberry Swirls from Hot Cakes, was she?

But Zoe knew it was her and Josie, just being there for her, that was actually helping. And that mattered even more than baking the perfect cake or pie.

Maybe Letty and Didi had screwed up. Didi shouldn't have stolen from Letty, but maybe Letty should have talked it out. Listened. Realized that a true friend was more important than butter and sugar.

Zoe couldn't really judge all that, but she did know that if Jane wanted and needed Hot Cakes to be okay, then Zoe wanted Hot Cakes to be okay.

———

"I, um, wanted to tell you I've heard everything you've said about Hot Cakes not being my competition and... I agree."

Zoe continued to cut heart shapes out of the rolled-out cookie dough, but she knew Aiden heard her.

It was him, Phil, and George in the shop. Aiden hadn't gotten home until late again last night, but Zoe was sound asleep by then anyway. She'd had more wine than she probably should have, and she'd been up talking to Jane and Josie until nearly eleven. But it had been worth it. Jane had decided she didn't regret stomping into the office to talk to the new boss and that it was a good thing he saw her as feisty and willing to stand up for herself and the other employees.

Of course, this morning, a little hungover, very tired, and pre-lemon-scone-sugar-rush, Jane had been less optimistic that being feisty was the right move. Zoe and Josie had given her a pep talk and a couple of extra scones to share with her new boss. They'd lifted the ban on employees buying from Buttered Up, so she didn't even have to put Jane's breakfast in a plain paper bag today. That had been nice.

"You agree?"

She lifted her head to find Aiden watching her from his usual seat by the window.

"I do. We offer very different products, and what they do with their business doesn't really affect mine either way."

He was up out of his chair and around the counter in a second. "I'm so happy to hear you say that." He moved in close but didn't touch her.

She looked up at him. "Yeah. Well, I realized I do want Hot Cakes to succeed. Jane needs it to."

"So do a lot of other people," he said.

"Yeah. I know." She went back to pressing the cookie cutter into the dough. "I hated you thinking I didn't care about that. I've just been so conditioned to think of Hot Cakes as synonymous with the Lancasters that I don't really think about the other regular people working there. What happened with Didi and Letty wasn't their fault at all."

"It wasn't really Whitney's either," Aiden said.

Zoe looked up with a frown. "Now you want me to be best friends with Whitney?"

He shrugged. "Not best friends. Maybe just not adversaries?"

"Why do you care about that?" she asked. "Have you forgotten what she did to my brother?"

Aiden gave a short laugh. "As if I could."

"It's okay for me to not like her for that, isn't it?" Zoe lifted the cookies onto a baking sheet with a spatula.

"You have a lot in common, you know," he said.

Zoe looked up again. "What do you mean?"

"She's just trying to keep her family legacy alive too."

Zoe opened her mouth but then shut it and swallowed. Okay, he had a point. Another point. Dammit. Finally, she gave a little nod. "I'll keep that in mind." She picked up the huge cookie sheet and turned toward the kitchen.

"Thank you." His smile was wide and bright. "I'm so glad you've given this some thought, Zoe. That means a lot to me."

She cocked her head. That was a strange thing to say. "It means a lot to you? Why?"

He seemed to realize what he'd said. His grin died. "There's something I need to talk to you about."

She set the cookie sheet back down. She didn't like the way he'd said that. "Okay." She felt nervous suddenly.

The bell over the front door jingled, interrupting them. She sighed and looked over.

It was Jane. Again. And she wasn't alone. She had a Hispanic woman by the hand, clearly pulling the woman through the door behind her.

"Jane?" Zoe asked. "Are you okay?"

She didn't look okay. She looked worried. Again.

"Aiden, I need to talk to you," Jane said, barely giving Zoe a glance.

Aiden started around the counter, frowning. "Of course. What's wrong?"

George and Phil even put their papers down.

"This is Maria," Jane said, putting her arm around the other woman's shoulders. "We work together."

"Hi, Maria," Aiden said, offering his hand.

The woman took it tentatively.

Zoe wiped her hands on a towel and moved closer, still behind the counter, but near where they were standing just inside the door.

"How can I help?" Aiden asked.

Zoe felt warmth spread through her chest. He would help

anyone who came to him. She hoped Maria felt as comforted by his confident presence as Zoe did.

"Maria's daughter was taken to Dubuque to the hospital last night," Jane said when Maria looked at her. "They think she has meningitis."

"I'm so sorry," Aiden said. "But I don't understand how I can help with that."

"She came into work this morning even though her four-teen-year-old is *in the hospital* with a serious condition," Jane said. "Because she's out of sick and personal days, and she can't afford to be docked pay or possibly even fired."

Aiden shook his head. "Oh, hell, you should absolutely go, Maria. Your daughter should be your only focus here."

"I told her she should just go and worry about the conse-quences later, but"—Jane looked at Maria again and gave her a little one-armed hug—"she doesn't feel like she can, and I totally understand that. I'm a little more able to say that since I don't have any direct dependents. I can't really get fired either, but it's a much bigger problem for Maria."

Aiden took a deep breath. "You need to go be with your daughter. You should never have to put work above your family."

"I can't lose my job," Maria said. "My husband's paycheck isn't enough. We have three kids. My older daughter is with my little one."

Jane nodded at Aiden. "Her oldest daughter is a junior in high school. She's missing school today to be with her sister because her mom can't be." Jane sighed. "Please tell us how to handle this. Do you know if there are employment laws or anything that could protect her job in this situation? I know I need to learn this stuff, but I thought coming to you would be faster than looking it up."

Aiden didn't say anything for a long moment. Then he said,

"I'm not sure, but I'll make a couple of calls. *But*—" he said firmly, looking at Maria. "I can assure you that your job will be there tomorrow, or next week, or next month. Whenever you come back, when your daughter is healthy again. Don't worry about that at all. In fact..." He turned on his heel and headed back to the table where his computer and phone were still sitting.

"Aiden, what are you talking about?" Jane asked.

"Just a second." He rummaged in his computer bag and pulled out what looked like a checkbook. He bent over it, scribbling, then tore the top check off and brought it back to Maria. He handed it to her. "This should get you a couple of hotel rooms close to the hospital. If you need more, please let me know."

Jane and Maria looked at the check then at each other.

"Oh, we can stay at the hospital. And they have a Ronald McDonald House," Maria protested, handing the check back.

Aiden held his hands up, refusing to take it back. "Leave those rooms for people who can't afford the hotel."

Maria started to cry. Jane looked up at Aiden, her eyes wide. "Aiden, I didn't mean for you to do that. We just need some coaching."

He let out a long breath. "No, you don't. All you should have to say is, 'I need time off because my daughter is sick,'" he told them.

"Well, sure, that would be ideal, but that would require bosses that felt the way you do," Jane said.

Aiden nodded. "Good thing you have that now."

Jane lifted both eyebrows. "You think the new guys feel that way? How do you know?"

"Because I'm one of them."

18

There was total silence in the bakery. Total. For several long seconds.

Then George set his coffee cup down on the table with a small *clack*. And Phil said, "About time you told them."

Aiden glanced over. "You knew?"

"We've been here every day listening to you on the phone. We figured it out." Phil looked at George. George nodded his agreement.

Aiden pushed a hand through his hair. Well, okay, so Phil and George had known. But he was certain no one else had.

Until now.

"Wait, *what*?" Jane demanded.

Aiden nodded. "I'm one of the new owners of Hot Cakes. Me and my partners from Chicago. The guy you met is Oliver. There's also Dax, Grant, and"—he took a deep breath—

"Cam."

"But..." Jane shook her head, frowning. "All the time you spent telling me how to talk to my new bosses..." She blinked several times. "*You* were one of them?"

"Yeah."

"You were telling me how to talk to *you* about all this?"

"Yes."

Jane opened her mouth. Then she looked at Maria. The other woman had tears tracking down her cheeks, and she was clutching the check to her chest like he'd just given her everything she'd ever dreamed of.

People shouldn't feel that way. People shouldn't be so desperate that a one thousand dollar check made them look so amazed and grateful. Dammit. He was happy to give the money. Even if he hadn't been Maria's boss, he would have written her that check. But the idea that this woman now worked for him and had been terrified of asking for time off even though her daughter was sick made his gut clench. Yes, of course people needed to be at the factory on a regular basis to make the Hot Cakes products. That's how it worked. People ran the factory. But *that* was the part that got to him. *People* ran the factory. And there were more important things in their lives, bigger things that would happen, things that made their lives worthwhile, that had nothing to do with the factory.

"When were you going to tell us?" Jane finally asked softly, looking back to him.

He swallowed. "Soon. I've been wanting to tell you all for a while. From the start. But..." He didn't want to look at Zoe. She was going to be so angry and hurt. But she'd told him, just a few minutes ago, that she understood Hot Cakes was not her competitor and that she wanted it to succeed. Maybe she would see what he was doing as a good thing. Maybe she'd be fine...

The sound of metal pans crashing together and then hitting the hard tile floor of the kitchen told him she was no longer at the bakery counter. And that she was *not* just fine.

Jane grimaced. "Right. She wouldn't have taken it well."

"No. And..." He was finally going to admit it out loud. "This is one game that isn't going according to the playbook. At all."

"No TD on your first long pass of the game this time, huh?" Jane asked.

"Not even close."

"Well, just be sure you've got your nut cup on when you walk into that kitchen."

Zoe's best friend didn't seem all that sympathetic really.

Aiden sighed. "You want to coach *me* on this one?"

Jane shook her head. "Not sure how. I think just... apologize?"

"I'm not sorry for buying the factory and keeping it open." He really wasn't.

In spite of the challenges he hadn't expected and the stress of the last few days, he felt good about what he was doing. Hot Cakes needed him. He was going to do right by these people, and it was going to be damned fulfilling. Even if he didn't make a lot of money and people were suspicious for a while, he wasn't sorry about taking over Hot Cakes over. He needed to help Zoe see that.

"Maybe don't lead with that," Jane said dryly. "Hear her out. Tell her you love her." She shrugged. "Tell her that *I*, for one, am happy it's you." She paused. "Though you could have told us."

"I needed to have a handle on things. I needed to know what I was doing first."

"You needed to be sure it was going to be a win."

He frowned. "What's that mean?"

"It means that you're very good at being a hero, and you aren't very good at not being good at things. You and Zoe have that in common."

"Well, that's—" He thought about it. Then sighed. "True."

Jane grinned. "You're a good guy, Aiden. But you need to figure out that people will give you points for *wanting* to do the right thing and for trying even if you don't get into the end zone every single time."

He nodded. "Thanks. I'll try to remember that."

"Now, go make up with Zoe."

His heart squeezed. Dammit. This was not how he'd wanted her to find out. He had *not* wanted to hurt her. This had all gone so crazy so fast. He'd been about to tell her just before Jane and Maria had walked in. Hell, he'd been about to tell her a dozen times since he'd come home. But he just hadn't made the words come out of his mouth.

That was on him.

He hadn't told her because of the touchdown-big-hero thing. Jane and Josie were both right.

"Thanks." He focused on Maria. "Go to your daughter. And please keep Jane updated, so she can let us know how things are going."

Suddenly the woman threw herself at Aiden, squeezing him tightly around the waist. "Thank you so much."

It took Aiden a second to recover, but he put his arms around Maria and hugged her back.

This was important. This was big. This was what his mom would have wanted him to do.

Zoe needed to be okay with this. He really needed her to be okay with this.

But he was going to have to go into that kitchen and talk to her about it.

He really didn't want to go into that kitchen.

Maria released him, smiling up at him like he was her best friend.

His chest tight, Aiden watched Maria and Jane until the bell jingled over the door as it shut behind them.

Now... the kitchen.

He stopped outside the swinging door. "Zoe! I'm coming in!"

He wasn't sure that giving her a chance to pick up a sharp

utensil was a great idea, but he didn't think surprising her was a good call either.

"Um... hey." Josie peeked out the door.

"How bad is it in there?"

"Hope you still have good athletic reflexes."

"What?"

Josie didn't answer. She slid past him and headed toward the register, presumably to watch the front while he and Zoe did... whatever they were going to do.

Fuck. He shoved his hand through his hair and then pushed the door open. He didn't see her at first.

"Zoe?"

She didn't answer, so he stepped the rest of the way into the kitchen.

He ducked as a cake ball came whizzing past his ear.

She was standing at the worktable, a tray of cake balls in front of her.

"Zoe."

He wasn't as quick the second time. The cake ball hit him right in the chest.

He let the door swing shut behind him. "Come on. Let's talk."

"Talk? *Now* you want to talk? Tell me all about Hot Cakes and everything?"

"Yes."

The next cake ball hit him in the cheek. He sighed.

"You could have been talking to me about this for *days*! Am I the last person to know about you and Hot Cakes?" she demanded.

"No. Hardly anyone knows," he said. "We've kept it quiet."

"Why?"

She was glowering at him, a cake ball smashed in her hand.

"Because..." He hadn't wanted the McCafferys to find out.

Shit. That was going to sound bad.

"Why, Aiden?"

Something in her tone told him she already knew.

"I wanted to have a chance to break the news to you and your family myself."

"And when were you planning to do that?" she demanded. "You've had plenty of opportunities."

"Right after I told you I was in love with you."

That seemed to catch her off guard for a second. She blinked then frowned. But she shook her head. "That's a *terrible* answer."

"*Seriously?*" he asked. "You don't think it was important that I lead with the main reason I was back in town *before* telling you I'd bought Hot Cakes—the thing you hate most in the world?"

"Yes! God!" She threw the mashed cake ball at him.

He dodged this one. Aiden stared at her. "I should have come back to town, said 'I'm buying Hot Cakes, but don't worry I love you'? *That* would have been better?"

"Yes!"

"You would have been pissed! You never would have listened to me tell you that I loved you and want to be with you and was back *for you!*"

"You should have kept trying, then! You should have *worked* to *make* me listen. To convince me. You could have put as much work into that as you did into convincing me over the past few days that *Hot Cakes* was important. You have been doing an *amazing* job convincing me that I needed to look at Hot Cakes differently and open my mind to that and give it a chance. You should have been willing to do that for us. For us being together."

"I *did* do that," he insisted, taking a step forward. "You gave me a hard time the minute I walked in here."

"I fought you on it for what? Thirty minutes? Isn't that about how long it took you to get me up against the fridge?" she asked. "You had to do a little talking and flirting and kissing, but you didn't have to fight. Because there wasn't *really* an obstacle. And you know why that was? Because you didn't *tell me* about the one thing that would have made me really shut you down. You didn't have to try to convince me that this"—she wagged a finger back and forth between them, clearly indicating "this" was their relationship—"was more important than my grudge against Hot Cakes. You would have had to work for it, yes, but you should have been willing to do that."

He took another step forward. She was within reach now, but he didn't try to touch her.

Her arms were crossed, and she didn't reach for him either.

"I'm so sorry. I know you're angry," he said.

She shook her head. "I'm not angry, Aiden. I... feel like a fool."

He flashed back to the first night he'd been in town, expecting her to be mad about Christmas Eve only to find out she'd been embarrassed about that night instead.

His gut tightened. He fucking hated that he kept doing this to her. And he didn't even realize it. "Why would you feel like a fool?"

She took a deep breath. "Because I didn't just have sex. I had sex with cream filling on the worktable where I learned to make *cookies* with my *grandmother*. Because—" Suddenly she pivoted and stomped to a cupboard. She threw the door open. "Because of this."

The shelves inside the cupboard were completely full. Of mason jars.

"I ordered five hundred of them," she said, slamming the door shut again. "Before I'd even made one cupcake or pie in one. Because... of *you*. Because, even though I fought it, you got into my head. And my heart. And I knew, deep down, that you would help me figure out a way to do this. Or you'd help me fix it if I messed it up. I—"

She threw up her hands. "*God*, I even opened my mind up and actually thought about *not* hating Hot Cakes. I worried my dead grandmother would come back and haunt me, but I still did it. I realized I *want* Hot Cakes to be saved and to stay in business, and I've spent the last couple of days hoping so hard that the new owners will be amazing and treat Jane and everyone well."

She glared at him. "I've been fucking *vulnerable* as *hell* with you. And because of you. Because I trust you. Because I believe in you. Because I thought you believed in me and wanted me to be... everything. Happy and fulfilled and open-minded and forgiving." She shook her head. "Over the last couple of days I've realized you were the *only* one who could have ever put cream filling where you put it on me, and you're the only person who could have gotten me to bake a damned cupcake in a jar. I listened to you about my business. Even the stuff I didn't want to hear. I... showed you my jar pies. And you couldn't even show me your Hot Cakes."

It flashed through his mind that that should be funny.

But it really fucking wasn't.

She was so damned amazing. And she was right. She *had* been vulnerable as hell with him. He was so damned humbled by that. He'd realized it, of course, on some level, but hearing her say that, admit it, *own it*, was incredible.

"I *do* want all those things. Zoe, I—"

"You haven't done *any* of that with me," she said, holding up a hand to stop whatever he'd been about to say. She clearly wasn't done.

"You didn't trust me enough to tell me about Hot Cakes and to let me be mad at you. You should have been willing to have those fights with me, Aiden. To have me tell you that you were wrong and selfish and greedy... or whatever I would have said. You should have been willing to take that. To not be Mr. Perfect Golden Boy for a few days."

"*And*—" she went on, when he opened his mouth. "You should have still *trusted* that you could convince me it was a good thing. You didn't even try. You've been trying to get me to be open-minded and think of Hot Cakes differently, not to help *me* be a better, more forgiving, grudge-free person, but because you thought it would make it harder for me to be mad at you when I found out."

He swallowed hard, his gut tight, his heart pounding so hard he could feel it through his whole body. "I wanted you to let go of that grudge so you could be happier and more confident in what you do here. You have to believe that. I *do* believe in you. I love you. I think you're amazing, and it kills me that you're afraid of *anything*."

"What I'm afraid of right now is that you won't ever really be vulnerable or let me see you not succeeding at something. You think I don't know what it's like to always want to throw touchdowns? I bake touchdowns in here every single day. I have a playbook that has never failed me. I hate the idea of not being good at something. But... I was willing to show *you* how that looked."

She had. That knowledge rocked through him. He and Zoe had a lot of things in common. Wanting to be the best at what they did and being damned stubborn in their determination to make that true were two of them. Her letting him see her not the best at something, worried about something, trying something she might fail at, was big.

His heart in his throat, he stepped forward again, right in front of her. He was scared. More scared than he'd ever been. Scared she'd reject what he was about to say. Scared he'd messed this up beyond repair.

But he had no other plays here. There was no other plan. There was no alternative. He had to say it anyway.

"Okay, I'm going to try this again. The way I should have done it before. Zoe, I've bought Hot Cakes. The people there need us. The town needs us. And I love you. I want to be with you. I've wanted that for a very long time. I want to move back to Appleby and make a life with you. A life that includes Buttered Up *and* Hot Cakes."

She didn't say anything. She just swallowed hard.

"Hot Cakes is really important to me, Zoe. This is the kind of business owner I want to be." He took a deep breath. "It's the most challenging thing I've done. It's the hardest. It's probably the first thing that hasn't just fallen into place because I wanted it. And it's also felt the best. I think *because* it's been hard. So you're right. I need to learn to be okay with not always having the answers right away or everything working out from the very first minute. I have to be willing to work at it."

He looked at her, his heart full of love but also pride. He was proud of her. "*You* are figuring all that out—with the jar cake and pies, with opening yourself up to the good things about Hot Cakes. You're willing to say that maybe you're not right all the time. Maybe you won't always like every part of everything that's happening. Maybe you won't always feel confident in every bit of it... but you're still willing to try. And I want to be like you in that way." He took a deep breath. "I should have told you. All of it. Day one. Minute one. I'm sorry. I really am." He swallowed. "And I do love you. So fucking much."

She didn't say anything for a long moment. Her eyes were wide and shiny. She was biting her bottom lip, and her arms were crossed. Nothing about her body language said she wanted him any closer to her right now. And she definitely wasn't *saying* that.

"I think you need to go," were the words she did finally say to him.

Aiden felt that like a punch straight to his chest. He sucked in a breath. He went through a million things he could say. But he'd come barging back into her life, swept her up, made her vulnerable, made her open up. Now it all had to be her choice.

If she wanted him.

Or if she didn't.

"Okay," he finally agreed.

"And maybe you should go stay in Dubuque tonight," she added.

Fuck. He blew out a breath. And nodded. "Okay."

For now. That was okay for now. He'd give her time and space. But this wasn't over.

He knew she knew that.

He headed for the back door of the bakery, but he paused with a hand on the knob. He turned back. "I love you, Zoe."

She met his eyes and held his gaze for a long, heart-wrenching moment. Then she gave him a single nod. "I know."

Aiden took a deep breath. God, he hadn't realized how tight his chest was until she'd said those words. He blew out the breath, nodded, and left the bakery.

———

After three minutes of just staring at Buttered Up's back door, Zoe told Josie that she needed to leave. Her friend had given her a sympathetic look, a hug, and assured her that she could handle the bakery until closing.

Zoe had headed to her car, but she'd just sat, replaying everything, expecting to cry. Or to feel angry. To want to rage bake. Or to go after Aiden and yell at him some more. Or to text Josie and Jane and insist they meet her at Jane's with lots of liquor.

But none of those things happened. She just sat there, thinking.

And feeling there was only one person she really needed to talk to right now.

"Hey, Mom."

Maggie looked over from where she was stirring something

on the stovetop as Zoe let herself into the house through the back door.

"Zoe. Hi, honey."

Maggie must have seen something in Zoe's face because she put her spoon down and turned fully.

"Aiden is one of the new owners of Hot Cakes." No sense in beating around the bush about it.

Maggie seemed to need a second to process that. Then her eyes widened. "What?"

Zoe slumped into one of the kitchen chairs. She was suddenly so tired. "Aiden, Cam, and their partners bought Hot Cakes."

Maggie took a deep breath. She turned back and started stirring again.

Zoe frowned at her mother's lack of response.

"Mom?"

"Two minutes," Maggie said simply. She kept stirring. "I need two more minutes."

"He didn't tell me because he wanted to make sure I knew he was in love with me first," Zoe went on anyway. "You know, before he told me he'd done something horrible."

But now, knowing that all the things Aiden had been working on over the last few days was for Hot Cakes, it didn't seem like he'd done something horrible. He was doing something pretty great, actually.

"And he doesn't think Hot Cakes is—or really ever has been —our competition."

The timer on the stove went off, and Maggie removed the pan from the burner. She shut the timer off then turned to pour the liquid from the pan over whatever was in the casserole dish on the counter next to the stove.

She covered the dish with aluminum foil, opened the oven, and slid it in. She reset the timer, wiped her hands, took a deep breath, then joined Zoe at the table.

"What you're saying is, he came back and made you fall in love with him before he told you all this," Maggie said.

Zoe shook her head. "He says he wanted to come back for me. Hot Cakes made that possible."

"Aiden is very rich. If he wanted to come back and settle down here, he could have bought any other business. Or started a new one."

Zoe studied her mother's face. Maggie looked upset.

"He could have," Zoe agreed.

"Knowing Aiden and Cam, they'll make it even better," Maggie said. Clearly, she was referring to Hot Cakes.

Zoe nodded. They would. That was just who they were. They were dreamers, but driven, smart, dedicated dreamers. Hot Cakes would grow and be even more successful with them at the helm.

"What are you going to do?" Maggie asked, meeting Zoe's eyes.

"What do you mean?"

"Are you going to break up with him?"

"I..." She supposed that made sense. He had lied to her—or at least kept the truth from her. He'd gone behind her back, for sure. He'd talked about their future without ever mentioning his future was Hot Cakes. He'd slept with her with all that between them.

"Well, those are your options, right?" Maggie asked. "You either forgive him and stay together and figure out a way to make it work, or you break it off and go back to how things were before he came back."

Zoe immediately knew that wasn't possible. She couldn't go back. Aiden had known back at Christmas—way before she had realized it—that if they slept together, let themselves fall, imagined a future together, there would be no going back.

Everything would change.

Everything *had* changed.

And she liked a lot of these changes. Seeing him every day. Smelling his soap in the bathroom. Having chunky peanut butter in her cupboards for his toast in the morning. Kissing him. Talking business with him. Having his input and help whether it was decorating cookies or looking at tax deductions. Watching him work and lead and grow.

She'd always looked at change as risk. When something was working, if you changed it, you risked it not working. You risked something going wrong, looking bad, being made to look like a fool.

That had happened with Aiden too. She'd let him change her mind. She'd opened herself up. And now she was...

Zoe frowned. What was she?

She'd told Aiden she felt foolish, and yes, she now blushed whenever she made cream-filled cupcakes, and she had a cupboard filled with mason jars, but... so what? Was any of that bad? She'd also had amazing sex, fallen in love, and made cake and pie in a jar that were, if nothing else, pretty cute with a big yellow bow and a Buttered Up sticker on the top. Nothing was hurt by being vulnerable with Aiden in those ways.

And she'd even decided that Hot Cakes needed Aiden. Before she'd known Aiden was the new boss. The way he'd helped Jane and Maria had been exactly what she'd been hoping their new bosses would be like. And... he was.

"I can't go back to how things were before he came back to Appleby," she finally said.

"You're going to forgive him for this? *He* is now your competition, Zoe." Maggie frowned. "And Camden. I'm going to have to have a word with my eldest son."

"He's..." Zoe swallowed. "He's not, Mom. He wouldn't do that to us. *They* wouldn't do that to us."

"But he kept this from you. He wasn't honest with you."

Yeah, Zoe hated that. But... She shrugged. "I didn't make it very easy for him to confide in me. I've always been so focused on hating Hot Cakes and feeling threatened that he couldn't trust me to look at it from his point of view." The more she thought about that, the worse she felt. She'd been so hard-headed. Whenever he'd brought Hot Cakes up, she'd complained and insulted it.

Now Maggie's frown was trained on Zoe. "I'm sure the sex is great, but don't let that mix all this up. This is business. Our family business."

Zoe stared at her mother. That was very unlike Maggie.

"That's not what this is."

"You weren't this big of a fan of Aiden's before you slept with him."

"Mom!" Zoe frowned. "That isn't true. I've always loved Aiden."

She heard her words out loud, and her heart thunked in her chest.

"I've loved him for a very long time. Yes, as a friend and pseudo big brother at first. But that... changed... at some point and became more. I don't even know when."

Huh, so not all change was earth shattering and scary. Sometimes it happened slowly. And ended up as something new and wonderful. Without you even realizing it until you really thought about it.

"And I trust him," she went on. "If Aiden had thought for a second that Hot Cakes would actually hurt us, he would have never gotten involved. He would probably work to shut it down even faster."

Maggie's frown didn't ease. "Your grandmother would be so disappointed. She's probably rolling in her grave."

Zoe reached out and squeezed her mother's hand. "I know she'd be upset." Zoe's chest felt tight. "But wouldn't she want me to be happy? Wouldn't she be happy that I had found love and a man I admire and respect and trust? Who feels the same way about me? Someone who cares about Buttered Up and will work to make it successful too?" Zoe swallowed. Aiden had done that. Even while he was in the process of buying Hot Cakes, he'd been helping her grow and make Buttered Up more. Better. "Or would she only see Hot Cakes as her enemy and not be able to look past that to all the good things Aiden means to me?"

Maggie swallowed. "I..." Maggie sighed. "I think she would have had a hard time seeing past her feelings for Didi and Hot Cakes."

Zoe's stomach knotted. "That's really sad." She looked into Maggie's eyes. "I don't want to be like that. I don't want to be bitter like that. Anymore. I don't want a grudge, that's not even mine, to make me miss good, happy things."

Maggie studied her face. Then slowly, she nodded. "He loves you. And you love him."

It wasn't really a question, but Zoe nodded. "Yes."

"Aiden loves our family."

"He does."

"So we're going to trust him?"

"Well, we have no reason not to," Zoe said, her heart feeling lighter. Maggie was coming around already. She loved Aiden too. That mattered a lot here. "He's never given us a reason to doubt him. He's trying to save the town. And... I think he's actually doing that."

She told Maggie about Maria and her daughter and how Aiden had been coaching Jane, how he'd been on all the guys to get things done, how hard he'd been working, and how much he'd been worrying.

Maggie was frowning again by the time Zoe finished. But she shook her head and laughed softly.

"What?" Zoe asked.

"Even knowing what he's working on and what he's worried about, now *I'm* worried about *him*. I want to make him a casserole and some of this new lotion I found a recipe for on Pinterest. It's supposed to help with relaxation. And I want to give him a pep talk and a hug and tell him it's all going to be okay."

Zoe felt her eyes stinging. "I know what you mean. This is really important to him."

"And he's really important to us."

Zoe nodded. "Yeah. He is."

"And he's doing it for the right reasons."

Zoe nodded again.

"Then we have to support him," Maggie said resolutely. "Because we love him."

Zoe agreed. Wholeheartedly. "Even if we think Grandma would be upset?" she asked.

Maggie smiled. "Well, the truth is, Grandma wasn't right about *everything*. I mean, she never put enough peanut butter in the peanut butter cookies and her lemon meringue pie was always too tart. And the stubborn woman wouldn't change those recipes even when I told her that."

Zoe sniffed, aware that her eyes were even more watery now. But she laughed. "Maybe that's why Didi didn't steal those recipes."

Maggie chuckled. "Maybe." She leaned over and cupped Zoe's cheek. "I *am* very happy about you and Aiden."

"Thanks. I am too."

"But I am still never going to eat a Hot Cakes snack cake. Don't even think of bringing any of those over here."

Zoe just nodded and smiled. She was *never* going to tell her mother that she'd cheated on the Buttered Up's cream filling with not one, but two, different Hot Cakes.

19

Aiden was very grateful that it wasn't winter. It got damned cold in Iowa.

Fortunately for him, it was a very pleasant sixty degrees as he approached the front door of Buttered Up in bare feet and nothing but a pair of pink silk boxers—the same pink as the teddy Zoe had worn on Christmas Eve—and a matching tie.

She did love him in ties.

Aiden turned the corner and hesitated for just a second when he saw the usual morning line spilling out of the front door of Buttered Up.

Then he took a deep breath and kept going. This was why he'd decided to do this now. The bigger the crowd the better. He needed to be vulnerable, take a risk, show her that he was willing to put himself out there even when he didn't know what the outcome would be.

A huge crowd of Appleby residents, mostly men, witnessing his apology and declaration of love in nothing but boxers and a tie was appropriate.

"Excuse me," he said, stepping through the line toward the door.

"Uh, line starts back there, man," someone Aiden didn't recognize said.

"I'm not here for the muffins," he said.

He got a couple of wolf whistles and heard someone behind him say, "I didn't realize this was a clothing-optional place."

Another voice responded, "I hope that applies to the bakery staff too."

Aiden thought for one second about stopping and turning back and explaining very loudly and very clearly that he would pummel anyone who said anything else like that. But he didn't have time. They didn't matter. Only Zoe mattered.

"What are you here for, then?" Zach Miller was the guy currently standing in the doorway, propping the door open, and more or less, blocking access to the bakery. His eyes scanned over Aiden.

"I'm here to make an ass of myself."

Zach nodded. "Well, then, so far, so good." He moved, giving Aiden a space to step through the bakery door.

"Thanks." Aiden hoped that none of the men in heavy work boots stepped back and onto his toes before he could get to the counter.

His arrival wasn't announced by the little bell that tinkled every time someone came into the bakery. But it didn't matter. The crowd parted for him as one after another of the men noticed the mostly naked guy in pink.

Aiden took a deep breath. This was definitely going to get around town. He doubted too many of these men had Instagram or Snapchat accounts, but he wouldn't be surprised if there were some photos and maybe even a video or two popping up after this.

That was all good.

Being vulnerable with Zoe was going to take him some time. And practice. He wasn't especially good at that. But he needed some gesture to show her that he'd heard what she

ERIN NICHOLAS

said, understood what she needed, and was willing and able to deliver.

The guy checking out at the register was the only one who hadn't noticed him. Well, that guy and Zoe, who was ringing up his purchase and chatting about his new granddaughter.

She looked so damned gorgeous.

Aiden had given her space last night. He hadn't called or texted, though he'd started to about twenty times. He'd hoped she'd reach out to him, but she hadn't.

He'd crashed on the sofa in Dax's suite. He'd also emptied six of the little bottles of liquor in Dax's mini fridge then borrowed several ibuprofen and charged room service to Dax's account this morning. But Dax had been the one to help him come up with this plan, and Dax had been the one to go out with him on the hunt for pink silk boxers in Dubuque, and Dax had been the one to sweet talk the sales guy at the trendy men's clothing store into rummaging through their storeroom even though it was closing time.

Aiden swore that Dax could charm a charging bull if he needed to.

Finally, the guy at the register moved, and Zoe looked up to help the next customer.

Him.

She froze. Then her eyes tracked over him, widening as they did. Her mouth dropped open.

"You were right," he said, before she could say anything.

He was aware of the crowd pressing in and spreading out, leaving the line so they could move farther into the bakery for a better view. And to better hear what was going on.

Josie came through the door from the kitchen with more to-go boxes in her hands. She froze, her eyes going wide, one box sliding off the top of the stack and hitting the floor.

"I'm not good at being vulnerable," he went on, focusing on Zoe. A draft of air brushed past his legs, reminding him of how little he had on. He ignored it and went on. "I always want to know the game plan ahead of time, and I want a sure thing. But I shouldn't have done that with you. I don't *need* to do that with you. I don't need a game plan that includes anything more than knowing you're on the field with me. I told you last night that I want to be like you. You've learned to take a chance, to put yourself out there, even when you're scared and have no idea how it's going to turn out."

He swallowed hard. His heart was thundering. Not because he was half naked in public in Appleby, but because he was about to give Zoe the chance to make a fool of *him*. He'd rejected her when she'd come to him in pink lingerie. She'd put herself out there with him and he'd shot her down. That had been behind closed doors, but that had been a very vulnerable moment for her. Then she'd come around and given him a chance to see her vulnerable again. More than once. She'd trusted him and he'd screwed it up.

Now she could get back at him for that. She could give him a taste of feeling like an idiot. She could shoot him down in front of all these people.

She was currently staring at him with an unreadable expression. But she wasn't trying to stop him.

"I have no idea how *this* is going to go right here and right now," he said. "I have no idea if this is going to be a touchdown or if I'm going to get knocked on my ass." He spread his arms wide. "I'm not good at not being good at things, but even if this turns out horribly, here I am. I'm ready to be vulnerable with you. To give you everything you've given me. I know this is small compared to what you've done, but this is the start."

Her expression softened, and he thought he saw a little sparkle in her eyes, but she crossed her arms and propped her hip against the counter, clearly waiting for him to go on.

So he dropped to one knee and held out the tiny velvet box

he'd been clutching in his hand. Unfortunately, that move put him down in front of the register, blocking her view.

He still went on. "Zoe McCaffery, I love you. I want to be with you, no matter what. I will give up Hot Cakes for you. I will work in this bakery for you frosting cookies and running the register if that's what you need from me. But whatever else, I just want to be with you and make you happy and remind you every single day that you're amazing and funny and smart and brave. Please marry me."

It felt like the entire bakery was holding its breath. No one said a word. No one even shifted their feet or cleared their throats.

Finally, Zoe shifted. She moved to the register and peered down at him over it. She took in the sight of him, kneeling on the bakery floor, in pink silk, holding out a ring box.

She drew a deep breath. Then she turned to grab something lying on the worktable before coming around the end of the counter to stand in front of him.

"You can't give up Hot Cakes," were her first words to him. She reached down and tugged on his arm, making him stand. "This town needs you to save Hot Cakes. And you need to do the town hall, and tell everyone that you're involved because it will reassure them that everything is going to be okay. Because you always make everything okay for the people you love." She held up the item she'd grabbed from the worktable. It was a tube of frosting. She uncapped the end and held it up. "And I'll be right there with you—and so will Mom and Dad and Henry —reassuring everyone that everything is fine, that the feud is over, and we are going to make both of these businesses a huge success."

She reached for his tie, ran her hand down the length of it from the knot at his throat to the end, where it rested on the waistband of the boxers. She smiled and flipped it over his shoulder.

"As for the rest of it, yes Aiden, I will marry you." She put the end of the tube of frosting against his chest and started drawing with it.

Aiden felt his heart thundering as relief and love and a definite feeling of holy-shit-I-don't-deserve-her-but-thank-you-God rushed through him.

"I can't imagine being with anyone else. Especially after everything you've taught me about frosting and cream filling."

She stepped back. Aiden looked down at his chest. She'd written MINE in pink frosting. On him.

"And no one will ever look better in pink than you do," she said, smiling up at him.

He reached for her then, pulling her in, tipping her back and putting his mouth against hers. "Except for you." Then he kissed her. Hot and deep and sweet, full of promises and apologies and gratitude.

The bakery erupted with applause and laughter, and Aiden felt people moving in closer, congratulating them and saying things like, "Well, damn, you don't see that every day," and "I'm going to need a dozen cupcakes with that pink icing to take home tonight," and "Hell, do you just sell the icing by itself?"

Aiden let her go after several long minutes.

The front of her apron was covered with sticky pink smears, but it was clear she didn't mind. She was looking up at him with a bright smile that was full of love and humor, and he knew that he was forgiven. Not that he was completely done making it up to her.

"Thank you," he said, his voice gruff and soft under the noise around them. "God, Zoe, thank you. Thank you for believing in me and trusting me. I love you." He shook his head, still overwhelmed himself over how he felt about her. "I love you so damned much."

"I love you too," she said. "I'm sorry I'm so stubborn and set in my ways."

"You act like I didn't expect it," he said with a smile. "Remember, I've known you for a very long time."

She nodded. "You have. You know me almost better than I know myself."

"I do," he agreed, relief and love and anticipation and a happiness he almost couldn't believe, rushing through him. "Like right now, I know that you really want to take the rest of the day off. With me."

She gave him a slow, sexy smile. "I really do."

"It's the tie, right?"

"It's definitely partly the tie." She took his hand and turned, starting for the kitchen.

"Hey, we need cupcakes and shit!" someone called.

"I can help with that."

Zoe and Aiden looked over to find Whitney standing to the side, in front of the bakery cases.

"Whitney," Aiden said, surprised. "What are you doing here?"

"Dax called and told me what you were planning. I wanted to come down and beg Zoe not to make you choose between her or Hot Cakes. Because I know we'd be the ones losing out on that one."

"But... you want to help wait on customers *here*?" Zoe asked.

"I think I can handle it," Whitney said, eyeing the bakery case. "Josie might have to run the register. I haven't done that in a really long time. But I definitely know the difference between scones and cookies, and I'm happy to serve them up to people." She looked up at Aiden. "I *really* want Aiden to stay in charge at Hot Cakes. We do need him. We all need him." She focused on Zoe again. "So I'm happy to help with what-ever it takes to keep *you* happy, so he doesn't have to choose. And it seems that maybe having him take you home right now —with that tube of frosting—is a good way to keep you happy."

Zoe laughed. And did not disagree. She looked up at Aiden. "You would really give Hot Cakes up for me?"

"I would." He didn't even have to think about it for a second.

"But that would be stupid. They need you and you love it."

"I love you more."

She shook her head. "You don't have to give stuff up, Aiden. Not stuff that's important to you. You just have to be willing to talk it out with me and convince me of your side."

"I'm so fucking glad you're willing to let me do that."

"Well, just keep the glove compartment in your car stocked, and I think you'll have plenty of negotiating power," she said with a sexy little smile.

God, he loved her. He held out the ring. "Put this on."

"My pleasure." She slipped the ring onto her left hand.

Aiden wasn't sure he'd ever felt as happy or possessive as he did seeing his ring on her hand, binding them together.

He bent and swung her up into his arms. They were done here for today. "Thanks, Whit. Just follow Josie's directions and you'll be fine," he said. "Oh, and you can talk to Josie about the cake pops."

Zoe looked back over his shoulder as he pushed through the swinging doors and into the kitchen. "You think she'll be okay?"

"The men come here for pastries and to flirt with pretty girls before work, right? Yes, I think Whitney will be just fine," Aiden said.

Zoe laughed.

"Oh, and by the way, last night we decided we should ply everyone with champagne and cake pops at the town hall. So you're about to get a huge order," Aiden said.

"Well... great," she said, clearly a little surprised, but also pleased. "But you're going to serve cake to people who *make* cake all day?"

"You think bartenders never crack open a beer after work or

that plumbers never have to fix pipes at home? I think the people who work at Hot Cakes probably eat cake at parties."

She shrugged. "Good point." Then she added, "And since you know me *so* well, you probably know that I'm going to charge Hot Cakes double for those cake pops."

Aiden chuckled. "That's my girl."

———

The second they got through the door to the house, Aiden kicked it shut and backed her up against it. He took her face in his hands, looking into her eyes.

"I love you."

"I love you too."

He kissed her, long and hot and sweet. Then he lifted his head. "You really will marry me?"

"Of course."

He kissed her again. Then said, "Get naked for me."

"Definitely." She reached behind her for the zipper of her dress.

He stopped her. "My bedroom."

"Christmas Eve do-over?" she asked, one eyebrow arched.

"The rest of our lives beginning," he said.

Her expression immediately softened. "Yeah."

He watched her for several seconds. "Zoe?"

"Yeah?"

"Naked. My bedroom. Now."

She took a deep breath. "I really love the bossy, dirty side of you."

"Good." He very much intended to keep up with all that. "But," he added. "I might be out of surprises."

"That's too bad. I was just starting to think about how much I like your surprises. And how much I like surprising myself."

Aiden's heart swelled. They'd known each other forever, but

they were still getting to know one another. And themselves. And that would never really stop.

"You know, scratch that," he said. "I think there are more surprises ahead. Neither of us is the person that we were even on Christmas Eve. Or when I walked back into the bakery a few days ago. Or when I walked in there this morning. Or who we'll be a year from now. Or ten years from now. Or even who we'll be after this town hall."

Her eyes were shiny as she smiled up at him. "That is a really good point. I love that," she added softly.

"Me too," he said, reaching for her zipper himself and drawing it down. "And promise that if I ever stop surprising you completely, you'll call me on it."

"Deal. And ditto," she said as her dress slipped down her body leaving her in only a tiny pair of panties.

Pink panties.

"And if I ever bitch about not wanting to change something, you remind me that if I hadn't changed, I wouldn't have you."

He skimmed his hands down her sides, resting them on her hips. "You've always had me. Even before I realized it."

She looped her arms around his neck. "You made me want to be better. More open. Thank you for that."

His breath stuck in his throat for a moment. He swallowed hard. "I came back for you. And because of that I'm so much better too."

She smiled. And hopped up into his arms. Aiden caught her with his hands under her butt. He started for the stairs immediately.

He nudged his bedroom door open and went straight to the bed. He laid her down and stripped her panties off in one smooth move. Then he pulled his tie loose and tossed it away before shedding the boxers. This was one definite advantage to not having more clothes on. He climbed up on the bed with her, covering her body with his, kissing her deeply.

Their hands were everywhere, stroking, squeezing, teasing. They licked frosting off of each other's skin. He kissed her neck. She arched into him. He sucked on her nipples. She ran her hands to his ass, pressing him close. They rolled and shifted, touching, kissing, nipping until Zoe was panting and begging, and his heart was thundering so hard he was sure she could hear it.

"You ready?" he asked, bracing himself above her, taking in the flushed pink of her skin, the rapid rise and fall of her chest, and her dazed, heated gaze.

She shook her head. "Not like this."

His eyes widened. "Uh… okay."

She shifted suddenly, rolling him to his back, and straddling him. Aiden drank in the sight of her. She looked like a goddess, and she felt like heaven as she moved, sliding up and down his hard length, letting him feel how hot and wet she was for him. Then she took his cock, stroking him firmly before positioning him and sinking down, taking him deep.

They moaned together, and Aiden's fingers dug into her hips. He gritted his teeth, giving her body a few seconds to adjust.

But it truly only took a few. Zoe started moving almost immediately, riding him as if she'd been doing it forever.

Dirty, loving words fell from their lips. "More." "I love you." "You feel like heaven." "I'll never get enough." "Deeper." "Harder." "Faster."

When he felt her inner muscles tightening, he thumbed her clit and sent her flying. The look on her face, and the sound of her calling his name was all he needed to follow directly behind, his body shuddering with the intensity of his climax.

After she'd slumped against him and they'd just concentrated on breathing for a few minutes, she said, "I've been dreaming about that. Doing that exactly that way."

Aiden stroked his hand up and down her back. "Since Christmas Eve?"

"Oh, before that. I was planning Christmas Eve for a couple of months."

He chuckled. "Dirty girl. Well, I've been thinking about this since I caught you ironing in your underwear."

She rolled to the side and propped herself on her elbow. "That's when I started thinking about you too."

Aiden lifted an eyebrow. "Really? Damn, all this time we could have been messing around."

She laughed lightly, but then she quieted, giving him a long, loving look. "Actually, I think our timing is perfect."

Her words hit him directly in the chest. They'd known each other forever, but *this*—this change, this shift, this new direction, could have only happened when they were both ready. Ready to think of their lives in a new way. Ready to change.

He nodded, nearly overwhelmed by the mix of emotions— lust, love, nostalgia about their past, excitement about their future. "You know, you're not so bad at the sweet talk."

She leaned over and kissed him then said against his lips, "Well, you do call me Sugar."

He nodded. "Sugar and spice. And I need both in my life."

"I'm both? You're not the spice?"

He laughed. "Uh, no. You're definitely the spice too."

"And what are you, then?" she teased.

He gathered her close and put his lips against her neck, feeling her shiver of pleasure and the way she arched into him. "Well, what else does baking need?"

"Cream?" she asked, giving a little gasp when he nipped her earlobe.

He squeezed her ass, rewarding her innuendo. "Only some recipes."

"Firm peaks?" she teased, rubbing her breast against his bicep.

He cupped one appreciatively. "Well, only sometimes and not what *I'm* bringing to the table."

"*Moistness?*" she asked, wiggling some more.

He laughed. "Not what I was thinking."

She giggled. "Then what?"

He rolled until she was under him, spreading her thighs. "Heat."

"Oh... yeah."

EPILOGUE

Three days later...

"Excuse me."

Jane froze in mid chew. She had an entire cake pop in her mouth and one in each hand. And now someone wanted to talk to her. Of course.

But it was even worse. This wasn't just someone. It was a male someone. A male someone who had come up behind her while she was perusing—and sampling—the dessert table. Whose voice she knew immediately.

Dax Marshall.

One of her new bosses. And the first man to actually make her heart trip by just smiling. Ever.

Jane was a little fascinated by that. But not fascinated enough to go up and talk to him. Or to put down her cake pops.

She didn't need anything making her fascinated or distracted. She just wanted to eat cake and not talk to anyone.

Dammit.

She chewed fast, wishing she hadn't put the entire thing in

her mouth. Wishing Zoe didn't make such amazing cake. Wishing she was the type to nibble on carrot sticks. Then realizing she did *not* wish that at all. And finally swallowing, wiping her mouth, and turning to face him.

"Um, hi."

He didn't just have a great laugh. He had a great... everything. The man was gorgeous. He had dark hair that was a little long on top and flopped over his forehead. He had deep-green eyes that had an actual, no-shit, twinkle in them. He also had a quick smile that had an edge of I'm-up-to-something. In addition, he was wearing a cake tie. A necktie that had pieces of various kinds of cake on it. It was entirely appropriate for the town-hall-slash-meet-your-new-bosses party for Hot Cakes while also being one of the most ridiculous things she'd ever seen. She loved it.

"How's the red velvet?" he asked.

"Um." She swallowed again. She probably had red velvet cake crumbs in her teeth. "Great. They're all great."

"I guess I'll have to take your word for it. Since you took the last one."

Jane glanced at the empty tray that had a tiny sign that said "Red Velvet" next to it. She reached over and knocked it face-down. "Sorry." She wasn't at all.

"I don't think you are. You ate two of the last three and have the third in your hand." He gave her a grin.

He'd been watching her eat cake pops? That was creepy.

She almost sighed with relief. He was creepy. Good deal. She could forget about him then and not worry about being fascinated or distracted.

"Sorry is just the polite thing to say." She swiped her thumb over her bottom lip. "I don't mean it."

He lifted an eyebrow. "I'm going to assume that means you're not going to share the strawberry one you're holding either. It's the last one too."

She lifted the strawberry cake pop to her mouth and took a bite. They really were two- or three-bite treats. Not stick-the-whole-thing-in-your-mouth-at-one-time treats. But you couldn't get through as many if you took the time to take three bites of each. "Nope."

His mouth dropped open in mock outrage. "Wow."

"I know. I'm the worst. You should definitely go find someone else to talk to."

But he didn't. He didn't move away. Or step back. He stepped forward. He also lifted his hand toward her breast.

She didn't so much as flinch away. *That* was fascinating too. She was pretty protective of her personal space. And her personal life. And her personal habits—like her cake addiction.

She did *not* want to be fascinated. Or stalked. Or fondled.

Still, she stood there, not moving, not kicking him in the balls as he lifted his hand, picked something off the front of her dress just above her right breast—it was definitely her chest, but her nipple didn't quite believe that because it tightened—and then lifted it to his mouth.

She watched as he licked the tip of his index finger.

"Mmm, the red velvet *is* good."

She looked down to where there was another crumb on the front of her dress. Her cheeks heated, and she looked up at him quickly. But why was she embarrassed? *He* had just picked a crumb off of *her* dress. That was very... presumptuous... or something... of him.

She stuffed the rest of the strawberry cake pop into her mouth, chewed, swallowed, and smiled. "Very good."

"Not the slightest bit apologetic?" he asked.

"Nope."

He grinned. "Good. Never apologize for stuff that makes you feel good."

Yeah, her nipples—and other parts of her—did *not* think "cake" when he talked about things making her feel good.

It was time to leave.

For one, she didn't need... any of whatever this was. People talked about having full plates and lots of balls in the air. Jane had *platters* flying around with those balls, and she knew that any second it all could come crashing down. And it would. It was just a matter of time.

She definitely didn't need to add this guy's balls to any of this.

"I'm just going to go," she said, taking a half step away from the table.

"I'm Dax."

Yeah, she knew that. Everyone knew that. He'd just been up on stage with Aiden and Whitney and Cam—the new owners of Hot Cakes, the company that 90 percent of the people in the Appleby Community Center tonight worked for.

He was a millionaire. A sexy, good looking, charming millionaire.

She really couldn't think of a guy she would *less* like to have picking crumbs off the front of her dress.

Okay, that wasn't true. There were way worse choices. There was also a lot to like about standing this close to Dax Marshall, and parts of her would very much like to have his fingers back on them. But he was the last type of guy whose fingers she should even be thinking about. Dax was rich. That was enough for her to know that they had zero in common.

Not that she was interested in any of the guys she had a ton in common with either.

She just didn't need any more balls. Of any kind. Period.

"I'm... late," she said. She grabbed one of the vanilla cake pops and started to slip around him. Then she thought about the three cake pops she held, turned back, grabbed another chocolate, *then* slipped around him.

"Do you work for Hot Cakes?" he asked, turning to watch her go, with a grin.

She didn't care what he thought of her cake addiction. Sugar wasn't the *best* thing she could be addicted to. She could be addicted to running or asparagus or meditation or herbal tea. Except... no one was addicted to those things, were they? Asparagus? Come on. The truth was, she did run. So she could eat more cake. She also ate asparagus, on occasion. She even meditated once in a while. But that was also to balance out the cake. And pie. And cookies.

She needed sugar in her life. There wasn't much figurative sweetness in her life so she substituted *actual* sugar.

She was thankful that one of her best friends owned a bakery.

She was also thankful that diabetes did not run in her family.

Bad decisions and progressive neurological disorders seemed to. But not diabetes.

Jane was very aware that her relationship with sweets wasn't healthy.

She didn't care.

"Are you okay?"

She'd been staring at Dax for thirty seconds.

Half a minute didn't usually seem like a long amount of time, but when you were staring at a stranger without making a sound, it was ridiculously long.

"Um, yes." She nodded. She was okay. Mostly. Right now. As far as he was concerned.

"You're sure?"

"Yes."

"You don't need another cake pop, then?" he asked, eyeing the four she held. "If I go for one, I'm not going to lose a finger or hand?"

"Nope, you're safe." She gave him a fake smile. He was flirting with her. She liked that. She wanted to flirt back.

Instead, she took a bite out of one of the cake pops. The chocolate one. Thank God for chocolate.

He picked one up. Also chocolate. "So do you work for Hot Cakes?" he repeated.

She sure did. But he didn't know who she was. And that was... nice.

She lived in a tiny town where *everyone* knew who she was. They knew all the reasons she worked for Hot Cakes. They all sympathized that this was how everything had turned out for her.

She really, *really* hated that. She took another bite of cake.

Should she tell him she worked for the company? He'd probably want to ask her questions about it if she did. Dax had been talking with the employees about what they liked and disliked about working for Hot Cakes, what changes they'd like to see, what they needed to make Hot Cakes their dream employer. The company had never been owned by anyone other than the Lancasters. This was a huge change that had everyone in the factory worried.

Until tonight. Tonight the new owners had held a town hall to introduce themselves, tell everyone their big plans, and feed everyone cake and champagne.

The smiles and laughter in the room told Jane this initial step had worked. Having Aiden and Cam in charge had also worked. Aiden and Cam were hometown boys. They'd left and made it big in Chicago, but they'd come back to save the factory, the three hundred-some jobs, and the town by buying Hot Cakes.

Knowing Aiden and Cam were at the head of the new ownership team definitely made everyone feel better.

She was proud of them. Happy for herself and her friends and coworkers. A little anxious about her new role as union leader. And really wishing she could take her bra off, kick off her shoes, and eat the rest of these cake pops on her couch.

"I'm... a friend of Whitney's," she said rather than confessing she'd been in his friend Oliver's office within five minutes of him stepping foot inside a Hot Cakes building. She'd demanded to see the new owner and had gone off about everyone's concerns and worries, demanding to know what he was going to do and how the transition was going to happen.

She knew they'd listened and taken everything she'd said to heart. She knew this town hall was partly a response to her first meeting with Oliver.

And that had been so out of character for her that she was still worked up about it.

She'd worked for Hot Cakes since she'd been in high school. It was all she'd ever done. But she'd done it as an aside in her life. She didn't want a job that demanded a lot of her energy or emotion. She wanted to go to work, do her job, and go home at the end of the day. She didn't want to meet with the owners and champion her coworkers and dress up for parties like this.

Yet, here she was. The main contact between the employees and the ownership. In a dress.

She did *not* want to talk about Hot Cakes with Dax. Or anyone. She felt like she'd been talking about it nonstop for days.

"Oh, Whitney's great," Dax said, finishing off the chocolate cake pop and reaching for another.

Good looking, rich, and had a sweet tooth.

Nice.

"She is." Jane nodded. It wasn't a lie that she and Whitney were friends. That just wasn't the reason Jane was here tonight. "So... it was nice to meet you. I need to go."

"You know if you don't tell me your name, I'm going to have to refer to you as Red," he told her.

She rolled her eyes. "Real original." She shook her head, her thick, wavy red hair swishing against her mid back.

"Because of the red velvet cake, of course," he said.

She actually laughed at that. "Oh, of course."

"Just that one little crumb, and it's all I can think about." His eyes and half smile said he wasn't talking about cake.

Dammit, had she given him a crumb? Of flirting? She had *not* meant to.

But the guy was clearly used to having women welcome *his* flirting.

"Zoe can totally hook you up with as much as you want," she told him, not sure why she wasn't just walking away.

"You're really not going to share that last one with me, are you?"

She glanced down, having forgotten that she still had one red velvet in hand. "Um..." She looked up at him. "No."

"Not even if I say please?" He leaned in a little.

"There are maybe two things in the *world* that could get me to part with a red velvet cake pop," she told him. "And hot millionaires with sexy smiles are *not* one of them."

His grin grew, and his freaking eyes seemed to twinkle again.

Oh crap. She'd just said he was hot *and* that he had a sexy smile. Either of those things alone would have been embarrassing, but of course, she'd said both.

"What *can* hot millionaires with sexy smiles get you to do? Because I'm thinking that cake pop may not be the most interesting thing you can give me."

Her eyes widened. He had *not* just said that.

"Are you seriously thinking I might give you a blow job? Does that happen a lot? You just meet a woman, know her for like five minutes, and she ends up on her knees?"

Now his eyes widened, and he nearly choked on the quick breath he took. "That is... damn... that's *not* what I was thinking."

Jane rolled her eyes. "It's a blow job. Guys think about those like twenty-seven times a day."

He half laughed, half choked again. "Wow, who are you hanging out with?"

"You *don't* think about blow jobs twenty-seven times a day?" she asked. She really should just walk away.

He seemed to be seriously considering her question. Jane felt the corner of her mouth quirk and fought to keep her smile under wraps.

"No," he finally said, shaking his head. "Maybe fifteen."

"Wow, that's it?"

"Well, I think about *other* things too. I'm a ladies-first kind of guy. And blow jobs are great, but they're not the *best* thing to be thinking about."

She had to fight her grin again. And to ignore the tingles that suddenly danced over her with the "ladies first" thing. "You're right," she said, nodding. "I mean, there's also cake."

"Right. Blow jobs and all the sweet stuff I like to put in *my* mouth."

Whoa.

"And by the way, that would all add up to *way* more than twenty-seven."

Jane shook her head and then held up the red velvet cake pop for him.

"Oh, I couldn't."

"Honestly, you have to, now," she said. "You have to add these to that list of sweet things you like to put in your mouth that you'll be thinking about tomorrow."

His grin huge, he took the cake pop from her. "Yeah, I've definitely got a couple of new things to add to those daydreams."

She felt a hot flush from her scalp to her belly.

"And *now*, I need to go," she said, taking a deep breath.

He bit into the red velvet cake pop then ran his tongue over his bottom lip.

"Still no name?"

"Definitely not." She hadn't meant that to sound quite so adamant.

But no, this guy did not need to know who she was. Or that she was going to be working just downstairs from the executive office suite.

"I don't think it will be that hard to find out in Appleby," Dax said. "Gorgeous redhead with a big sweet tooth. It will probably take me two minutes."

He was right. Especially if he asked Zoe or Whitney.

"You don't need to know," Jane told him. "Zoe can keep your mouth full of all the sweet stuff you could possibly want."

"Yeah, I don't think so," he said, his voice a little husky and his gaze on her mouth.

She needed to stay away from this guy.

Because she didn't need any more balls in her life.

She started to turn, planning to hightail it out of the community center and away from the hot millionaire with the sexy smile. But she stopped, quickly grabbed another cake pop, and *then* hightailed it out to her car.

Cake balls were the exception to her no-balls rule.

———

Thank you so much for reading! I hope you loved Zoe and Aiden's story in *Sugarcoated!*

Dax and Jane's story is next in **Forking Around!**

A Cinderella story with a hot boss so charming even a fairy godmother couldn't do better!

———

The Hot Cakes Series
Forking Around
Making Whoopie
Oh, Fudge (Christmas)
Semi-Sweet On You
Gimme S'more

———

If you love sexy, funny, small town romance and, well, hot kitchens and baked goods ;) you should also check out my **Billionaires in Blue Jeans** series!
Triplet billionaire sisters find themselves in small town Kansas for a year running a pie shop...and falling in love!

Diamonds and Dirt Roads
High Heels and Haystacks
Cashmere and Camo

Find all my books at
www.ErinNicholas.com

———

And join in on all the FAN FUN!

Join my email list!

http://bit.ly/ErinNicholasEmails

And be the first to hear about my news, sales, freebies, behind-the-scenes, and more!

Or for even more fun, join my **Super Fan page** on Facebook and chat with me and other super fans every day! Just search for Erin Nicholas Super Fans!

ABOUT ERIN

Erin Nicholas is the New York Times and USA Today bestselling author of over thirty sexy contemporary romances. Her stories have been described as toe-curling, enchanting, steamy and fun. She loves to write about reluctant heroes, imperfect heroines and happily ever afters. She lives in the Midwest with her husband who only wants to read the sex scenes in her books, her kids who will never read the sex scenes in her books, and family and friends who say they're shocked by the sex scenes in her books (yeah, right!).

Find her and all her books at
www.ErinNicholas.com

And find her on Facebook, BookBub, and Instagram!